USA TODAY bestsell author **Caitlin Crew** teaches her favourite classes at places like Writers' Program, w MA and PhD in Eng from the University of York in England lives in the Pacific Northwest, with her very own hero and too many pets. Visit her at caitlincrews.com.

Margot Radcliffe lives in Columbus, Ohio, right now, but surrenders to wanderlust every couple of years, so it's hard to say where she'll end up next. Regardless of location, her apricot dog will be by her side while she writes fun romances that hopefully make readers laugh and space out for a bit. With heroines who aren't afraid to take what they want and confident heroes who are up to a challenge, she loves creating complicated modern relationships. She can be found @margotradcliffe on Twitter and @margot_radcliffe on Instagram.

9112000416789

If you liked *The Risk* and *Friends with Benefits*
why not try

In Too Deep by Taryn Belle
Matched by Kelli Ireland

The Risk is the second instalment of
The Billionaires Club series,
which began with

The Debt by Jackie Ashenden

and continues with

The Proposition by JC Harroway
The Deal by Clare Connelly

Join an exclusive, elite, exciting world and meet the
globe's sexiest billionaires!

Discover more at millsandboon.co.uk

THE RISK

CAITLIN CREWS

FRIENDS WITH BENEFITS

MARGOT RADCLIFFE

Friends with Benefits © 2018 Margot Radcliffe

MIX
Paper from
responsible sources
FSC
FSC C007464

This book is produced from independently certified FSC™ paper
to ensure responsible forest management.
For more information visit www.harpercollins.co.uk/green

Printed and bound in Spain
by CPI, Barcelona

MILLS & BOON

All rights reserved including the right of reproduction
in whole or in part in any form. This edition is published
by arrangement with Harlequin Books S.A.

This is a work of fiction. Names, characters, places, locations
and incidents are purely fictional and bear no relationship to
any real life individuals, living or dead, or to any actual places,
business establishments, locations, events or incidents.
Any resemblance is entirely coincidental.

This book is sold subject to the condition that it shall not,
by way of trade or otherwise, be lent, resold, hired out
or otherwise circulated without the prior consent of the publisher
in any form of binding or cover other than that in which it is published
and without a similar condition including this condition
being imposed on the subsequent purchaser.

® and TM are trademarks owned and used by the trademark owner
and/or its licensee. Trademarks marked with ® are registered with the
United Kingdom Patent Office and/or the Office for Harmonisation
in the Internal Market and in other countries.

First Published in Great Britain 2019
by Mills & Boon, an imprint of HarperCollins*Publishers*
1 London Bridge Street, London, SE1 9GF

The Risk © 2019 Caitlin Crews

Friends with Benefits © 2019 Margot Radcliffe

ISBN: 978-0-263-27389-2

BRENT LIBRARIES	
91120000416789	
Askews & Holts	20-Sep-2019
AF ROM	£5.99

THE RISK

CAITLIN CREWS

MILLS & BOON

CHAPTER ONE

Darcy

ONCE I WALKED through the door, there was no going back.

I stood there on the Paris street in the thick, rich darkness of an autumn night, staring at the discreetly unmarked door in question. I was breathing hard and felt faintly dizzy, as if I'd danced a difficult night of several shows on very little food.

I was used to the feeling. It was the reason for the feeling that was making my heart pound tonight.

I had signed all the documents, in triplicate, from the straightforward performance contract to several different NDAs that would make certain I never dreamed of telling a soul what happened within the walls of the M Club. *To* me or *around* me. I had practiced the burlesque routine that was my entrance into this excruciatingly private club in Paris—though I'd been informed there were many other locations scattered across the globe—until I could do it in my sleep.

"All you have to do is dance," my friend Annabelle had told me with an eye roll when she'd asked me to take her place here at M Club. "Or whatever you want to call it."

We'd laughed, because we were proper, professional ballet dancers, not burlesque performers. We dedicated our lives to perfecting lines and steps, counts and patterns, in a world-renowned ballet company. We didn't play pretend with feathers and bloomers or whatever it was burlesque was meant to do when, really, it was just a striptease. Emphasis on *tease*.

And, yes, we were maybe a little full of ourselves. Annabelle and I had met in the *corps de ballet* of the prestigious Knickerbocker Ballet in New York City when we were both seventeen. Ten years of dancing and struggling through injuries and setbacks, occasional partying and rooming together in a tiny walk-up in New York City, and we were still hanging in there.

That we were both still—and only—members of the company meant, of course, that we were not likely to be promoted to principal dancers, despite whatever dreams we'd had as younger, newer dancers. It also meant that our inevitable retirements were looming, whether we wanted to stop dancing or not.

No one wanted to stop dancing. I certainly didn't. But the body could only take so much, and nothing but sheer greatness in the eyes of the world—and demanding artistic directors—ever seemed to combat the ravages of gravity. Soloists and principal dancers were more likely to fight their way toward the age of forty before retiring—when their bodies finally gave out after too many surgeries and untreated injuries and the daily toll of so much pointed use. Or when they could no longer maintain the preferred form and appearance required by most of the major ballet companies, no matter what lip service they might give to a newer, more body-positive approach. Ballet was about precision. And even the most celebrated principals were forbidden the creeping ravages of age.

But dancers who had never made it out of the *corps* in the first place? They leaned in hard, made themselves indispensable and became ballet mistresses when they could no longer perform, like the Knickerbocker's much-feared and widely respected Miss Fortunato. Otherwise, they tended to give up the fight sooner, usually after a steep downward spiral from an esteemed company like Knickerbocker through far less demanding organizations until even those wouldn't have them.

That I knew my own future didn't make it any less grim. I did my best to focus on the day before me, not the future I couldn't change no matter what I did.

It didn't surprise me that Annabelle had found yet another new and strange way to get her center stage fix, while crossing as many lines as possible in the process. She had always been the adventurous one.

For every lover I took, Annabelle took three. At once, whenever possible. Annabelle's boundaries were fluid, smoky. One year, between seasons, she beguiled a well-known older Broadway actress who still called our apartment, all these years later, begging for one more night. Another year, while nursing a broken ankle that took her out of the company, she had entertained two princes and a number of politicians on the sort of Mediterranean yachts that were forever appearing in the tabloids.

Last year, when rent money had been scarce between our performance seasons, Annabelle had decided that she might as well monetize her dating life. She'd found the initial experience electrifying. She liked to indulge herself on nights we didn't perform, and liked to tell me every scandalous detail of the men who paid her for the privilege of touching her.

Others might call it *escorting*. They might use other, less euphemistic words. But Annabelle didn't care what anyone else thought of her. And I was the one who pretended to find her stories scandalous…and then, when I was alone in the dark, imagined it was me starring in all those dark and dirty scenes.

"And if you're not too afraid," she'd told me, when we'd finished laughing about burlesque and the idea that it was on a par with what we did, "who knows? Maybe you can finally do something about your own prudishness."

"Your definition of a prude is anyone else's definition of a lusty, committed whore," I pointed out drily.

It had been a morning last spring. We'd been limbering up before the daily company class, which we took every morning before the afternoons of rehearsals and the evening shows. We stood in the back of the studio space behind the Knickerbocker theater, because everything in ballet was a hierarchy, even where we practiced. I was trying to pretend that my body was as supple and invincible as it had felt when I was seventeen and had believed that, truly, I could fly. And had, here and there, across stages in my toe shoes.

These days, my hamstrings and hips protested a lot more than they used to. And my feet were so battered that it was never a question of whether or not I was in pain but what, if anything, I planned to do about it. That day.

Everyone was injured, always. We all had to

pay attention to these injuries, taking care not to let minor flare-ups become major problems.

That day I flexed my toes as I went into my first split, failed to wince and decided I was about as good as I could expect to get.

"You know what I mean," Annabelle had been saying.

She was holding on to the barre as she worked her way through a few positions, her willowy body flowing as she moved. To the untrained eye, every move she made was deserving of applause. I could see my own reflection in the mirror and knew it was the same for me. But we did not dance for untrained eyes. We danced for beauty and learned judges. For precision and grace. We chased perfection, and were willing to starve and slave, whatever it took, to get as close to the sun as we could for as long as we could.

Annabelle's hair, bright and red, was in the typical bun on the top of her head. Next to her, I always felt dimmer. My dark hair never seemed glossy enough to combat her brightness. And my eyes certainly never shone like that, wicked and insinuating.

Annabelle might not be a *prima ballerina* any more than I was, but she always captured attention. Though that was not always a good thing in company class, where those of us in the *corps* were working on uniformity, not interpretation.

"I don't understand why you think your kink has to be my kink," I told her, perhaps a bit loftily. It was an old argument. "As I think we've established in the past decade, you like things that I definitely do not."

"How do you know if you won't try?" she asked, as she always did. Her gaze was wicked, as usual, but steady on mine in the mirror. "And believe me, Darcy, you will never find more controlled circumstances than these."

"Annabelle." I was afraid that the sudden roughness in my voice would give away the startling truth that this conversation felt emotional to me. Which I was terribly afraid meant that, as usual, my fearless, impetuous friend had poked her finger directly onto the sort of button I preferred to keep to myself. As if she knew exactly what fantasies I toyed with in the dark. Alone. "I have no interest whatsoever in selling myself."

She sniffed, then grinned cheekily when our friend Bernard, another member of the *corps*, looked over his shoulder at us with his eyebrows raised.

"You sold your body to the ballet ten years ago," she told me, with the brutal practicality that made me love her no matter how little I understood her. "Selling a fuck or two is far less wear and tear on your body, pays more, and unlike a lifetime in the *corps*, will make you come your face off."

But all my face did that day was turn red, which got me a sharp rebuke from Miss Fortunato when we were called out into the floor to begin the class.

All through my rehearsals that day and the show I danced that evening, I pretended that I'd put Annabelle's nonsense out of my mind the way I normally did, whether she was claiming she'd seduced the chiropractor or pretending she might at any moment become a stripper, instead.

But that night, I dreamed. Of a private dance in a dark room, and the hot, demanding stare of the man I danced for. I imagined peeling off my clothes and embracing the true vulnerability of my performance, around and around until I landed between his legs. I dreamed I knelt there before him, alive with need.

I could feel his hand like a brand against my jaw, lifting my face to his, and what I saw there made my body tremble.

Because he saw me as his. A possession. An object.

Something he could use for his pleasure, however he wished.

My whole body clenched. My thighs pressed tightly together. And a wild, intense orgasm woke me from a sound sleep and left me panting there in the dark.

In my bed. Alone.

"There are some fantasies that should never

become reality," I told Annabelle a few mornings later.

We'd set out on the run we sometimes did in the mornings before company class, if we weren't in the mood to swim or hit the elliptical. That left our break times free for the more pointed bodywork or extra rehearsals we might need as the day wore on. That morning we'd followed our usual loop, running up a few blocks from our nondescript street on the Upper East Side, along Fifth Avenue, then into Central Park.

Annabelle and I lived in a studio apartment in the low 70s we'd long ago converted into a makeshift two-bedroom—which was to say we'd put a few bookcases and a screen here and there to create a little psychological space. It meant that no matter how often I might hear Annabelle crying out her pleasure or making her lovers sob her name I didn't actually have to witness any of it unless I wanted to.

"Why?" she asked me then. "Making fantasies reality is the point of life, as far as I can tell."

Neither one of us liked running that much, though we dedicated ourselves to it the same way we did everything else: with intense focus and determination because of course we needed the cardio. We always needed the cardio. We were still in our twenties, but our metabolisms were already shifting and we were certainly no longer the

seventeen-year-olds we'd been when we'd started.
A few miles every morning helped, and went by
quicker with a friend and some conversation. But
soon I was much too aware nothing would help.
Time came for us all, whether we wanted to face
it or not.

There were no elderly ballerinas in the Knickerbocker.

"Why?" I repeated. "Let me think. First of all,
safety."

"You're a grown woman, Darcy," Annabelle
said with a laugh. "I feel certain that you can make
yourself safe, if you want. Or not so safe, if that's
hotter."

"Just because you sell yourself without blinking, it doesn't mean that kind of thing comes easily
to others. It's a social taboo for a reason."

"I consider myself a world-class performer.
Why shouldn't a lover pay just as they would if
they were coming to see me dance at the theater?"
She laughed again when I made a face. "I always
forget that you have this traditional streak. This
is what happens when you grow up sheltered in
Greenwich, Connecticut, the toast of all those desperately preppy boarding schools."

"I was not the toast of Miss Porter's."

"Miss Porter's," Annabelle repeated, pronounc-
ing the name of my high school alma mater as if
she was belting it from the center stage. While also

mocking it. "I'm just saying that I had fewer moral quandaries at good old Roosevelt High."

"To hear you tell it, your tiny little high school in Indiana was ground zero for debauchery."

"It's *Indiana*. What's there to do except get a little twisted and dirty?" Annabelle blew out a breath as we sped up to pass a group of nannies. "Your trouble is, you think that if you actually got what you wanted, it would ruin you."

"I do not."

I did. I really, truly did.

"Here's the deal, Darcy," Annabelle said, coming to a stop when we'd only done the first of our three miles. She rested her hands on her hips, and I knew she was serious when a good-looking man ran past and looked at her admiringly and she didn't look back at him. "I've spent years trying to get inside this. Any branch, anywhere."

"Then you shouldn't give up your opportunity to do it this time."

"I'm understudying Claudia," Annabelle said, naming one of our soloists. She shrugged. "I can't be flying off to Paris during our season break, indulging myself, and possibly miss an opportunity that both you and I know is unlikely to come again. Not that it will come this time, either. You know Claudia. She won't miss a show. She'd dance through the plague."

I did know Claudia, younger than us and far more

ambitious. I also knew Annabelle. And I'd been hearing her talk about the pleasures to be had in this exquisite M Club of hers for at least two years. There was no applying for membership. There was no showing up or waiting in a line. The club was by invitation only, membership was rumored to be extended only to the wealthiest individuals alive, and clearly, the only possible way that someone like Annabelle or me was getting inside was as the help.

Or in this case, as the talent.

"If they're so fancy, why wouldn't they hire real burlesque dancers?" I didn't even smirk when I said it. Because, between Annabelle's first mention of it and now, I had accidentally spent a little too much time researching the art form. "There are world-renowned burlesque dancers who I'm sure would leap at the chance—"

"For exactly that reason. World-renowned, professional burlesque dancers would likely perform burlesque, then go about their business. M Club is looking for dancers who might do a little bit more than that."

"You mean dancers who want to be whores."

Annabelle tipped back her head and laughed at that loudly. Once more drawing attention from passing men and women alike. And ignoring the attention entirely, which was unlike her.

"Keep your morals to yourself, please." She waved a hand over the sports bra and tiny running shorts she wore. "This body is my instrument. I've honed it, beaten it into submission and gloried in it. But what I choose to do with it, who I choose to do it with, and what I want in return is entirely my business. I don't think that makes me a whore."

"Please stop saying that word so loudly," I said. Through my teeth.

Annabelle smiled. "My understanding is that the club wants dancers who are open to using this opportunity as more than just a simple performance. Dancers who will push the envelope and give themselves over to the fantasy."

I wanted to dismiss the whole notion of M Club out of hand. I wanted to laugh, much as Annabelle had, all lust and delight. I wanted to start running again, stop talking and chalk this up to one more of Annabelle's predictable flights of fancy.

But my heart was kicking inside my chest as if we'd sped up instead of stopping. Between my legs, I was slippery. Too hot and trembling again, as if on the verge of another intense orgasm like last night's.

I didn't know what was happening to me.

I didn't want to know.

"You need to call the number I already have. You will have to update them about our little cast change. Tell them who you are, answer all their questions, and they will ask you to share your deepest, darkest fantasies with them." Annabelle smirked at me. "I think we both know what that is."

"I don't know what makes you think you have the slightest idea what I fantasize about. For all you know, I'd like nothing more than to zip-tie a room full of domineering men, then make them crawl around and serve me."

"Yes, yes," she murmured. "Anyone who's ever suffered through rehearsals with François has entertained a thousand fantasies of tying up men just like him and torturing them within an inch of their lives." François was the Knickerbocker's most temperamental male soloist and a diva beyond compare. "But that's not quite the same thing, is it? That's a revenge fantasy. It's not what haunts you. It's not what makes you moan in your sleep. Rhythmically. Waking up with a gasp—"

I could feel my face turning red again. Bright and obvious, even outside on a sunny spring morning.

"You must be thinking of yourself," I countered. "Or either one of those twins you had over last night."

"I exhausted the twins long before I heard you, Darcy. But tell yourself any fiction you like." Annabelle reached up and adjusted her ponytail. "I don't need an answer until next week. You're welcome to say no and condemn yourself to your usual life of mediocre scx and a thousand fantasies that you will soon enough be too old and too decrepit to enjoy."

"I don't have mediocre sex—how dare you— and I have no intention of becoming decrepit."

"It's one night, Darcy. In Paris." Annabelle sighed as if she, too, played out some fantasies in her head instead of hurling herself headfirst into every last one of them. "You dance suggestively for strange men and women whose names you will not know. You show them as much of your naked body as you like, but only on your terms. Then, afterward, if you are so moved, you let the man who most captures your fancy draw you into a private room. You let him purchase you for the rest of the night and then do with you, to you, absolutely everything and anything he desires."

Her gaze was hot. Demanding. I told myself that was why I couldn't breathe.

"Just think about it," Annabelle said.

It took me much too long to remember I was in New York in the bright light of day, not under a dark Parisian night sky with a relentless stranger… I repressed a shiver.

"I'll be thinking about the ballet we need to perform," I told her loftily. "Not your latest sexcapade."

But I thought of nothing else.

And one of the reasons I loved Annabelle as

much as I did was that when I went to her one
largely sleepless week later and couldn't quite meet
her eyes as I muttered that yes, in fact, I could go
to Paris in her stead, she only smiled.

I'd undergone the written interview. The intru-
sive background check. I'd signed away every right
I could think of and several I had not.

I had met with a woman who had never offered
me her name in a brownstone just steps from Fifth
Avenue. She was obviously meant to be intimidat-
ing, but I'd been contending with famed dragon
ladies like the Knickerbocker's formidable ballet
mistress most of my life. I'd smiled politely as we
sat together in a room bursting with understated
elegance and just enough wealth to seem acces-
sible instead of off-putting. I'd answered what had
seemed to me like an excruciating set of personal
questions.

What were my fantasies? Why? What would
happen if I discovered that the reality was something far different than what I'd dreamed?

"Well, ordinarily, I would demand everything
stop. Then leave." I'd blinked at the woman. "Is
that allowed?"

"Of course it is allowed," the woman replied,
with that faint accent I couldn't quite place. She
was regal, silver-haired, and with the sort of bearing that it was tempting to ascribe to rampant
plastic surgery and a life of ease but was far more

likely, I was certain, to be a simple combination of genetics and rigorous discipline.

She reminded me of my first ballet teacher all those years ago in Greenwich. Madame Archambault had been unflappable and much, much kinder than she'd looked. She had once danced with Balanchine. She had brought out the best in all her students, and she'd made a dancer out of me. Maybe that was why I told this stranger, who knew everything about me though I knew nothing about her, my most secret, most tightly held fantasy.

The one Annabelle had guessed but which I'd never admitted out loud.

"It is not a fantasy for everyone," the woman said when I had finished, feeling dirty and ruined and torn apart by my own black-and-white morality, just as Annabelle had long accused me. "It is easy to get lost."

My heart was a lump in my throat. "That's why I've never done it."

"I think what you seek is surrender," she said, smiling slightly. "For a woman who has always kept her body so tightly controlled, it would be something, would it not, to be under the control of another?"

"You could argue that I've been under the control of this or that instructor, director or choreographer for most of my life."

The woman shrugged and she did that, too, with

an innate elegance that made me wonder if she'd
ever danced herself. "Ballet is your art. Your ambition. You submit to the tyrants of your daily life
in service to your ego, your determination. It will
be something else entirely, I think, to truly surrender your will to another's."

"Or pretend to." My voice had cracked on that,
and it was a measure of how far I'd already fallen
that I didn't flush with embarrassment or try to
clear my throat as if it was a trapped sneeze instead
of emotion. "Isn't that what we're talking about?
A game of pretend?"

"If you like." The woman's gaze was steady.
And she saw entirely too much. "Let us be clear
what we're talking about here, shall we?"

"I love clarity," I managed to say, though my
lips were numb.

"You wish to sell yourself to a man. A stranger."

And there it was, stark and unmistakable. I told
myself it was an ugly thing, this strange fantasy
that had flirted with me for as long as I could remember.

But it didn't feel ugly. Not here. Not in the face
of this woman's matter-of-factness.

Here, and inside me, it felt beautiful. Pure.
Relationships were always muddied by so many
external factors. Feelings, histories. Schedules. Re-
sentments. But this fantasy was all about *simplicity*.

My body. His. Sex and lust, need and surrender, and a deep, intimate dance that ended in the most glorious flight of all.

All unsullied by the mud of our lives outside the space we carved out for our indulgence.

I couldn't look away from the woman sitting across from me in that hushed, watchful room.

"I do," I said. And I sounded far more certain than I'd expected I would.

"There are certain expectations in such a transaction," she said, and her very briskness felt like an acceptance of me, of the dark needs that coiled inside me, of this. I felt my overly straight back ease. "Certain rules. What he wants. How he wants it. When he wants it. And for however long he wants it. He will not ask after your feelings. Your family. He might suspect that you have a history of dancing, but he will certainly not know. Or care. All he will see is something he wishes to possess. Use. Then discard."

My throat hurt from whatever I was holding back. A sob? A cry of joy and excitement as she outlined precisely what I wanted most? "Are you trying to talk me out of it?"

"My dear girl, I can see your arousal written all over you," she told me with the detachment of a doctor, which kept me from surrendering to the same mortification that had made me blush when I'd discussed these things with Annabelle. "This excites you, and well it should. Fantasies are powerful. I find it is when you begin to second-guess yourself that the trouble comes."

I was shaking. I felt jittery, as if I'd downed too many cups of coffee and eaten nothing but sugar for days.

"I understand that you don't want someone who might back out—"

"You will not back out of the performance, as you are a professional," the woman said. "But I encourage you to take advantage of the opportunity that you are being given to explore your darkest desires. This is normally a privilege of membership. You will not be hurt in any way, unless you request it. The members of our club who choose to purchase what we call 'party favors' have all agreed to a certain framework that ensures your safety and theirs. I feel certain that momentum will carry you through this encounter handily. What concerns me is how you will handle it on the other side."

"You don't need to worry about that," I told her with tremendous confidence. If I could stop shaking, I was sure I'd be able to feel it, too. "I get butterflies before I go onstage, but I never think about the show once it's over."

Once again, that enigmatic half smile. As if she knew things I did not.

"I hope very much that you enjoy your time

in our club in Paris," she said quietly. And that was that.

I practiced the burlesque routine at home on those summer nights after we got out of ballet rehearsals. Annabelle threw dollar bills at me to "set the scene," and we laughed and carried on as if it was all a big joke. The required costume came, what little there was of it, fitted so perfectly to my measurements that it almost felt like a lover's hands when I put it on. And even more so when I took it off, there in our living room that we'd made a stage. As summer gave way to fall I grew comfortable with it. It was another show, that was all, if more naked than anything the Knickerbocker put up.

Still, it seemed like a lark. A story I would tell, the way we all did when we strayed a bit from the ballet, then came back. We always came back. Because the ballet couldn't last, so we were addicted to what little piece of it we had while we had it.

And now I was here, across an ocean from the place I danced my heart out, always knowing I wasn't good enough to find myself elevated from the *corps*. The night I'd been working toward in my scant free time was upon me, and yet I was frozen in place outside. Staring at a door.

It's only stage fright, I told myself. *Just a few butterflies.*

All I had to do was the routine. And no one would be looking for missed steps or bungled counts—they'd be looking at my flesh. And then, afterward, instead of tending to my sore muscles and preparing to do it all over again the next day, I could play out one of my more deeply held fantasies.

My pussy was melting hot and slick already.

"You don't *have* to do anything but dance," I reminded myself. Sternly. "You can go straight home after the performance if you want."

This was my choice. My yes or no that made it happen, or didn't.

The only thing required of me was the performance, and I knew I had that down. Everything else was icing.

I walked the last few remaining steps until I was square in front of the unmarked door, a world away from the fancy entrance out front. I reminded myself that I was a professional. This was what I did, no matter the costume or lack thereof. I had nothing to fear.

Except surrender, a voice inside me whispered.

"There's nothing to be afraid of if I choose it," I told myself, my voice sounding harsh and rough against the night.

I reached out my hand. I took a breath.

Then I rang the bell as I'd been directed, and sealed my fate.

CHAPTER TWO

Sebastian

I WOULD ORDINARILY avoid a burlesque show or anything resembling such a thing like the plague.

I was a man of discipline. I had been ruled by my passions precisely once, and it had cost me. Now I indulged them as I pleased, but only as far as I could control them. I did not leap heedlessly into spontaneity. I did nothing heedlessly at all.

And I certainly did not vie for the attention of women.

I preferred directness to coy flutterings and anything involving glitter or bejeweled bikinis—which was the only thing the woman descending from ribbons in the ballroom appeared to be wearing as she writhed about—but I found myself watching the M Club burlesque show anyway. I was a longtime member of the world's most exclusive club, membership by invitation only and based entirely on net worth, and these charity displays were part of the package. The membership made charitable gestures a few times a year, the better to disguise the true purpose of the club as far as I was concerned.

Which was business. And when business was concluded, excess in controlled circumstances. Meaning no press, no scrutiny, and no possibility of anyone emerging later with blackmail fodder.

I had not been expecting to see my half brother tonight.

I hadn't been expecting to see Ash anywhere, for that matter. He had suffered the most from my one and only hotheaded decision all those years ago and had hated me ever since—a feeling he expressed by competing with my luxury hotel business, disrupting what deals he could and generally making sure I knew he would never, ever forgive me my error.

I didn't forgive myself, either.

Ash Evans had been my best friend and closest, most trusted ally during our boarding school years, a relationship that had flourished despite—or because—we both knew our father had intended for us to hate each other. Ash was my father's illegitimate son; his very existence, and the affair right under my mother's nose that had made him, had been the final hail of bullets that had broken my mother's heart and made her the brittle, fragile woman she was to this day.

Our friendship had been unlikely. Its end inevitable.

Ash had saluted my surprise at seeing him here tonight in a manner only he could, with one finger raised high at the bar. In the scruffy jeans and a T-shirt that extended that same *fuck you* to the entirety of the club and all its members. Much as the Ash I'd known well when we were kids had always done in our aristocratic boarding school.

If he wasn't so dedicated to my downfall, I might have admired him. The way I always had.

After Ash stalked off—no need to speak when he'd already been so eloquent—I found myself restless. I normally saved that sort of drumbeat and drive for my business, especially when I so often had to fight off Ash's attempts to steal deals out from under me.

Making money was my religion and I its high priest. But it was not until tonight, when the brother who called me his betrayer stirred things up like a stone tossed into a quiet pool, that I realized how much I had come to view the club as my sanctuary. For both business and pleasure.

There were very few places that a man like me could indulge himself, in a controlled manner or otherwise, without having to fear the consequences. There were no tabloids within the M Club's walls in a handful of major cities across the globe. No stray mobile phone cameras to record indiscretions and use them for extortion or favors. This was a place where names were known, but rarely spoken. Where kings brushed shoulders with self-made captains of industry, we all played as hard as we bargained, and the outside world faded to irrelevance.

I had learned from my mistakes. I kept my temptations transactional.

And I confined them to the walls of the club.

I had come here tonight to smile for the paparazzi outside on one of the few nights the club permitted them access. And much as I knew the club liked its members to show up for their charity events, I wouldn't have come if there hadn't been another, more strategic reason. There was a man, John Delaney, with Caribbean islands for sale and I wanted them for my next five-star resort. I'd seen him in the bar and had been talking to his assistant when I'd seen Ash.

And Ash had flipped me off.

Which was as good as a billboard announcing that Ash had come for the same reason I had: he wanted those islands.

In that moment, a familiar swell of emotions had charged through me. Guilt. Temper. But it all swirled around to the same end. Ash would never forgive me. He would take whatever he could.

And I would let him, because I had brought it on myself.

I had been so cocky about my friendship with Ash when we'd been young. It had been a burr in my father's side, and I'd enjoyed that because I had hated him. Not only because young men must hate their fathers at one point or another if they wish to grow, but because of how he'd hurt my mother.

It hadn't occurred to me then that my friendship with Ash had hurt her, too.

All I did was hurt those I loved. I understood that now. And I loved no one and nothing. I cared for my mother, who confined her alcoholism to the walls of the listed house in Surrey that had become her very own prison, but called me almost nightly with her slurred accusations and tears. I did not mourn my father. And I cared for my angry half brother, too, in my fashion—by now and again bowing out of negotiations like this one because I kept imagining that if he took enough from me, his hatred of me would ease.

Ash had to have crossed the line to become a billionaire to enter these premises and he showed no sign of stopping.

But I would keep paying my penance.

And I would never love again, no matter what.

I had made myself one of the most powerful men in the world by following those two cardinal rules.

And tonight I decided I needed a little some-

thing extra to soothe away the sting of my unac-
knowledged atonement.

I left the bar, and avoided the ballroom with its
caterers and aerial displays. I wanted something
less public. I made my way through the crowd,
choosing not to meet the gazes of any acquain-
tances as I headed for one of the smaller rooms off
the ballroom. Rooms that were called by anodyne
names like *the study* or *the library* but were, like
tonight, transformed into more intimate venues.
The club never threw one show when ten would do.

I was focused on what small slice of oblivion
I could court while still retaining my faculties.

I settled myself in the dark in the library, in
one of the plush booths that were supposedly for
reading or business but often played other roles on
nights like this, when the library had been made
over into a performance space. I ordered the finest whiskey, grimacing in respect as it burned,
then warmed me. But then I found myself in the
suggestive shadows of the long, high room, much
closer to the stage than I'd intended.

The music was hypnotic. Beneath it, the faint
sounds of pleasure from the booths around me. A
gasp here, a groan there.

I didn't know what to do with the edginess
in me. It felt almost brutal in its intensity. So I
watched the show before me and ordered another
drink.

The woman on the stage was beautiful, but I expected nothing less. Unlike the aerial performers in the ballroom, this woman did not soar overhead. She was performing an elaborate striptease that held as much humor as temptation, and I wondered idly who the act was aimed at.

My cock did not require costumes to get hard.

I swirled my drink in my hand, liking the dark and the relative privacy of the booth. I didn't want anyone—especially my half brother—gloating over the agitation I was sure was visible on my face. One of the reasons I loved the club was that it permitted me these opportunities to disappear in plain sight.

I had been running the family corporation since my father's unlamented death, not long after I had lost both Ash and my savings. A stupid move that would have haunted me whether Ash hated me or not. I had believed that our too-good-to-be-true investors were on the level, because I'd wanted so badly for the deal to work. Instead, they'd walked away with all of our money and we'd been left with nothing to show for it.

Ash had warned me. I'd ignored him.

Thanks to that loss, I was a much more careful CEO than I had been an upstart junior executive cutting his teeth in the big leagues. I'd been so certain that deal was Ash's springboard to legitimacy in the only realm that mattered to our father—the corporate world. I'd thought it would prove my mettle, too.

Instead, it had made everything worse.

My father had died thinking I was an idiot and Ash was unscrupulous. The failed deal had wiped Ash out and made him hate me. My mother had spent six months pretending to dry out in an exclusive facility somewhere in America while recovering from the shock and betrayal she'd felt that I'd been in business with Ash in the first place.

I'd been made CEO amid plunging stocks and a thousand articles in business journals smugly predicting that I would run the company into the ground just as I'd lost all my money once already in a stupid, speculative gamble. I hadn't.

But it had required a long, extended fight. It had taken everything I had. It still did. I had enemies and business associates, nothing else, and depending on the deal they were often one and the same. I'd learned to love the fight.

And these days I didn't take unnecessary gambles without performing exhaustive risk assessments first.

It was only in the dark, in rooms like this, that I could simply…be. No fight. No fury. No high risks with even higher consequences.

The woman on the stage, too perky and blond for my tastes tonight, faded off. The music changed, becoming brooding and sensual.

A new dancer took the stage.

And everything…shifted.

One moment I'd been idly wondering how anyone found shows like these provocative, something better suited to the kind of hearty stag nights I was happily never invited to attend.

In the next, I was as hard and ready as if the woman on stage had leaned forward and wrapped her hands around my cock, then bathed me with her tongue.

I sat forward, my drink forgotten.

She looked tall, though she wasn't. There was a certain willowy quality to her, lithe and slender. She wore the same bejeweled bikini that all the others did, but on her, all I saw was the sparkle. The sensual shine. Even the headdress she wore was captivating, feathered and inviting.

And she had wings. Great, feathered white wings that she used to conceal and then reveal her exquisitely toned body as she danced.

Like an angel already decidedly fallen.

She danced like liquid. She was art and sex in sultry motion, a feathered being that couldn't possibly be real. But I was so close to the stage I could see her breathe. I could very nearly smell the scent of her. Her eyes were luminous and wicked, her hips were a wonder, and her sultry mouth wasn't hitched into an unconvincing smile.

It was pure temptation.

I was vaguely aware that she was doing some routine. A shifting of hips and dance steps of some description that only drew my attention to what little she wore beneath those feathers she opened and closed as if she was tempting me, personally. Sparkling stones covered her breasts, holding them aloft and leaving the sweep of her glorious abdomen bare. More bright, shining stones covered her pussy and rippled as she did. Her legs were like poetry. She wasn't simply toned. She was strong.

I felt her everywhere.

And at some point during her performance on the intimate stage before me, she saw me there in the audience.

I felt the electric pulse of the connection. The crackle of it. I was certain every hair on my body stood on end.

What I felt was like a fury. That driving. That impossible. That dark and all consuming.

Soon it became clear that she danced for me. She still didn't smile. Her eyes seemed heavy to me, thick with secrets, and she found me in the dark.

Again and again, she found me.

As if she knew.

Who I was. What I'd done.

What I needed.

When she was done with her routine, she

walked down the stairs at the side of the tempo-
rary stage and was almost instantly swept up in a
throng of admirers. I couldn't blame the men and
women who wanted a piece of her. Who wouldn't?

But I was having none of it. I wanted her.

I wanted her with that all-consuming fury that I
was very much afraid was desperation. But a desperate man was a determined one, and I'd built an
empire on the strength of my determination.

What was one night?

I cut my way through the crowd, and I knew she
was aware of me coming. I could feel that awareness like my own blood in my veins, thick and insistent. And then I was before her.

Her gaze locked to mine and I couldn't breathe.
And, oddly, didn't care.

I was dimly aware that I must have looked angry.
Menacing, perhaps, given the second glances others
threw my way.

But my dancer—*my* dancer—didn't look the
slightest bit afraid.

"I want you," I told her baldly. "Now."

That sultry, pouty mouth did not curve, and I
wanted it beneath mine. And all over my body. But
her eyes sparkled. "Do you always issue orders like
that? Do you just…snap your fingers and watch
your minions jump to do your bidding?"

I was surprised she sounded American. No one
walked around the club with a name tag on, it was

true. Still, it was a long while since I had gotten the impression that someone did not recognize me. I was Sebastian Dumont. I had been born rich, and had made myself infinitely wealthier after that one, early failure. After losing my fortune, I'd doubled it before I was twenty-five. Tripled it by thirty. And I very rarely succumbed to *want*.

Because there was so very rarely something to want that I didn't already have.

"Yes," I gritted out. "Is that how you jump? I like your dancing better."

I was vaguely aware that the rest of her fans had peeled off, no doubt recognizing the ferocity of my claim.

Or, more likely, the fact that she looked only at me.

It would have felt like a triumph if I'd already been inside her.

She gazed at me a moment. Something indefinable moved through her dark eyes. I could have sworn she hesitated, when the women who came to the club as part of its offerings were usually far more overt.

But then she tipped her head, the feathers on her headdress swaying as she moved, and it was hypnotic. She was.

"Aren't you going to ask me how much?" she asked.

This was familiar ground. I liked the purity of a

transaction. Compensation for goods and services, no muss and no fuss. But this woman was already like a madness in my veins. I had the strangest thought that there was nothing I wouldn't do to have her. Nothing at all.

I wanted her no matter the cost.

I didn't care that the club normally handled these things far more discreetly and behind the scenes. There was something refreshing in discussing it openly. It put us both on the same page, with no possibility of later confusion.

Better still, it made my dick ache.

"I don't care what you charge," I growled. "Name a price."

"That would be vulgar."

But then—at last—her lips curved, and there was something wicked and innocent in it. Angel and devil and, my God, I had never wanted anything as much as I wanted her.

I leaned forward, unable to keep my hands to myself. I traced her lips with my thumb, and that electric charge between us ignited.

Her lips were soft, with a hint of wetness that drove me wild and had me imagining what sort of dance she could perform with that mouth. She smelled sweet, with a hint of musk that reminded me she'd just performed.

I wanted a far different performance.

I wanted everything.

I wanted.

I lifted a finger and a member of staff materialized before me.

"Whatever the price," I told the man without looking at him. "No cap."

"Very good," the man murmured. Then he pressed a key into my hand. "Please enjoy Suite Six, *monsieur.*"

I took her hand in mine, marveling at the slide of skin on skin. It was a lush little preview.

"Very good," she said, as if daring me.

Challenge accepted, I thought.

I drew her with me. The private rooms of the club were accessed through the sweeping stair out front, and I didn't care who watched me take my prize with me to the second floor. I wasn't sure I would have cared if it ended up in the tabloids. That was how much I wanted this woman.

We didn't speak as we walked. I held her hand, led her behind me and wondered how I could possibly keep my cock from unmanning me as I moved.

When we reached the suite I drew her inside. As with all things involving the club, the private suite was exquisite. Quiet elegance in all its details and Paris at our feet and, far more important for my purposes, privacy.

She was mine.

I had bought her for the night.

And I had never felt something as primitive as the dark thing that beat in me then.

Need. Desire.

Destiny, something whispered, but I shoved it aside.

"Strip," I ordered her, hardly trusting my own voice. "I want to see you."

Again, I thought I caught a moment of hesitation. The cynical part of me chimed in then and told me it was because she was a professional. She knew how to inflame a man's desires with these little bread crumbs that hinted at an innocence she might never have possessed.

Her regular punters must like it.

I liked it, and I was no punter. Regular otherwise.

Anyway, I didn't care that she hadn't left the show onstage. I wanted her too much.

We were standing there in the grand foyer of the suite, with a chandelier sparkling above and a marble floor at our feet. Just beyond, there was a living area with sturdy couches and thick rugs. A million surfaces on which to enjoy her, but I needed her naked. Right now.

When she didn't move, I only lifted a brow. And waited.

She didn't smile, but she started with her headdress. She pulled out a few pins, then lifted it up and off her head. She held it aloft and looked at me inquiringly.

I nodded toward the ground between us.

My little dancer set it down gingerly, then released her hair, rubbing her fingers through the thick length of it, releasing into the air between us the scent of ripe apples. Her shampoo, presumably.

I hissed in a breath as if the scent would send me over the edge. It nearly did.

Bread crumbs, I snarled at myself.

She leaned down much the way she had onstage to unlace one shoe. Then the other. Then she stepped out of them, leaning to one side and balancing her fingers against the wall, her eyes half lidded and fixed to mine.

And lost about six inches, making her even tinier than I'd imagined.

Perfectly sized to lift and move and handle as I wished.

Her wings were dispensed of with a few tugs behind her shoulders, which she did herself. Showing me all the ways she was flexible. Limber.

My mouth was dry.

Her hair tumbled around her shoulders as she reached behind her and unwrapped those shining jewels from around her breasts.

"That's enough," I growled.

Because I knew that if I saw her fully naked right now, this would end far too soon.

This round, I amended.

She would be no businesswoman at all if she

didn't take me for the fortune I had offered her, and that meant I intended to get my money's worth.

Again and again.

But something else had happened as she stood there with her angel's wings in a feathery cloud around her and that stark, wicked invitation on her face.

It had suddenly become wildly important to me that she want me, if not as much as I wanted her, then at least enough.

Enough to shiver. Enough to ache.

Just as I did.

"Show me," I commanded her. "Touch yourself, little dancer, and show me exactly how much you want me."

CHAPTER THREE

Darcy

IF IT HADN'T been for my burlesque performance earlier, I wasn't sure I would have been able to handle this.

Any of this. All of my darkest, most-hidden fantasies coming true. At once.

At last.

The club had been better than I'd imagined it. Everything that carefully nameless woman had promised in New York, and then some. All the staff had been excruciatingly professional and, better still, polite when I'd rung the bell to the quiet staff entrance a world away from the fancier entrance at the front of the building. I'd been greeted, then ushered to a private dressing room several floors beneath the Parisian street, surprised to find it significantly more luxurious than most of the makeshift, communal dressing rooms I'd spent my life in at the ballet. The other talent I'd seen in those downstairs halls hadn't been amateurs, as I'd feared when I'd received an instruction packet that indicated the show tonight was more than just me. The dancers and performers I'd met were reticent about their names and their current gigs, as was I, but we recognized each other just the same.

Professionals, in one form or another. I could identify others in my line of work at a glance. It was how we stood. How we held ourselves. I knew the others I saw were just like me. Here to work, then play.

It was the "play" part I was trying to get my head around now.

I'd practiced my routine so many times that I'd expected my actual performance to flash by. Or maybe I'd hoped it would. Annabelle and I had laughed about what we'd both called my "snobby striptease" so many times that my emotional response while I was actually doing it in front of an audience took me completely by surprise.

Alone onstage. Centered in the spotlight. Nothing but the pumping, seductive music.

And me.

Just me.

I felt…walloped by it.

I could never tell Annabelle this when I got back home, but there was something about the burlesque that got to me in a way I wasn't sure I understood.

Or maybe I did understand. Too well.

Because there was something about the freedom. No one knew the steps except me, and that meant I could embroider upon them as I pleased. For the first time in as long as I could remember—maybe in my whole life—I could do whatever I wanted while dancing onstage.

I felt powerful. It was *thrilling*.

It was like a wave crashing over me, then carrying me out to sea—

And then I saw him.

That sensation intensified. Until I became the sea or it ate me alive, and either way I was still dancing.

And somewhere in that hot, electric moment between one breath and the next, I forgot that I was on a stage at all and found myself dancing only for him.

He sat in one of the closest booths to the stage they'd set up in what I'd been told was usually a library. I could see him perfectly over the stage lights, and he never took his eyes from me. I danced for the man in the perfectly cut suit, his gaze as brooding as it was bright, and the cut-crystal lines of his beautiful face.

I danced as if we were alone. As if I was there for his pleasure and nothing more.

Until that was all I felt.

And then, afterward, he came to me as if we were magnetic halves, drawn together no matter what.

I'd always secretly dreamed of handing myself over like this. Offering myself for purchase, and then surrendering to whoever bought me. Not the way I did, in one way or another, in my career. Surrendering to the demands of my ballet over-lords…hurt. Always. The pain was an accepted part of life in the ballet.

In my dreams, I could hand myself over, make myself nothing more than a possession and feel nothing but pleasure. The ultimate dance of plea-sure and need. Everything the ballet promised but didn't deliver. Surrender and greed, lust and long-ing, all made real. All available if I but dared.

The taboo made me shiver. The fantasy made me hot.

But I wasn't Annabelle. I had never wanted my fantasies to become real, not in the real world. No yachts or monetized "dates" for me, because I knew I would never, ever feel safe enough to go through with it.

Fantasies in my head were glorious when I was alone in my bed. But I knew a little some-thing about making fantasies real in my actual life. There was always a price, and that price was often pain. I had never wanted to test the thing that made me hottest out there in Annabelle's world of risky nights and reckless lovers, because I'd always known on some level that reality would ruin it.

Until tonight.

Because the beautiful blue-eyed man might be a stranger to me, but he was known to the club or he wouldn't have been permitted in the audience. One of the numerous documents I had signed had made that clear. The club knew everything about everyone, including medical records and sexual preferences. Everyone was deemed safe for playtime or they weren't allowed to partake. And no abuses would go unpunished, assuming they even occurred—which was, I was told, so unlikely as to be well-nigh impossible.

This wasn't me in my bed at home taking myself on a little fantasy journey. But it wasn't quite reality, either. That made it perfect.

It felt like a dream, but I knew I was awake. Awake enough to feel myself jolt and shiver when he touched me, there beside the stage. Awake enough to make it clear I was for sale and extract a purchase agreement, a notion that made me... ache. Everywhere. And more than awake enough to follow him up the sweeping stairs to this suite.

I wasn't going to sleep through a single moment of this fantasy-made-real. Not now that I was stripped down to nothing but the sparkly bikini bottoms I'd worn onstage, though I didn't feel exposed or naked. I felt completely dressed in this man's hot, demanding gaze.

And he wanted me to prove I wanted him. He wanted me to *show* him.

I wasn't sure my knees would hold me up as I imagined—in bright detail—how I could do that.

"Haven't I already proved it?" I asked. We both still stood in the marble foyer of the suite, my costume in heaps at our feet. "If I didn't, we wouldn't be here."

"I prefer certainty to innuendo," he said, a faintly sardonic note in his voice.

It kicked through me. A megawatt jolt in my chest and a helpless shuddering below.

My being present here tonight—on that stage and now here with him—should have been enough. There was no one here who hadn't asserted their willingness in triplicate. That was part of what the club offered.

But that wasn't enough for this man.

He wanted my explicit consent.

It made me dizzy. It made me wet.

And as that surge of molten heat left me slippery and achy, I felt the same wild wave that had taken me over on the stage nearly take me from my feet here, too.

He didn't know who I was. I was a woman he'd bought for the night, that was all. He didn't know a single thing about me; he didn't care and wouldn't pretend to care as long as he was certain I wanted this, too, and that meant… I could be anyone.

I could be as free as I'd felt on that stage, strutting around to steps of my own design, following my body instead of forcing my body to follow rigid protocols to suit someone else's aesthetic.

I was no longer an indistinguishable member of the *corps*. I was no longer the perennial understudy, condemned to the back of the stage and judged harshly should I in any way stand out from the crowd. Tonight I would not be judged, for once, on the position of my wrist or the turn of my ankle.

Every lover I'd ever taken had known exactly who I was before we'd touched. And some men loved the idea of a ballerina. A little doll, they thought, who could spin around on command and show off her splits in bed. But what they expected from that little doll was her shyness. A docile willingness to please that tipped over into fragility. Tears, vulnerability and an eating disorder.

I was many things, but meek wasn't one of them.

And if I was fragile, I never would have made it into the *corps* in the first place, much less maintained my place for a decade.

But surely no call girl would be expected to be anything like meek.

I smiled at this dark, mouthwatering man who wanted what he'd bought so much that his face looked tight with it. Hungry.

The way he looked at me made me hungry, too.

"I could have had anyone in that room," I told him, almost unconsciously letting my body move as it liked. And what it liked tonight was the burlesque. The jut of a hip. The exaggerated curve at my waist. The feminine knowledge I could feel in me and all over me, like his hands would be soon, I was sure. "I chose you."

"And here I thought I was the one who had done the choosing."

"This isn't a street corner. Last I checked this was the most exclusive club in the world."

"You are American," he said, and it wasn't a question. If anything, it sounded like an accusation.

"You are British," I replied. "And apparently very wealthy, to be a member here and to offer me any amount of money I choose. Does that mean you come with a title attached?"

His mouth curved. And here in this quiet, hushed space where he would take me as he liked and I would surrender entirely—a notion that made me feel as if I teetered right there on the edge of an orgasm without his even touching me—I couldn't help but find myself dazzled by all of his male beauty. He was a hard man, because the fact he was beautiful did not make him pretty. And there was something about the cut of his jaw and that simmering heat in his bright blue gaze that made me want to sink down onto my knees. And *show* him exactly how much I wanted him.

"I'm not that kind of British, nor that kind of wealthy," he said, though his accent made him sound like the earl of this or the baron of that. "But you can call me 'sir,' all the same."

That made me even wetter, and I had the strangest sensation that he could tell. That he knew.

That he might think I was some kind of hardened prostitute who did this all the time, but still I was soaking my panties for him.

Maybe that was his fantasy.

"Very well," I said softly.

I moved toward him, the marble soothing beneath my feet, then hard enough to leave bruises when I sank down on my knees before him. But I was a ballet dancer. I wore my bruises like badges of honor, counted them, and sometimes gave them names. I already knew I would love these wholeheartedly.

I swayed forward, resting my hands on his powerful thighs, and then I tipped my head back so I could meet his gaze up above the impressive length of his toned, muscled body.

Above the thick rod of his cock, which pressed out against the front of his trousers and made me feel something like giddy.

"How's this?" I asked. Then smiled. "Sir."

I saw his nostrils flare. His blue eyes glittered like an afternoon sea. And he did nothing but incline his head.

It was an order, not an invitation.

My mouth was watering. My hands felt as if

they were shaking, though I could see that they were not. I moved to unzip him, easing the metal teeth carefully over the thick heat of him, so big and so hot to the touch that I felt almost giddy.

I finished with the zipper, then ran my hands over the silk he wore beneath his trousers, getting my first feel of him.

His cock was huge. Heavy. The ridge beneath the silk grew as I rubbed it, and whatever notion I might have had about playing with him a while shivered off into a bright, hot lust.

"Take me out," he ordered me, his voice a low growl. "I want to watch you while I fuck your mouth."

People did not say things like that to sweet, meek, *fragile* ballerinas, that was for sure.

Again, it wasn't a request.

My nipples pulled so tight a sharp little pain stabbed through me every time I breathed. My breasts felt heavy, my pussy was scalding and soft, and I couldn't seem to keep myself from pressing my thighs together to give myself a little bit of friction.

And I did what I was told.

I pulled that beautiful cock out from the silk of his boxers, reveling in the textures. The soft, warm silk, then the heat of his satiny flesh stretched over the thick iron beneath.

I moved even closer, pressing my knees against

the marble floor to make sure I got that bruise. His hands moved to tangle in my hair, holding me right where he wanted me.

This was what I'd wanted, all this time. This was what I'd dreamed about and feverishly imagined, hidden away in the privacy of my own bed, playing out the stories Annabelle told me in my mind with my hands busy between my legs.

I couldn't seem to help myself. I let him support my head with those big hands tugging at my hair and keeping my head high. I slid my own hands beneath the sparkling bikini bottoms I wore, finding my way through all that molten heat to my greedy clit.

And as I found myself, I opened my mouth and sucked him in.

He tasted like salt and man; he was *big*, and I took as much of him as I could. Even though he came perilously close to triggering my gag reflex.

But the truth was, I liked that, too.

I could feel tears form in the corners of my eyes. I wanted to cry, but not because I was sad.

But because his hands controlled my head, holding me as he began to thrust.

He didn't ask if I was ready. He didn't consult my feelings. He just took what he wanted and, my God, did I nearly come all over myself in my eagerness to give it to him.

He eased his way in, then pulled out, letting me

feel every thick inch of him. My mouth was wide, my tongue busy against his satiny length, but he didn't wait to see what sort of acrobatics I might perform with it. He didn't wait to see if I was a licker or a sucker. He took charge and control.

And there was nothing I could do but stay where I'd knelt, keep my mouth open and let him fuck my mouth as he chose.

That hard, uncompromising slide, a little deeper each time, like a test.

I was filled with him. His cock in my mouth and my hands between my legs—two fingers, then three—as I pretended he was fucking me there, too.

And then I was coming. Flooding my own fingers as he maintained that same bossy, insistent rhythm. Once. Then again.

As if I really was an object.

And I'd spent my whole life learning how to be a specific kind of movable, flexible object, set here and there in the choreography of every creative director I'd ever danced for. I was a company dancer, trained my whole life to be interchangeable. My job was to blend. To be indistinguishable from the girl beside me.

I fought for that privilege. I fought to disappear every time I went onstage. I beat myself up, suffered the critiques, and staggered into the studio every day with my aches and nagging pains and protesting limbs to do it all over again.

We are nothing but game pieces they move around their little boards, my friend Winston had said before he'd left the ballet two years back. We'd all pretended to be supportive of what he called a lateral move into contemporary dance, but we'd all viewed it as a death. A suicide.

I prefer to be one of the prettiest, most perfect pieces, Annabelle had said afterward. *Or why not just go home?*

And here, now, on my knees in a hotel suite in Paris with a man whose name I didn't know, it was that very objectification that made it all so hot.

He wanted me because I was that object. Because we could play this game, where he did with me as he pleased because it pleased me, too. And I didn't have to know any steps or worry about perfection.

All I had to do was let him fuck me as he liked.

I came and I came, bucking against my hands, and the man who held me so securely in his grasp growled his approval, but didn't stop.

He didn't speed up. He didn't change his rhythm at all.

He was inexorable. Relentless.

And that, too, made me come.

He fucked my face while my eyes overflowed with my gratitude and my pussy wept and shook.

And when he came, he flooded the back of my throat, and there was nothing to do but take it. Nothing to do but swallow him down, again and again, until he was done.

He pulled me off his cock, then dropped his hands, and I sighed because I wanted them back. Holding me. Controlling me. Making me burn bright beneath his control.

"Take your hands off your pussy," he told me, dark and intense, only another layer of roughness in his voice indicating anything had happened. But I could feel it inside me. "And lick them clean."

I shuddered. I stayed on my knees and slowly pulled my hands from beneath my sparkling bikini bottoms. His gaze was bright and hot, and my nipples tightened even further as I lifted one hand and slowly, carefully, licked each finger clean.

I tasted myself, tart and sweet, and felt lust and need coil tightly inside me.

All over again.

He stripped himself of the dark suit he wore, watching me lick my fingers clean of my own need.

By the time I finished he stood before me naked, gloriously male, and packed tight with hard muscles. He was built along powerful lines thicker and more solid than any dancer. I thought I might actually die if there wasn't more. A lot more.

And that cock of his that I could still taste in my mouth, deep inside me at last.

"Come with me," he said, another one of those harsh, delicious orders that danced around inside me, kicking up light and heat and more of that dark, dark need I hadn't understood could boil in me so quickly. "And bring your wings."

He moved farther into the suite, not bothering to turn the lights up higher than where they sat already, low and inviting. There was the sparkle of Paris in the windows before him, but I was mesmerized by the play of muscles in his fine back, and his high, gorgeous ass.

I would have followed him anywhere. For free.

"Little dancer." It took me a fuzzy moment to realize my gaze had dropped to admire that ass, but he had turned his head to look back at me. And when I lifted my gaze I found his mouth in a stern line that made my heart wheel about in delight and a kind of erotic anxiety bubble inside my chest. "You really don't want to keep me waiting."

CHAPTER FOUR

Sebastian

I WAS HARD again almost instantly, as if I hadn't emptied myself down my little dancer's lovely throat.

She was glorious.

I'd controlled the way I fucked her, watching in a kind of greedy disbelief as she rode her own hands and then came. Again and again, red and shuddering as her hips rocked.

It was the hottest blow job I'd ever had.

There was a part of me that was tempted to repeat the experience, again and again, until I couldn't take it anymore.

But I changed my mind as she rose.

Because that body of hers was like one long, perfect muscle. And I already knew that she was flexible. Lithe and lovely onstage, and even more so naked.

She made my mouth water.

And she did as I asked, reaching down and picking up those feathered wings of hers from the gleaming marble in the foyer, then dragging them behind her as she came toward me. I wondered if she knew the picture she made, my distinctly fallen, sulky angel swaying toward me on her bare feet, her breasts jutting high on her chest with her nipples hard. That mouth of hers swollen from my cock.

And her eyes all over me, filled with a kind of bright, hot wonder that I wanted badly to be real.

I tried to shove that urge aside. It was naive at best, and I was not a naive man. This was a transaction, not a romance, and I needed to remember that. I'd never needed to remind myself such a thing before, but this woman was like a drug. The kind of drug I never permitted myself to sample, too certain was I that it would wreck my control.

And I was nothing without my control.

Or so I assumed, having never released my grip on it after the singular, epic failure that had destroyed my relationship with Ash.

I certainly wasn't going to lose it tonight because of a woman, no matter how she danced or what she did with her talented mouth.

She stopped before me, there in the middle of the suite's great room. There were wide, inviting sofas all around, and handy side tables, but no inconvenient coffee table perched on the soft rug in the center. Nothing to work around.

I didn't speak. I wasn't sure what I wanted to say, and that, too, was a first.

Instead, I helped her tie those wings onto her shoulders again. Then I crouched down to hook my fingers in that sparkling bikini bottom she wore, tugging it down from her hips.

She lifted an absurdly graceful hand and rested it on my shoulder with the lightest possible touch as she swayed to help me, lifting one leg, then the other. I had the distinct impression that she didn't actually need my help to balance herself. That she was touching me because she wanted to touch me.

Maybe I was a fool. But I couldn't seem to care when my own personal angel was so close to me, smelling of sex. And me.

I'd had some vague intention of doing this or that to her delectable body once I'd finally got her naked, but now that she was I found myself transfixed by her pretty, swollen pussy.

"Hold on," I told her.

That was all the warning I gave her.

I drew one of her legs up and over my shoulder, and she made a soft sound that might have been a sigh. Then she shifted, and I felt her balance again in an instant—confirming what I'd thought before, that she didn't need any help finding it. That if she held on to me, it was because she wanted to.

I didn't let myself bask in the pleasure of that, because there was far more pleasure right there before me. And I thought that if I didn't get my mouth on her, I might die.

I wrapped my hands around her ass, bringing that sweet, soft pussy to my lips at last. She didn't simply *meet* me. She bent back. All the way back, arching herself like a bow.

She was the hottest thing I'd ever had my hands on. And she tasted like sugar.

Sugar and cream, and I growled my lust and approval as I took her clit between my teeth. I tugged at her, then bit down gently.

She came again, flooding me with her scent and taste and impossible heat.

I bent to the task. I ate her like a starving man, growling every time I heard that hitch in her breath or felt her pussy quake against my tongue.

There were ways to fake almost anything, but not this. Not the way she flooded me. Not the way her clit pulsed in my mouth, and not even the way she shook and then ground her pussy against me, as if she wanted to fuck herself straight into oblivion.

Her body was a marvel. She stood with only one foot on the ground, her other leg hooked around my shoulder, and her hands on me from time to time. But she wasn't gripping me in any way. She swayed with me, as if this was another dance. A beast devouring a beauty like every fairy tale I could recall, and all she did was arch herself back and raise her hips.

I was so hard again it was as if I hadn't had sex in years.

And she wasn't simply coming now in those sweet, hot bursts. She was crying out as she did it, her voice getting hoarser with each cry.

If she was faking this, she was the best I'd ever seen. And if she was faking this, she was far better at fucking than she was at dancing, and God knows watching her dance had nearly killed me where I'd sat.

She came again, her whole body flushing with the heat of it. She went red and pink everywhere as she rocked herself against my mouth and let out one of those raw little cries.

I pulled away from her, shifting to set her other foot on the ground. As I rose, she swayed there before me but stayed on her feet. She looked dazed. Drunk, almost.

Something roared in me, triumphant and hot.

"Do you come like this with all your customers?" I asked her.

I didn't know where the question came from. I had never been a possessive man. I never compared myself to others, and not because I worried comparison might steal my joy or whatever the fuck motivational nonsense people liked to splay all over their mugs of tea. Quite the opposite. I felt confident I had no peer.

If I'd had one at all, he'd stopped speaking to me years ago when I'd lost all his money.

And I wasn't precisely *jealous* now, either. It was something else. I wanted to mark her, perhaps. I wanted to leave an indelible mark on her supple, remarkable flesh. I wanted her to remember this—and me—forever.

I did not want to analyze why I had this urge. I just wanted it.

She blinked, then smiled. "Wouldn't you like to know?"

And I don't know which one of us was more surprised by that, her or me. But I was shocked when I…laughed.

I wanted to throw her down and bury myself inside her—right now—but I didn't. My own laughter felt like a tension breaker. Like another kind of coming and, oddly enough, it made me feel something like… Exposed.

I studied her body instead. I had been too consumed with the need to bury my cock in her before to take a good, hard look.

I remedied that now. And took my time.

"What kind of dancing do you do?" I asked. Because she was a lithe, taut column of muscle, but she was bruised here and there. And sported the kinds of scrapes that spoke of a body well used.

And her feet.

Her feet were a disaster.

"Don't look at my feet," she said, and when I looked up I thought I saw something on her face for second, but it was gone too soon to name it. "I have a horrifying addiction to high-heeled shoes."

"High-heeled shoes do…that?"

Her feet were so battered that they called to mind something inside me, some memory I couldn't quite place, of an image—

"You have to be brave to be beautiful," she told me, with another one of those wicked, mischievous smiles that I wanted to taste. "That's what my mother always told me."

"Is your mother dead?"

My little dancer let out a laugh. "I certainly hope not. As far as I know, she's alive and well and competing for the title of best hostess in the whole of—" She stopped herself, and her smile was rueful. "I apologize. The last thing you want, I'm sure, is a whole lot of unsolicited personal detail."

This would ordinarily be true, no matter how I'd met the woman in question. But she was…different, somehow, from all my previous dates and conquests.

"It's not unsolicited. I literally solicited it. Just now."

Another tilt of her head. "Do you talk about mothers every time you buy a woman?"

I laughed again, but surely none of this was funny. And stranger still, it only made me harder. "What if that's my kink?"

"Then you can call me Mommy while you come." Her eyes were alight with a wicked sort of promise I wanted to lose myself in. "If you must. But somehow, I don't think that's your thing."

"Indeed, it is not." Still, I studied her. "Does your mother know what you do?"

"Of course." Her smile widened. "She supports my dancing wholeheartedly."

That made me laugh again, and it was like a light switched on inside me. From pitch-dark to blazing, laughter and secrets and need, and I was done. I needed to fuck her, hard and long and now. Right now.

I rose then, and she must have seen my intentions on my face, because she sobered as she tipped her head back to look at me.

"Time to fuck, little dancer," I told her. Softly.

And I watched, in pure delight and no little wonder, as goose bumps broke out all over her skin.

There were things I could do if I was willing to take my time…but I couldn't wait. Not now, with her taste in my mouth and the evidence that she wanted me as desperately as I wanted her written all over her flesh.

I felt edgy and wild. So close already, as if I

might explode or topple over some cliff and lose any semblance of control.

That set off an alarm, deep inside me, but I didn't care. Not now.

I couldn't wait another second. I reached down and slid my arm around her waist, then lifted her into the air.

She was a little thing, though she was all muscle. Still, she felt like air, particularly as she flowed with me, wrapping her legs around my waist as if I'd ordered her to do it. And then she held herself there, with thigh muscles that made my head spin around and around with lust, and her arms around my shoulders.

My God, she was a wonder.

I gripped her ass again and began lowering her, but for a heady sort of moment I couldn't tell which one of us was doing the work.

Was I holding her up? Or was she the one holding herself against me, then lowering herself down, with a kind of impossible precision that made the blood in my cock pulse?

"You have a lot of muscle control," I managed to say as she inched down my torso the slightest bit more, then the slightest bit more than that, so I could almost feel the heat of her with the head of my cock.

She let out a laugh, her hard nipples brushing my chest. "For a whore, you mean?"

"For anyone," I managed to get out.

"You saw me on that stage. What did you think? It was all smoke and mirrors?"

Something inside me tore open. Something greedy and dark, an uncontrollable storm of need and longing.

And instead of fearing such a thing, I wanted to lose myself in it.

In her.

"Prove it," I dared her. "Fuck yourself silly."

A smile broke over her face, wicked and bright and all mine.

"Yes, sir," she said, her voice rough and husky.

And then, at last, she obeyed me.

Darcy

Being lifted was nothing new for me. But this was different.

Everything about this was different.

He held me easily, and it was almost like dancing. It was almost like the *pas de deux*.

Almost.

I adjusted my hold on him and let myself slide until I could feel the thick head of his cock at the opening of my pussy.

I had the mad thought that all those years of ballet training had been for this, all along.

For this moment, when I could look up and hold

his bright blue gaze, then lower myself down on that hard, hot length of his.

I was so wet it should have embarrassed me though it didn't. I was wildly soft and deliciously hot, and even so, I had to adjust to the size of him. He was thick and long, but I dedicated myself to the task of taking him.

One hot inch after the next.

Slowly, carefully, I lowered myself. I waited for my body to accept him, then I went farther.

And we were both sweating by the time I finally made it all the way, my pussy flush against him.

And that glorious huge cock of his buried deep inside of me.

I felt myself begin to quiver. And his gaze shifted, his expression turning almost cruel with hunger and command.

"Don't you dare come," he told me. "You need to work for it this time."

One hand gripped my hair again. The other shifted to my waist, holding me against him as I arched back a little.

But nothing else was up to me.

And I loved it.

First, I had to fight off my own orgasm. And once again, it was years of fighting back my body's various urges that helped me. I didn't dare to disobey him, but I didn't ask myself what I thought he might do if I did.

I fought the need to come. I caught myself at the edge, shook with the effort but pulled myself back.

"Good girl," he murmured approvingly.

And that went through me like another shudder.

I glanced to the side, thinking a break in the intensity might help me maintain my control.

And I could see us in the window's reflection. Whoever we were.

A big, strong man. And an angel.

My wings flowed over the backs of my arms, and I arched my back to make them fall even more beautifully toward the floor. A move that lifted me up and got his cock even deeper inside me.

And then I rolled my hips, experimenting with the feel of it and ignoring the protest in my thigh muscles.

I didn't care if it hurt.

All I cared about was doing exactly what he told me to do.

Again and again, until it swept us both away.

I used my thighs and my core, and my grip on his wide shoulders. I lifted myself up, using my internal muscles to grip his cock all the way. And right when I got to the tip, I settled myself down again.

And that felt so good, so deep and full and glorious that I laughed a little.

I saw him look to the side, taking in that same reflection. I arched back even farther, dramatically, then gasped a little when he put his teeth to the side of my neck.

And then I did what I'd come here to do.

What he'd told me to do.

I fucked myself silly on him.

I found the count, the pattern. The lift and then the settle. The shimmer in my hips.

Again and again I rose up, then dropped myself down, until I lost track of the fact that this was another kind of performance. I was too drunk on the sensation of it. Too wild.

"Please, sir," I said, then began to chant. "I need to come."

"Too bad," he growled in reply.

So I fought my body even as I shook and grew wetter, hotter. Wilder by the moment.

There was no sound in the room save the two of us.

Our bodies, wet and hot, coming together over and over. Harsh breathing, his or mine, I could hardly tell.

I was used to orchestras, but this was a symphony all its own, and I couldn't tell the difference between the blood pounding in my head and the sounds I made.

"Please," I begged him. *"Please."*

I thought he would ignore me. And he did, for what seemed like forever.

Then he shifted. He wrapped his hands around

my ass, easing the tension in my thighs, which felt like its own release.

"Come, little dancer," he ordered me. "Now."

Before I change my mind, he didn't say. But I heard it all the same.

And I exploded. I burst into flame and fury and a thousand pieces of glorious shrapnel.

It was as if all the orgasms that preceded this one didn't count. They were insubstantial. Releases, that was all.

This was a bomb.

This was life altering.

I felt the way I had the first time I'd danced in my point shoes, spinning around and around as if made of light and air. I felt like I was flying.

The orgasm walloped me and kept going. I thought I heard myself scream.

And then he was turning us around, falling back against one of the sofas, bringing me down astride him with my wings all around us.

He waited until I stopped sobbing against him, there where my mouth had fallen against the crook of his neck.

I lifted my head, though it felt too heavy, and looked down at him.

He was beautiful. He was hard inside me and cruel in all the right ways.

I felt soft all the way through. Even in my heart,

though I cautioned myself against such nonsense as best I could when my head was still spinning.

He smiled then, this man who had bought me and had already given me more pleasure than lovers who'd claimed they knew me.

And his smile was a dark, erotic promise.

"My turn," he said.

CHAPTER FIVE

Darcy

I MADE AN involuntary sound.

I had made many sounds already—some I couldn't believe had come out of me—but this was different. I realized it even as it escaped my lips, but I couldn't take it back. I watched that dark, intent expression on his face as it altered slightly at the evidence of my vulnerability still echoing there between us.

I'd spent my whole life denying that I was capable of vulnerability. I smiled, instead. I danced until I bled, then I danced some more. Only actual broken bones made me stop, and sometimes not even then. And I certainly never *made vulnerable noises*. Ballet dancers were tough. We had to be, or we could never look that graceful.

"Problem?" he asked, his voice gritty.

Less a question than a demand.

I felt my breath shudder through my body, as if I'd forgotten how to breathe. I could feel the ache in my thighs, reminding me that I was splayed open as I sat astride him. And I could feel him, deep inside me, hard and hot. Still.

It made a different sort of shiver curl its way down my spine.

Every part of my body was sensitized. Overly raw and mad with it. Awake and alive in ways that made my head spin. I couldn't make sense of it. Of him. Of this fantasy brought to life at last. All the sex I'd had before this seemed dull, dim. Unsatisfying in a thousand ways, and we weren't even finished yet. It was as if this was my first time, as crazy as that was to imagine.

I felt words I shouldn't say swell inside of me—

But then I remembered myself.

This was the fantasy I had chosen.

And no man—or woman—bought an experience like this so they could hear about someone else's emotions. I understood that full well. The fantasy was in the anonymity. In the taking. This was a place for only certain kinds of intimacy.

My emotions were my own business. As were his.

That was what made this so hot.

"Of course not," I said, trying to sound serene and in control. I even managed what I thought was a passable smile. "How could there be a problem?"

His eyes were so bright I was sure they were punching holes right through me. I wondered if when I looked down I would see not only myself impaled upon him, but see those marks, too. Like scars.

And I wanted those scars. I wore the ones ballet had given me like badges of honor. Audiences had no idea what it took to look that effortless onstage. We covered our scars and danced straight through them.

I wanted whatever this man would give me. I wanted to wear his marks forward, like brands.

I expected him to start fucking me again, much harder this time—a notion that made me quiver—now that he called it *his turn*.

Instead, he moved one of his big, strong hands to fit against the curve of my cheek. It wasn't gentle, particularly. It felt like the very brand I'd just been imagining. A mark of ownership, especially when his thumb moved over my lips again.

As if he'd seen the raw, unbound truth behind my smile and was rubbing it away.

"You don't have to worry about anything," he told me then, and there was something in the way he said it. So dark. So intent and sure. So *certain*. That, too, made me quiver. "You have one job. Do you know what that is?"

"I thought I was doing it."

His blue eyes sharpened. "All you have to do

is what I tell you to do, little dancer. No more. No less. I will tell you what I want. What I like and what I don't. You don't have to worry about anticipating my needs. I'll make sure you know what they are. Do you understand?"

A thousand responses to that swirled around inside me, each one as raw and powerful and emotional as the next, but in the end I chose the only response that mattered.

"Yes," I said. He watched me, something expectant and commanding on his face, and I felt myself flush. "Yes, sir."

"Good girl."

And then he showed me what he meant.

His hands smoothed their way down my torso to grip my hips. I thought he would order me to move, but he didn't. Instead, he lifted me up, an easy slide along the length of his cock because I was so wet and hot and melting. He lifted me up, then slammed me back down.

Sensation exploded inside me, and he did it again. And again.

I didn't have to do a thing. He was using me like his very own fuck toy.

Something else exploded in me then. Something so bright and sharp and beautiful that I wanted to *grand jeté* straight into the center of it. I wanted to spin around and around and around until I *became* it.

I wanted this to last forever.

Still he lifted me, then slammed me down against him. Faster and faster. Harder each time.

I didn't know if it was aftershocks or a new tremor all its own, but I shook. Each slam of my body against his, with his cock so deep inside me, made my whole body hum in a sort of startled delight that spread everywhere until I was lit up with it.

And inside, I understood exactly what it was I felt. What all that rawness and wildness was.

Joy.

Freedom.

Because this was not the ballet. There I was an object valued for the pain I could withstand in my ability to make it all pretty and perfect for the audience. But here I was a different sort of object altogether.

Made for pleasure, not pain. And there was no putting a foot wrong. There was no messing up a step or ruining the perfect uniformity expected of the *corps*.

There was only this man's needs, his imagination and what he told me to do. Or did himself with my body as his instrument.

It was like magic.

He slammed me against him until I couldn't tell where I ended and his iron control began. There was only the sweetness of total surrender. And all the while, the building crisis of sheer delight inside me.

"Come once more," he ordered me, and it didn't occur to me to do anything but what I was told.

I let my head tip back, my breasts jutting forward as I curved my back into the arch.

And the cries that came out of me as I convulsed on his dick once again, as ordered, seemed to bounce back from the marble floors and the carefully brocaded walls. Calling me out. Calling my name when I didn't know his.

But the true music was when he finally roared out his own release, coming deep inside me in what felt like a scalding flood.

That tripped off another shock inside me and I sobbed with it, riding it out until I finally collapsed against him.

If I was on a stage, I would have to remove myself from it. I would have to dance my way off, no matter how I felt or what had happened to me up there. Or I would have to crawl off—maybe even ask someone to pull me off if I was really hurt—once the lights went down. The stage was an addiction, and there were times the price it demanded seemed impossible to pay. And no matter what, the show had to go on. The music would swell and the next act would take their place. That was the nature of the business we called show.

But this was no stage. There was no spotlight. This was a far simpler transaction.

The price had already been paid, and not by me.

And somehow, that notion made me feel safe. Enough that I hardly moved when he stirred beneath me, then swept me up with him as he stood.

I assumed he meant to set me on my feet. And then…who knows? Slap me on the ass and tell me to leave? Tell me to collect my things and go? Whatever he did, it certainly couldn't be worse than standing before the ballet master—or any one of the fierce teachers I'd had in my career—fighting to control my breathing while also trying to pay attention as they ripped my performance to shreds. Step by step.

Was there a critique in a transaction like this? Notes?

I wasn't sure what it said about me that my nipples hardened at the thought. As if all this time, all I'd really wanted was someone to take all these brutal little pieces of the life I'd chosen and turn them into sex.

Not just anyone, something inside me whispered. *Him.*

He didn't set me down. I thought the wiser course of action was to close my eyes, the better to avoid looking at the overwhelming perfection of his face. Not to mention the impossible blue of his gaze.

I rested my head against his broad shoulder as he carried me. And I peeked from under my lashes as we left the main room, moving through a bed-chamber with a crackling fire in a picturesque grate and on into a seductively lit bathroom suite. It was there that he set me on my feet, propping me up against the nearest tiled wall as if I really was no more than a sex toy.

The same delirious heat curled in me again. I stood where he'd put me, happy to wait and see how he would use me next.

That this was a suite set aside for sex was obvious, because the bathroom was clearly arranged for seduction first and hygienic purposes second. There was a door across the room with a WC written on it, but everything in the chamber where we stood was either gold, marble or dark wood, all of it as beautiful as it was functional.

Like me, I thought. My career in a nutshell.

He moved around the tub, which was vast and tall and clearly made to service at least four people. The water spilled out of the faucet like a waterfall, quick and quiet. The room grew steamy, scented with lavender and something spicier I couldn't identify. I breathed it in, deeply.

He looked up, then tilted his head toward the water in silent command. I had never been waited on in this fashion before. No one saw to my physical needs after a tough class, no matter how many muscles I'd pulled. It was up to me to care for my body, always making sure it could withstand the demands of all that dancing.

And even if I'd imagined someone tending to me, it would never have occurred to me that someone could perform the tasks he did while making it seem like some kind of *noblesse oblige*. The lord of the manor ministering to his underlings, but certainly not *serving* them.

My limbs felt deliciously heavy. I hadn't had sex in a while, and I'd never had sex like *that*. I could feel the ache of it, the longing deep inside and the actual sensation of use in my pussy. I could feel aches and pains all over, just enough to indicate I'd done something—and a lot of it—but not nearly enough to qualify as actual *hurt*.

Truth be told, I wasn't sure I'd ever felt better.

"Do I need to ask you twice?" His voice was silky then, but I didn't mistake the erotic menace in it.

And even that rolled over me with a delicious sort of ripple. I tried to hide my smile as I moved off the wall. He watched me—supervised me, maybe—as I climbed into the expansive tub, sighed at the embrace of the hot water, then sank down into it.

"Stay there and soak," he ordered me.

Then he strode from the bathroom, leaving me there to do just that.

The huge tub was set up on a dais, with a bank of windows splayed out before me, showing me Paris at night. I twisted my hair into an easy knot on the top of my head. I sank down as the water rose, letting it cover me to my chin. And I just... soaked.

As ordered.

I expected to start questioning myself. For the second-guessing to take me over, storming around and around inside me until it made me raw. I expected all the usual voices of doubt and worry to swamp me then and braced myself a little in anticipation.

Because it was one thing to fantasize about something and another to do it. I already knew that all too well. It was my life. Every little girl dreams of being a ballerina at one point or another. But the actual doing of it was something else entirely. Everybody wants the tutu. Everybody imagines themselves starring in *Swan Lake*.

Nobody wants the reality of practicing the same step over and over and over, day in and day out, ignoring your body screaming, your exhaustion, and all those same voices in your head forever telling you that you can't make it. That you can't do it. That no matter what, you'll never get there. All that to be good enough in your local ballet school.

The reality was that being the best in your ballet school was still not necessarily good enough

to make it into the *corps*, much less out of it to become a principal.

Fantasy was always *en pointe*, graceful and
light like a sylph. Reality was the state of my feet,
battered and ugly forever, and that kick of sharp
agony every time I used them that told me who
I was.

I turned off the water and sank deeper into the
tub. I waited for my body to finish cataloging its
reaction to what had happened, and for my emotions to catch up and wallop me. I waited for my
heartbeat to tip me over into sheer horror at what
I had not only allowed tonight, but encouraged.
Enthusiastically.

I waited.

But it was as if his order to sit here, to do nothing but soak, and his earlier command to lose myself in what he told me to do...*held me*, somehow.

It wasn't that I was numb or hiding from any
feelings. I could feel all kinds of things. The silky,
warm water against my skin. Every little tug here
and sharpness there, each with its own story to tell.

What I didn't feel was shame. Horror. Self-
recrimination or disgust that I had crossed every
line there was and, worse still, enjoyed it.

I had taken one of my deepest, most secret fantasies, made it real, and it wasn't over yet.

And I had no urge to jump up and run. I could
have, of course. There were panic buttons in every

room, I'd been told. *Should anything get out of hand*, my intake counselor had told me what seemed like a thousand years ago when I'd rung that bell and set all this in motion. I looked around now and, sure enough, beneath the discreet panel of light switches beside the bathroom door, there was another button. It was big and shiny and glinted like steel. If I didn't like what was happening, all I needed to do was get out of this tub, go over there and press it.

Nothing was keeping me from it. He had left me in this room all alone. I had nothing to do but consider each and every one of my options. Or even the fact I had some.

I wondered if he'd done it deliberately. I was used to the mind games of famous choreographers and my various ballet masters, who always insisted that we *choose*. In each and every moment, every step and every note of music, they demanded it. *Choose to be here*, one of our teachers liked to shout. *Choose to be better than yesterday. Choose perfection.*

Maybe he wanted me to keep choosing tonight, too.

I didn't hear anything, but something in the air around me changed. I glanced over, and he stood there in the door, that blue gaze of his as intense as when he'd been deep inside me.

Again, the freedom of this felt heady. I was a

little high on it, if I was honest, though I hadn't touched anything but water since I'd arrived here. Because if he was any other lover, I might have asked him where he'd gone. What he'd done in the other room while I'd sat here, soaking. Why he'd left me in this room in the first place.

But he wasn't my lover.

This was a different arrangement altogether. There was no reason to ask him a thing. He'd told me so himself. He would make sure I knew what he wanted. All I needed to do was what he told me to do. No thinking or worrying required.

So instead of interrogating him, I smiled. And said nothing.

"Give me a name," he said.

I noticed he did not ask for *my* name. I considered. "You can give me one. Whatever you like."

"If I wanted to give you a name, little dancer, I would."

I didn't know what it was about his voice that got to me, like a length of chain coiling inside me, wrapping itself around me and pulling tight. And all those tight links gleaming bright.

"You can call me Darcy," I said.

That had to be a mistake, surely. I didn't know where the urge to be honest came from. Why had I given this man my real name? Even if I had tried to dress it up like it was an alias of some kind?

But even as I asked myself the question, I knew the answer.

I wanted him to know me.

Annabelle took great pleasure in handing out fake names wherever she went. *Tonight I'm Caroline*, she would announced grandly, sweeping into this bar or that party. *I'm a disappointed society girl from Beacon Hill, whose inheritance is nothing more than a crumbling old brownstone and three ancient VW bugs.* And then she would spend the rest of the night acting and fucking the way she imagined her fictional Boston Brahmin Caroline would.

But I didn't want to play Annabelle's games. This was my fantasy, and I didn't want to spend the rest of my life replaying it in my head with another woman's name on this man's perfectly cruel mouth.

I already knew that I would hoard this night like treasure. I would lie in that bed of mine back in New York, run my hands over my own body and imagine this. Him. The blue of his eyes and the particular scrape of his voice all over me.

I would live this again and again.

It was only one night. But it would have to last me a lifetime.

Because I knew that I was never going to feel safe enough to repeat this, because I certainly couldn't afford to make myself a member of this club. This was my one chance.

A part of me whispered that it wasn't only the safety…it was him. This particular man on this specific night.

And if I wanted to make sure that I could hold this close to me forever, in all the years that followed, it required I give him my real name.

"Darcy," he said, as if he was tasting the syllables. As if it was a fine wine that required its own ritual before he could drink deeply.

I was sure it probably was a mistake to give him my real name, like bread crumbs that might lead away from this enchanted room in this decadent club straight back to my real life. But I would have to beat myself up for that later, when my emotions caught up with me. When I was back in reality, across the sea in Manhattan again.

Because here in this gleaming tub, with Paris like a sea of light outside the windows, all I could think about was the way it felt to hear him say it.

Darcy.

As if I wasn't just another object to him, as hot as that was.

As if I was *his*.

CHAPTER SIX

Sebastian

SHE CALLED HERSELF DARCY, and her eyes were big and brown and shaded with what looked like vulnerability.

I told myself that was what she wanted me to see. That it was not cynicism to remember that she was a treat I'd bought myself, an act to witness rather than a date to attempt to trust. It was reality.

Though, of course, I came to the club because I liked my reality filtered by their expert selection of possibilities. I wasn't the kind of man who was turned on by purchasing a stranger off a street corner. It was more accurate to say I wasn't turned off by transactional sex—in the right setting. With the correct controls in place. I didn't have to ask my dancer if she was safe or sane, or whether this encounter was consensual. I knew it was or she wouldn't be here.

But *consensual* didn't necessarily mean she

couldn't keep her hands off me. It was entirely possible what turned her on was my net worth, not the magic I could work with my cock.

There were some nights I might have cared about that. Tonight wasn't one of them.

Whatever had brought her here to me, I couldn't take my eyes off her.

I felt like a new man. As if she'd cleansed me, somehow, of all the darkness and guilt that had hung over me earlier. As if she'd made me brand-new.

It should have been just sex, quite a lot of it. But it hadn't felt like *just* anything to me.

And I had spent so many years trying to atone for my rashness. My mistakes. I'd spent a lifetime making myself responsible and dutiful to make up for the one time I'd been neither.

But tonight I felt filled with rashness. Hollowed out by greed.

All I wanted was…more.

I ignored the alarms that set off. I dimmed the lights and hit the other switch that lit up the electric candles that sat in sconces all over this room. Then I went to the tub that was more of a small swimming pool and climbed in, letting the hot water envelop me. The world I'd left outside this suite could wait. Ash. The endless negotiations over this deal or that. My mother's endless demands. The life I'd built so deliberately, so carefully. I knew it would all be there after I lost myself in my lovely little dancer.

I found a seat on one of the interior benches, then pulled her toward me.

"Kneel here," I said, low and dark.

And the way she moved was endlessly fascinating to me. It was as if she didn't have a bone in her body. As if she was entirely made of supple, glorious muscle and grace. She didn't slosh around in the hot water. Instead, she flowed as she moved from where she'd been sitting to kneel in the place I'd indicated, between my legs.

She'd piled her hair on top of her head, and the steam from the tub was making curls of the strands twist down. I knew it was humidity, that was all, but it seemed like magic. As she settled there on her knees between my outstretched legs, the water caught her at her breasts. And once again, I found myself unable to look away from her nipples, hard and proud. I reached out and found one of the soft, porous sponges along the rim of the tub, squeezed some of the provided gel into it and handed it to her.

"Make yourself soapy. Squeaky clean, Darcy, if you please. We have a long night ahead of us."

She laughed, but she didn't argue. She didn't throw out something suggestive, as I half expected. She only took the sponge I offered her, dipped it in the water and kept her melting brown gaze on mine as she slowly began to work it down one side of her elegant neck.

My mouth went dry.

It was another performance, I knew. Another dance. She might not have been removing her clothes, but she still commanded the stage. And every last bit of my attention.

I watched her, as wildly greedy as a man who hadn't just come—so hard it had left me something like dizzy, so I'd had to remove myself until I'd regained my control. She smoothed the sponge down the length of one arm, over each of her fingers, then up the other arm. Then she knelt up higher and arched her back in that way of hers that I thought might haunt me for the rest of my days, tracking hot water and soapy bubbles across one breast and proud nipple, then the other.

It was the most erotic thing I'd ever seen, especially because I knew how she tasted. How her pussy gripped me when she came. And all the hungry noises she made while she fought to take all of my cock.

"How are you enjoying Paris?" I found myself asking her, perhaps because it was the sort of question a man might ask a woman in more innocuous circumstances. Over a sedate dinner, perhaps. While pretending not to notice the stultifying boredom. "Will you be staying here long?"

"Maybe I live in Paris." She grinned. "In a

charming garret, the way you're supposed to live here. Or maybe I have no particular home at all. And merely roam about the planet, wherever the wind takes me. Then again, maybe this is my secret life and I spend the rest of my time as a very junior accountant in an unremarkable suburb somewhere."

"Pick a life, Darcy," I drawled, enjoying the way she played with herself, arching this way and that with all of her mouthwatering flexibility. "And tell it to me like a bedtime story."

"Are we going to bed?" she asked, and there was more than simple feminine awareness in her gaze, then. It was shot through with something else. I wanted to call it *delight*, but I told myself I was making that up. Putting it where it didn't belong. Making this something it wasn't. Something I shouldn't want it to be. "That's not where I thought this was heading, sir. If I'm honest."

"Make sure it's a good story, then. And who knows where we'll end up?"

My own words seemed to sit in me strangely. As if they were too heavy, or too ripe with something I refused to call foreboding. As if I was talking about something else altogether.

I shook that off because she swayed closer, balancing herself—though I felt certain she didn't need any help to balance herself—with her fingers on my thigh beneath the water. She dipped the sponge in the water and began to run it slowly over the thigh she wasn't already touching.

"Once upon a time there was a girl named Darcy," she told me, and there was laughter in her voice and in her gaze. It was like sunshine to me, who had been born and bred in the rains of England and the cold of my father's house. I wanted to bask in her. "Unrelated to anyone present here tonight, of course."

"Of course," I agreed, caught somewhere in the heat of the steam, the water and the sensation of her hands on me. Her body, slippery and lithe, and the sound of her voice like a spell.

That was the secret I didn't want told, not even to myself. I wanted to be enchanted, if only for the night.

"Darcy lived in a house big enough to be a castle, though it wasn't. It had tennis courts. Its own bowling alley, though no one ever actually bowled in it, because bowling was considered low-class. There was an indoor swimming pool that no one ever used, but was always mentioned in public anyway, especially in the winter. And there were miles and miles of lawn, always green and manicured. And quickly Darcy learned that though she had come into the world as a daughter, her true purpose in the castle was to be a doll."

"A doll?"

"Dolls are collected. They're dressed perfectly and can be left to their own devices for years at a time if necessary, remaining pristine. Dolls never talk back. They not only do what they're told, they don't do anything at all unless someone does it for them. Darcy was more of a puppet, really. And where there's a puppet, there are puppet masters. I think you know the puppet masters make the rules." She laughed, though it held less sunshine than before. "And if the dolls don't obey, they get set down and ignored. Possibly replaced."

She wrung out the sponge, then dipped it in the water all over again and started on my other leg.

If she noticed that my cock was hardening again, she gave no sign.

"Darcy decided that if she had to be a puppet, a doll, she might as well be the best of all the dolls. The prettiest. The most accomplished. The kind that was so universally beloved that she belonged in the puppet masters' favorite music box, twirling around and around whenever the box was opened."

"This does not exactly sound like an uplifting bedtime story."

"That really depends on how you think about dolls and puppets, I guess."

"I don't."

"But you're British. Punch and Judy and all those terrifying pantomimes. Puppets are in your blood, surely."

"I have never paid the slightest attention to dolls, puppets, or bloody pantos."

"Haven't you?"

Her mouth curved at that. And she moved again, sliding that soft, warm sponge across my chest, rubbing me like she was polishing me to a shine.

I didn't care that she was challenging me.

On the contrary, I liked it.

"Dolls exist to be bought," she said. "To be played with. To dance while the music plays, then be put away until they are useful again."

Her voice changed at that last part, melting a bit as she spoke. Not quite singsong, but close enough.

I found my hands moving of their own accord. I spun her around so her back was to my chest and her ass was snug against my cock. She braced herself, one hand on each of my thighs, and she moved in a sinuous, delicious little wiggle that made me groan.

"You can keep talking to me about dolls," I managed to say, though I wanted to roar it. "But do it with my cock inside you."

She arched against me, and I filled my hands with her breasts, small, but perfect. And those nipples that I could pluck and roll between my fingers until goose bumps broke out all over her neck. She tilted her hips and impaled herself on the tip of my cock. Then slowly, rolling her hips, worked herself down my full length.

And her pussy was scalding hot. Far silkier than the bathwater all around us.

"I told you to keep talking," I growled against her neck, and raked my teeth across the goose bumps I'd raised.

I could feel her shudder from where she clenched tight around my cock to the breasts she pushed harder into my palms.

"This is how a doll dances," she told me, a catch in her voice. "Music box dancers are all the same, you know. You must nail them down on some kind of peg or pole." And she demonstrated by clenching me tight with her internal muscles. Locking me inside her in such a fierce grip that for a tumultuous moment I thought I might come there and then. I gritted my teeth, bit her a little in warning and held on. Barely. "And as long as the music plays, they dance. Like this."

And she rocked against me then, her hips the enchantment I'd been looking for. Pure magic. Lust and light. She rose, then settled back against me, each sweet, sexy wriggle taking me deeper.

Beneath the surface of the water, I could see the way she looked splayed against me like this. Riding my cock, open and abandoned.

She was most beautiful thing I had ever seen. There was no possible way that one night with her could ever be enough. I accepted that, and the regret I would feel when this was over.

But it wasn't over yet.

"Our Darcy takes each and every music box she finds herself in seriously," she told me, tipping her head back so she could lean into my mouth against her neck. "One way or another, she still wants to be the favorite doll. Everyone's favorite."

"I think that's really down to her owner, don't you?" I asked.

I left one hand where it was, toying lazily with her nipple, and let the other one fall down to the place where we were joined. I felt my own cock, and I felt her. That sweet, hot pussy, greedy and lush.

Then I found her clit, and began to play with it the way I was playing with her nipple. Lazy enough to make her flush. Intense enough to make her moan.

"I like the way you dance," I told her as she began to make those choked noises that I knew meant she was close to coming again. "And I had no idea how much I like a music box. I like to turn it on. Then turn it off, at will. My will."

I stopped playing with her nipple and moved my hand to hold her pussy flush against me, so she couldn't keep rocking us both toward bliss.

"On," I growled against her neck, and resumed what I'd been doing. Pinching her nipple and her clit in turn. She sobbed out something that could have been words, and moved again. More jerk-ily this time, her body trembling in my hands. "Then off."

Again I stopped. Her breath sawed in and out of her. I could feel her pulse beneath my mouth, thundering in her veins.

"Darcy." I said the name she'd given me because I liked it. And because it made her shudder. "I don't play with dolls. But a music box? That's something I could get my head around. I like to collect pretty things, after all. But there's something you should know. When I take something and make it mine, I don't like to let it go."

I didn't know why I said that. Or why I raked the soft, sweet skin of her neck with my teeth until she cried out, then bucked against me wildly as if she'd lost all semblance of control.

"Please, sir. I want to come. I want to dance. I want whatever it takes—"

"You get what I give you, little doll. Maybe that's the shelf for you, cast aside with nothing to do but watch."

I pulled her off me then and set her before me, turning her around again until she settled back down on her knees.

And this time, her eyes were unfocused. She was panting, her lips parted, a pretty flush all over her cheeks.

She was so beautiful it hurt. I reached over and helped myself to some more of the bath gel.

I wrapped my hand around my cock, made a fist and pumped myself as she watched.

And very nearly lost myself entirely when that unfocused look turned greedy. Hungry.

"Sir…?"

But I shook my head, enjoying myself. And her need. "I want you to stand up. Climb out of this tub and wrap yourself in a towel."

She swallowed. "Can I make you come first?"

I felt my cock pulse in my own hand.

"Did I ask you to?" I demanded. Severely.

She blew out a breath as if that hurt her, which only made me harder.

Then she did what she was told.

And that was when I knew.

No matter what, no matter what it cost or how foolhardy it was, there was no way in hell one night with this woman who called herself a doll— and who I wanted to call mine—was going to satisfy me.

I wanted more.

And I was Sebastian Dumont. What I wanted, I usually got.

My little dancer didn't stand a chance.

CHAPTER SEVEN

Darcy

SOMETHING WAS DIFFERENT.

I wrapped myself in a towel as ordered and watched as he did the same. Then I followed him out through the sumptuous bedchamber to the main room again, where an elegant meal had been set up on the table for two, placed to take in the breathtaking views of Paris all around us.

It looked romantic. Intimate. And I felt something tug at me, because there was a part of me that wished it was—

Stop, I ordered myself. I needed to remember my place. The transaction I'd agreed to, no matter what it looked like.

But I couldn't keep myself from trying to make light of it, somehow. I laughed as we walked toward the table. "Is this a date? I think we're doing it backwards."

"Do you have dinner with all your dates without

your clothes on?" He didn't wait for my answer. He pulled out a chair for me, helped me sit in it with distinct courtesy, though I didn't require assistance, and then took my towel from me.

I should have protested. I meant to, surely. Instead, goose bumps prickled all over my skin in a new kind of delight and I…didn't.

When he sat down across from me, he kept his towel knotted loosely around his hips. That meant I could still admire that beautifully formed chest of his. I could marvel at the clean, masculine line of his jaw. I could watch his hands as he used them to pour the wine and remember what they felt like on me. In me.

It was possible I sighed a little. Happily.

"Surely this night is whatever I want it to be," he said as he filled one crystal glass, then the other. "Or did I misunderstand what I paid for?"

On some level, I imagined that was meant to be a slap. But I liked it. It was good to be reminded of what this was. Who we were. Every dancer had to know the limits of the stage, after all. Or she risked toppling off into the orchestra pit.

"Are you hungry?" he asked after a moment, when I didn't respond.

And I understood the difference in him, then. It was this sudden solicitude. I could see the same greediness in that blue gaze of his that had held us both so tightly before. The same driving hunger I'd seen from the stage. But first he'd had me soak. Now he wanted to feed me.

"It really isn't a dinner date," I said. Sternly.

Because I wasn't worried he needed the reminder; it was me.

"Thank you, Darcy." And there was a gleam I suspected was amusement in his bright gaze. "I am aware. I have a great deal of money and even more influence, and even I cannot dine out wearing so little."

For some reason, that calmed me. And it wasn't until I felt calm again that I understood I hadn't before. Not really. There had been too much sensation. Too much *feeling*. Too many emotions circling around and not quite landing. Too much *soaking*.

For a little while, there was silence. If this had really been my job, I probably would have leaped to fill it. I would have attempted to entertain him with my sparkling personality and wit—assuming I could access either, after all that astonishing sex—but then again, that wasn't what he'd signed up for. The burlesque was a lot of things, suggestive and saucy in turn, but it didn't involve *conversation*. At least, not the way I did it.

And the truth of the matter was, I was ravenous.

I hadn't paid much attention to the hollow feeling in my belly, because we'd come up to this room right after I'd finished my act. And I'd had other, more pressing concerns. And with all that ruthless, glorious fucking, it was like my performance had just…kept right on going. I was used to controlling any flashes of hunger while I danced, in class or rehearsal or in strange little pockets of my performances. It was to be expected when using my body with such intensity.

And this night was a very different kind of performance, but it wasn't over yet—and it was already requiring just about all the intensity I could stand.

He had taken the ordering upon himself, but there was a variety to choose from on the table between us. Meat, fish. Salads and sides. I helped myself to a little bit of everything, and ate. Heedlessly.

With the table manners my mother had drilled into me since birth, in deference to my opulent surroundings, but heedlessly all the same.

"You eat the way you fuck," he said when I finally sat back and sighed, happily full. "But you are so slight. You cannot possibly eat that way all the time."

I shrugged. "When I allow myself to eat, I eat whatever I want."

"And what are your allowances?"

I grinned, not in the least put off by this line of questioning. No matter how progressive the ballet pretended to be to get in line with the times, we were all obsessed with food. Eating too much or too little of it. Eating the wrong things that would adversely affect our performance or stamina.

We did what we had to do to keep attention on how we danced, not our shapes while we did it. People didn't like to admit these things out loud in these welcome days of body positivity out there in the real world, but I had always been of the mind that my body belonged to the company. The company was responsible for its aches and pains, its sometime ability to *almost* fly, and so too whatever shape was best to fit into their costumes and blend into their backgrounds. It was only when I strayed outside the confines of the ballet that I remembered the rest of the world viewed these things rather differently.

Because the rest of the world didn't have to dance beautifully enough to disappear, night after night after night.

But this man was not the world. I had the distinct impression that if he could, he would take the place of the company. And mold me to his own specifications.

The notion thrilled me, like his hands on me again.

"I usually eat after a performance," I told him. "But I don't like to eat much beforehand. It makes me feel…heavy. And cranky. And no one likes a cranky—" I remembered myself. And my anonymity. "Dancer."

His gaze was as sharp and incisive as it was blue. "And when you speak of performance, you mean the burlesque?"

I felt as caught in his gaze as I had been in his arms. My throat was dry. I had the strangest urge to tell him my whole life's story—and not in the form of a thinly veiled fairy tale this time.

Instead, I smiled airily. "What else could I mean?"

I expected him to smile back at me. To acknowledge that we were both playing this little game of masked identities, secrets and lies. Wasn't that the purpose of a single night like this? Everyone could be who they pretended to be for this little window of time. You could do anything for a night, after all. Anything at all.

"I want another night," he said.

He might as well have tossed a grenade across the table. I lowered the linen napkin I'd pressed to my lips and set it beside my plate. I swallowed hard. And suddenly, I couldn't bear all that bright blue regard. "That's not our arrangement."

"Is it money?" He lifted a shoulder. "I will pay you whatever you wish, of course."

"It's not the money." The moment I said that, I thought better of it. What enterprising prostitute said such a thing? Of course it was about the money, as it should be. "Every night is the same price, rest assured. But this? You? One night only, as agreed."

A brow lifted in a way that told me he was used to great swaths of underlings vaulting about to tend to his every whim, expressed or not. "Why?"

It would have been different if he'd seemed upset. Or too…determined, in any of the ways that might have tripped alarms in me. But he didn't. Instead, he lounged back in his seat as if this was all a foregone conclusion, and I had the impression of a predator trying to hide in plain sight. The intense focus in those bright blue eyes didn't fade in the least.

"Our arrangement was for one night," I reminded him primly.

"Then let's change the arrangement."

"I don't think so."

"Darcy." The folly of telling him my name was all too apparent then, because it was exactly as I'd intended. He used my name, and it felt intimate. It felt real. I might cling to these things later, but they only made this moment harder to navigate. "If an item is for sale, and I have the money required to purchase it, there is no reason I shouldn't have it. Is there?"

I made myself laugh, bright and sparkling. "My feeling is that a performer should never commit to more performances than she knows she can do well."

And I tried to smile the way I imagined a burlesque dancer would. More earthy, less regal. More happy hooker and less hungry princess.

When his expression took on that intent look again, I figured that whatever I was doing, it was working.

"I've been doing this awhile," I continued. I meant dancing, of course, but he could think whatever he liked. "There's a certain point where the spirit might be willing, but the body can't quite keep up. I prefer to make sure I get all the beauty sleep I need."

"Why do I not quite believe you, little dancer?"

He asked the question in such an idle, offhand way that I almost confessed the truth. That he was right not to believe me, because I was full of it. Apart from the practicalities and the papers I'd signed, I knew I couldn't let myself have another night with him because it was a high possibility that I'd forget myself completely. I'd tell him who I was. I'd beg him for more. I'd ruin this fantasy by shoving it too far into reality, and that would destroy the whole thing.

I didn't want the reality of him, because I wasn't sure I could handle it. I wanted this high-octane night of endless sex and happy obedience. I wanted his cock in my mouth and my knees on a hard floor. Not the mundane reality of another man I wouldn't have enough time for and who would irritate me before the month was out.

This was the only way I could have him just like this, forever. It was my fantasy. It belonged in the dark, in my bed, and in reality for only one night. I didn't want to bring it out into the light where it would inevitably spoil.

No matter how much I thought I might like to roll around in the sunlight with *him*.

"One night," I said quietly.

"Very well. If that's what you want."

"It is."

My hands were in my lap and I laced them tightly together, then squeezed, to remind me that this really wasn't a dinner date of any kind. I was not here to ask his name. Or to question him at all. I was here to do what I did best: look pretty, bend in every direction, and smile at the applause.

I'd expected the fantasy to be potent, no matter the man. I hadn't expected *him* to be as potent as the taboo.

He was still studying me as if he could *see* what he wanted that way. He toyed with stem of the wineglass before him, using those same strong fingers that had made me weep with passion. And I wanted to break the mood. I was naked and entirely too aware of my body. The tightness of my nipples pulled into points. The melting, slippery heat between my legs.

That trembling thing, deep inside, that I knew had nothing to do with the fantasy and everything to do with me.

I slid from my chair, sinking down to my knees beside it. Then I tipped myself forward onto all fours and kept my eyes on him. There wasn't much space between us, but I made the most of it. I crawled, sensuous and deliberate, from my chair to his.

"What are you doing, little dancer?" His voice sounded darker than before, but indulgent.

"It was such a good dinner." My voice was husky when I reached him. I ran my hands up over the hair-roughened muscles of his thighs, pushing the towel out of my way as I went. "I thought there had to be dessert."

He didn't order me to stop. He didn't tell me to sit back, drop my hands, or await his orders. He only stared down at me, heat and greed and something darker on his hard, beautiful face. I followed my gut feeling, and that trembling thing inside me. I cupped him in one palm, and wrapped the fingers of my other hand around the shaft of his cock. He was already hard, and he thickened even more as I gripped him.

I kept my eyes locked to his as I leaned closer, circling the plump head with my tongue.

"Don't tease," he growled.

I smiled. Then I sucked him in deep.

And for long moments, there was nothing but this. Communion. Consolation.

This fantasy made real in the best way imaginable.

He tasted male. And like me. I couldn't get enough. I wished I could take all of him and I did my best, triumph washing through me when his hands moved to fist in my hair.

And I moaned out my pleasure when he lifted his hips, gently fucking my mouth.

I rocked my hips from side to side, desperate for some friction, but I was too busy holding on to him to tend to myself.

I liked that almost more than I could bear. Aching for him even as I serviced him. Leaving myself needy while he grunted out his pleasure, then came hard, salt and man down the back of my throat.

I sat back, feeling dazed and delicious. There was moisture in the corners of my eyes and that lovely used feeling making my mouth feel like his, not mine.

His eyes glittered as he looked down at me, still kneeling there beside his chair. He smoothed my hair back with those hard hands of his I knew without question would haunt me for the rest of my life. He wiped the excess moisture away from beneath my eyes with his thumb, then kept his hand there. He cupped my cheek, holding my face tilted toward his.

And it was so easy to forget how I'd come to
be here. All the necessary lines between fantasy
and real life. In this moment, I was a woman and
he was a man, and everything else felt like make-
believe.

I was tempted to forget myself.

I wanted more than one night. I wanted a thousand nights. I wanted to take this fantasy, make
it real all the time and, more than that, make it
work. Whatever that meant. I wanted what I knew
I couldn't have. I wanted things I couldn't name
and wouldn't know how to ask for. I wanted the
sheer ecstasy of this to transcend this transaction
we'd agreed upon.

But that was the beauty of this situation. There
was no changing it. He was a member of this club
and could do what he liked, but I had signed very
specific contracts. I was not to take the initiative
and contact anyone I met here afterward. I was
certainly not to make my own arrangements. And
if I wanted to come back to the club, to continue
what I'd started here tonight, as I was informed
many "fantasy guests" did, I would have to pay
them for the privilege.

The price they quoted to me had made my eyes
water and my stomach twist in a kind of panic.

I would not be coming back here on my dime,
that was for sure.

"I don't know what you're doing to me," he said,

his voice low, his hand hot and strong against my jaw. And there were too many things I was afraid I understood all too well in his gaze. "I am a man of duty, not debauchery. I blow off steam only under the most controlled circumstances, and I never lose myself. And you have me imagining things I would have told you were impossible eight hours ago."

I knew there was no hope in it. No happy ending, save the ones we gave each other here. Orgasms aplenty, but absolutely nothing else. I told myself that made it safe.

I leaned my cheek into his hand. "What do you imagine?"

"You don't understand." His voice was even darker now. Something far more dangerous than a mere growl. "My father was a man who broke things because he knew he could always buy more. He particularly liked to break companies down into parts, sell them off at a profit and enrich himself. Still, the thing he broke most often was my mother."

He shouldn't be telling me something like that. Something so real it seemed to hurt him as he said it. I wanted to tell him to take back those words. To steer us in a different direction altogether, back to *yes, sir* and the stark honesty of sex, but I couldn't seem to make my mouth work. I could still taste him on my tongue.

I told myself that it was better, maybe, that he

should talk to me as if he was nothing but a man. Any man at all. The kind I could find annoying after a few weeks. Maybe this way I'd believe it.

"Everything I know about emotion I learned from a broken, bitter woman whose only friend comes in liquid form and keeps her drunk around the clock. She keeps a good face for the public, which means I'm usually the one treated to her drunken displays. She taught me that love means always, always, being the victim."

"You don't have to talk about these things," I murmured, not sure why my instinct was to soothe him.

His smile was merciless. "I keep my life in strict compartments. Work. Play. Family on one branch, my social life, such as it is, on another. And these branches never, ever cross."

"I think everybody does that."

I thought of my own parents, chilly and remote. Never quite pleased, no matter what. They had attended my early recitals—if the dates didn't conflict with their social calendars—but I'd always thought they supported their ballet-dancer daughter because that made them seem more sophisticated to their friends. It meant I had worked that much harder, as if I needed to prove myself to them. As if that might make them love me. I was almost thirty and I wasn't sure they did. I never asked them about it. I just…danced. With more focus and intensity. And I had never considered introducing Annabelle to them, for example. It was unimaginable that they might have access to my *actual* life.

"Families are like secret wounds that never quite heal," I found myself saying, there in a suite in Paris while a man watched me too closely with eyes like every summer I'd missed because I'd been too busy rehearsing. "Sometimes they leave scars. But I think those scars mean you're lucky. For the rest of us, there's no hoping that the scar tissue fades from pink and becomes white over time. For most of us there's no healing. There's only coming to terms with the maintenance and the bandages as best we can."

"Why, Darcy." His hand moved against my cheek. "I had no idea someone who moves the way you do could be so cynical."

"It's not cynicism, it's reality. No one can work in fantasy without a serious grounding in reality. Not if they want to survive. Much less succeed."

I surprised myself, because I was talking about ballet. And what it took to live the life I did. The kind of life that strangers assumed they could imagine when all they saw was pancake makeup and costumes floating across the stage, never the years of work that went into looking that effortless—

But he thought I was talking about sex.

"And here I thought it was your emotions that made this work."

"Emotions are fuel," I said lightly. "Let them take control, and they'll eat you alive. Use them as fuel, and they'll help you burn brighter." His thumb moved along my jawline, hypnotically. "But then again, I am not drunk."

"Indeed, you are not." His mouth flattened. "I cannot imagine a woman like you ever allowing a man to break her the way my father broke my mother. Over and over again."

"I break things all the time." That happened to be true. "What are a few broken bones among friends?"

It occurred to me after I said it that possibly that was the sort of joke better confined to the ballet rehearsal halls.

"Bones heal. Marriages? Not so much." Again, that smile without any mirth. "I promised myself I would never make myself so vulnerable to another. I would never allow anyone close enough to break me. And I never have."

"Forgive me," I murmured then. "You do not strike me as particularly…unbroken."

He let out a sound at that, though I would not call it a laugh. "Tell me, little dancer, why do I have the impression that you will be the wound I cannot heal?"

"I can give you what you paid for," I whispered,

my heart pounding in ways I refused to analyze. "Nothing more."

"I want another night. The whole bloody weekend."

"No," I whispered. "That will only make it worse."

"I don't think it will. I don't think it could." He lifted me up and settled me on his lap, and for a moment there was nothing but the electricity between us. The crackle of that connection. Heat and longing. "But this will. I'm sure of it."

I held my breath, not sure what he was about to do. And not prepared when what he did was wrap his hand around the nape of my neck.

Then slowly, inexorably, he drew my mouth to his.

"You can't…" I began.

"Did I buy all of you? Or only a small part of you?"

It was a silken challenge. Dark and hot.

"I don't even know—"

But I cut myself off. Horrified that I'd nearly given myself away.

And something far more complicated than merely *horrified* that the very thought of his kiss… panicked me. All the sex we'd had must have gotten to me. But not like this.

His blue eyes flashed a warning, but I didn't pull away. And not because he'd paid for me. But because I wanted him to kiss me more than I'd ever wanted anything. More than breath.

And when he took my mouth, it wasn't as if he owned it. Or me. It was as if kissing me was the answer to a question neither one of us wanted to ask. An answer that thudded in me like stone.

But I didn't pull away.

His kiss was sweet and hot at once. It was searing. And yet it filled me up like a sob.

He pulled back, his mouth close to mine, and I knew.

That nothing would be the same. Least of all me.

"My name is Sebastian," he said, because it turned out there was always a way to make it worse. To make it hurt. "Sebastian Dumont. I want more, little dancer, but if you won't give it to me, all I can do is make sure that every single moment we have together, tonight, counts."

And that was exactly what he did.

Again and again and again.

CHAPTER EIGHT

Darcy

BACK HOME, I told myself that everything was exactly the same.

New York was as noisy and exhilarating, anonymous and comfortable as I'd left it. I had the same life, the same responsibilities, the same routine. Morning class and endless, intense rehearsals as we geared up for the new season.

I was the same person who had left for a weekend in Paris.

I was *fine*.

"You're welcome," Annabelle had purred when I walked into our apartment after my long flight home. "I told you that you needed this and I was right. Think how much fun we're going to have here now that you—"

"I'm not doing it again." I dropped my bag on the floor and wanted to frown at her. Sternly. But I made myself smile instead, because I didn't want her to know that I was…rocked. I wanted her to think I was like her and completely at my ease. "I wanted to do it once. And I did, so I'm done."

Then, no matter how much she begged, I didn't tell her a single thing about Sebastian. I told her about the performance. I commiserated with the fact she'd stayed here to understudy when, of course, Claudia hadn't had so much as a stray sniffle and likely wouldn't. I talked about the thrill of the burlesque, the unwieldy costume, and how *different* it had all been. I told her every detail I could recall about the club she'd been dying to see for years—at least, all the ones I could share under the conditions of the NDA.

But I kept Sebastian to myself.

Sebastian, who had been absolutely true to his word. Sebastian, who had kissed me and fucked me, made me cry his name, made me sob, and made me laugh. Over and over again.

We hadn't gotten any sleep. After that meal and my refusal to extend our arrangement, he had applied himself to the task as if bent on leaving his mark on every square inch of my skin.

And he did.

But the fantasy was over. I'd walked out of that club into a sullen, wet Parisian morning—and the rest of my life—and I hadn't looked back. I'd forced myself to stay awake and reasonably alert, and had marched through a few museums before whiling away a couple of hours at a café. I'd checked my bank balance and had just about fainted.

Then, finally, I'd gone to the airport a far richer woman than I'd been when I arrived, and slept all the way home on the plane.

I'd left the fantasy where it belonged. In a club I couldn't access, across an ocean from me. I told myself that in time all that sensation would fade. My memories of it would become less vivid. That intense longing in me would dissipate.

I could comfort myself with the money I'd earned, and I did.

But one week passed, then another, and I kept waiting for my body to feel like...*mine* again.

Because, try as I might, I felt...different. And I knew it was me, because life in the *corps* was as it always had been and always would be. We danced. We obsessed over a wrist here, an ankle there. We practiced our steps, mastered our timing. As the weather grew colder, Annabelle and I spent less time running in Central Park and more time on elliptical machines. Sometimes we swam. It didn't matter what I did, I didn't feel right. I *looked* fine. As close to perfect as I could get, as required.

But I didn't feel like me anymore.

I could feel that night in Paris in the way I danced. In every step and every tired muscle in my body. And maybe, I thought as yet another week passed and I still couldn't quite inhabit my own body the way I used to so easily, it wasn't Sebastian at all. He had touched something in me I hadn't known was there, that was true. I didn't try to deny that even to myself.

But I was beginning to wonder if the burlesque had changed my dancing for good.

Or not the dancing, not really. I could perform at the same capacity and did, because if I didn't I'd get cut. I was *fine*. But my drive had shifted.

Before I'd gone to Paris, my life had revolved around a certain grim acceptance that this was the way it was and nothing could change it. I would dance until I was cut from the *corps*. I would never ascend to a higher level as a soloist—always a bridesmaid and never a bride, my friend Winston used to say—and I would call that a career. I would be grateful for it, and someday I feared I would miss these days.

If I had any future plans, they were dim and insubstantial. There were those who parlayed their time in the company into teaching for the Knickerbocker. But that, too, was a political quagmire, and I already knew that I would have to be far better than I was—far better, yet still not good enough to bloom into a *prima ballerina* role—to shift over to company staff, much less become a ballet master in my own right. I'd once seen a TV show about a former ballerina who went off to some picturesque village somewhere and opened her own ballet school, and when I imagined anything at all after these years of the *corps*, I imagined that.

Late at night, while Annabelle and her lovers made their typical ruckus, I didn't lie in bed with my hands between my legs any longer, getting myself off on my fantasies. Sebastian had far outstripped any fantasy I might have had. And I didn't really see the point of pretending my fingers were him when I knew better. Instead, I lay awake and tried to imagine myself as one of my early ballet teachers. I tried to imagine myself patiently molding little girls without crushing their dreams. Or attempting to see the beauty in their waddling, ghastly attempts at ballet's contradictory willowy crispness. Trying all the while to pretend I wasn't desolate for the life I'd been forced to leave behind.

But no matter how I tried to imagine it, I couldn't quite see myself in that role.

The next time I took the train north from the city, using my day off for one of my command performance dinners with my parents, I tried to imagine that this was my commute home. That I'd come down into the city to see Annabelle, perhaps, and was now returning to my small little suburban life. Back to the Darcy James Ballet School, where ambitious mamas would bully their little girls into tutus, bully me into pretending they could dance, and calling all that failure and imperfection ballet.

It made me feel hollow.

I took a taxi from the train station when I arrived, the better not to inconvenience my parents, and stared out at the Connecticut countryside that I knew so well. I had grown up here. I didn't dislike it, or go to great lengths to separate myself from its suburban grasp the way I knew Annabelle did. But by the same token, when all was said and done, I had never imagined myself here.

I had always imagined myself onstage.

I tried to snap myself out of it when the car turned into the long drive that led to my childhood home. I made myself breathe properly as the stone house, fashioned like an opulent farmhouse, came into view. It was lit up bright and cheery against the autumn night, and I told myself that I was, too.

But no visit to my parents was ever without tension.

I was a grown, independent woman, but I still dressed for them instead of myself. A smart pair of flats instead of the comfortable boots I preferred. Black leggings, but not worn as pants, as I knew that was one of my mother's pet peeves. I wore a little A-line shift dress over the leggings, and it wasn't until I glanced at myself in the hall mirror in the foyer that I realized I already looked like the suburban ballet mistress who haunted my future.

I'd draped myself in several scarves to break up the relentless black and pulled my hair back into the ubiquitous ballet bun, but that didn't change the facts. I had never seen a woman either in the ballet or adjacent to the ballet—of any age—who didn't dress…exactly like this. As if we spent our lives in *corps* whether we were dancing or not.

Welcome to your life, I told myself sharply. *Better get used to it now.*

I wandered farther into the house, following the sound of my parents' favorite classical music station into the back of the house. Evenings were always conducted in the chic, sophisticated kitchen complete with sofas arranged around a cozy fireplace and the sort of dramatic flower arrangements that could only be maintained by twice-weekly visits from the florist. Sure enough, my mother stood at the counter, putting the finishing touches on a meal I knew she hadn't cooked. That was the province of the housekeeper. While she added her own little flourishes to the dinner she needed only to warm, my father sat near the fire, lost behind *The New York Times*.

I hovered in the wide archway a moment, not sure why it had never occurred to me before that I had first learned the rules of performance here. In this house, where the appearance of perfection had always been valued far above any kind of honesty or emotion. This was where I'd learned to dance long before I'd learned the basics of the five positions that were the foundation of ballet.

But maybe that was straying too far into the

cynicism I had so boldly told Sebastian I didn't possess.

My mother was slim, her hair more silver than black these days. Even though this was a dinner at home, she was dressed elegantly. She was always dressed elegantly. Dark, exquisitely tailored pants over flats that gleamed. And above, the sort of fitted, understated jacket that was undoubtedly sourced from some designer recognizable by a single name. She wore pearls at her ears, a simple gold chain at her neck. On her left hand, she wore one exquisite diamond that my father had placed there some thirty years ago. She was the kind of woman other people, who didn't dance professionally, always claimed *looked* like a dancer. They meant she stood tall, was thin, and carried herself with a certain air of purpose.

I really was a professional dancer, but I'd never come close to my mother's elegance. And looking at her now, I felt a familiar ache inside me that reminded me I never would. I could dance myself silly, and I had. And would, as long as I could. But it was my mother who commanded rooms with an arch of one brow.

If she'd taken to the stage, I knew beyond any shadow of a doubt that my mother would have easily become a *prima ballerina*. Sometimes I suspected she knew it, too.

Maybe that was the sharp little thing beneath

my heart that always pulsed so painfully when I was near her.

"Do come inside, Darcy," she said then, her voice a cool reproach. "I'm not sure why you're lurking in the doorway like that."

"Hi, Mom," I replied, fighting to keep from sounding like a petulant child. "It's nice to see you, too."

Dinner wasn't strained, because my mother was always the consummate hostess. My father, who had been exactly this stout and stern and mustached as long as I could remember, told carefully curated stories that gave the appearance of joviality. My mother steered the conversation from his stories to topics of general interest, then back again. She always asked questions, then pretended to be interested in the answers. He always pretended to be as entertained as he was entertaining.

I sat there dutifully and pretended to be perfect.

It was like every dinner I could remember in this house. We sat stiffly in the sophisticated dining room with its gleaming mahogany table, the hand-polished chandelier, and my grandmother's silver.

"You must be excited about the new ballet season," my mother said. Her formidable gaze met mine. "Is there any hope that this is your year at last?"

She meant, *When can I tell our friends that you're dancing a solo instead of merely leaping around in the back?*

"It's been almost a decade," my father chimed in, as if I'd missed that. "You deserve a promotion."

"It doesn't really work like that."

"Have you tried, dear?" my mother asked.

She didn't ask it snidely. There was no edge to her voice at all. She sounded as cool, composed, and carefully neutral as she always did.

There was no reason whatsoever that I should feel this...*thing* erupt inside of me.

I wanted it to be a cleansing sort of rage, but it was far more frightening than that. It was emotion. Thick and ugly and *everywhere*.

And I knew why. I could see Sebastian's bright blue gaze as if he sat there across from me at this excruciatingly polite dinner. I had kept myself in little boxes my whole life. Perfect daughter. Straight-A student. And the best ballet dancer that I could be, which was never good enough.

"It's actually extremely hard to make it into the *corps* at all," I heard myself say, all that emotion making my voice too thick. "Much less stay there, dancing perfectly day in and day out, for years."

My mother did not express disappointment in my words. Instead, it was in the angle of her head. The faint lift of one brow. "No one is prouder of you than we are, Darcy. Was that in doubt?"

And just like that, I felt like a bull in a china shop. I set down my heavy silver fork and fought to compose myself. For some reason I thought of Sebastian again, somehow handling a drunken, broken mother. Maybe we were all reduced to this, no matter our accomplishments. Maybe we all acted like children when faced with the only people on earth who still saw us that way.

But telling myself it was normal didn't make it feel any better. It didn't make me *feel* any better. And all I ended up wanting to do was...rebel. Somehow. When the most rebellious thing I'd ever done was talk back a few times as a child, right here at this same table. Or fail to disclose every detail of my whereabouts when asked. Small-fry stuff, if that. Mostly I'd spent my childhood in ballet studios and boarding schools.

Maybe that was why what I said then felt like such a bombshell.

"Ballet is only one kind of dancing," I heard myself say. "It's just a style. There are other styles."

Sacrilege.

My parents looked appalled, as if I'd started shooting up heroin at the dinner table.

"Such as?" my mother asked, frostily.

"Please don't tell me you're planning to run off and join one of those Cirque du Soleil troops," my father muttered, no longer the least bit jovial. "Dress it up anyway you like, it's still the circus."

"Cirque du Soleil performers are acrobats of the highest level," I replied. Possibly through my teeth. "And no, I would not be running off to join

them, because I'm not an acrobat. It's a completely
different form of bodywork."

"I don't recall anyone using the term *bodywork*
in your ballet classes, Darcy," my mother said in
repressive tones.

"That's because they use French names so they
can sound fancier," I replied in much the same
tone, as if we were fighting. When I knew very
well we were not. Because my parents didn't fight.
They exhibited their reactions through the use of
temperature. Cold or frigid, generally. Right now
there was a wintry wind blowing in this dining
room, but for some reason, it wasn't having the
effect on me it normally did.

"I've spent my whole life trying to be perfect,"
I heard myself say, though no one had asked. My
parents looked glacial. "That's what ballet is. It's
rigid. Exact. And I love it, I do. I always will. But
every now and again I wonder if it might not be a
whole lot more fun to just…dance."

My heart was pounding. My ears were ringing.
My head felt thick and fuzzy.

I had never said something like that out loud
before. I wasn't sure I'd ever dared *think* it.

"Just dance," my mother echoed. She and my
father exchanged a chilly look. "I'm not sure I understand what that means, Darcy. As far as I was
aware, that is what you do. As a profession—one
you worked very hard to achieve."

"There's more to dancing than just classic ballet, that's all I'm saying. Modern dance. Contemporary dance. Folk dancing. Postmodern dance. Personal dancing in clubs. Burlesque dancing."

"Burlesque dancing." This time, the way my mother repeated the words dripped icicles. "Do you really think a…*cabaret show* is an appropriate use of all the years you've spent studying proper dance?"

She said *cabaret show* as if it was a filthy curse word more commonly employed in truck stops.

"Is 'cabaret' how you say 'stripper' in Connecticut, Mom?"

I shouldn't have asked that.

My father's face turned red. My mother's hand rose to her neck, and if she'd been wearing a strand of pearls I was sure she'd have clung to them. Not because I'd said something so distasteful, I knew. They read grittier things on the front page of *The Wall Street Journal*. But because it wasn't appropriate dinner conversation.

"I'm not saying I want to be a stripper—not that there's anything wrong with that," I hurried to say. "I'm just pointing out that there are other forms of dance."

My mother seemed to take an ice age or two to lower her hand back to her lap.

"Your father and I have season tickets to the New York Philharmonic," she said evenly. "The

Metropolitan Opera. And the Knickerbocker Ballet. We do not have season tickets, or any tickets at all, to a burlesque revue. Why do you think that is?"

I wanted to say, *because you're snobs*. But that would be drastically upping the intensity of the bomb I'd already thrown into the middle of the dinner table. I wasn't sure I really needed to up the ante with the nuclear option.

Or you're too afraid, said a voice inside me that sounded entirely too much like a very dangerous Englishman I needed to forget. *Too much of a coward*.

So instead, I fumed about it all the way back to the city on the train. And when the fuming wore itself out, I wondered why I'd lost my temper in the first place. I didn't fight with my parents, as a governing policy. There was no point to it. I didn't fight with anyone, for that matter, because there were so few areas of my life that allowed for any conflict. Not when what was required to survive my schedule was discipline, endless discipline.

And yet since I had returned from Paris, I'd felt constantly *this close* to an explosion. At my parents. In rehearsals. Even at Annabelle.

People liked to claim artists were temperamental. In my experience, *temperamental* was an act. An indulgence. When it was time to work, the professionals got down to business and left the dramatic carrying-on to the amateurs. There were no divas in the *corps*. There was no room for any theatrics but the ones we were being paid to perform.

And yet there was too much inside me these days. Too much wildness and recklessness. As if I was seconds away from snapping back every time the ballet master corrected me, which would not be good.

As the train charged through the night, I faced the inescapable fact that I was different now, whether I wanted that to be true or not. I'd lost something in Paris a month ago, even as I'd gained the sheer joy of actually living out my wildest, most insane, most delicious fantasy. I'd lost the single-minded focus and drive that had fueled my life and my discipline for all these years, and I couldn't seem to get it back.

There had always been a pleasure in surrendering to the tough little march of my days. I loved what I did, especially when I let go of my ambition and lost myself in the sheer, fierce joy of dancing. But there was so much pain that went with it. You had to be some kind of masochist to build your life around it. I'd accepted that a long time ago, and I'd surrendered.

Because every once in a while, the suffering disappeared, and there was only the breath inside me and flying. Without wings, light and free.

And as the train pulled into Grand Central Station, it hit me. I wasn't sure that having made myself an object devoted entirely to pleasure for one long night in Paris, and having loved it as much as I had, that I could give myself back to the pain again. Not even for the gift of flight.

That tore me wide open, like an earthquake.

Maybe it was the aftershocks from that that made me get on the subway instead of walking home the way I had planned. I didn't question what I was doing. I headed to Chelsea and found myself walking quickly toward a theater tucked away on a side street. I bought a ticket at the box office in front, then ducked into the back.

The show had already started, but I didn't mind. I felt vulnerable and exposed already, even there in the darkness of the audience, and I was glad there were no house lights on to expose me.

Because this was the contemporary dance company my friend Winston had joined two years ago, and at which he had become a principal. And Winston himself was there on stage, barefoot and beautiful as he danced to the kind of throbbing music that would give our Tchaikovsky-loving audiences the vapors.

He looked happier than he ever had in the *corps*.

More than that, he looked…free.

That was the word that pounded through me, in time to the hypnotic beat. *Free.*

There wasn't a hint of ballet on that stage. And I loved it.

When the curtain lowered, I was shaken. Tears poured down my face, but not because I was sad. I wasn't. I was electrified. I had seen sheer joy on that stage. Art and beauty. And I knew that if I hadn't gone to Paris, if I hadn't given myself over to that one night of burlesque and fantasy, I would have failed to see what was happening here. I would have judged it through the lens of the Knickerbocker and found it sadly lacking.

Because if you didn't know what you were missing, you couldn't see it. You would never see it. You could flap your wings all you liked, make all the right noises about *flight*, but you stayed in the same cage.

But I knew better, now. I'd stepped outside the cage, and maybe it had been silly to imagine I could ever go back. That I could ever pretend I *didn't* know the difference when I was back behind the bars.

When I made my way backstage, Winston took one look at my face and let out a deep, joyful belly laugh.

"I know that look," he said, catching me in a hug. "Welcome to the dark side, Darcy. Anytime you want a place out here dancing for the fun of it, you let me know."

"The *corps* is life," I replied lightly, as if it was all a joke.

"That's the marines, sweetie." Winston rolled

his eyes. "And don't listen to those grim old sadists at the Knickerbocker. It's not the same thing."

Maybe it was as simple as having options and choices instead of the same well-documented decline that made me feel so drunk all the way home. It was a cold night, but I walked anyway, because I wanted my feet on the ground. I wanted to feel the world the best way I knew how: by moving through it and in it, breath in my lungs and my toes against the earth.

Nothing had changed, and yet everything was different.

I had changed, and that made *everything* different.

I thought of bright blue eyes, cruel lips, and his hands in fists in my hair.

Right on cue, I melted. I went breathless and slippery, here in a different city a world away, with no hope of ever repeating that one glorious night. I thought of him, and I melted the way I expected I always would.

And then everything changed again.

Because when I turned the corner and started down the street to my building, the door to a sleek, low black car opened right in front of me.

And then he was there.

Sebastian. My Sebastian.

Not a fantasy this time, lost somewhere in Paris with angel wings and the magic of the burlesque.

Big and real and *right here*, in my real life.

CHAPTER NINE

Sebastian

IT HAD BEEN a shite few weeks.

At first, I told myself everything was normal and I was fine. Because everything *was* normal and I bloody well should have been fine.

I'd left the club that following morning and I hadn't charged about the streets of Paris like a madman, looking for a woman who wanted neither me nor my money. I hadn't begged or pleaded with her before she left, or given in to any of the equally appalling urges I was horrified to discover clambered there inside me. She had left, then I had called for my car, and I had resumed my life with nary a ripple.

That was the point of the club, after all.

But no matter how hard I worked to stop thinking about that night—and that woman—I couldn't quite make it stick.

I thought about my little dancer in meetings.

During negotiations. When I woke in the morning and all throughout the day, when I should have been thinking about other things—from macro concerns like the corporation I preferred not to run into the ground due to my inattention and more micro concerns, like John Delaney's islands that my brother, Ash, was doing his level best to steal out from under me. I castigated myself for these lapses in the strongest possible terms.

And then, every night, I dreamed about her in vivid color—sound and scent and the silken feel of her skin against mine—and woke to begin the mad cycle anew.

I hardly knew who the hell I was.

Maybe I didn't have to fear becoming like my father, which had always been my gravest concern—especially after my great failure, which he'd openly sneered at. It had been easy enough for me to keep everything and everyone at arm's length after the disaster with Ash, because my father had been a huge fan of *pretending* that he was capable of relationships. Fidelity. Fatherhood. My solution was not to pretend.

But maybe the true worry was how easy it was for me to become like my mother, instead. Obsessed forever with a person who had forgotten her long ago.

Everything I had told Darcy was true. My mother had never tolerated my father's infidelities well, but it was Ash's existence with which she found it impossible to make her peace. It was Ash who had rendered her distraught—for years. Not Ash himself, whom I doubted she had ever met, but the *fact* of him.

My mother had believed herself special among my father's many liaisons because she alone was the one my father had married. She'd imagined that she was the only one to bear him a child, too. And even all these years later, she couldn't stand the idea that Ash's mother had been doing the same thing. At the same time.

She had viewed my friendship with him in school as a betrayal. And after everything had fallen apart, I had agreed. I should never have let myself imagine that I—or Ash and I—could overcome the curse of my father's blood. I should never have allowed my youthful naivete to hurt my mother, whose only sin was in wishing my father was a different man.

I paid my penance to this day. That was why I subjected myself to trips home to the unhappy house in Surrey where I had been raised—between terms at my various boarding schools, that was—and danced attendance on the woman who acted as if I'd wronged her yesterday. And was capable of turning operatic when distraught.

I was no longer friends with Ash. He considered me an enemy now and had for years. My father was dead, and my mother had received the bulk of his estate. He had not recognized his host of mistresses in that way. Only my mother got to live in style with the old man's ghost.

I would have preferred to burn the house and its memories to the ground, I reflected as I drove up to the sprawling old house that day. That I hadn't yet done so was a monument to my strength of character, I liked to think.

Especially when I knew my mother would spend our visit as she spent every visit, regaling me with tales of her victimhood as she sat surrounded by all the luxuries my father's money could buy and mine could support. But that was part and parcel of the penance I paid her. She behaved as she liked and I took it.

I strode inside, nodding curtly at the butler. "Is she downstairs today?"

"I'm afraid not, sir," the man replied, without inflection.

That wasn't a surprise. I took the grand stairs two at a time, then made my way down the hall toward my mother's private rooms. And found her where I expected I would, swaying as she stood behind the settee in her drawing room, shakily fixing herself a drink.

It was clearly not her first.

That wasn't remotely surprising. My mother did not work. She did not even dabble at the sort of "work" women in her tax bracket normally did—meaning hosting charity events with high profiles. What was surprising was my own irritation with it today. I normally viewed interactions with my mother as a kind of hair shirt. Not comfortable, certainly. But mine to suffer anyway.

I should have been focused on my mother today, a week or so after I'd left Paris, but all I could think about was Darcy.

She had given me one night. I shouldn't have wanted more.

Yet I dreamed of her every night—and was daydreaming about her even now as I greeted my mother and sat across the room in the chair closest to the door. Because sometimes she liked to throw things.

"If you have better things to do, Sebastian, don't let me keep you," she said when her glass was full. Her voice was the typical mix of petulance and malice that only got worse—and more shrill—the more she drank. I could tell by her pitch that she'd been at it all day.

There were other clues. My mother was a beautiful woman whose vanity had increased with age and insecurity in equal measure. Her version of day drinking involved dressing as if she planned to attend a black-tie ball at any moment, with hair and cosmetics to match. Today she wore a flowing gold gown that made her look like a statuette.

Her dark hair was arranged into an elegant coiffure that I knew her staff made certain could withstand a selection of gales.

It was the smudged lipstick that gave her away. The unfocused gaze. And the shadow beneath her eyes that told me she'd already raged and cried, then had tried to wipe the telltale mascara runs away.

I forced myself to smile. "What could be a better thing to do than spend time with my mother?"

"Everything, apparently. I haven't seen you in ages."

"I was here last month."

"Last *month*," she said, to the walls. As if it hurt her. "*Last month*, if you please."

"Mother." It was harder to keep my voice level and pleasant than it should have been. Harder than it had ever been before. "You know full well I have a company to run."

She drank from her glass, then sauntered out from behind the settee—and the bar that was always stocked with the finest liquors for her to toss back at will. She swept to the center of the settee and then settled herself, likely imagining she looked regal and haughty, like the queen she sometimes fancied herself. When, instead, she was obviously unsteady, and sloshed whatever she was drinking today over the rim of her glass onto the cushion beside her.

"You spend too much time working. And not nearly enough time with your family."

She had no idea how I spent my time, but I didn't bother to point that out. I had long since come to terms with the fact that when my mother addressed me, she was seeing her late husband, not her son. I gave her what he never had: the courtesy of remaining in the room to hear her out, and a response.

"The company is my responsibility," I said evenly. "It takes up most of my time, but then, it should."

It took up all of my time and I liked it that way.

All of my time save one memorable night in Paris, that was.

I blinked. Surely I was not going to daydream about my little dancer here and now. In the presence of my *mother*. I might enjoy shattering taboos now and again in the safety of the club, but that seemed a bridge too far.

"I think it's high time you found yourself a wife, Sebastian," she said, high color on her cheeks and something hectic in her eyes as she regarded me. "A good one to settle you. And I don't trust you to pick her. You're far too much like your father."

It always ended this way. On good days she would shower me with love, then smother me with her various protestations. Too quickly, she would veer into insults. I was too much like my father. I was cold, withdrawn. Being near me was like being staked out in a field in the middle of winter, and so on.

Apparently, we were fast-forwarding straight into the insults.

Normally, I took this as part of my penance, too. Because I'd always understood that I really was too much like him. It had been my needing to be too much like him that had led to my attempt to put together that deal. It had been my unearned certainty that I could pull it off that had lost Ash's money. And lost me Ash in the bargain.

I thought of his raised middle finger across the club bar. Eloquent as always. And I wasn't sure why that old hollow feeling swept over me again. It was as if I'd left my best armor behind in that suite in Paris. As if Darcy had taken it with her when she'd left me.

She haunted me.

And in all that mess, as always, there was my mother. Needy and demanding, lonely and shrill.

"Why would I ever marry?" I asked, though I knew better than to engage. "I have seen no evidence that you enjoyed your marriage. Or that anyone else does, either."

"A man like you needs a wife," she replied. She sniffed. "You can stash her away in a place like this. After all, you will need her to produce an heir at some point."

"Yes, that was a lovely childhood. I remember it well."

"You had everything you needed, Sebastian.

This is about what I need. A daughter-in-law will fill the space nicely when you're not here. And I fancy I'd make a darling grandmother, don't you?"

"I have no intention of marrying," I said, amazed she was still going on about it. "The notion has never crossed my mind."

"Sebastian." Now her expression had turned scornful. "You are a Dumont. Of course you must marry. And pass all of this along to your children. Or what will become of everything you've built?"

I had never thought about marriage. Or children. Or any of the supposed joys of domestic bliss that the rest of the world treated like an inevitable hangman's noose. And yet later, after I escaped my mother that afternoon, I couldn't think of anything else.

I had always thought of marriage in terms of my parents'. My mother had been in love. My father had been quickly bored. I'd never wanted any part of that. But why not buy what I wanted instead of hoping I happened upon it emotionally?

The more I thought about it, the more I knew that I'd found a solution. Because my mother wasn't wrong. Men in my position generally produced a few heirs, hoping to train one up behind him. I didn't want a relationship like my parents'. But then, I didn't want love or even the pretense of it. I'd stopped believing in love long ago, likely during one of my mother's unhinged, drunken rants when I was still a child.

That was fine. I preferred the clarity of money. My only friend—my brother—had cut me off because of money. My father had loved nothing but money. And money—a whole lot of money, according to my bankers—had bought me the best night of my life.

Why couldn't it buy me everything else I needed?

A woman who would sell herself once might just do it again, and with far better incentive this time. And no need to perform a public striptease, either.

The more I considered it, the more I congratulated myself for my brilliance.

And then I set about trying to find her.

I expected it to take a day or so. Instead, it had taken weeks.

But I was here at last. In New York City, standing in a chilly night on a busy sidewalk.

And she wasn't dressed in feathers, or better still, naked—but there was no denying that it was Darcy. My Darcy.

Whose name, it turned out, really was Darcy, after all.

I had taken that as a sign. I'd given her my real name. And unbeknownst to me, she had done the same.

"What are you doing here?" she asked me, her eyes wide and that fascinating heat climbing into her cheeks. "How did you find me? It's not supposed to be allowed, is it?"

"I didn't find you through the club. I found you in spite of the club." Imogen Carmichael, owner and director of the club, had been surprisingly unforthcoming. She kept quoting contracts I didn't care about at all. It had been irritating, but I'd persevered. I always did. "I took everything you told me and everything I'd observed about you, and found you."

I had started with every dark-haired dancer, which was an impossibly wide pool. But I had been so certain that she couldn't possibly have given me her real name that I didn't bother to search for it. It wasn't until one week had turned into two, then a third, that my frustration led me to search for American dancers named Darcy.

I'd found the Knickerbocker Ballet, and her, quickly.

"I have a proposition for you," I told her.

"I'm not for sale." She looked wildly around the street where we stood, as if she expected to be overheard in a city that specialized in deliberately not hearing most things. "I shouldn't have to say that, should I? You asked for another night before and I said no. That's not going to change just because we're on the other side of the Atlantic Ocean tonight."

But she didn't turn on her heel and walk away. She didn't order me to stay away from her. The color in her cheeks intensified and her dark eyes seemed fathomless, but she stayed where she was. Right there in front of me, at last.

"I heard you," I assured her. "I assume that means you sell yourself only under specific circumstances."

"Once." She threw that at me, and I didn't know which one of us was more surprised at how fierce she sounded. "I sold myself *once.* I have no intention of doing it again."

I knew I wasn't a good man. I'd been told so a thousand times, often by my own mother. But that truth was made clear to me then as her words pounded in me. Like heat. Like sex. Like a victory drum.

Once.

Meaning, she had only ever sold herself to me.

As far as I was concerned, that made her mine.

"Are you married?" I asked her. Because her presence in the club meant she was acting out some kind of fantasy, and I needed to establish what it was. There had been no mention of a husband in the materials I'd found about her, but that didn't mean anything. It wasn't for me to judge another person's extracurricular activities outside of their marriage—but if that was what she was doing, she wasn't for me.

"Of course I'm not married!" She rubbed a hand over her mouth and I saw it was trembling slightly.

"I would never… No. I'm not married. Or any-where close to married."

"Boyfriend?"

She frowned at me. "What did I just say?"

"Habitual sexual partners?"

Her hand wasn't trembling anymore. She dropped it. "How is any of this your business? I think we can both agree that you got your money's worth. That doesn't give you the right to come here, throw yourself into the middle of my life, and start interrogating me."

"I apologize." Though, really, I wasn't sorry. "It's not my intention to upset you."

"I'm not upset." She looked around again, then scowled. "Come with me."

She wheeled around, then stomped off toward the intersection. I followed, bemused, because she wasn't quite the biddable burlesque dancer I re-membered. I wondered whether that woman had ever really existed. If she had been as much a part of the act as the suggestive dance and her wings.

A wise man would cut his losses and leave. But when it came to this woman, I discovered I was many things. None of them the least bit wise.

She ushered me into a small dive bar around the corner that seemed remarkably empty.

"It's early," she said when I pointed that out. "This is the kind of place you go to on your way out or on your way home. Not in between."

She lifted two fingers at the bartender as she headed for a U-shaped booth on the back wall, then slid into it. I sat across from her, my initial worry that this had all been foolish fading as she scowled back at me.

Because even scowling, dressed like a real, live woman instead of a wet dream, she made my body...hum. She made me feel alive. She was even more beautiful than I remembered, effortless and elegant with shawls wrapped around her in a way that struck me as far more European than American. And much as I'd liked her on her knees, on all fours, astride me and beneath me, I couldn't deny the fact that I liked her just as much now that she faced me. Dressed.

My dick just liked her. Full stop.

"Fantasies are just that," she said after a moment. "Fantasies. They're not supposed to be real. And the point of that night was that it was meant to be anonymous."

"You told me your name."

"You were never supposed to know it was real."

"But I do know." I studied her. "Why did you give it to me at all if you were concerned about preserving the fantasy?"

Her scowl deepened, but I could see that flush on her cheeks and after the night we'd spent together, I knew it was the truth of what she was feeling. "It was a regrettable impulse, nothing more."

"I don't think so," I said quietly. "I think you wanted me to know you. And to find you. And Darcy, I have."

I expected her to scoff at that. But when she only huffed out a breath, then looked down at her hands before her on the table, I knew I was right.

That pounded in me, too. Drums on drums, and my pulse like heat.

The bartender slid two shot glasses filled with clear liquid onto the table between us, and Darcy nodded her thanks. She picked up the small glass nearest her and tossed it back. She didn't cough or choke. She only blew out another breath, then nodded at me as if she'd settled something.

"Vodka makes everything better. Even unexpected reappearances on the street outside my house."

I followed suit, feeling the top-shelf liquor burn a smooth, hot trail through me. Then I sat back, still watching her closely. "I've never had sex like that in my life. I want more. A lot more."

Her cheeks burned, but she shrugged. "I already told you, I'm not selling myself again."

"I'm not asking you to. Or not like that, anyway. As it happens, I also need a wife."

I didn't know what I expected, but all she did was sigh. Then roll her eyes. "Of course you do. Also, no."

"I will eventually need an heir," I said as if she'd

asked. "It occurred to me, as my mother was lecturing me on this topic, that I have no interest in any of the women I've ever met. I like them well enough in the moment, but I never think about them again. You, on the other hand, I can't seem to get out of my head."

"Maybe you should see a doctor."

"You have a lovely pedigree, for an American."

"Be still, my beating heart."

I ignored that dry little comment. "And even if you did not, the fact remains that I cannot imagine that there's even the slightest possibility that I will ever draw breath and *not* want to fuck you. In every possible way."

She regarded me steadily. Too steadily. "That's not a good basis for marriage. You must know that."

"It's a better basis than most have, as far as I can tell."

She poked at her shot glass with one finger. "I have received several marriage proposals, you know. One was a desperation sucker punch of a proposal from my first serious boyfriend after I found him in bed with his college study buddy. The other three were from much older men who had never really spent any time with me, but wanted a ballerina to add to their collection. Pathetic, really. And yet all of them seem more romantic than yours."

I didn't know why I was smiling. "I'm not a romantic man. I told you. I've been surrounded by emotion my whole life, and I want nothing to do with it. But I want this. I want you."

"I understand that you're very rich." Darcy made that sound vaguely sordid. "You're not the only one who knows how to search the internet. But I have to wonder, what exactly went through your brain as you came here to confront me? What made you think that a woman you don't know— who you purchased for the express purpose of having sex with, nothing more—could possibly make you a good wife? Even if she wanted to try?"

There were a hundred things I could have said to that. Instead, I decided that there was too much space between us. The booth was shaped like a horseshoe, so I slid over until she was right next to me. I stretched one arm around her shoulders and dropped the other below the table, resting my hand on her thigh.

Then, holding her wide gaze with mine, I slid my hand up her thigh until I could cup her pussy through the sheer leggings she wore. Slowly. Deliberately.

Waiting for her to say no.

But she didn't.

"Why not?" I asked.

I could feel her heat. Her need. And a surge of dampness that told me everything I needed to know about that night we'd spent together.

It hadn't been a fluke. She hadn't been pretending.

"I was playing a role," she told me now. Primly.

"You can consider marrying me a long-running private theater appointment, if you like."

"With you in charge, then?"

"Darcy. You like me in charge."

"People don't roam around the earth asking strangers to marry them," she argued. "Not after *one night*."

"They don't typically sell themselves for that night in an exclusive club, either. But here we are."

"You don't even know me." That came out of her in a different kind of voice altogether. Wispier. Quieter. More real, I thought. "And maybe if you did, you wouldn't think that sex is enough. Because guess what? It's not."

"Fair enough." I smiled at her, while beneath the table, I squeezed her pussy. Once, then again. And I continued, building a rhythm. Feeling her dampness in my palm and the restless motion of her hips. As if she couldn't help herself. "Let's do this the old-fashioned way. Darcy James, I want to date you."

"No," she said, but her voice was barely there and she was grinding her pussy into my hand.

"What's life without a little risk?" I murmured, moving closer and getting my mouth on her neck. "I'll take that as a challenge."

CHAPTER TEN

Darcy

"I DON'T BELIEVE IN LOVE," Sebastian told me solemnly that first night of our second act. "But I will care for you. I will support you. I will give you anything and everything you desire. This I can promise you."

"People don't say that on dates," I replied, but I wasn't scowling at him anymore. He'd taken care of my temper with his hand between my legs, right there at the table in my favorite local bar. I'd rocked against him heedlessly, and I'd come almost too fast to believe, hiding my face against his wide shoulder as I fought to hide what was happening. "I think you'll find it's considered a little creepy."

"A risk I'm prepared to take," he said drily.

I had never intended to see him again. Oh sure, I'd dreamed about him. But before I met him, I'd dreamed about the fantasy that we shared. I told myself that dreaming about him had nothing to do with *him*, personally. It allowed me to put a face to the fantasy, that was all.

A particularly gorgeous face, as it happened.

"Okay," I said later that same night, while we fought to catch our breath in the vast king-size bed in the penthouse he stayed in when he was in Manhattan. Because, naturally, he was the kind of man who had property everywhere he might wish to go. Which was lucky, because it turned out our connection hadn't dimmed any now that we knew each other's names and were outside the confines of the club. "I guess we can date."

"You guess?"

"I *guess* it would be okay. As an experiment. Probably a short experiment."

"Then I will tell you the rules," he replied, as if he'd been waiting for me to say that. And more, as if he'd known all along that I would. His mouth curved as I propped myself up, my hands beneath my chin as I sprawled there across his chest. "There will be no one else. Just you and me, you understand?"

"You can make all the rules you want," I said lazily, because I felt deliciously limp and wrung out. "You're about to find out that I already have a demanding lover." I smiled when something dark and hot flashed in those bright blue eyes of his.

"The ballet. I've yet to meet anyone it docsn't make wildly, madly jealous. And fast."

That hot gleam in his eyes changed. He reached over and took a strand of my hair between his fingers. And tugged a little. Not entirely gently.

"You have the ballet. I have a Fortune 500 company. Somehow, I don't think jealousy will be an issue."

I didn't argue, though I knew better. These things always followed the same pattern. Within a month, I would feel smothered. Too many dramatic phone calls, wondering why I never had any time to lavish on him. Too many demands that I skip this or that to spend a little more time together, as if skipping my workouts didn't directly impact my dancing.

It always came down to a choice. I always chose the ballet, and regretted only the time I'd taken away from it while attempting to appease a new lover.

But Sebastian was beautiful. Dark and demanding. And my half-formed fears that we would only find each other electric within the confines of our Paris fantasy disappeared almost immediately. He'd come to find me here in New York, which I couldn't pretend I didn't love. And I had never fit anywhere better or more securely in all my life than in his arms, with him surging deep inside of me, turning me inside out.

Over and over again.

"No other people." His voice was stern. Just the way I liked it. "And no lies."

"Has there been a rash of lying that I'm unaware of?" I laughed. "I thought our relationship was remarkably straightforward, actually. Given that until tonight it was literally a transaction."

"I'd like it to stay that way, as much as possible. I prefer the clarity of commerce. I favor direct conversation over missish half truths."

I raised a brow at him. "I prefer less male posturing and more applied emotional intelligence."

Sebastian blinked. "Did you just obliquely suggest that I'm…dumb?"

"Not dumb. Just a man." But I grinned to take the sting out of it. "If you feel something, say so. Don't grunt it out, pick a fight, then storm off because you don't know how to say what's bothering you."

"Have I given any indication that I might be likely to do such a thing?"

"I thought we were laying out our ground rules for…whatever this is. Not making pointed commentary. I can do pointed commentary, too, if you want. Just say the word."

There was something like steel in his gaze, though it was much, much hotter. But he didn't argue.

"We have a deal," he said, instead.

And he showed me exactly how he liked to celebrate it.

When I made it in to our morning class the following day, I was a wreck. Miss Fortunato was appalled by my arabesque, and I was so delirious that I only laughed in reply—which was not wise. But it was worth the grueling, painful day that followed, because the night with Sebastian had been that good.

It's been a total of two nights, I told myself later as I dragged myself home after the show. *Two nights are always good. Two nights suck you in and make you believe. It's the day in and day out that ruins everything.*

"That's life, though, isn't it?" I ranted at Annabelle a few mornings later. We were on side-by-side ellipticals at the gym, and I was going much faster than usual. Too fast, you might even say, but I didn't stop. I courted the ache in my quads and glutes. "Everyone wants center stage. The spotlight. They think they're going to wake up one morning, and boom! There it is. Everything they ever dreamed about, right in front of them on a silver platter. You and I know that's not how it goes. There's no such thing as an overnight success. There's only years upon years of practice. Failures. Rejections and reinvention, over and over again. That's what success *is*."

"You need to stop yelling at me," Annabelle

replied, sounding grumpy as her red ponytail swished back and forth. "You're making me feel hungover and I didn't even drink last night."

I slowed down and bit my tongue. I started counting days. It had never taken more than about two weeks to know that I was wasting my time with a man, and another two to extricate myself. And I expected that a man who would go to the trouble to hunt me down outside of the club's anonymity would insert himself into my life with a vengeance and stay there, expediting that timeline with all of that arrogance he wore so well.

But Sebastian Dumont wasn't like any man I'd ever known.

When he told me that he was busy himself, and that it was unlikely he'd find himself jealous of my work or my life, he'd meant it.

I couldn't leave New York, not as fall rolled on and the season started in earnest. Sebastian's business took him all over the world, so he spent the week attending to a hotel chain here, a negotiation over some islands there. He flew back in at some point on the day before my weekly day off, and I would always leave those shows amped and way overexcited as I headed for the penthouse overlooking Central Park, where so far, we spent almost all of our time naked. Or nearly naked.

He would greet me at the door and most of the time, we didn't make it much farther. We needed each other, hard and deep and *now*. We tore off each other's clothes. We fought to get close. He lifted me against his body and I wrapped myself around him, anchoring myself to him and groaning out the unbearable pleasure of it when finally—*finally*—he was inside me again.

It was only after we took the edge off—sometimes more than once—that we moved on to other things. Conversation, for example.

At first, it was almost hesitant. Like it really was the early stages of dating someone, without sex or the club or the rest of it.

"I didn't realize you had a brother," I said on one of those nights, wearing his shirt like a robe as I sat in the spacious, modern kitchen. Sebastian, it turned out, might not be a gourmet chef, but he could throw together a basic meal, and usually did, because I was always hungry after a show. And after our extended greetings. He always had big plans for the rest of the night, which went on into my one day off each week that required I keep up my strength. "By which I mean, you seem to have kept that pretty quiet on the internet, which is hard to do."

"It's not a secret," he said. I'd gotten to know him better as October had rained and blustered its way into November, weeks passing without the usual irritants—which I opted not to pay too much attention to, in case that made it change. I'd gotten to know him well enough that the shift from how he normally spoke to me—open, focused, and always commanding—to this stiffness was...jarring. "But it also isn't something that either one of us likes to talk about if we can avoid it."

"Why?"

He slid the omelet he'd made onto my plate and set it before me on the granite countertop. He raked his hand through his hair, then frowned. "We aren't close."

"Is that a good thing or bad thing?" I asked. It had been a good show and even better sex, and I was buzzing along nicely. But I could feel my stomach growling, so I picked up my fork and dug in. "Siblings fascinate me. I always wanted one."

"When I discovered I had a brother, I was overjoyed," Sebastian said, almost idly, when he was never *idle*. "It was all I had ever wanted."

"When did you discover it?" Because that was a weird way to talk about the arrival of a baby brother, surely. Usually there were stories about mommy's belly and the hospital and all that baby wailing. Not...discoveries.

"When my father saw to it that we were both enrolled in the same boarding school in the same year," Sebastian said. His blue gaze met mine, and I froze. That was how cold it was. "Ash and I do not share a mother. But no son of my father's could be raised without the benefit of the education my father values above every other thing on this earth, save money. And if I'm honest, I always suspected that what the old man really liked was the idea of the two of us at each other's throats. Because that meant he was always the focus, as he believed he deserved to be."

I was still hungry, but I put my fork down. Especially when Sebastian's lips twisted.

"But Ash and I became best friends, instead. It was my rebellion, I suppose."

"Best friends. But you said you weren't close…?"

"We were close in school. Inseparable, in fact. My mother is a drunk who periodically pretends to dry out but never does. My father was cruel and delighted in it. In many ways, Ash was the only person I was ever close to."

That was sad enough. But what struck me was that he didn't say it as if he expected pity. He just said it. Matter-of-factly. That broke my heart all the more.

Even though I knew my heart wasn't supposed to be involved in this.

"After university, we decided we should take it a step further and go into business together. Our success would be yet another two fingers to the old man. We each put up half the capital. Ash urged caution. He wasn't sure he liked our potential investors or the fine print. But I didn't care. I wanted to get the deal done, so I could throw it into my father's face."

He was silent for a long moment, a faraway look on his face that struck me as…sad.

I wanted nothing more than to go to him, and hold him, and try to somehow make him less alone than he seemed then. But I didn't quite dare. He was too remote. Too self-contained and forbidding. I liked those things about him, especially during sex.

But for the first time, I wondered what it must have cost him to become those things. And what he'd lost.

"I'm guessing it didn't go well."

I tried to keep that ache out of my voice and off my face.

"We lost everything." He shook his head. "But when I say that, what I mean is that Ash lost everything. I lost my savings, my father's respect, and the confidence of the corporate world. But Ash didn't have what I had. My father might have paid for his schooling, but he didn't pay for anything else. Whatever I might have lost, I still had a roof over my head and my job in the family company, no matter what. I was not only reckless and out of control, it had literally never occurred to me how much more Ash had to lose."

He winced at that, all these years later. And my poor heart kicked at me, foolishly.

"Sure," I said. "But you didn't lose all your money *at* him, right?"

Sebastian frowned at me. "As far as Ash was concerned, I was a liar. Untrustworthy and despicable, just like our father, or how else could I have ruined us both so completely? Maybe on some level he was waiting all those years for me to prove that I was no better than the old man. And how could I argue with that? He didn't want my explanations. Our father died not long after, and left everything to me. It doesn't surprise me that Ash reckoned I might have known that would happen. Maybe I even went so far as to set him up to take that fall, knowing I'd have it cushy enough in a few years' time."

"That sounds a little far-fetched to me. This is your life you're talking about, not a soap opera."

He let out a short laugh. "You didn't know my father. When I tell you he was cruel, I mean that. He held grudges forever, but none so potent as the grudges against his own sons. If he was alive he would tell you that had all been in aid of toughening us up. But I doubt it." Sebastian shook his head. "I think he liked causing us trouble and pain, the more the merrier."

"He sounds awful," I said quietly. Suddenly, my father's cherry-picked stories and endless mustached years seemed almost cute in comparison. "And I know what it's like not to have a brother, Sebastian. But I have to think it's much worse to have one, then lose him. Is there no way...?"

Sebastian's expression shut down, like a door slamming shut. "None."

"If it makes you feel any better, I don't think my parents know how to love anything, either," I said. Brightly, even. "Especially not me."

And it wasn't until the words were sitting there between us, like a garnish on the omelet he'd made me, that I realized I'd never said it *quite* so baldly before. Not to another person, certainly.

"Maybe that's not fair," I continued in a kind of panic before he could say anything. And before I could think better of it. "They might very well love their sophisticated friends. Their summers in Bar Harbor and their season tickets to the opera. But not their daughter." I pretended I couldn't hear the catch in my voice. "Definitely not that."

"Then they're fools." Sebastian's voice was dark. Stirring. And when he looked at me, that shut-down look faded, to be replaced by a heat I recognized. "And you need to eat, little dancer. You'll need your stamina."

The weeks kept passing. We spent what little time we had free with each other. And slowly but surely, we communicated more the rest of the time. He liked to call me before I went to bed, sometimes purely to hear my voice. Other times so he could whisper filthy things down the line, and the two of us could drive each other crazy while apart.

I couldn't possibly say which I liked better. *Yes,* I would think. *Both.*

And it wasn't until the run up to Christmas—which was to say, *Nutcracker* season—that I realized it had been more than a month. More than two months, in fact, and going on three. Now and again I daydreamed about throwing it all in and joining Winston's company. But the bulk of my daydreams were spent on Sebastian.

And in acting them out.

I still wasn't sick of him. He hadn't irritated me at all.

But the holidays meant the Knickerbocker put on *The Nutcracker,* which meant even more shows than usual to meet the demand for Tchaikovsky's music and the traditional Christmas story. I was impressed that Sebastian had lasted as long as he had, really I was, but there was a reason we call it *Nutcracker* season.

Because walnuts weren't the only nuts it cracked.

It took out would-be lovers left and right.

"I'm exhausted," Annabelle said as we sat on the bench in the studio one December afternoon in what little downtime we had between matinees. "I've hit that point when I'm so tired I don't even want to have sex."

I laughed. "A fate worse than death."

Annabelle rolled her eyes. "You joke. But losing my libido is like losing a piece of my soul."

"Who gets the luxury of a soul this time of year?" our friend Bernard asked from Annabelle's other side as he bandaged up the calf that was giving him trouble. "You're lucky if you get to survive. Soul or no soul."

And a few nights later, after the third consecutive night in a row that I hadn't gotten on the phone with him and hadn't had the energy to respond to a text—after a previous week of much the same—I wasn't particularly surprised to find Sebastian waiting for me at the stage door after our last performance.

"Bye-bye, Mr. Penthouse," Annabelle murmured in my ear as she left me there to deal with the stern, beautiful man in his exquisite suit who stood there next to a long, low car that gleamed beneath the streetlights. But she didn't say it unkindly.

I hadn't told her that I'd met Sebastian at the club. I doubted I would tell anyone that I had ever been to M Club, and certainly not what I'd gotten up to while I'd been there. Instead, I'd told her that I'd met him around the corner from our apartment in our favorite dive bar. Which wasn't entirely untrue.

Just my luck, she'd grumbled. *I've slept with most of New York and I can't find a man like that. All you have to do is have a single drink on your way back home from a tedious dinner with your parents and it's Goodbye Yellow Brick Road, hello Central Park West.*

But she was Annabelle, so her grumpiness had quickly turned into support.

We all knew how rare it was for something to survive our grueling schedule. I got more than a few sympathetic looks from other members of the company as they streamed past me, until they were swallowed up in the cold New York night.

I was bone tired, so tired that I thought I might actually burst into tears, and I didn't want that. Not when I was very much afraid that he was about to break my heart all on his own. *You need to save your tears, Darcy*, I told myself sternly.

I let him usher me into his car, and slumped there bonelessly on the wide back seat as he slid in after me. The car pulled away from the curb and I squeezed my eyes shut, wishing that I had paid more attention to those rules he'd laid out at the beginning. Mainly the part where he'd said that he didn't believe in love and had little tolerance for feelings.

Because I felt neck deep in feelings and drowning, as it happened. But I figured that whatever he was about to say—however he was going to do it, this inevitable breakup that I didn't want at all—it was the time to share them.

"Sebastian," I began.

"Quiet, little dancer," was all he said, in that

voice that I remembered from Paris. Strong and sure. Controlled.

I didn't realize that I'd fallen asleep until he was lifting me into his arms and carrying me out of the car. He didn't put me down as he stepped into his private elevator with its own private entrance to the building, and I was more than okay with it. That meant I could pretend a little while longer. I could rest my head on his shoulder. Lose myself in his arms.

Pretend this could last forever, the way I'd started to imagine it might.

I expected him to let loose when we walked inside the penthouse, but he didn't. He carried me through one high-ceilinged, scrupulously elegant room after the next, until he brought me into the bathroom next to the master suite. He didn't have a giant pool masquerading as a bath like the club had offered us in Paris, but it was an elegant, claw-foot tub all the same. It wasn't until he sat me down beside it that I realized it was already filled. And the water was steaming. Ready.

"Sebastian. I don't…"

"Get in," he ordered me. "Soak."

And I didn't think I was the only one who shuddered a bit as the echoes of Paris swirled there between us.

Just like I had in Paris, I obeyed him.

Because it felt good to let him take control. It

felt like freedom to simply…surrender. The way that fearsome woman in that Fifth Avenue brownstone had suggested so long ago.

After the bath, he fed me. He iced my feet, then helped me apply my favorite ointments and bandage them up. He didn't speak. I thought that certainly he would exact some form of payment in the currency we both liked best—but instead, he merely put me to bed.

And in the morning, he was gone when I woke.

But he had left strict instructions with his staff. And from that night on, whether he was in town or across the world, I was met after every performance. There was always a tub waiting, and all the ice packs and easily digestible protein a girl could want.

It lulled me into a sense of security.

Christmas came and went. *Nutcracker* season was almost over. Sebastian had arrived two days before from his Christmas with his mother in England, and I would have known that he'd seen her even if he hadn't told me.

He held himself differently. His mouth was tighter, his eyes bleaker.

The great benefit of what I did was that I had to do it on Christmas Day. Which meant I couldn't head up north to celebrate the holiday with my parents. An arrangement that had suited all of us for years now.

"I can't wait for New Year's," I said, because I had it off. I smiled at him. "I'm hoping it will snow you in and we can sit here, just like this."

We were in the study, my favorite room in his penthouse. There was a fireplace with a delightful fire, the cold weather outside held at bay, and I had wrapped myself in one of the soft cashmere throws that lay over the leather furniture. Sebastian sat beside me, a tumbler of whiskey in one hand and his brooding gaze on the dancing flames.

We were both, for the moment, sated.

"We can do that," he said. He shifted that brooding gaze from the fire to my face. "But I need you to marry me."

This time, I laughed, though my heart leaped inside my chest. "You realize you're talking about a lifetime of tending to these feet. A lifetime of *Nutcracker* season, when you're lucky if I rise to the level of brain-dead for the entire month of December. At least."

His mouth curved, and I got the sense—as I often did—that he surprised himself when he smiled. "I understand what it is to do what you love. And what sacrifices it requires."

His hand was on the nape of my neck, because he liked to hold it there. As if he liked to know exactly where I was at all times when we were together. And I liked the weight of his hand there. It centered me. Connected me to him and reminded me of Paris. All these weeks since. And the mad fire that still roared between us. No matter how many times we surrendered to it, stoked it and immolated ourselves, still it burned on.

"*Do* I love it?" I asked, and I wasn't sure as the words came out of my mouth whether the question was as rhetorical as I'd meant it to sound. "It's a complicated love, at best. Sometimes I think I hate it. You dream of being a ballerina. You don't dream about being that girl in the back. Especially when the amount of work is the same. But you're doing it, so you dance. And you give it everything you have. And the sad truth is that some people have that *thing*. That spark that sets them apart. And others don't, no matter how hard they work. Maybe it's not about work. Maybe it's luck. The right dancer and the right choreographer and the right ballet... I don't know."

Sebastian's gaze seemed to sharpen on me. "Does it matter how your success can be measured? Or does it matter that it's what you love?"

"I love ballet." I didn't understand why it felt as if I was making vows. Here, now. And at some great risk that made my chest feel tight. "I love everything about it. The obsession with form. How strict it is. How rigid. All in service to that flow. That perfect flight. But it doesn't matter how much you love some things, does it? Loving them doesn't mean they bring you any joy. The act of loving something doesn't make it good for you."

"Are you talking about ballet, Darcy?" His voice was crisp. His eyes burned. "Or me?"

I was flustered suddenly. "I'm just talking."

"I never told you I would bring you joy. Or that I would be *good* for you, whatever that is." He sounded fierce. Remote. "I guaranteed you orgasms. And anything else you could possibly want, the moment you want it. Why isn't that enough?"

"I didn't say it was or wasn't enough." I studied his face. "Is this about me? Because I was talking about ballet." Or I thought I had been. "Is this what happens when you spend time with your mother?"

"You don't understand." Sebastian got to his feet, moving restlessly toward the window. Outside, the city looked cold and bright. As if it was filled with chilly light, not all those lives. "It's not her fault."

"Yes, yes. Your father was cruel." I rolled my eyes. "But he died a long time ago. And she's a grown woman. At what point does a person have to take responsibility for their own happiness?"

He turned back around. And he looked like a stranger, then. Something in me, some kind of panic, coiled tight.

"Why do you continue in the ballet if you don't love it, Darcy?" he fired back at me. "If it doesn't make you happy, why do it at all?"

That felt like a kick, as if he'd taken out a knee, and I found I was curling my hands into fists in my lap.

Are you really lecturing me on happiness? I wanted to shout, but I didn't. I made myself stay calm—or look calm, anyway. "Do you even know what happy *is*, Sebastian? Your mother's horrible to you and you let her do it. Your brother stopped talking to you years ago, and you accepted it. You don't love me, as you make sure to tell me in case I get *ideas*, but you still want to marry me. Why?"

"What would you have me do? Throw my mother on the street? Force my brother to revisit the most painful time of his life when that's clearly not what he wants?"

I noticed he didn't touch the marriage thing. And that made me clench my fists even harder.

"All I'm saying is that if we're talking about pursuing happiness tonight, you could start with yourself." There was something wild in that bright blue gaze of his that seemed to match that panicked thing in me. I should have stopped. I told myself to stop. But I didn't. "Maybe try to practice what you preach, Sebastian."

"I thought you understood," he said, and he sounded…different. Something like foreboding prickled down the length of my spine. "I thought it was clear. Happiness is for other people. I don't deserve it."

CHAPTER ELEVEN

Sebastian

I DIDN'T UNDERSTAND what was happening. But then, when it came to Darcy, I didn't understand much of anything and wasn't sure I ever had—a sensation that hadn't gotten any easier to bear over the last few months.

I hadn't expected to feel like this. I hadn't expected to *feel*.

I'd imagined the initial madness would fade, but it hadn't. If anything, I hated being away from her even more now. Even in these last weeks, when being with her had meant making sure she was fed and cared for and could sleep. Almost as if the sex was secondary, no matter how fantastic it continued to be.

I didn't like to use words like *joy* or *happiness*, because what did I know of either?

If I viewed her as a particularly prime deal I needed to close, it was easier. Or it all made better sense, anyway. I just needed to get the contracts signed and settled. That was what would make things more palatable and less overwhelming, I was sure of it.

But she still wouldn't marry me.

"What do you mean, you don't deserve it?" she asked quietly now.

I already regretted my outburst. And everything that had preceded it, like telling her about my family. About me. Something about this woman made me forget all my own rules.

"I'm not a good man, Darcy," I said when I could be sure I was under control. And I was absurdly, ridiculously glad that I had moved over to the window, because I wasn't sure what would become of me if she touched me just now. "I haven't hidden that from you. But you don't seem to want to accept it."

"Maybe you're really not a good man. But you've been nothing but good to me, so I can only take your word for that."

"I bankrupted my brother. I betrayed my mother." When she only stared back at me, I upped the ante. "I purchased you. For sex."

I expected her to look poleaxed. Instead, she looked as if I was making her sad. "I sold myself. To you. For sex. Does that make me dirty and undeserving of happiness, Sebastian?"

"Of course not."

"It might have been hard for her, and of course you feel badly about that, but you didn't actually betray your mother by choosing to have a relationship with your brother." She shook her head when I started to argue the point. "Your father might have betrayed her, and you, but he's your brother. It makes sense that you wanted a relationship with him. It makes sense that she doesn't. But you're not actually required to hate him just because his existence reminds her of a dead man's sins."

When she said it like that, it landed differently. It even felt different. It was almost as if—

But I knew better.

"I've been paying penance as long as I can remember," I told her, my voice low and full of all the ways I'd let down the people closest to me. And all the ways I'd earned their enduring dislike and disdain. It was the axis that kept my world spinning. "But I welcome it. I can't change the past. I can't make my father faithful. I can't restore Ash's trust in me. Most of all, I can't be the man you want me to be."

She sat up a little straighter on the leather couch, drawing the soft throw tighter around that body of hers that regularly made me imagine I was a religious man. "I don't recall asking you to be one way or another."

"Do you truly think I don't know that you feel

things for me?" I demanded. "Do you suppose I can't see it?"

She didn't flush. She didn't look the least bit flustered. She tilted her head to one side, regal and beautiful and entirely too composed.

God, she was so beautiful it hurt. All these months later, it still hurt.

"I could say the same, Sebastian," she said quietly. As if she was rendering a judgment. "The only difference between you and me is that I'm not over here lying to myself about it."

And the storm in me…broke.

"I can't be that man!" I thundered at her. "*I can't.* I told you from the start that I want you. But not this. Happiness. Joy." And that other thing that filled the rooms we inhabited, no matter how hard I worked to ignore it. I decided to stop pretending I couldn't see it, couldn't feel it. "Love is for other people, Darcy."

I braced myself for a storm in return, but all she did was sigh.

And then she rose to her feet before me, sinuous and mesmerizing. She wasn't wearing those wings of hers tonight, but I could almost see them there. Not as part of a costume, just a part of her. Angelic in the fiercest, most gloriously fiery way.

Her gaze on me was intense. It made that storm in me rage all the more. "I have a radical idea, Sebastian. What would happen if you accepted the possibility, just for one second, that you actually deserve to be loved?"

I would have preferred it if she'd hauled off and punched me. Then kicked me a few times for good measure.

"I don't want to have this discussion."

"Because let me tell you what this has been like for me," she continued in that same ferociously calm way. "I went to Paris to live out a fantasy. And now, looking back, I realize that none of it would have worked at all if it hadn't been you. I looked up from that performance and I saw *you*, Sebastian. I think I fell in love with you then and there."

There was so much thunder in my head it should have drowned her out, but instead it seemed to amplify her.

"Stop it," I managed to grit out.

But she didn't. Instead, Darcy unwrapped the throw from her perfect body and dropped it to the side with a certain dramatic flourish. Or maybe it was a dare.

Because she didn't need to hide a thing. I was the one who felt as if I needed to lock myself away somewhere until I could figure out how to handle this. How to handle her. And not just metaphorically.

"I can't believe I actually imagined that I could just…have sex with some stranger like that," she was saying, as if she was knocking down all the walls inside me on purpose. "Because of course I couldn't have. Don't get me wrong. It might have been fun. Erotic, certainly. I would have been glad I did it, no matter who it was, if only so I'd stop fantasizing about it. But it was you, Sebastian. And it changed everything."

I wanted to shout at her. Or whatever else would make this stop. Make *her* stop. But I couldn't seem to move, much less make noise. I felt frozen solid and rendered mute, there before the window with the cold, careless city at my back.

Maybe I should have known that I could never have her. Not the way I wanted her. And not because she didn't want me. But because deep down, as everyone who had ever been close to me had discovered at one point or another, I was defective. No one who truly knew me wanted anything to do with me.

That was why I'd wanted to marry her before she could get to that point. That was why I'd hoped that sex could confuse the issue and keep her from realizing what everyone else had.

"Sometimes," she was saying, as if she was wholly unaware of what she was doing to me, "it's easy to get lost in a rut even when it doesn't feel good any longer. And particularly if it hurts, because you're so desperate to make the pain *mean something.*"

"I'm fine," I seethed at her.

"Congratulations," she shot back at me. "I'm not. I love ballet, but I'm tired of it. I don't want to dance the same thing over and over and over again, particularly when I'm always at the back of the stage. There are other ways to dance. My contract is up in March, and I'm not going to renew it."

I saw the way she swayed a little after she said that, as if she hadn't meant to let that out. Not like that. Not tonight. Maybe not ever.

"Darcy."

Her gaze was wide and faintly shocked, but she lifted her chin.

"And I'm not going to marry you unless you love me," she said, her voice soft. But that didn't make it any less fierce. "I'm not going to torture myself with one more thing that doesn't love me back. I'm not going to batter my body and break my heart against another brick wall."

My chest hurt. "Darcy…"

"I think you love me already," she said, and the catch in her voice almost wrecked me where I stood. "You promised me you'd be honest. Can you do that, Sebastian? Now, when it counts?"

Everything inside me was mad storms and wild earthquakes, and still, somehow, I kept my feet beneath me.

And then I was moving. There were words on my tongue, but I couldn't seem to find them. Instead, I found her.

I wrapped my hands around her strong, slender shoulders, then stared down at her face. Her beautiful face that haunted me even when she was right there in front of me.

Her lovely face that I knew would haunt me forever.

She had already wrecked me. Or I had wrecked myself. And I didn't know what to do with all the wreckage.

So I set my mouth to hers.

She surged to meet my kiss as if she was returning a punch, and she wound her arms around my neck.

And I couldn't pretend I didn't feel the desperation. The loss.

The love, something in me whispered.

She pulled away, and I thought she would turn and run, finally. Was that what I'd wanted all along? But this was Darcy. My little dancer, as brave as she was beautiful.

She pushed me back onto the sofa and I let her do it. I let myself fall, feeling greedy and nearly delirious with it as she followed me down, climbing on top of me as we went.

I would never get over the way we fit together. Electricity and need, skin against skin.

I lay lengthwise on the couch and waited, teeth gritted, as she knelt over me. Her pussy brushed against me, molten hot. I didn't know how I managed to stay still as she lifted herself up, then worked herself down on my cock.

We'd fucked a thousand times by now. More. Several times today already.

But this was different. Everything was different. My hands circled her hips and she braced herself against my chest. Her gaze locked to mine, and I saw too many things there.

I told myself I didn't know what they were.

And then slowly, deliberately, she drove us both insane.

A slick, slow lift, then that hot clasp of her sweet pussy as she glided back down.

Again and again, until there was only the sensation. The joining.

And all the things I couldn't feel. Or wouldn't let myself feel. Or more precisely, wouldn't let myself name.

There was only Darcy. And this dance she taught me.

And it didn't matter who knew the steps and who didn't. All that mattered was that it lasted forever. That was all I wanted. Darcy. This.

But all too soon, I felt her shudder. And that ripple washed over her, down into her tight, hot pussy, then threw her over that cliff.

And me along with her.

It was a long time later when she stirred, then

pushed herself off me. She got to her feet and gathered the throw around her like a robe again.

"Darcy," I started.

She had already begun to head for the door, but she stopped then and looked back over her shoulder. Her black hair spilled down her back in abandon, the way I liked it. But her melting brown eyes were filled with loss.

"You deserve love, Sebastian, no matter what you think," she told me, her voice hushed. "No matter what you've convinced yourself all these years. You deserve it. But so do I."

"Don't do this."

It was as close as I'd ever come to begging. And her gaze only grew sadder.

"I don't need you to love me," she said. "I wish you would, but I've lived without it all these years. I'll be fine."

I knew that I was never going to be the same. I wasn't even sure I'd make it to *fine*.

But I couldn't seem to say a thing. Much less the thing that would stop this. The thing that might keep her.

"I'm going to love me for a change, Sebastian," Darcy said. "Not the ballet. Not a man who's happy to pay for me but refuses to love me. *Me*. And I don't care if anyone likes it."

And then, again and for good, I watched my little dancer walk out of my life.

CHAPTER TWELVE

Sebastian.

FIRST I LOST my temper, having already lost my woman.

I let the kick of it propel me across oceans and continents alike. How dare she issue ultimatums? How dare she leave me—again? When it was obvious how good things were between us. When she was the one who had changed the game, not me.

But the trouble with temper was that it faded. And sooner or later, there was no more hiding from myself. No matter how I tried.

I found myself in Surrey some ten days after my last night with Darcy, in the foyer of that same cold house where I'd grown up. The New Year had rolled in. The world had been ripe with resolutions and vows, many already broken. Yet here in this house, everything was the same as it had always been.

Upstairs, I could hear my mother hurling things around, and the sound of shattered glass. It was my own personal symphony.

I climbed the stairs slowly. It took me longer than it should have to make my way down that same old familiar hallway. I knew this was my duty, but it sat heavier on me today. In the bright glare of this new year.

And when I stood in the door to her private drawing room, this interaction with my mother didn't feel like penance anymore. It didn't feel like a hair shirt.

It felt sick.

"Finally!" she shrieked at me when she saw me. "You dare to show your face here, after abandoning me the way you did? What kind of son are you?"

Normally, I would sit down. I would endeavor to be calm. Soothing. *Something.*

Today I stayed where I was.

"Things have to change," I told her, in a voice I'd never used before. Not with her.

"*You* need to change, Sebastian," she fired back at me, unsteady on her feet. "But I know you won't. You're too much like your father. It's how you're made. So cold straight through it's like frostbite when you enter a room."

I had accepted that as truth my whole life. And why? Because a drunk woman told me so?

"You're a grown woman." And the funny part was that after all the rage and fury that had held me in its grip since I'd last seen Darcy, today I felt quiet straight down into my bones. "I'm not going to tell you what you can and cannot do, Mother. But I will tell you this. I'm finished standing by while you indulge in yet another drunken tantrum. If you want to get drunk and throw a tantrum, go right ahead. But if you want to see me, you cannot be drunk. If you can't do that, you can't see me."

I didn't wait for her to respond. I turned and headed for the stairs.

And with every step I took, I felt lighter. Brighter. As if tethering myself to her downward spiral had made it mine, too.

How had I not seen that? I wasn't paying penance. I'd been suffering through a prison sentence, maybe, but it had allowed me to lock myself away. It had kept me from feeling anything. It had made me distant and cold. My father by default.

And it was time I took responsibility for my own damned life. For what I had made it simply by standing by and letting these things go on.

My phone rang in my pocket as I stepped outside into the gloomy English January afternoon. I glanced at it, but it was never who I wanted it to be. This time it was my secretary.

"I don't mean to bother you while you're with your family," he said, sounding harried. "But we've received another bid on the Delancy islands. Your brother has taken it upon himself to—"

"Enough," I said.

"Sir?"

"Give him the islands," I ordered my secretary. "He can have them. I don't care. I'm not fighting with him anymore."

"As you wish," my secretary said, and rang off to do as I asked.

I made a mental note to send him an extra bonus for not mentioning that I'd waffled back and forth about this deal for months.

I had extended these olive branches before, of course. I'd stepped away from negotiation tables and left deals to Ash. I'd waited for him to recognize those gestures for what they were. I slipped my phone back into my pocket and heard something crash inside, but I didn't look back.

None of this was mine. It never had been. It was my mother's to hold or put down, as she chose.

I folded myself into my sports car and fired up the engine, but I didn't drive away. I sat there for a moment. Considering olive branches and grand gestures.

I had made myself into a martyr. Ash hated me, and I knew he had a right to those feelings, so I'd done nothing, directly. Periodically, when he'd fought me for business, I'd handed over the thing he appeared to want and then I'd sat about, waiting to see if he did something else.

I'd done exactly nothing on my own. I hadn't followed up. I hadn't reached out to him. I expected him to divine from the ether of a business deal that I regretted what had happened between us and wished it could change.

And when he didn't respond, because of course he didn't respond, I used that as further ammunition that I was precisely as wretched and unlovable as my parents had always made me feel.

I was thoroughly sick of myself, in fact. The only thing martyrs were good for, as far as I was aware, was kindling. And I was tired of letting myself burn.

I pulled my phone out again and stared at the screen.

And then I punched in a number I hadn't called in years.

It rang once. Again. Then shifted to voice mail.

I wanted to hang up. Because it was easier by far not to change. It was easier to keep doing what I'd always done. But the only place that had led were these ruins I'd made of myself, my life. This sad wreckage.

And I was tired of living my life like a salvage operation.

The voice mail beeped.

I cleared my throat. I had no idea how to do this.

Which meant I had no choice but to go ahead and do it anyway.

"Ash," I said. I blew out a breath and told myself the only olive branch that mattered was the one I extended with my own arm. My own hand. Not a series of corporate sallies through intermediaries that meant nothing in the end. "This is your brother. I think it's time we talked."

Darcy

It was a brisk, blustery morning in the beginning of February, and I would normally have felt grim and deeply aggrieved as I walked toward a restaurant behind the New York Public Library to meet my mother.

But this was a different sort of New Year. I'd decided. I was a different Darcy from the one who'd seen out the last year with more of a whimper than any kind of bang.

I'd already had my initial discussions with the Knickerbocker. And I knew that I'd made the right decision when their protestations that they would miss me only made me smile. Maybe because I knew that they weren't *lies*, necessarily. But that they also weren't the truth. Not really.

The thing about the *corps* was that if you wanted to leave, they were happy for you to go.

You needed to go. It was a hard enough life when you loved it.

Annabelle felt betrayed.

"I don't understand this!" she cried, when I told her that I'd informed the Knickerbocker that I didn't want to renew my contract with them this year. And worse, that I was planning to go over to the dark side, after all. "Why would you blow up your entire life? Is this what happens when you do burlesque?"

But it didn't feel like blowing up my life. It felt like living it—at last.

Winston's dance company required an audition no matter my résumé, and I thought I should have been far more nervous than I was. I hadn't auditioned for a new company in a decade. Instead, I felt excited.

That was the burlesque, I thought, though I didn't tell Annabelle. It hadn't blown anything up. It was the key that had opened a lock at the front of a cage I hadn't known was holding me in. Now the door was open and I could do anything.

Thinking about burlesque dancing made me think about Sebastian, which I still did far too often. And I might have known, without a shred of doubt, that I'd made the right decision. That I wouldn't change anything if I could.

But that didn't make me miss him any less.

My mother had come down to the city for some

or other charity thing today. She knew perfectly well this was my day off, so I'd had no option but to agree to meet her for lunch when I would have preferred to work on my audition routine.

I walked into the restaurant, saw her at once, and started weaving my way to the tables toward her. She looked as she always did. Perfectly put together, her hair elegant, her expression haughtily serene.

I couldn't help thinking about the odd ties that held us together. Mother and daughter. Obligation and disappointment, love and hope. I understood how those things moved as one and made a whole when it was a dance company. Why did I think a family was so different?

When she looked up and saw me, a faint frown marred her smooth forehead. I knew she did not approve of what I had chosen to wear for our lunch. My favorite boots, clunky and a little bit motorcycle-y. Leggings without a tunic covering them up, making them the pants she abhorred. And the cropped leather jacket that showed off entirely too much of my body without even attempting to conceal any of it. I could hear her objections from across the room.

But she said nothing as I sat down opposite her and we exchanged greetings.

I waited until we'd ordered our food, a sensible salad for her and a grilled cheese for me, because

I liked to live dangerously. These days, anyway. Then I sat back in my chair and smiled at her.

"I'm glad you wanted to have lunch, Mom," I said, before I lost my nerve. "I have something to tell you."

Up went that brow. But I refused to be cowed.

"I'm leaving the Knickerbocker," I said.

My mother stared back at me, her face frozen. "I beg your pardon?"

"I understand that you don't appreciate other forms of dance the way you do ballet," I said as diplomatically as possible. "But I'm going to join a contemporary dance company. It actually has quite a sterling reputation, though of course it doesn't have the Knickerbocker's grand history. Anyway, it's time to move on and that's what I'm doing."

"I don't understand."

"You don't need to understand this, Mom." My voice was harder than it needed to be, maybe. But I wanted to get my point across. "I hope you'll support me either way."

My mother blinked. "Darcy."

I braced myself for the lecture, but she only shook her head as if I was a mystery to her. It made my heart hurt.

"*Of course* we'll support you," she said, with that cultured *certainty* that had always made me feel grubby and unhinged in comparison. "You behave as if you think your father and I don't know how difficult it is to be a professional dancer. But of course we do. We see exactly how hard you work. If you see any hesitation on my part it's because I thought you loved ballet to distraction. Why else would you dedicate your life to it?"

"I do love ballet." Though I felt unsteady, suddenly. As if I'd never seen my mother before. As if I'd broken my own heart. "But it doesn't love me back, Mom. It never will. And I think there's only so long you can live with that."

Maybe I wasn't talking about the ballet anymore. Not entirely.

"I know it's the fashion to tell young people that they should do what they love, damn the torpedoes, and so on," my mother said, after a moment. "But you've done that. And you've always combined your passions with intense discipline. It's why you've made it as far as you have."

"But not far enough," I finished for her. Before she could get the jab in. "Not a soloist."

"Will you be a soloist at your new company?"

"Yes." It was amazing how much satisfaction it gave me to say that. "I believe I'll come in— assuming I nail the addition—as a principal."

"It's what you've always wanted," my mother said. "It doesn't surprise me, Darcy, that having gone so far down one road without getting where you wanted to go, you decided that you might prefer another. You were the most determined child

I'd ever encountered. While my friends' children were getting into trouble, with drugs and sex and all the rest of it, you never wavered. Ever."

"I'm wavering now." Though really, the only thing wavering was my voice. "I guess if professional ballet is a game of chicken, I lost."

"Nonsense." And this time, when my mother's brow rose, I felt that she was doing it *for* me, not *at* me. "Ballet might be rigidly hierarchical, but love is not. Or it isn't love. It expands. It changes when necessary—that's called growth. And so will you." She even smiled. "I will look into season tickets for your new company at once."

And in case I thought that she had been body snatched, when my tears welled up she looked aghast, produced a tissue from her bag, and told me to pull myself together.

I couldn't remember ever feeling so at peace after an interaction with my mother before. I walked back to my apartment afterward, feeling... solid. Connected. I would dance out the rest of my contract at the Knickerbocker. I would nail my audition. And I would start a whole new chapter of professional dancing.

I would grow. This was *growth*. It was good.

The only thing stranger and more dizzying than not getting what you wanted, I was discovering with every step, was actually getting it.

I was going to have to figure out a way to be all right with center stage for a change.

I thought of Sebastian then and sighed. But I refused to let myself dwell on the things I couldn't change. On the man who loved me—because I knew he loved me, so far as he was able—but couldn't admit it.

And when I came around the corner of my street, I was so busy *not dwelling* that I almost slammed into the person standing there. Standing still in the middle of the sidewalk, as a matter fact, which should be illegal on New York City streets. Everyone knew that.

"Sorry—" I began.

But I knew that blue gaze, bright and beautiful.

And this time it was real, not a dream.

It was Sebastian. Live and in person and in the glorious flesh. And he took my breath away as surely as the periodic gusts of frigid wind rushing in from the East River. He cut through me that easily. He turned me inside out without laying a finger on me or saying a word.

"You can't come back here and do this to me again," I threw at him, hoping I sounded fierce enough to hide the sharp kick of longing inside.

"Quiet," he told me, bossy and stern the way I liked him, though he wore an expression on his face I'd never seen before. "This time, little dancer, I'm going to do it right."

And then, to my astonishment, he sank down onto his knees. Right there on the dirty, frigid February street.

It took me a long moment to realize that he'd reached into his pocket and pulled out a box. A small box in a recognizable shade of blue. He cracked it open, momentarily blinding me with the manic sparkle of the ring within.

A ring.

"Darcy James," he said, dark and certain and still delightfully bossy. "I'm an idiot. I don't deserve you, but I can't seem to manage without you. I can't think of a single reason why you should marry me, but I'm hoping you will all the same."

I wasn't sure my heart could take it. It was the hope that about killed me, swelling up inside and making my eyes tear up.

"I already told you why I can't." I wanted to touch him. I wanted to love him, forever. It was possible I already would. And did. But I wanted everything. *Everything.* I couldn't stop loving myself, the way I knew I would if he didn't love me back. "I just can't—"

"I love you," he said, low and urgent. "Of course I love you. You electrified me the moment I laid eyes on you in Paris. I would have paid six times what you took from me for another taste. I love you, Darcy. Madly. Impossibly. There's no point to any of this without you. You don't just make me wish I was a better man, you've already made me one."

"Sebastian…" I whispered.

"Marry me, because I've never loved anyone else," he urged me. Ordered me. "And I have the feeling I have a lot to make up for. I can't promise you that I won't drive you crazy. I'm sure I will. But I can promise you that the makeup sex will always be fantastic."

"I love you," I said helplessly. "I can't help it. And I love that you keep showing up here and making these sweeping pronouncements. But a big, dramatic showstopper isn't real life. If you want a ballerina doll of your very own, you should know that I can't do that anymore. I'm not that person. I'm quitting the Knickerbocker."

"I don't care if the only place you dance is naked, for me," he growled at me. "In fact, I encourage it. You look fierce and happy, and that's what I want our life to feel like. You don't have to be ready to marry me today. Just give me *someday*, Darcy."

He took the ring out of its box and slipped it onto my finger.

A key into a lock.

It fit my finger the way we fit together. Perfectly.

"I want it all," I whispered. "I want everything. With you."

His smile broke my heart again, smashing it into pieces, then knit it back together again.

"Then everything is what you get," he promised me.

He rose then, pulling me into his arms, and it was like coming home at last. I was vaguely aware that we'd drawn a crowd, but I didn't care about them. I couldn't even see them.

What mattered was Sebastian. He was all I could see. All I wanted. The two of us together and the life we would build, one brick at a time.

It was most important dance of my life, and it started now.

And unlike every other dance I'd ever learned, this one would last forever.

CHAPTER THIRTEEN

Sebastian

THE THEATER WAS FULL. There were the sounds of soft conversations, programs rustling in people's hands and the orchestra—or perhaps, more properly tonight, the band—tuning their instruments.

I couldn't remember the last time I had allowed myself so much as the faintest hint of nerves, but this was different. This wasn't something for me to win or lose. This was Darcy's debut in her new company.

I was a wreck, though I would die before I'd show it.

Darcy's parents sat to one side of me, cool and polite, as ever. We had gone up to Connecticut to celebrate our engagement with them, after a fashion. It had been restrained, but still far more loving than any family dinner I could recall. And I really didn't care how ferociously manicured and distant they both were as long as they were kind to their daughter.

On my other side was my mother, which I would have told the world would never happen. And had. She wasn't sober all the time, but she was sober tonight. We weren't exactly bosom friends. I wasn't sure that was possible or even desirable.

But when my mother didn't drink, she was a different person. One, I was surprised to discover, I might actually like. We'd spent the last month or so being very, very careful with each other.

Still, I couldn't help being optimistic.

To my great surprise.

It was one more gift my beautiful dancer had given me.

These had been the best months of my life. The hardest, in many ways. I might have discovered my heart and handed it over to Darcy on a winter street in New York City. But that didn't mean I knew how to use it.

She'd moved into the penthouse with me, if not quickly enough to suit me. She told me she'd set a wedding date in a year's time, assuming things continued to grow and bloom.

I'm a ruin of a man, I'd shouted at her in one of our fights. They came like storms, flaring up hot and blowing themselves out again.

Ruins are where the flowers grow, asshole,

she'd hurled right back at me. *Try that, for a change.*

And I'd kept my promise about the makeup sex. It was blistering, always.

Day after day, together, we worked it out.

Just as, slowly and carefully, I thought Ash and I were working it out, too. At long last.

My life was unrecognizable from the one I'd had when I'd walked into the club last fall.

There was love. There was hope.

And in the middle of it, making it all possible, there was Darcy.

I got a life of her smiles. Her occasional silliness and her iron discipline. I got her dancer friends, and their camaraderie that sometimes baffled me as much as I admired it. I got that body of hers and all the ways she could use it. I got to care for her and protect her and let her do the same for me.

She understood my drive because she had her own. She supported me in ways I'd never really understood a partner could. And should. She listened. She felt for me and with me. She made things I would have said were only mine brighter because I told her about them.

And every once in a while, when I greeted her at the door dressed in a suit with a credit card in my hand or a stack of crisp bills in any currency, I got to buy her for another night, too.

We would marry when the time was right. And

then, forever, I would get to do this thing with the one person who made it all matter.

If I could just survive opening night.

As if on cue, the lights in the theater went down.

I heard an ear-piercing whoop of joy and support and knew it was Annabelle, Darcy's irrepressible best friend, from her favorite seat in the first row of the balcony with a group of other dancers.

Then everything was silent.

A spotlight punched through the inky dark, lighting up the figure who crouched in the center of the stage.

For a moment she looked like the doll she'd never been, not to me.

She moved in a sudden, liquid rush, from that crouched-down position into a bold, impossible leap—as if she was scaling a wall only she could see—

Then she was flying, with those wings of hers that I could always see on either side of her. Tonight, it wasn't only me who could see them.

And I knew they were feathered bright and pure, made entirely of joy.

Pure joy.

But then, to me, she had never been anything else.

I let out the breath I'd been holding as the music kicked in. Then I sat back and watched my little dancer do what she loved, as if she was doing it just for me.

The way I would insist she do later, for my eyes only, naked and flushed.

And, best of all, mine.

* * * * *

FRIENDS WITH BENEFITS

MARGOT RADCLIFFE

MILLS & BOON

To Catfish,
for giving me a valid reason to not bring carrots into
my home.

CHAPTER ONE

ALEXA LAWSON STEPPED OUT of the plate glass elevator onto her casino floor. While her uncle was out of the country on business she was the head bitch in charge at Halcyon, the newest and hottest den of decadence in Las Vegas. She was known in town for running all three of her uncle's casinos, but this one was her baby because she'd designed it on her own.

Halcyon was the only casino in Vegas with a true woman's touch. Twinkling fairy lights draped sensuously from the ceiling like long ropes of iridescent pearls, their reflection dancing across the lavish white marble floors. Gold finishes and furniture glittered like starbursts under brushed-brass chandeliers, and luscious greenery with exotic cream and peach blooms burst from the walls as reminders of the earthly pleasures one could find when people lost their inhibitions.

Designed after a wedding Alexa had been to in

Athens, the casino was old-world romance with a touch of new-world naughtiness.

On her way out the door for the day, she snagged a chocolate-covered fig from the tray of a passing waiter. Wearing nothing but a pair of beige linen pants and a leather wristband with *Halcyon* embroidered in gold on it, this new waiter with his chiseled abs was a customer favorite.

His name tag read Apollo, but she doubted that was his real name.

"I see you're taking the casino's theme seriously," Alexa told him. She glanced down at the tag hanging from the gold chain around his muscled neck and back up again to his sexy grin.

"Yes, ma'am," Apollo returned, giving her a jovial wink that made her smile.

"Are you flirting with your employees?" a familiar voice said from behind her. His voice was deep with just a little grit in it, like a rich and chalky cabernet sauvignon.

Her best friend, Carter Hayes, appeared beside her looking supremely amused.

She thanked the waiter and he left to spread the wonder that was his abdominal region to the paying customers.

"Hey there, darling," she said, biting into the fig. She met Carter's eyes as she caught a smear of chocolate in the corner of her mouth with her tongue. "To what do I owe the pleasure of this visit?"

He shook his head at her deliberate provocation. Teasing him was one of her favorite pastimes. He could be so uptight. It was one of her responsibilities as best friend to make sure he lightened up sometimes.

Shoving his hands into the pockets of his worn chino pants, he frowned. "We should talk somewhere else."

"Is that so?" she asked. She took another bite of the fig, letting her lips linger on it just a moment longer than required. "Sounds important."

A corner of his full mouth quirked. "You know you're turning me on, right? I'm not made of stone."

She laughed. "Trust me, I know." One of her girlfriends had bragged to her only days ago about how much of a real live man he was. She'd stopped Maggie before she shared any real details, but it had been enough.

Carter plucked the fig out of her fingers and popped the rest of it in his mouth before she could torment him with it again. His strong jaw chewed, the muscles methodically clenching and unclenching, his eyes on hers. Then he swallowed, his Adam's apple bobbing up and down in his tanned, corded throat. He'd been her nerdy, shy neighbor who'd once asked her out with a "check YES or NO" note, but he'd all of a sudden grown up into one of the richest people in Las Vegas as well as its most eligible bachelor.

"Was it good for you?" she asked, her eyes sliding to the fig stem in his hands.

"Always," he told her with a wink.

Shaking her head, she started walking toward the elevators. It wasn't unusual for Carter to show up at one of her casinos. He'd created a facial recognition software that took pictures of customers and then matched them to a database to make sure dealers and customers weren't working together to win money from casinos. It did a lot of other stuff, too, but that was the part she understood. It had been over a decade since he'd done the grunt work of programming software, but his right arm had a sleeve of binary code tattoos to remind everyone how he'd built his fortune.

Inside the elevator, she stuck in her key card to go to her private office floor.

"I see you're wearing my favorite hoodie today." When he was out with other girls he wore bespoke three-piece Savile Row suits that hugged his broad shoulders and cost more than a down payment on a house, but she didn't warrant that kind of effort apparently.

He looked down at his navy blue sweatshirt. "You have a favorite?"

"Of course. That one brings out your eyes."

He laughed. "Whatever you say, Alexa."

"I pay attention, Carter. You give me far too little credit."

He crossed his thick arms over his chest and raised a judgmental sandy brown eyebrow that winged up over the top of his round tortoiseshell glasses. "You haven't returned a single text I've sent you in the past three weeks. The only reason I know you're alive is because of social media. The photo montage of your current dating spree is impressive even for you."

"Now, Carter, let's not argue," she appealed, giving him a jovial pat on the shoulder. "I'm sorry I didn't answer your texts, but I am running three casinos in Uncle John's absence, you know."

"And playing just as hard, apparently."

Alexa shrugged again. "It's Vegas. I have a reputation to maintain. Besides, at least I haven't chosen any of your friends to sleep with. That's a little close to home, don't you think?"

He had the decency to look embarrassed. "I didn't know you and Maggie were friends until afterward."

"For a man so interested in my social media presence, it would have only taken a quick search to find out." She should keep her mouth shut. It wasn't any of her business who he slept with. It wasn't like she was scrolling through his follower list before she slept with someone.

The elevator dinged open and they stepped out onto her floor. They suspended their conversation until they reached her office. She loved what she thought of as her sanctuary in the middle of the chaos. Sprays of cream roses, peach peonies and blue hydrangeas graced her desk and sitting area, while ivory velvet curtains framed the large window overlooking the Vegas Strip.

"Dinner?" she asked, making them both dirty martinis at her minibar.

"Mexican?" he suggested.

She recited their orders to her assistant over the phone, then handed him a drink.

She took a seat on the white velvet sofa next to him. "I see you haven't brought me a gift, so I hope the news you're intending to share with me isn't too bad."

He pulled a small package out of his sweatshirt pocket and she blew out a breath. She didn't want bad news when she'd been having such a good day.

"There are two things, but I'll tell you the mostly good one first. We're building a satellite office in San Francisco, so it looks like I might be gone for a while."

Alexa stared at him, jittery anxiety pooling in her middle. "You're leaving Las Vegas?"

"Not permanently, but for probably at least a year."

"An entire year?" she spluttered. "Are you serious?"

At his affirmative nod, she tried to digest his bombshell, but the wrenching in her gut made it hard to think. She stared blankly at the sign on the coffee table in front of her of a famous singer/dancer who was starting Halcyon's first residency in a month. She'd worked day and night to put the event together, enticing the performer to her casino instead of one of the more established places, but the accomplishment felt like dust in her mouth now.

Carter was her best friend, her rock and her brother all rolled up into basically the most important person in her life, and they'd been together since elementary school in the same city. She didn't doubt the strength of their friendship, but a lot could happen in a year. They'd miss so much of each other's lives—the small, mundane details of the day-to-day, late-night drinks and quickie lunches that made their friendship tick. Plus, he'd been right earlier—she'd barely seen him the past couple of months as it was.

"But it's not final yet?" she asked hopefully.

"The final plans for the office need to be approved by the board, so it'll be a month or so before we can start officially hiring, but it's definitely happening."

"Well," she managed, her voice unnaturally cheery to cover up the sudden urge to cry, "congratulations on the expansion, but you really should have brought me more chocolate considering the circumstances."

He handed over the package, a small box wrapped simply in silver paper with a periwinkle satin bow. Pulling it off, she lifted the lid and found eight delicate and colorful chocolates. "I know these didn't come from anywhere around here," she told him.

"I got back from Paris earlier in the week."

"Parisian truffles," she cooed, slightly mollified by his typical thoughtfulness. "A man of taste and sophistication as usual." She closed the box and stuffed it into her purse. "Were you planning on giving these to some other girl before you found out you were leaving?"

He met her eyes, amusement dancing in his. "You're the only woman I give truffles to, Alexa."

That rang true, since he gave other women more expensive gifts. He'd sent Maggie an Hermès scarf after they'd slept together. Of course, that was the last time Maggie had ever heard from him, but still, an Hermès scarf was an Hermès scarf for pity's sake.

"How nice to know I'm special," she returned.

Their eyes met, the muscle in his jaw twitching, and it looked as if he was about to say something but changed his mind. "Unfortunately, there's more bad news," he told her, his expression mild again. "Chris Miller is stealing from you."

"Chris Miller?" she repeated, completely floored. "My best general manager? That Chris Miller?"

At his solemn nod, she digested the truth of the news even though she was loath to. However, she trusted Carter literally more than any other person in the world, so there was no way he was lying, which meant she needed to accept the inevitable.

"How? How long? And how much?"

"He's been working with one of the new poker dealers, having him lose to one of their friends. The three of them are splitting the takes. Probably two days and over $100,000 so far."

Alexa laughed because it was an insignificant number for Chris to risk his job over. He made over three times that as his yearly salary. "He must be in some kind of trouble," she speculated.

Carter shrugged. "You need to fire him. And the dealer."

She bristled at the order. Of course she would fire them, but she didn't need Carter to tell her so.

"Would you like to tell me how to do the rest of my job as well?"

He rolled his eyes. "You know what I mean. He could be down there right now overseeing another run."

"I'll fire him after we eat," she assured him, taking a much-needed sip of alcohol. She liked Chris and he'd been a good general manager, but she'd learned not to take this kind of stuff personally. The lure of so much free money was quite frequently too much temptation for employees to resist. She did, however, instruct the other general manager on duty to send the poker dealer in question on break.

"I'm sorry about this," Carter told her. "I thought you'd rather hear the news from me instead of one of your tech guys."

"That's nice of you, but it happens."

Besides, she was more broken up by the fact that her best friend was basically moving light-years away even though he hated San Francisco and the whole Silicon Valley scene. Just two months or so ago after a particularly nasty client meeting, he'd literally spent an entire evening ragging on everything about it, including the relatively blameless and objectively delicious sourdough bread.

Carter responded to a text, which was a thing he did all the time while they were hanging out. His undivided attention didn't really exist. She assumed it was work-related, but when she glanced over, she saw that a cute blonde girl had literally sent him a nude picture. She looked away quickly since it wasn't any of her business, but the image was burned in her brain.

Instead of being embarrassed like she was, Carter looked as if getting nudes was just an everyday occurrence for him. And maybe it was. Lord knew her DMs were crammed with dicks both figurative and literal. Of course, unlike Carter had just done, she never responded to said dicks.

"That's one way to say hello," she joked.

"Yeah, and a pretty effective one, too."

She laughed, but the fact that Carter might be dating someone was inspiring something new and terrible in her—pure and simple jealousy. Maybe it was PMS hormones or something, because she'd never cared who Carter dated before. Of course, he'd never been leaving before, either.

Thankfully, a knock sounded and Carter got their food from the delivery guy before she could analyze her wayward emotional state.

While he set out the food, she texted her uncle about Chris Miller's theft, making sure he knew she had everything under control.

"You got a hot date tonight?" Carter asked, referring to her texting.

She shook her head, setting her phone aside and piling a couple of tacos on her plate. "Nope, tomorrow."

"So I get woman-about-town Alexa Lawson to myself for an entire night. I can't remember the last time that happened."

She snorted. "We hung out just last month."

"On a Tuesday," he pointed out. "For coffee."

"I think we can admit we've both been guilty of getting bogged down with work lately," she acknowledged. "Why don't we go back to my place and catch up on some movie time? I've had to wait for you to finish that documentary series we started and I definitely resent you for it."

Deep-cut documentaries were one of the first things they'd had in common as kids and had sustained them ever since.

"Sounds perfect," he agreed.

CHAPTER TWO

THEIR DINNER, FROM their favorite Mexican place, was fantastic as usual, and a comfortable silence fell as they ate, wherein Carter wondered if Alexa was going to say more about his move to San Francisco. She seemed upset, but since she basically never admitted she had emotions it was typical of her to pretend everything was fine.

Their history was littered with complications. The fact that all those years ago he'd created a program for her casinos mainly so he'd always be in her life should have been clue enough for her that he wanted to be more than friends, but she'd been willfully oblivious. After college, he'd even told her straight-out that he loved her, but she hadn't taken the admission seriously, which had been the wake-up call he'd needed.

She hadn't been interested in the pudgy nerd he'd been back then so he'd gotten a gym membership and started his company in the crappy studio apartment he'd rented on the Strip, and the rest was history. He'd moved the fuck on and any boyhood fantasies he'd had about Alexa had gone in the trash along with the majority of his oversize hoodies. His reputation with women was legendary, which was saying a shit-ton for a town with the highest population density of fuckboys in the country.

He and Alexa both were two of Vegas's notorious players, but over the past few months he'd been considering showing his hand. He'd accomplished his goals and now he was ready for something else, a new challenge before things got stale. He didn't want to be that creepy old guy out on the prowl.

And if there was ever a challenge to be had, it was Alexa Lawson, who was currently living up to his boyhood fantasies in a painted-on black pencil skirt and silky red camisole.

"Let me take care of that other little problem and we'll get going," she informed him, rising from the couch and shrugging back into her suit jacket. Her demeanor already signaled that she had returned to business mode, which was equally as sexy as her relaxed mode. As far as his dick was concerned, she actually didn't have a non-sexy mode.

Carter installed some updates on her assistant's computer while Alexa dealt with Jason and Chris. Both men were shouting angrily and he suppressed the urge to rush in there and protect her, but she didn't need him. Before too long the room got quiet and she must have shown them the evidence. His software had uncovered Chris's friendship with the customer who kept winning and video evidence of them talking and splitting the take. It was a cut-and-dried situation.

He was impressed that Alexa never had to raise her voice, she just got shit done. However, when the cops showed up, he realized just how serious the matter was. Software company CEOs like himself generally didn't deal with the police even though, ironically, his software literally caught thieves. Watching the men in blue cart Chris and Jason away in handcuffs was awkward to say the least, especially considering the way Chris sneered at him. Everyone knew what his software did, so while Alexa did the firing he was technically the one who put Chris in jail.

When they were gone, Carter returned to her office as she was pouring herself another drink.

"You didn't tell me about the police," Carter said, scratching the back of his head.

"They're thieves," she said simply, joining him on the sofa. "Thieves go to jail."

Her phone rang and her uncle's face appeared on the screen.

She put him on speakerphone, and John Lawson's perpetually jovial voice crackled through the international phone lines loud and clear as a bell.

"Well, Alexa my love, thank you for taking care of another snake in the grass."

She grinned at Carter and he returned it. Alexa's uncle was a big personality but also a man of integrity, which was hard to find in Vegas. Like Alexa, he'd admired him all his life.

"I know you're going to be upset, dear, but like we talked about, I'm ready to retire. I think we should put the casinos up for sale," John said, shocking both him and Alexa.

"What?" Alexa burst out, her eyes wide and stunned. "Uncle John, I thought you were joking about that. You just went to France to scout out new casino locations."

Alexa jumped off the couch and started pacing, clearly about to lose her shit as she turned the speaker off and held the phone to her ear. He ignored the urge to comfort her because he knew she wouldn't let him.

"Yes, of course, Uncle John. The next news article you read about me will be about my heroic dog rescue or helping an elderly widow find love again."

She sank back down onto the edge of the sofa next to him and tapped the phone to end the call.

"What the hell was that?" Carter asked, resisting brushing away the piece of hair stuck in her red lipstick.

Alexa shook her head, mystified. "Like you

heard, he wants to retire and sell the casinos, but my reputation is causing a problem with potential buyers. If I clean it up and he can sell the Wild Nights and Hard Eight casinos, he'll give me Halcyon outright."

Carter refilled her glass with the last of the martini from the shaker. Even though it was a good deal for her as far as Halcyon was concerned, he knew she'd rather die than lose the other casinos, too. Alexa *was* Las Vegas and those casinos; she'd lived and breathed them her entire life. As kids, they'd run the floors of Wild Nights and Hard Eight instead of their backyards, as teenagers they'd worked whatever odd jobs they could, and as adults they'd enjoyed the casinos as they were meant to. But she'd also do whatever her uncle needed no matter how it might hurt her.

"So what's the play?" he asked, handing her a glass. He often felt like he lived to serve Alexa. Whatever she needed, he did. It was a mutual codependence, as long as he never tried to press her to talk about feelings. Ever since her parents died she'd cut herself off from anything too serious.

"I don't know," she said, sounding a little lost. "I have to clean up my image, I guess."

"So how do you want to do that? I can take over the media aspect of it, make sure content of you doing wholesome stuff gets shared in cyberspace."

She nodded. "That's good, but I need to do more.

Like practice abstinence and wear a chastity belt, apparently."

He laughed at the impossibility and she smacked his arm, unamused.

She slumped down into the back of the couch and he put his arm around her shoulders, breathing in the light apple scent of her hair. She'd used the same shampoo and conditioner since high school and it tugged at his gut like it always did.

"I'm sure you'll figure something out," Carter told her, letting go of her to take a fortifying drink of his martini.

She stilled then, looking over at him speculatively.

"I don't like that look," he drawled.

"I need a fake fiancé," she announced, clapping her hands together. "That would solve everything!"

"And exactly how would that solve everything?" he pressed. Perfect, he thought. He was about to leave for a year just as she decided to get fake-engaged to some random Vegas loser.

"Think about it," she insisted, kneeling on the couch and facing him. Her hair fell over her shoulders in thick chestnut waves as she moved. "For example, if you and I got fake engaged, it would solve all my problems. We don't have to invent a backstory because everyone in town already knows we're close, and spending more time together wouldn't be terrible because we actually like each other. It would be the quickest way to get everyone to believe that I've settled down."

"Wait, you want *me* to be your fake fiancé? Uh, no way in hell."

"Why not?" she asked, her head doing that cute little tilt it always did when she was curious about something. "If you're worried about San Francisco, I think a month is more than enough time to convince people I'm a changed woman."

Why wasn't it a good idea for them to pretend to be engaged? he mused. Maybe because their friendship had become a game to see how long he could be in her presence without throwing her down on the nearest surface and fucking her until they both couldn't remember their own names? Yeah, maybe that was why.

"I just don't think I'll have time. There's a lot to do before the move."

She looked slightly crestfallen, but a fake engagement was just too much to ask of him.

"You could stop dating for a while," he suggested. "You'd get the same result."

"Maybe," she agreed. "But it will take longer."

"Yeah, but that's a good thing, right?" he reasoned. "You don't want your uncle to sell the casinos right away. In the meantime, maybe you'll think of a way to change his mind."

The possibility seemed to at least distract her.

"I'm too wired to talk about this now. Let's get out of here."

He nodded and followed her out of the office, relieved that he'd put an end to the fake fiancé thing.

They stepped out of the elevator onto the ground floor and the crush of the Friday night crowd was instant sensory overload. The electronic whirring of machines, the tinny clink of coins and the underlying bass beat of rumbling conversation was enough to drive a decent person to recklessness. The anonymity was liberating.

When they finally stepped outside into the bright lights of Vegas, he could tell that Alexa needed to blow off some steam and wasn't surprised when she grabbed his arm.

"Come on," she urged, pulling him across the street to Elysium. "Let's gamble and make bad decisions."

"So much for reinventing yourself," he pointed out.

"Tomorrow," she promised with a wink, shoving open the front doors to the towering casino.

CHAPTER THREE

As SHE'D KNOWN he would, Carter waited for her while she played several hands of blackjack even though he hated gambling. She won her last hand with twenty-one and turned around to celebrate with Carter, but he wasn't there.

She collected her winnings and left the table, roaming around until she finally found him in the grand lobby talking on his cell. As he spoke, a deep crease formed between his eyebrows and he ran an agitated hand through his already mussed hair. He was completely oblivious to the women around him doing everything but stripping to try to get his attention.

She waded through the crowds, intending to apologize for ignoring him, but when she reached him he didn't notice her, either.

It was positively demoralizing, as she was literally right in front of his face. Both of them were married to their jobs, but he could at least acknowledge her existence. She put an arm around his waist just to see if she could get his attention away from work, but he barely glanced at her. Instead walked out of her arms as he barked at someone about profit margins.

Flustered, Alexa watched him walk away before turning her attention to the rest of the lobby.

Her gaze stuck on the glass art installation. It was an explosion of color and light and fanned out over most of the lobby's ceiling, the flower pinwheels stunning in their intensity. Customers' phones all pointed up to capture the joyful riot of bold-colored flowers. But the pictures people took wouldn't capture the significance of the glass sculpture, the subtle striations of color in the individual pieces, or the delicate and thoughtful way the flowers had been arranged and hung to maximize the light. So much of it would be lost in translation.

Her parents had taken her to see it as a teenager when the casino first opened. It was one of the last things they had all done as a family before her parents died.

She glanced back at Carter, but he was still on the phone.

Skirting the perimeter of the display, she found the piece she wanted. The bright magenta flower with a dark red center that fanned out to the palest of pink on the ruffled edges had been her mother's favorite. She'd been Alexa's best friend. She'd told her mom everything, from getting her period, to her first crush, Perry Knightly, who now sat on the Las Vegas City Council, and all the little inconsequential things that made up her life. But since her parents died, she'd had trouble opening up to people, because having to wade through the abyss of that kind of grief to get to happiness again felt insurmountable.

She blew out a frustrated breath and gave the flower a final look. It was still beautiful, but rather than grounding Alexa as it usually did, the memory of her parents made her anxious. She would never stop missing them, but she loved her life and was thankful for everything she still had. Her uncle had made her work her ass off doing every job in the casino, including scrubbing toilets, which wasn't a pretty picture in a casino that gave alcohol away for free. She'd worked hard and was making her mark on Vegas. Life was good.

However, now Carter was leaving town, quite possibly her uncle if he was serious about retiring, and even Halcyon might be out of her life if she didn't get her shit together. Where did that leave her? Alone in Las Vegas without her best friend and only living family? That sounded awful.

A man in faded, ripped jeans and two full sleeves of tattoos comprising vivid Mexican sugar skulls and raging flames stopped next to her to study the sculpture. His tight black T-shirt hugged imposing biceps and pecs that practically begged to be touched. Just the kind of guy she liked to have a good time with.

"Impressive, isn't it?" she asked him, following his gaze upward.

He glanced over at her, and she felt him take her in from bare legs to ample cleavage. His deep brown eyes met hers with an appreciative twinkle.

"I'll say," he drawled, his voice gruff and a little rough around the edges, like his outfit.

She smiled up at him, loving the chance to flirt with someone. It was so easy. *Men* were so easy.

"Do you ride?" she asked, nodding to the chain on his pants and the scuffed black motorcycle boots.

He nodded. "You?"

Head tilted, she gave him a coy smile. "Of course. But not usually on the first date."

"Set you up for that one, didn't I?" He grinned, taking a step into her space.

The smell of leather and oil tickled her nose as she breathed him in, vaguely thinking that she preferred Carter's fresh and spicy scent. It reminded her of laundry and money. Not that biker guy didn't have his own appeal based on sheer muscle mass alone.

"You did," she agreed, glancing up at him. "So are you here to gamble or just look at the art?"

His head tilted. "Would you believe me if I said just to look at the art?"

It was her turn to give him a once-over then, which he visibly enjoyed, the corners of his eyes crinkling with amusement. "I'd say there's a fifty-fifty chance," she concluded.

"I'm a tattoo artist. Sometimes I come look at this to get inspired." He lifted up the front of his shirt to reveal a massive tattoo covering his washboard abs, the bombs of color similar to the flowers above them.

She reached out a hand and traced one of the blue shapes with a finger. "That's...unexpected," she murmured, marveling at the artistry of it and the myriad of colors and shapes winding over his skin like a trippy Pollock painting.

"Yeah, I'm only a hardheaded motorcycle dude like sixty percent of the time," he joked.

She pulled her hand back and his shirt fell down, which made her nearly sigh out loud in disappointment. Abs and art like that should never be covered up.

"What about you?" he asked, taking her hand in his like a pro, tracing the same fingertips that had touched his chest. "You here to gamble?"

She didn't necessarily feel a spark between them, but that didn't mean there couldn't be one later. He was just the kind of distraction she needed. "I'm always ready to gamble."

His thick arm slid around her waist then and her eyes slid closed in anticipation of a kiss that never came.

Her eyes popped open to see Carter standing there, his arms crossed and mouth knotted into a sinister frown.

"What do you think you're doing?" Carter demanded, looking more pissed off than she could ever remember him being. Especially at her. He never got angry at her.

Biker Guy released her, but kept a hand on her back. He didn't look scared of Carter, but he should be. Though Biker Guy's muscles were larger, Carter had been studying jujitsu since he was a kid and could kick a lot of ass in very little time. Specifically, he'd put a football player in the hospital for grabbing her ass at a party in college once.

Alexa wasn't exactly sure who Carter was addressing, but before she could answer, Biker Guy did it for her. "Who are you?"

Alexa stepped in front of Carter, imploring him to be cool with her eyes. "I'm busy, Carter. Can I just catch you later?"

Carter's blue eyes darkened dangerously under the lenses of his glasses. "I don't think so."

Biker Guy gave Carter an assessing look. "If the lady wants to be left alone, I'd say that's what you should do."

Alexa sighed. As much as she was annoyed by

Carter's intrusion and high-handedness, this interaction needed to end before it turned into a scene that would get back to her uncle. That was exactly the last thing she needed at the advent of her reputation-cleanup initiative.

She held out her hand to the Biker Guy. "Mind if I see your phone?"

A corner of his mouth lifting, he reached into his back pocket and handed it over. She programmed her number into his contacts, showing him the face where she'd typed in her name as *Your Best Ride.* Someone sue her, he was hot.

"Call me soon," she instructed.

"I look forward to it," he said with one last once-over. "You take care."

When he was gone, Alexa returned her attention to Carter, who was still standing with his arms crossed over his chest and looking murderous.

"What the hell is your problem?" she demanded.

"I was gone for all of three minutes and you're hitting on some random guy who by the looks of it could be a serial killer?"

She doubted serial killers were lovers of rainbow glass, but she could be wrong. More importantly, that wasn't the point at all.

"First of all, you were completely ignoring me to open up your new office in Seattle or whatever other hipster town you're leaving me for. Secondly, I'm allowed to hit on whomever I like."

"I am not leaving you, Alexa. I'll just be out of town for a while."

"An entire year," she clarified.

"I don't know why that's a problem for you. I'm sure that extra from *Sons of Anarchy* will keep you busy."

"Why are you so bothered by him? You were busy so I flirted with a cute guy. It's been known to happen before."

He ran an agitated hand through his sandy blond hair. "Because we were supposed to hang out tonight, and instead you chose to gamble for over an hour and were just about to go home with some dude."

"Okay, I'm sorry for that," she allowed, trying to calm him down. "Let's go back to my house now. It's not a big deal, Carter."

She took a few steps toward the exit, but he remained rooted to the spot, his expression still uncharacteristically dark and moody.

"Are you going to pout all night?" she prodded. "Or are we going to salvage this evening and actually spend some time together before you leave?"

He stalked toward her, his blue eyes flashing with anger as he grasped her arm. "You're not the one giving orders here, Alexa."

A shiver of awareness danced across her skin, sending up a wave of goose bumps in its wake.

Carter suddenly pulled her toward the back of

the casino. They passed a startled concierge as he led her into a remote stairwell with a big staff-only sign on the front, but as a contractor for Elysium's security system he had access to all areas of the casino.

The concrete stairwell was cold and quiet, but they were in a standoff, eyes clashing in anger, confusion and denied lust. She didn't know exactly how she'd gotten so angry so fast, but she was plenty pissed off at his attitude and the fact that he'd dragged her across the casino like she was his property. She wasn't the one who was leaving town for some bullshit extension office that could be handled remotely or by his countless executives who would love to relocate to San Francisco. In the course of several hours the life she loved was in danger of becoming extinct and he was upset because she was flirting with some guy? He needed to check himself.

"You have no reason to be pissed right now," she bit off.

His eyes widened in incredulity. "I don't have a reason to be pissed off? You're supposed to be fixing your reputation and you can't even do it for one fucking night."

She bristled at the censure. "You're not my boyfriend or my dad, and I'm allowed to flirt with guys. If you're not going to be my fiancé, then my reputation is none of your business either."

"Why are we even here in the first place? You talk a good game of being sad that I'm leaving, but you can't even spare a couple hours off from flirting and gambling to hang out with me. You know I hate crowds and casinos."

"If you didn't want to gamble, you should have spoken up and we'd have gone home. I'm not a damned mind reader."

Her blood was raging now and she shivered. Something was different here. The tension that always simmered below the surface was so second nature it was easy to ignore, but now it was reaching a boiling point. She wasn't sure whether she wanted to shake the living daylights out of him or rip his clothes off.

Carter pulled her into his arms and her breath caught. "I'll speak up then."

CHAPTER FOUR

CARTER'S LIPS MET hers and the world suddenly felt like the glass flower exhibit, upside-down and chaotic. His lips were firm and confident as he threaded strong fingers through her hair and held her tightly against his solid body. The body of her friend, whom she'd lusted after for years. She'd denied herself for such a long time, only imagining what it would be like with him, but those daydreams were incredibly vivid now.

She moaned against his mouth as he took the kiss deeper, opening her up and invading her with gentle but insistent explorations. It was methodical and thorough, just like the man himself. Carter was the most intelligent and inventive person she knew and she wanted him to apply all of those skills to her while they were both naked and in her bed. Or his bed. She wasn't picky.

His strong, steady hands drifted down her back and gripped her ass just tightly enough to let her

know he meant business and drew her hard against
his erection so that she was cradling him right
where she wanted him. He was big, and she rocked
her hips against him, wanting to feel the length of
his cock against her wet heat. She arched into him,
needing to be closer and feed the feverish ache between her legs, but he only gave her a fraction of
what she wanted, his hands stilling her hips when
she wanted nothing more than to ride him to her
own release.

One of his hands caressed up her side, the rough
calluses dragging against the silky fabric of her
blouse as he cupped her breast in his hand. He
drew a blunt thumb lightly over her beaded nipple,
and she groaned in pleasure as liquid heat poured
through her like the first sip of rich hot chocolate
on a cold day.

His lips crashed onto hers again as they fought
for dominance in the kiss, tasting each other, their
tongues invading and retrenching, teasing and
commanding.

She found his chest under his shirt and stroked
along his abdomen, the fact that she'd done this
to another man just moments ago not lost on her.
Carter felt perfect under her fingers, taut and
smooth and hot.

"Mine better be the last chest you touch tonight," he growled, lifting her into his arms.

The new height put them face-to-face. The hard

length of his erection finally pressed against her core and she closed her eyes against the onslaught of desire that stormed through her insides.

"You'd better make it worth my while then," she told him, nipping at his bottom lip.

Their lips locked again, the heat rising between them like a bubbling geyser. He pulled her shirt over her head, leaving her exposed in a red silk bra. In response she scored his thick hair with her fingers and guided him to her peaked nipple, which he drew into his mouth without hesitation. Bolts of desire roared to her clit and her hips rolled against his erection, creating a maelstrom of sensation. Just a few more seconds and she could come just from some innocent dry humping like a teenager in the back seat of a car.

"Carter," she whispered against his lips.

Tracing a thumb over the corner of her mouth, he coaxed her to let him go deeper, explore and taste all there was to discover.

"Touch me," he murmured against her lips.

"Are you telling me what to do?" she asked, drawing back with a raised eyebrow.

"Yeah," he grinned. "Now stop being so damned contrary and do it."

"Oh, this so is not how we're doing this," Alexa declared, waving her pointer finger as she attempted to climb out of his hold. Orgasm be damned, she wasn't his servant.

He let her go, but then crowded her underneath the stairwell until she was flat against the wall. Anticipation danced up her spine.

"Hey!" she snapped, pushing at his shoulder. "What are you doing?"

"You think this is going to be like our friendship, where I look the other way when you try to boss me around, but Alexa, what we're about to do isn't friendship."

None too gently, he spread her legs apart with his knee, pinning them there until she squirmed.

"Now touch me."

She obliged immediately, her soft fingers gliding up his abdomen.

"Someone's been working out," she purred, scraping her nails over his dark nipples.

"I've looked like this for years."

"I know, but this is the first time I get to touch," she explained, grinning as her fingers brushed down his sides. "I liked your old body, too, you know. I'd take your brain in whatever package it came in."

A weird look passed across Carter's face for an instant before he grabbed her wrists and pinned her arms to the wall. "Stay."

Then he knelt in front of her, pushed her skirt up to her waist and revealed the smallest scrap of a black lace thong.

He licked up the inside of her thigh, spreading

her legs wider as he went. He threw one of her legs over his shoulder and pushed the thin piece of underwear out of his way. But then he stilled for a moment, and she thought she might die from want.

"Do it," she commanded, clutching at his hair.

Smiling at her bossiness, he obeyed, setting his lips to her. His tongue found its way into her, leaving no inch untouched. He explored her vagina as thoroughly as if he were going to make a damn map of it afterward. She didn't give a shit what he did as long as he kept it up. The long strokes of his tongue, the teasing brush of his thumb—he was a man on a mission, and her desired destination was pleasure.

"Carter," she rasped, trying to catch her breath. "I want you inside me."

Her skin was on fire, as hot as a car hood on a Vegas desert summer afternoon, unrelenting and merciless. His fingers replaced his tongue and he pumped inside her, the slick channel offering no resistance, only friction and anticipation. She squirmed underneath his ministrations, unable to control herself as his thumb and tongue worked in tandem to drive her in-fucking-sane.

"Not until I say," he told her, biting down gently on her engorged nub as he added another finger. He pistoned furiously, his tongue laving the spot he'd bitten, soothing the bolt of electricity he'd delivered to her core.

She'd had sex before, even been ordered around, but it was different with Carter. Everything he was doing was better, more considered. His shoulders were wide, keeping her legs pinned to the wall when she would have tried to take control of the situation. The brush of his thumb on her clit was practiced and precise, the angle calculated just right to touch her where she needed to be touched the most.

The rush of pleasure hit her hard, shoving her off the edge of the cliff with wild abandon.

Her cry of climax rent the still air of the stairwell. Carter soothed her gently, tonguing her lightly until she stopped shuddering and regained some measure of normalcy.

"That was really great work, Carter," she joked, giving his shoulder a friendly pat to try to make it normal when she felt anything but. She had no idea what this meant for them, but it was too late to stop now. He'd knocked down the door and she didn't have the tools to put it back up at the moment.

His blue eyes turning smoky, he rose and pulled her into him. She fought for the kiss this time, aggressively sucking his tongue into her mouth and running her hand over his straining erection. She wanted more of him, wanted the heavy weight pulsing under her hand inside her.

Unzipping his pants slowly, her eyes met Carter's.

It was officially the last gasp of their friendship, because there was no going back now.

She hesitated for just a split second, enjoying her new view but also to tamp down the terror that edged her buzz that Carter would want more than she could give if they went through with this. Adding sex to their friendship was basically putting them into relationship zone, which generally included those messy emotions she liked to keep in check.

She pushed the worry aside because she was sure Carter didn't want anything serious, either. He was even leaving town, so they were safe. Switching their positions, she pushed him back against the wall and ran her hands over his chest.

She met his eyes as her hands moved lower and lower, and his flared as she came to his kelly-green boxer briefs. The color delighted her since she knew it was his favorite. She pulled them down and let his cock spring free.

Grinning at him and what she'd revealed, she murmured, "I just didn't know what I was missing, did I?"

He kissed her hard, letting their desire rage out of control.

Her heart beating rapid-fire, she tore away from the kiss and nipped and licked her way down his chest and abdomen and finally ran her tongue up the length of his impressive cock. Thick, long and gorgeous, she wrapped her hands around him, feeling his hardness and heat as he throbbed against her hand in time to her own pulse.

Breaking eye contact, she leaned down and took the tip of him into her mouth, loving his growl of pleasure. She fell in, taking his length, tasting, sucking, caressing until his muscles tensed. Increasing the pressure, she slid up, almost letting him slide out of her mouth before taking him all the way in again. She loved the feel of him on her tongue, his skin, his musky smell. Her core squeezed in pleasure as the first salty drops of come greeted her tongue.

His big hands ran through her hair, pulling just a little. The time for slow was over; she was too turned on for finesse and she handled him easily, alternating between hard and soft pressure, fast and slow speed until his whole body froze against her.

"Alexa, stop, I'm there," he growled, his voice raspy and strained.

She didn't listen, sucking harder until he came apart in her mouth. It was the least a best friend could do. The pressure of his fingers on her skull intensified and she swallowed him down, licking around the tip to finish.

Lifting her head, she met his eyes, seeing a fierceness she'd never witnessed before in them.

Just then the door creaked open and her heart

stopped. In an instant, Carter had himself zipped and her pushed behind him so the two uniformed Elysium employees didn't see her face.

The two men exchanged greetings with Carter and her heart felt like it was going to beat right out of her chest. Christ, she'd had sex in weird places before, but never this public and never with Carter.

Once the two men had reached the second floor, Carter helped put on her shirt. He watched her, his deep blue gaze intent and focused on her face as he straightened out the hem of her camisole. They were both breathing hard.

"You okay?" he asked, tucking a strand of hair behind her ear.

She nodded and the moment of awkward silence seemed to stretch out for minutes instead of the actual seconds it was.

"Well, that's a first for our friendship," she tried, giving a forced laugh.

He shook his head at her lame attempt at humor. "My place or yours?"

The question jolted her back to reality. Sleeping with Carter would be the biggest mistake of her life if she lost him afterward. Her love life track record wasn't exactly filled with functional long-term relationships. For Christ's sake, her nickname in Vegas was literally the Disposal, because that's where all her men ended up, thrown away and emotionally mangled beyond recognition.

She also had serious doubts about whether or not she could be in a real relationship. Her parents' deaths had turned the entire trajectory of her life around. One minute she'd been a carefree sixteen-year-old, and the next she was the girl who everybody pitied because her parents died. It had taken her years to feel like Alexa again and not just a pity case. It made her extremely hesitant to enter into a relationship where not only would she have to deal with someone leaving her again, but that it would be Carter. He was her last link to what she would always think of as the happiest time of her life.

He took her hand in his, giving it a squeeze. "Don't chicken out now."

"Sleeping together would hurt our friendship," she entreated, catching his gaze.

He drew her back into his arms and heat again, and it felt natural and right. "You don't know that."

"Yes, I do," she insisted. "I don't like the way you fold your clothes in rolls. It would drive me nuts to be in a relationship with you."

He laughed and shook his head. "I didn't know your excuses could get any lamer. We'll figure it out."

"Maybe I could wear a wig or something."

She felt his chest rumble against her as he chuckled. "What?"

"You know, like I'll wear a wig and sneak into your house and have my way with you and then we'll pretend I was a girl named Marci and never speak of it again. Then we'll return to our regularly scheduled friendship."

He nudged her chin up so she could see him. "Is this something you do with guys?"

"Yeah, it's called role-playing and it happens, Carter."

"Jesus, Alexa, you're fucking killing me." He took her mouth again, quick and rough.

Taking a deep breath, the familiar scent of his clean cologne hit her like a brick wall of need.

Then her phone rang. Pulling it out of her bag, she saw that it was Carter's mom. The woman who'd, for all intents and purposes, filled in for her own mother after she died. Carter's mom had been the one to buy Alexa the dress she'd worn for the funeral, the one who, along with her uncle, had held her hand during the service as the priest droned on and on about people he only barely knew. For an instant, Alexa thought about not answering, but it was the second call she'd missed from her today and she felt ashamed.

Carter saw who was calling and blew out an annoyed breath.

By the time the conversation was over and Carter's mom had reminded her to bring her famous brownies to Sunday dinner, Alexa realized what a mistake she'd been about to make. Carter and his family were her family. If she and Carter didn't work out—and all signs pointed to her not making an actual adult relationship work—she wouldn't just be losing him.

She stepped out of his arms and out from under the stairwell.

Meeting his eyes, reading the disappointment already there, she said it anyway. "I'm sorry, Carter, but we can't do this."

CHAPTER FIVE

ALEXA WOKE UP with a pounding headache, knowing she'd totally fucked up. She grabbed at her phone on the pillow beside her, cringing at the eleven missed calls and ten urgent text messages from her uncle.

After her parents died, Uncle John had raised her with unconditional love and support and all she ever wanted was to make him proud. She'd been an okay student, but as soon as Uncle John told her she'd only have the casinos one day if she applied herself, she'd gotten her shit together and graduated at the top of her business class in college. He'd given her a purpose at a time in her life where she'd felt rudderless, and it was absolutely killing her that she was basically crapping all over the opportunities he'd given her.

His first text was a link to the local paper, so she tapped it with enough trepidation that a pit of dread opened up in her gut. Glaring at her in bright white light on the homepage of the *Las Vegas Gazette* was an enormous picture of her and Carter in Elysium's stairwell. Her legs were wrapped around him and they were basically sucking each other's faces off. In that light, the rest of her uncle's text messages, which were some variation of *FIX IT*, made much more sense.

She groaned, a sound from deep in the bottom of her chest. And she'd thought yesterday had been a shitty day.

Calling her uncle, she prepared herself for his disappointment and the reiteration of his earlier directive to clean up her image. It was exactly what he delivered.

"I'm calling Carter, too," her uncle expounded, fuming. "The Carter Hayes I know has more respect for women than to put them in compromising positions like that. He should be ashamed of himself."

"I think—" she started, in an attempt to explain that neither of them had been thinking straight, but her uncle wasn't interested in excuses or equivocations.

"You need to fix this, Alexa, or we're both out of a lot of money," he grumbled.

"Understood," she told him, her heart clenching with the thought of hurting the investment her uncle had worked his whole life to build. "I will take care of it."

"Please do," he instructed, some of the steam going out of his bluster. It wasn't like her uncle to be mad, but seeing his niece semi-nude in his daily newspaper would probably put anyone in a less-than-gracious mood. "And Alexa, if anything else like this happens, the deal we had about Halcyon is out the window."

Her heart squeezed at the thought of losing Halcyon, too. "I promise I'll make it right," she reiterated. "Please just enjoy the rest of your vacation."

She expected her uncle to hang up, but he stayed on the line.

Finally, he spoke again. "You and Carter, of all people, know that there are cameras everywhere in a casino. What the hell were you thinking, dear?"

Alexa so did not want to have this conversation. Especially since the moment she'd walked into that stairwell she'd known there would be a camera. She just hadn't given a shit.

"We got into a fight. It didn't, um, end like I expected it to," she explained lamely.

Uncle John chuckled softly and some of the panic in her chest subsided. Business or not, he was still her uncle.

"Well, seems like this is a problem you two could work on together."

Alexa blew out a breath. Unfortunately, he was

right. After that photo in the news, Carter was her only solution.

Running a hot shower and scarfing down some pain relievers, she tried desperately not to think about just what had happened last night. Carter knew everything about her, stayed up late with her after her parents died and she couldn't sleep, been her confidant about guys, her trusted friend as she'd learned how to run the casinos. And they were one bad breakup away from losing all of it.

She changed for work into a charcoal skirt and an aqua sleeveless blouse, hoping she didn't look as awful as she felt. She had no idea what she'd say to him now. Maybe, "Hey, I know we almost boned, but I got scared because I'm an emotional kindergartner, so do you mind if we just get fake-engaged instead?"

The drive to the bakery and then to Carter's was short, but thankfully gave her enough time to think of a plan of action. If heavy and shameless groveling was, in fact, considered an actual plan.

His house was ultramodern; the standard Southwestern adobe tile roof and white stucco didn't interest Carter. Instead he'd designed a three-story building with sharp angles of steel, glass and countless windows. Five stone columns reached from the ground to the top floor, the middle floor cantilevering out into the air over the floor beneath.

It wasn't really her style, but it was very expensive and creative, the latter of which probably most appealed to Carter. He'd always been a little bit of an odd man out, never quite fitting into the crowd. In high school, he'd carried a briefcase instead of a backpack. That fact had subjected him to a fair amount of ridicule to the point where Alexa had to step in a couple of times, except it never seemed to matter to him. If people made fun of her, she would have switched to a backpack, but the next day, Carter doubled down and added a pocket watch to his briefcase. It was one of the reasons she liked him so much. He was always himself, and there was a lot of comfort in that for her, especially in a place like Vegas where everyone wanted to be something else.

His house doors had smart locks and her fingerprint was already programmed in, so she let herself in without ringing the bell. It was a much better idea to not give him a chance to slam the door in her face before he could hear her best groveling.

She stepped into his foyer, a wide-open space with dark wood floors and an enormous modern brass light fixture hanging down from the high ceiling. Just as she headed in the direction of the kitchen to set down her bags, a youngish girl in her twenties tiptoed down the suspended staircase, silver stilettos dangling from her hand. It was clearly the commencement of a walk of shame.

When the girl saw Alexa, she froze mid-step, eyes wide with an arrested expression on her face.

"Don't worry," Alexa offered. "We're just friends."

The blond-haired girl blew out a relieved breath. "Thank God."

The two exchanged another brief smile before she bolted toward the front door, taking a moment to slip on her shoes before she opened it.

The girl had her hand on the knob when Carter appeared at the top of the steps. Looking from his guest to Alexa, his eyes shuttered, as if he couldn't handle the sight of what was happening.

Alexa attempted to rein in her rage, because Carter had every right to seek out someone else last night since she'd basically left him high and dry. Except, wait a second, no, he damned well didn't because she'd given him a fucking amazing blow job.

More importantly, had it meant that little to him that he could turn around on a dime and sleep with someone else? They had been best friends for over fifteen years and their actions last night had changed everything.

Her heart stopped for a second at the thought that he might be seriously dating that girl, but he would have told her and she wouldn't have been sneaking out the door at first light.

So basically she was just pissed again. The door closed shut behind his late-night date.

"It's not what you think," Carter began, holding a hand up as if to halt her train of thought.

Alexa was a power player and she'd spent years perfecting her poker face, which was just what she gave him.

"What you do is your business, Carter," she said, meeting his eyes as he came down the steps. "We're just friends."

Jaw ticking, he crossed his arms over his bare chest and stared her down but she didn't give anything away.

"Alex, you can pretend you're not pissed all you want because far be it from me to presume that last night meant anything to the man-eater of Vegas, but I promise nothing happened. You fucking know me better than that. Now would you like to tell me why you're skulking around in my house so early?"

"You know why I'm here," she threw out, walking briskly into his expansive kitchen, where slate countertops and butter-colored eco-friendly wood cabinets lined the space. She sat her purse on top of the island along with the bag of pastries and fruit salad she'd picked up from his favorite bakery, vaguely irritated that she'd brought breakfast for a person who at the very least slept in the same room as another woman. "And since you now seem to be in a position to owe me a favor, I'm very glad I did stop by so early."

"Nothing happened," he gritted. "She was here when I got home—"

Alexa raised a hand. "Like I said, your love life is not my business."

"Right, how can I forget that we're just friends," he mocked. "Your lips are wrapped around my dick every day."

A bolt of heat shot up Alexa's spine, which enraged her because she wasn't interested in revisiting last night. She might not want to do it again, but it had meant something to her. A whole hell of a lot, in fact. Clearly, he didn't feel the same way, which felt a little like a vise mercilessly squeezing her insides and jiggling them around at the same time. Additionally, she did not at all appreciate his sarcastic tone considering what he'd done, sexual penetration or not.

"Well, apparently that wasn't enough of an evening for you," she said, kicking herself for not being able to hold it back. "Nevertheless, it's for the best because you're going to have to pose as my fake fiancé."

CHAPTER SIX

CARTER WAS ASTONISHED to see Alexa in his house this morning at all, much less with pastries, witnessing a near indiscretion on his part and proposing a fake engagement. It was a less-than-ideal wake-up call.

When he'd gotten home last night, Kelly had been waiting in his driveway. She was an old friend who'd just shown up with an expectation that usually he was up for, but they hadn't slept together last night. He should have sent her away, but he'd been just pissed off enough to hope Alexa got wind of it to let Kelly stay. He was still pissed now, as a matter of fact, because last night had been some pretty epic bullshit even from Alexa, who was never honest about what she was feeling.

However, the call he'd gotten from his board just minutes before she arrived was the reason he'd nudged Kelly out the door. His company's stock had risen in value today after the story of his and Alexa's stairwell indiscretion hit the national news circuit. Apparently, the tech world loved that one of their geeky own had conquered the closest thing Vegas had to royalty. The increase had more to do with the fact that he was about to launch a product to expand his business, but his board would say anything to maximize their investment. They'd gone so far as to suggest him making the most out of his relationship with Alexa even though they'd previously been against his friendship with her because of her rep. It was nonsense that he ignored, so he wasn't about to take their advice on his personal life now, either.

"You really want to get fake-engaged?" he asked Alexa.

"You know it would work," Alexa contended. "Uncle John is madder than I've ever heard him. He threatened to sell Halcyon, too, if I didn't clean this up."

It figured. John knew that selling Halcyon would be just the incentive Alexa needed to take the threat seriously.

"Alexa, I still don't think it's a good idea," he said, shaking his head.

He would literally give her the shirt off his back in an ice storm, but they needed to talk about what had happened last night. Unfortunately, now that she'd seen Kelly this morning, Alexa was closed up tighter than one of her casino vaults.

"Come on, Carter. You're my best chance to turn this around quickly."

"Do you really think that after last night we can be in a fake engagement?" he asked. "Despite you getting scared at the end, we started a physical relationship. And now you're proposing that we also carry on a fake engagement? That's blurring the lines immeasurably even for us."

"I did not get scared," she argued. "Besides, the lines won't get blurry because we won't be having sex. Problem solved."

"Then I'm out." She was batshit crazy if she thought they were going backward now.

She was totally running scared. The look in her eyes last night when his mom had called was as if she'd fallen into her own personal horror movie, only the murderer was wielding an engagement ring instead of a gun. If there was a thing he could do to assure her that no matter what, they'd still be friends, he'd do it. She'd wrecked his heart as a kid and he was still here, which was proof they could weather anything. Unfortunately, that probably wasn't the best example to use to not incite more fear.

She folded her arms across her chest, lifting her perfect breasts even higher. "So you're saying that because we nearly slept together you can't help out your best friend in need? That you'd rather sleep with me than continue our friendship?"

"Of course I'd rather sleep with you!" he burst out.

Alexa shook her head, looking disappointed. It pissed him off almost as much as it tugged at his higher sense of integrity.

"Carter, I really need your help right now."

He dropped his head onto the cool slate of his kitchen island, trying to rein in his irritation. Then realizing something, he lifted his head and pointed at her. "Alexa, if we're fake-engaged and also not sleeping together, that means you can't sleep with anyone else, either."

She shrugged. "I'm okay with it."

"Really, Alexa?" he asked doubtfully. "You're out with a different guy every week."

She pointed an angry finger at him, fire back in her eyes at the implication in his words. "We both like to have fun. There's nothing wrong with it, but it's not as if I can't go for a few months without sex."

"Months?" Carter croaked, shaking his head. "No fucking way I can do it and no fucking way you can, either."

"Do you want to bet?" she challenged, hands on hips.

"No!" he shouted, throwing his arms up. "That is the worst bet I've ever heard! *Winning* is actually *losing*!"

She just rolled her eyes at his outburst, but Christ, a couple of months? Not that he couldn't do it, but why would he?

"You can sleep with people if you're discreet," she said, folding her arms over her chest. "So are you helping me or not?"

"You know I am," he muttered. He also ignored the offer, because any idiot would know it wasn't true and just a ploy to get him to agree to this ludicrous plan of hers. She was pissed about a sleepover and they weren't even fake-engaged yet; she'd have his balls in a vise if he actually had sex with someone. "But we need to talk about last night."

"I thought last night was amazing," Alexa offered, surprising him considering that she'd ended it before they got to the best part. "But apparently, it wasn't amazing enough."

Ah, right, he thought, that admission made much more sense now. It was passive-aggressiveness. Something Alexa normally eschewed, which meant she must really be pissed. Good thing she needed him for this fake fiancé thing so badly or he'd probably be hanging from a spit over a fire by now.

"Alexa," he said, catching hold of her eyes. "Kelly's just a girl I hang out with sometimes. You know, in the middle of the night. She showed up and I was pissed at you, but nothing happened. You can call her if you don't believe me."

Alexa didn't look totally convinced.

"I want what was happening with us last night to actually happen. I wouldn't jeopardize that."

Shaking her head, she sighed. "Last night was

obviously a mistake. I'm already acting like a jealous bitch."

"Last night was the best idea we've had in years and it's nice that you're jealous. I like it. This fake engagement, however, is going to be a mistake of meteoric proportions."

"Maybe, but I don't have a lot of choices," she acknowledged grimly.

Despite the fact that this idea was basically turning his life into a dumpster fire, he felt for her position. It wasn't fair or right that her reputation was damaging the possibility of selling the casinos, and it wasn't lost on him that she didn't even want to sell them to begin with. And even if all that weren't true, he'd still do what she needed him to do because that's what best friends did.

"Come here," he told her, waiting as she hesitated, but finally came to him.

He pulled her into his arms, threading his fingers through that silky curtain of chestnut hair. "Before we're officially engaged, let's at least finish what we started."

Before she could argue, he caught her lips. The spark kindled again immediately and he fanned the flames as his tongue tangled with hers. He lifted her onto the kitchen island, right beside her bag of pastries, and stepped between her legs, never breaking contact with her mouth. Her fingers tugged at his hair and his dick throbbed like the devil as they ground against each other. He made easy work of her blouse and bra and threw them to the floor, taking her exposed breasts in his hands, kneading the soft globes and circling the taut nipples beneath his thumbs until she was squirming against him.

He gave her what she wanted, finally focusing his full attention on her nipples. He pinched them just a little too hard for comfort, and she met his eyes, surprised. He gently pulled one hard nipple and twisted it just the slightest bit to show her he was full of surprises. At her whimper of pleasure, he leaned down and took the pink nub into his mouth, soothing the bit of pain with his tongue.

Pushing her skirt up, he found her center, hot as hell and dripping with moisture. She wanted him just as much as he wanted her. Fuck the fake engagement shit. Fuck the friendship she was trying to maintain. They weren't going to make it without blurring the hell out of the lines. He dropped to his knees before he took her right on the island. He slid a finger in her, the sweet smell like a siren's call for him to devour her. He ran his fingers along her slick clit, increasing the pressure as she clung to him, powerless to the conflagration between them. Eye level with her core, he pulled her panties off, a green thong today. That couldn't be incidental. Greedy for what it might mean, he pocketed the bit of silky cloth in his shorts. He parted her engorged pink folds, exposing her to the air and to his gaze. Their eyes met as he put his mouth to her, lapping at her, loving the taste, like heat and spice and need.

Her moans echoed in the empty kitchen as he took her higher and higher until she stilled against him, coming with a cry of pleasure. He licked and stroked lightly until her fingers uncurled from his hair and she sighed.

He stood then, pushing a lock of hair from her flushed face behind her ear.

She gave him a weird look, then hopped off the island and pulling down her skirt and sliding on the bra and blouse he handed her.

Her purse in hand, she smoothed the lines in her skirt. "I'll accept that as your apology."

After treating her to a morning delight, he definitely wasn't going to let her have the last word.

"I'll see you tonight for our first public date to announce this ill-conceived engagement to the world. Do me a favor and wear a garbage bag or something so we don't end up on the front of tomorrow's newspaper, too."

Within an hour of leaving his house, Alexa received a flurry of texts from Carter. He'd updated his social media with news of their engagement and sent an email out to all the casino owners on his mailing list, and the homepage of the *Las Vegas*

Gazette now had something else to post along with that incriminating stairwell picture.

Smiling at Carter's customary diligence, she returned his texts with copious heart emojis, but he didn't bother to respond. She knew he was still pissed about having to pretend, but she was too relieved that he'd agreed to help her to regret it. This morning had been challenging because of his unanticipated visitor, but it had inadvertently taken out the possibility of the awkward morning-after kind of conversation she'd been anticipating. She loved Carter a lot, and this morning in the kitchen had been another stellar performance, but she wasn't ready to be in a real relationship with him. There was no "dating" Carter. They were so close it would be like going straight into a marriage when what she needed was dating training wheels.

She picked up her phone to remind him to get an engagement ring for her, but set it back down. Uncle John had given her a diamond ring when she'd graduated from college that would work. It might not be as flashy as some would expect the co-owner of three casinos to wear, but the sentiment of two old friends getting married would probably erase anyone's suspicions. Besides, an engagement ring, fake or not, felt like too much to ask of a person.

She went back to her house to grab the ring along with a dress for tonight and then drove to Halcyon.

Whatever reception she thought she was prepared for was nothing compared to the excited response to the engagement from everyone in the casino. From the bouncers to the cashiers to her administrative assistant, the congratulations were effusive. It didn't hurt that everyone knew Carter Hayes was a catch. And not a single person even mentioned the fact that she was half-nude in the news, so mission accomplished.

When she finally made it to her office it was already noon and she vowed to not give Carter another thought. Running three casinos was enough to drive the most organized person crazy and that's what she needed to focus on. For the rest of the afternoon, she succeeded in getting work done.

She didn't realize how much time had passed until an alert dinged on her phone, reminding her that Carter was picking her up in just over an hour. She shut her computer down for the day and popped into her office's en suite bathroom to get ready. Eschewing the requested garbage bag, she'd chosen a sleeveless bloodred sheath with an open back. She slid into a pair of gold peep-toe heels, did a double check of her makeup and grabbed her gold clutch.

By the time she made it down to the front of the casino, Carter was pulling up in his cobalt-blue Bentley convertible with the top down. He hopped out and assisted her into the passenger's seat.

"Couldn't find a garbage bag, huh?"

"I wouldn't even know where to look. My housekeeper is on vacation this week."

He closed the door. Instead of a hoodie, Carter wore a navy blue suit with a crisp white shirt and shiny tobacco wing tips. Buttoned up and sleek, he looked like a rich designer piece of chocolate.

He settled into the driver's seat and she looked him over. "So I get the mogul treatment as your fake fiancée?"

"We're on a date. I wear suits on dates."

She grabbed his tie, drawing him close. "Can't you just take a compliment?"

"I didn't actually hear one in there," he drawled.

She could smell the mint on his breath. "You look sexy in that suit."

"I know," he said. He pulled a small box out of his jacket pocket. "You'll need this for people to believe we're engaged."

Her eyes widened at the *HW* for Harry Winston emblazoned on the top of a small square black box. Pulling open the two sides, she revealed a huge emerald-cut diamond engagement ring with a platinum band. She didn't pull the exquisite ring out of the box, marveling at how it glittered under the flashing rainbow lights of the Strip.

"Holy shit, Hayes," she gasped. "This is insane. Tell me it's a loaner."

It was a perfect piece of jewelry and the kind of ring she'd envisioned for herself all her life. Mar-

riage she could be indifferent about, but there was
no question about her love of bling. It was a simple
ring, just a single diamond on an unadorned band,
but it was no less glitzy for it. The diamond was
at least six carats, would nearly dwarf her finger,
and it came with the kind of unparalleled clarity
Harry Winston was known for. It was like some
"John Jacob Astor on the Titanic" shit for sure.

Glancing over at her, Carter took the box from
her hands and pulled the ring out. "Alexa Marielle
Lawson, will you be my fake fiancée?"

"I thought you'd never ask," she returned cheekily.

Carter took her hand in his and removed her
uncle's ring and handed it to her. As he slid the
new one onto her finger she thought of anything
else besides the fact that he was literally putting
an engagement ring on her finger.

"Did you pick this out or did your assistant?"

"How would I have my assistant pick out a ring
I was to supposed to have given you last night?"
he asked blandly.

Aw, hell. It figured. One fake engagement ring
and her critical thinking skills had already de-
serted her.

"Well, it's a lovely choice. Were I your real fiancée, I'd be very impressed."

"I remembered your mom's ring was an emerald-
cut, so I thought you'd like it."

Just like that, tears pricked at the back of her

eyes. Even after all these years, thinking about her parents sometimes caught her wrong. The fact that Carter remembered her mom's ring at all and had gone so far as to replicate it was the very reason they could never be together. If she lost Carter... well, she couldn't even contemplate it.

She took his hand and squeezed. "Thank you."

Their eyes met and his held hers for a moment. "You deserve the best."

Then he leaned in and kissed her full on the mouth in front of her own casino, treating her valet guys to quite a show. She grasped at the lapels of his jacket to bring him closer, jolts of lust sparking between her thighs. His hands tangled in her loose waves as he angled her head for deeper access, exploring her as if they had all the time in the world. He tasted like mint and citrus and hot-blooded man, and she couldn't get enough. Pleasure thrummed through her veins as he gently nipped her bottom lip before diving back in for a final taste.

He broke contact and put the car into gear. "That ought to get the rumors going."

They pulled away from the curb and she fell back into the seat. She was having serious doubts that they could make it through a fake engagement with no sex and both their friendship and sanity intact.

CHAPTER SEVEN

GOING TO THIS fake dinner with Alexa was the last thing Carter wanted to do right now. Seeing her with his ring on her finger was fucking with his head, because while the ring itself was exactly what he would have picked for her in reality, everything else was a sham.

"Where are we going?" she asked, oblivious to his disquiet.

"Sinatra," he replied, naming a favorite tourist spot.

Alexa laughed. "We're really doing this, I guess."

"Yep," Carter said, but he couldn't keep the tightness out of his voice.

"What else did you do today besides shop for jewelry?"

"I worked out and then launched the full-scale internet rollout of our engagement news, in case you hadn't noticed."

"Of course I did. Maybe you overlooked the twenty heart emojis I sent you."

He raised an eyebrow.

"I mean to say thank you, Carter," she said, moving her hand to pat his arm but drawing back at the last moment.

That was a good move on her part. Touching was a bad idea at the moment.

"I know you don't want to do this," she continued, because that's how this game had always been played between them—never let on how much you actually wanted your best friend to touch you. "And you have no idea how much it means to me."

"You're welcome, but for the record, I'm still in this begrudgingly."

"Noted," she said, hiding a small smile.

It only took a minute or so more to arrive at the restaurant, where he handed the car off to the valet.

The host, dressed in formal black tails, showed them to their seats, tucked away in a dark corner of the restaurant. They passed tables with red herringbone tablecloths and red metal lattice chairs, the style quintessentially 1950s Vegas.

Before they sat, Carter took Alexa's hand and pulled her into his arms. "I'm sorry I've been in a shitty mood. You look absolutely stunning tonight."

He took her mouth in a showy kiss in front of the entire restaurant. It was to add authenticity to their story, but it didn't feel fake. Tongues tangled together in an age-old dance of desire as his hand moved from her back to her ass. He wanted so much more of her touch, her soft curves against him, her tongue in his mouth. Everything about her felt like coming home.

That single thought had him releasing her. Those thoughts were dangerous territory considering he was already too close to caving to her wishes and staying in Vegas. That's what he would do as her friend, which is exactly what he was trying to avoid.

"Well, that got out of hand," she whispered when he'd taken his seat across from her.

"It needed to be authentic," he informed her. "I saw at least six people recording it on their phones."

"Great," she murmured under her breath.

Carter thought she looked vaguely disappointed and wondered if she had any idea what a dangerous game they were playing. If she thought that either of them was walking away from this without feelings getting engaged, she was delusional.

After the waiter took their orders, Alexa started tapping on her phone.

"I met with a member of my board today for lunch and he expects them to approve the California satellite office," he blurted, because he needed the distance after that kiss.

Alexa's water glass made an audible thunk as it hit the table. "What? I thought the meeting wasn't until next month."

He shrugged. "Well, they've already approved the office, but the final plans are still being reviewed."

A furrow appeared between Alexa's eyes and she frowned. "I don't understand why you're even doing this. The cost of living and the property rental for the office in San Francisco has to be astronomical compared to Vegas. Plus, those employees could work remotely if you want them."

He grinned, because those were the exact same considerations he'd gone over in his head as well before making the final decision.

"True, but I've already lost some of my best people to Cisco and Symantec, mostly because of the locale. Programmers aren't huge Vegas people." That wasn't entirely true, but he still wanted a presence in the area. More importantly, he needed a change, to take his life and business to the next level. He'd never lived anywhere except for Vegas. He'd gotten accepted other places for college, but Alexa had been staying in town and UNLV was good enough for him. But it was time to move on with or without her.

"Well, I don't want you to go," Alexa said, displeasure darkening her hazel eyes. "I would think your fiancée should have a say."

He raised an eyebrow and paused as the waiter appeared with their drinks.

"I promise I won't be gone forever," he assured her.

"You'd never leave Vegas forever. It's in your blood," she declared, as if trying to convince herself. But then maybe she just assumed it, that he was so far up her ass that he couldn't possibly make a decision that didn't involve her. That might have been true before, but the role of dependable best friend wasn't one he was playing anymore.

He hated what he was about to do, but it needed to be done. Or maybe he was actually looking forward to it. This charade was already torture on his sex life, which was nonexistent now, and if he didn't carve out some space between them it would be even worse.

"You know," he said, not denying his affinity for his home in the desert, "I've been thinking all day today what I get out of this arrangement."

"Besides the pleasure of my company and the notoriety that comes along with getting the city's most un-gettable girl, you mean?"

Grinning at her stunningly deep, yet not unfounded, well of confidence, he drawled, "Yes, besides all that."

She took a sip of her martini, her plump red lips closing over the rim of her glass and reminding him of how they'd looked wrapped around his dick last night.

"Well, what is it? What can I do for you, Carter?" She licked her lips, completely on purpose to drive him fucking further into insanity.

"When we break up, I want you to set me up with Monroe."

Nothing had ever pleased him as much as the pure and unadulterated rage that transformed Alexa's smug face. Monroe was a friend of Alexa's, one of her best ones, who, on paper, was a perfect match for him. She owned her own successful start-up and was a fellow computer person. And like Alexa, she came from a renowned casino dynasty. Her father was the only man in the history of Vegas with enough balls to build a casino outside the Strip and still make it wildly successful.

He expected her to balk at the request, but she gritted her teeth. "Fine," she ground out. "But it's going to be difficult to date her when you're halfway across the country."

"Las Vegas to San Francisco is not nearly halfway across the country," he pointed out.

She glared, if not daggers then certainly a sharp set of kitchen knives, at him.

"I'm not going to let you distract me with pedantry. I'll set you up with Monroe, but that does bring me to my own agenda. The rules," she began.

Taking a drink of his whiskey, he waited for her to expound.

"Obviously, this engagement only lasts a month since you're cutting out on me."

"I'm not—"

She stilled him with a raised hand, palm out. "Cutting out."

He rolled his eyes.

"Second," she said, lowering all except two fingers, "during that month, we can't see other people publicly. As discussed, you can do whatever you want on your own time as long as you are discreet."

He nodded, and then she muttered, "Of course, this morning was not discreet enough."

"For fuck's sake, Alexa," he growled quietly, leaning across the table into her space. "I swear to you, nothing happened."

He didn't know why he was even saying it since he didn't care if she believed him or not. Frankly, if he was going to have to be celibate for an entire fucking month, he should have slept with Kelly and not let her out of his damn bed for days. Christ knew he was regretting it now.

Alexa met his eyes then, her hazel ones considering whether or not to believe him.

He saved her the worry. "I promise. I'll be on my best behavior."

She didn't look completely convinced, but he also couldn't bring himself to give a single fuck.

Their food came, her lobster risotto and his filet mignon. Despite Sinatra's being a shameless tourist trap, the food was pretty good. Plus, since

Vegas itself was a shameless tourist trap, it was hard to get around the stigma.

They dug in, setting aside the rules conversation for a moment. Alexa always ordered risotto when she could. He remembered her uncle telling both of them at dinner one night that a good risotto was the mark of an excellent chef, and Alexa was always looking for chefs in the area to poach for her own restaurants.

About seven bites in, she frowned and took a drink of water.

"Not going to steal this guy?"

She shook her head. "Gummy."

"Ah," he said, slicing into his perfectly cooked filet mignon like butter. "Mine's perfect."

A dark, unamused eyebrow raised as he shoved juicy bite of beef after juicy bite into his mouth. Normally, he would have offered to share his own food with her since she wasn't going to finish the risotto, but meh, no sex for a month meant he deserved the entire steak.

He pushed the basket of bread her way. Taking a piece, she gave his steak a longing glance she tried to hide.

Finishing her piece of bread, she sat back into the cloth booth. "There are two more rules," she informed.

"I'm all ears," he replied around a bite.

She met his eyes again, letting him know she was in on the joke.

"We're not going to get through this entire month without touching each other," she said, stating the obvious. "But we both agreed that we can't blur those lines. So the only time we can be physical is in public, where there's a clear purpose of convincing people we're really engaged. Like earlier, with that kiss."

"Agreed." As if he had another choice anyway, but at least this way he'd get a little action, even if it was PG.

"The last thing is, I think you should move in with me. Or I should move in with you if you don't want to leave your place. It would look weird if we don't do that, being friends for so long. And people do that before they get married now."

"Nope."

Without thinking, he shoved a whole stalk of broccoli in his mouth. So when she said, "You know I'm right," his only response was to double down with an emphatic head shake.

"Carter," she pleaded. "You know it makes sense. This really needs to be believable if I'm going to change my reputation. Do you know today I signed up for a knitting class? Knitting! You can't even wear sweaters in Vegas!"

He swallowed. "I don't care. That's way more than I agreed to."

"Come on, we'll have separate bedrooms and we're on totally different work schedules. We won't even know the other is there."

Crossing his arms over his chest, his eyes drifted down over her delicate bare neck and exposed cleavage. "I will know."

She sighed, a wispy piece of hair blowing to the side of her face. He wondered if she'd worn this particular dress on dates before with the same hairstyle. Had getting ready for their date tonight been any different for her or was it just another bullet point on her work to-do list?

In college, she'd had two different date dresses, one that she wore for dates she was excited about and one for the dates she was dreading. He'd been a dorky kid so in love with a dreamed-up version of his best friend and wanted to be the one she was on a date with. Watching her get ready had been painful and awesome all at once, and now here he was, finally on the other end with the exception that they were so much further from any kind of real romantic relationship than ever.

Her red lips pursed in an impressive pout. "You're going to make me beg, aren't you?"

"You can beg all you like. It's not happening."

"We'll see," she said, challenge twinkling in her eyes. "I'll give you one hundred grand to move in with me."

He choked on his whiskey. He didn't need the money, but shit. "Alexa, don't be ridiculous."

"I am deadly serious."

"You know I don't need money."

She shrugged. "Neither of us needs money, but that doesn't mean we wouldn't like more of it. Besides, you said you wanted something out of this arrangement. I can deliver cash."

A hundred grand was certainly a tidy sum, especially for something he would have done two days ago for free, and gladly.

"I'm going to pass on the money. What else you got in the way of bribery?"

She grinned, loving the game. "Dates to all future weddings and work functions."

"And?"

"Sex."

His ears perked up.

"One time and one time only. You pick when and where."

It was tempting, but once wouldn't be enough. "Pass."

A flicker of surprise crossed her face before she covered it up. He had to admit, fucking with Alexa was cathartic. He'd spent far too much of their friendship waiting for scraps of the affection she gave so freely to other guys, and now she needed to actually accept that he wasn't the taciturn and awkward friend she could keep at a distance.

"Listen," he said, putting an end to her campaign to assuage her nonexistent guilt, "when I think of how you can pay me back for this favor, I'll let you know, but the thank-you for a favor this immense doesn't exist yet."

She raised a dark eyebrow. "Is it because of the celibacy thing?" she asked. "Because I said you could sleep with other people as long as you're discreet."

The back of his neck heated in anger. It was the second time she'd made the proposal and it was just one more piece of evidence that she wasn't at all affected by it. After what had happened between them in the stairwell and his kitchen, it pissed him the fuck off.

"I'm not going to sleep with anyone. I wouldn't do that to you."

She shook her head emphatically. "You don't have to do that for me, Carter. I don't want to interfere with your life that much. Besides, I might get the urge as well."

"If you sleep with someone else, this is over," he bit off, furious with the fact that she would sleep with other people while engaged to him. Yes, he knew it was fake and it wasn't as if his reputation would take a hit if she made him look stupid. This was just good old-fashioned jealousy and he wasn't stubborn enough to think otherwise.

"That wasn't—"

"These are *my* terms. You've already made yours very clear."

"Carter—" she began again.

"You'll move into my house tomorrow."

Her mouth dropped. "You just said—"

"I changed my mind," he clipped. "I'm allowed to change it. That's part of the favor you owe me."

Her bare arms crossed over her chest. "Anything else you want to throw in?"

He pinned her with a look dead in her eyes. "Not right now, no."

Then he took the last bite of his steak.

She fished out a chunk of lobster from her risotto, chewing on it listlessly. Eventually, the waiter came and removed his empty plate and her half-eaten dinner.

"Is that all your rules or was there something else you had in mind to restrict my general freedoms as a human being?"

She laughed. "Come on, now that's too far!"

He leaned into the middle of the table again, keeping his voice hushed. "For an entire month, I can't date, can't fuck, can't sleep alone in my own house, have to go to your insipid casino functions and make small talk with slimy owners, have to lie to my own family, company heads and coworkers, and in exchange you've offered me one night of sex, some money and dates. And I'm your best friend. I hope this isn't how you negotiate at your job."

She looked stricken, her hazel eyes wide. "I'm sorry, Carter. I just kind of thought it was a chance for us to hang out more. Like we used to before our jobs took over our lives."

"It is like that, but it's also all those other things, too."

"Two times for sex?" she offered with a cheeky grin. "Would that make up for it? I'm really good at it. Like, the best you've ever had kind of good."

The waiter arrived with their check. When she grabbed for it, he got there first.

He signed over an enormous tip and helped her out of the booth, murmuring in her ear, "You might be good, but I'm better."

"That's what all guys say," she told him, leading him through the restaurant.

He caught up with her, laying a hand on the small of her back, which happened to be mostly bare. Her skin was warm and soft, but the textured cloth of the booth had made gentle impressions in her smooth skin. He ran a thumb over the raised bumps as he guided her to the exit.

He held the front door open, following her past the valet station and into a small courtyard with a ten-foot-tall privacy hedge. Pruned with ruthless precision, it blocked them from the busy street beyond.

"I don't suppose you want to go to Encore?" Alexa asked. "It *is* Friday night. I'm not usually home yet."

"You want to go to a casino again?" Considering that was how he'd gotten into this predicament, he wasn't super eager to return to one.

She shrugged. "This is a date. What do you usually do on dates? Go to dinner and that's it?"

He had no response to that.

"You go straight from dinner to sex?" she presumed with a disbelieving laugh.

He shrugged. It was often what he did.

"What if you have a heavy meal, like cheese or something?"

"Stop it," he warned, heading toward the entrance to Encore, the casino Sinatra was attached to.

"You just ate sixteen ounces of steak. You seriously think you could deliver the best sex of my life right now? I highly doubt it," she kept on badgering.

This was why friends didn't have sex. Because there were no boundaries.

It goaded him into asking the question he didn't want the answer to. "What do you normally do on dates? You just ate a bowl full of carbs and cheese."

"You're the only person I eat carbs and cheese with."

"How did I get so lucky?" he muttered as they followed the wide marble pathway to the casino entrance.

Low-hanging trees laced with twinkling lights and delicate red-and-white paper lanterns arched over them, creating a small haven of intimacy.

"If I'm on a date," she answered, "we usually do something after dinner, like a show or something. Remember when that guy flew me to Rio? That was amazing. I definitely did not eat risotto then. Because, you know…"

"Okay, I get it," he told her, ducking so his head didn't hit one of the lanterns. "Tell me again, did you give that guy a second date?"

"Yeah, but then he got serious too fast and I had to break things off."

"You didn't pick up on that when he flew you to Brazil on your first date?"

"I bet you've done something like that before. You gave Maggie an Hermès scarf after one date. That's the cost of a first-class plane ticket somewhere."

His eyes slid away from hers for a moment. "I've never flown a date to another country. Nor do I own a jet."

"Maybe that's why you can't get a girlfriend," she teased.

He took her hand in his as a noisy group of people rounded the corner.

"You think I can't get a girlfriend?" he asked, pulling her off the main path and deeper into the garden.

"No," she said carefully. "I never said that."

He backed her up into the corner where two hedges met, their view of the path cut off so that it felt isolated and private. "I can get a girlfriend if I want one."

"I didn't mean—"

"I know exactly what you meant."

He pulled her hard against him and found her mouth. If he could only touch her in public, he might as well make it count.

Her lips were soft and lush and she smelled like she always did, like smoky vanilla and green apples. She'd been wearing the same perfume forever; he imagined he smelled it when he got off with her on his mind.

Her arms wrapped around his neck and he went deeper, tasting her mouth and giving it the attention they hadn't bothered with last night in the stairwell or in his kitchen this morning. Their tongues stroked each other, testing and teasing and learning.

She sighed against his mouth and he tightened his grip, hiking up her leg around his waist so his perpetual hard-on could find a measure of relief. His hand found the side of a bare breast and he thanked some generous deity for the miracle of naked skin. Sliding a thumb over a silken nipple, he growled and tightened his hold on her hair, deepening the kiss until their teeth knocked against each other.

He thought he heard something but ignored it, but when what might have been throat-clearing happened again he finally looked up and saw John Lawson standing just off the main path with a group of well-dressed businessmen.

"Shit," Alexa whispered, stepping quickly away from him when she saw what had caught his attention.

"Long time, no see, John," Carter said, taking Alexa's hand and leading her back onto the main walkway.

John shook his hand, a big grin on his face. "My boy, it's been too long. My vacation was excellent, but I had to come back and wish my two favorite kids congratulations on their engagement!"

"You must have hopped on a plane right after we spoke this morning," Alexa observed.

John pulled her into a hug, giving her a kiss on the forehead. "I did, indeed, when I heard the good news." John held out a hand to his friends, who must be investors since Alexa's uncle was putting on such a show for them. "This is Carter Hayes, the man who is single-handedly reforming my niece."

Carter could only imagine how incensed that comment made Alexa.

However, the men did suddenly look interested in him, their assessing gazes swinging from Alexa's cleavage to him. With their Tony Soprano suits and greasy hair, every single one of them looked like a smarmy asshole, but Carter kept this mouth shut and played the part he'd been assigned.

When her uncle invited them to have drinks with the group, he opened his mouth to refuse, but Alexa had other ideas.

He'd forgotten for a moment that this was all about business to her.

CHAPTER EIGHT

ALEXA WATCHED, ARMS crossed in irritation, as the two uniformed men carried her hastily packed suitcases from her house to the moving van Carter had sent over. While frugal was not a term that could ever apply to her when it came to clothing, she didn't think a monthlong slumber party at his house warranted an entire moving van.

But then the point was to irritate her, and he'd succeeded.

She stood in her living room wondering what else she could possibly take with her. Was she meant to take her couch? She'd already packed up her home office, which was just her laptop and a box of books she never found the time to read. Tackling the kitchen, she struggled to even fill a freezer bag, only locating some protein bars, the rest of her bowl of fruit, two bags of salad and a couple of yogurt cups. After she filled up a second box of shoes and packed her toiletry case, that was pretty much all she needed.

Giving her bedroom a last once-over, she turned off the light with a sigh. Today was the day that she became a fake fiancée and Carter's roommate. Never would have thought to write that in their high school yearbook. *Thanks for the memories, can't wait to be adult roommates with you in a semi-platonic semi-sexual fake engagement. Keep in touch!*

Even though she'd suggested it, and with good reason, she hadn't been prepared for what moving in together actually meant apparently, because she was feeling jittery and anxious. Now that she was packed up and leaving her home, reality was setting in. Every moment of her life was basically going to be spent with Carter. As if the lines delineating their friendship and public ruse weren't blurry enough, now she would have nowhere to hide.

One of the ways she and Carter had been able to stay friends all these years without sex getting involved was knowing when to give the other distance. Now there would be no distance, no space, no way to pretend that the only thing between them was friendship.

She followed the movers outside, watching with a certain amount of trepidation as they pulled away from the curb with her stuff.

By the time she got to Carter's house, still dressed in faded yoga pants and an old sweatshirt, because when one had a slightly percussive hangover that was what one did on Saturdays, she'd worked up a good rant. He had no right to, well, make this move easier on her, actually. But still, his behavior was high-handed and presumptuous. She'd move into his house when she was damned good and ready.

The garage door was open when she pulled into his driveway and his cars had been rearranged to leave her an open spot in the front. Some of her irritation evaporated. This was Carter, and regardless of how sexually frustrating and confusing this next month was going to be, she needed to remember that. They took care of each other. Sometimes that was smothering, and yet other times, it was lovely.

She parked in the spot and grabbed the coffees and bag of bagels she'd picked up before heading out onto the front walkway where the movers were already carrying the boxes into the house.

Carter stood in the foyer, looking very much himself in a pair of khakis and a black hoodie, a lightly scruffy beard forming on his face. Secretly, she liked to think of this as his Mark Zuckerberg look, but he'd hate it if she told him that. Mostly because of vanity, but also because he hated Facebook and the very idea of interacting with other humans. Despite his reputation with women, he wasn't a people person.

She waved to him as he directed the men up the stairs and to the left.

"I put you in your regular room," he informed her, referring to the second master suite on the opposite side of the house from his. She'd claimed it on their first official sleepover when he'd bought the house and his only furniture had been an old leather recliner from his parents' basement and a computer desk and chair. "If you want a different one, just tell the guys."

"The usual is fine," she said. "How did you even get movers to do this on such short notice?"

He looked at her as if she'd literally been born yesterday. "Money."

"Okay, smart-ass," she returned. "How much was it, so I can pay you back? It's the least I can do."

"Don't worry about it. We'll just lump this in with the other favors you owe me."

She pursed her lips. Someone was in a mood this morning. Holding out his coffee for him, he took it without a word and only looked mildly interested in the bagels she offered. Her guilt about this fake engagement had really settled deep in her gut last night while they sat through round after round of drinks with her uncle's sleazy investor friends. Even her social limits had been tested, so she couldn't imagine how awful it had been for Carter, who prided himself on perfecting the Irish goodbye.

Unfortunately, it was about to get worse for the both of them.

"There's an Autism Awareness charity gala tonight," Alexa told Carter. "I already bought tickets so I need be there." She'd also had another date lined up, but she'd obviously canceled that.

"And that means I have to be there, too," Carter guessed.

When she nodded, he winced but looked resigned. She didn't blame him. She'd rather snort cocaine with her mouth taped to a tailpipe than go to what amounted to an expensive school dance for grown-ups. Especially since she'd be playing the girl on Carter's arm, gushing about their engagement like a woman desperately in love. If she did too good a job, she didn't want Carter to get confused about what it meant. If she did too good a job, she didn't want her own self to get confused, either.

"Yeah," she said with a friendly pat on his back. "I'm sorry, Carter."

The words didn't quite make up for the reality of Las Vegas's so-called elite society. Aging men with baked-on fake tans and women who wore enough makeup to make drag queens look like ladies who lunch. The gala was everything Carter hated about Vegas. But she had to be there to do damage control, and this stuff was a part of her job even if she weren't trying to sell the casinos.

Plus, if she didn't go to these events, what had all her shopping been for?

"Well, I'd give you the tour, but you know everything already," he told her, gesturing to the house at large.

"Breakfast?" she suggested, then led him into the kitchen. She slid the bagel slices into his futuristic toaster. Its severely sloped sides made it look like a bullet and it fit in his ultramodern kitchen.

While the bagels toasted, she leaned back on the counter and met his eyes. "So what's your plan for the day? Want to do something?"

"I've got work stuff right now."

"On a Saturday?"

He shoved a hand into his pocket. "I can help you unpack, but then I need to work if we're going out tonight."

"What are you working on?"

"You really want to know?" he asked, regarding her over the top of his coffee cup.

She nodded. "Of course."

"As you know, we're set to release a new program soon, but we're having some problems."

"A new software for casinos?"

"Yeah, it's a program that analyzes the hands played and win data from table games. It would help casino owners determine what kinds of incentives to offer for play and tell them if they're making their money back on their current incentives based on money made at the tables."

"That would be awesome!" Alexa grinned. "Why didn't you tell me about it?"

The bagels popped up so she plated them and set them on the island between her and Carter with the tub of cream cheese.

He took the sesame bagel, just like she'd assumed, and spread a very precise layer of cream cheese over the top, making sure it touched the entire surface of the bagel and was uniform in thickness all the way around. She bit the side of her lip to stop from smiling at his typically precise behavior.

"I didn't not tell you," he explained with a shrug. "It's just work. I try and fail at different stuff all the time."

"Well, we're fake-engaged now so I need to know this stuff. You used to tell me about your work all the time. Before you got all tech mogul on me." Maybe they'd both become too obsessed with their work over the years. More probably, though, the time they'd spent together had tapered off as they'd built their careers so that when they were together it was the last thing they wanted to talk about.

"You used to talk about the casinos all the time, too." He gave her a mock salute before biting into his bagel.

One of the movers, the burly bearded one, poked his head into the kitchen to let them know the job was finished. Alexa grabbed her purse and shuffled off a huge tip for them.

The man held up the fistful of money with a wide smile. "Anytime you all need movers, you let me know. I'll be happy to do it."

Then he saw himself out.

"You didn't have to do that," Carter said. "They probably made more on this job than they do in two months."

Alexa shrugged. "They were nice and didn't bang my stuff around."

Carter gave her a look. "Let's go unpack."

After unpacking and getting ready, Alexa met Carter downstairs. She stopped halfway down the steps when she saw him because he looked nothing like the guy in the hoodie from earlier. In a nontraditional navy tux, he looked like Ryan Gosling at the Oscars, his sandy blond hair slicked back off his face and his glasses replaced with contacts. The lapels of the jacket were shiny as well as his bow tie and the openings of his pockets. He looked expensive and confident, and it was going to be a long night.

"I ordered us a car," he informed her. "There's not a version of me in any timeline or universe that doesn't need to drink irresponsibly tonight."

She took the last step to the floor. "One might

argue that ordering a car is actually drinking responsibly."

He raised an eyebrow.

Then he took a look at all of her, and instinctively, she turned in a full circle to show off the dress she'd bought months ago for this occasion. It was a sleeveless bronze Badgley Mischka with horizontal sequins, and it clung to every inch of her before flaring into a gentle trumpet skirt. "Good enough?"

"Yeah, good enough," he laughed. "You look unreal and you know it."

"Thank you. You look good, too."

Their eyes met then, a quiet acknowledgment that they'd never had an exchange like this before where they admitted to each other that they found the other attractive. There had always been teasing and joking, but the out-in-the-open part was the difference. All those lines they'd drawn were being erased one by one. More to the point, they were lines that she'd drawn because she wasn't going to be the one who led Carter on. She'd been very careful about that over the years. She wasn't good for him.

"Who was your original date to this thing?" he asked, moving to the front door.

She thought about lying, but she didn't ever lie to Carter. She might not tell him everything because she certainly didn't want to know who he was out with every night, but she didn't lie. "Hugh Matteson."

He nodded, recognizing the name of the retired football player who now owned a couple of restaurants in town. "Too bad, he would have been a good pull."

Opening the door for her, he stepped aside as she went through.

"I'm aware," she agreed. "And he was gracious when I called to cancel. Even congratulated me on the engagement."

A black town car waited at the curb and Carter helped her in. It was a short drive to the Revel casino, the sister casino of the one they'd been to last night. It was also a silent ride. For her own part, Alexa felt awkwardness pulling at the edges of their comfortable camaraderie. Even more so than last night when they'd gone out for the first time as engaged.

She glanced down at the ring on her finger, sparkling and beautiful and perfect. As they embarked on their first public appearance as a real couple, a small part of her wondered how she'd feel if it wasn't all fake. Would Carter be smiling at her now instead of typing away at his phone? Would her stomach be full of butterflies instead of weighty resolve, though she couldn't deny that there were some butterflies? Maybe they'd dance under the soft light of the ballroom's numerous chandeliers until the sun came up, never too tired to gaze into each other's eyes.

But that wasn't real life; that was a fairy-tale world that Alexa knew didn't exist. From the day her parents died, she'd learned not to dwell in daydreams. Real life was there to be lived.

The car came to a stop and Carter held his hand out for her, the expression on his face so carefully blank she knew he was mentally preparing for what for him would be a genuinely torturous evening.

He dutifully escorted her into the Lafite Ballroom, where rich red carpet and matching inlay on the walls made the expansive rectangle somehow feel warm and decadent. Twinkling candelabra chandeliers caught the copious gold embellishments in the floor and ceiling, creating the kind of drama the night demanded.

The party was already a crush considering tickets were a pricey thousand dollars a head. Couples crowded together on the dance floor, diners chatted among the ivory linen–covered tables, and groups milled about around the strategically placed open bars in the four corners of the room. The same low thrum of excitement pulsed in her chest like it had the other night at Elysium. It might be tacky and crass and an overpriced school dance, but she lived for the energy of making a deal. She'd make the sale for her uncle one way or another, and if that meant she had to manipulate and cajole every creep in the room, she'd do it gladly. Sure, she didn't want to sell the casinos at all, but the thrill of making money was a drug she never denied herself.

"You ready?" she asked Carter.

A muscle in his angled jaw twitched. "Yeah," he finally said.

Then he leaned down to kiss her. It was just the quickest of pecks to show the world they were together, but it sent a white-hot jolt of awareness through her chest. It also triggered a fair amount of alarm because she was in grave danger of losing sight of the lines herself. With every touch, kiss, laugh, they were heading further into what was an actual relationship. Something she didn't know how to extricate herself from smoothly.

He stepped away, looking just the slightest bit smug at the surprise she knew was on her face. She took a deep breath to collect herself.

Far too quickly, they were greeted by her uncle and his companion, a gentleman named Arthur Hendricks, a shipping magnate who apparently liked to look at breasts and was also looking to diversify. Her uncle noticed and his eyes flickered dangerously as they met hers.

She shook her head to dissuade him from calling attention to it, because Arthur Hendricks was just the kind of easily maneuvered blowhard they could sell a casino to.

CHAPTER NINE

CARTER HAD ASSUMED he'd have a shitty time at the gala, but it had already exceeded his expectations. Watching this douchebag with his comb-over and over-tan skin stare at Alexa's tits for the past ten minutes was not only a chore, but a lesson in restraint. He had no idea how John was doing it, but Alexa had clearly telegraphed for them to shut their mouths and that's what he was doing, so shut that his teeth were grinding.

When a call came in from work, he nearly audibly sighed at the excuse to escape. A voice mail from Greg, his right-hand guy, had informed him that someone was leaking the code to their new software to another security company. He found a seat at their empty table and called Henry Mueller, his board secretary.

"Carter," Henry boomed jovially, "Congratulations on your engagement! I thought you guys were just messing around, but this is wonderful news."

"I'm just doing it to help Alexa's reputation, Henry," Carter explained.

"Well, either way, that's good news for us. Have you set a date for the wedding?"

Was Henry having a stroke? "We're not actually engaged," Carter said again. "We're just doing this for a month to clean up Alexa's reputation so she can sell her casinos."

"I heard you," Henry laughed.

"Okaaay," Carter said, slowly, confused. But he didn't have time to explain further. "Listen, we might have a problem."

Carter gave him the express version of what was going on with the leak, wondering what this would mean for the new office.

"Well, we anticipate this kind of thing, obviously," Henry began, his voice calm. "But we should go ahead and announce the new office to change the narrative before the press has a field day with the leak. In the meantime, I've been talking to some other board members and we agreed that it wouldn't be the worst thing for you if this engagement were real."

Carter snorted. "Henry, it's 2019. I don't need to be married to run a company."

He caught Alexa's eye then, and if he'd worried that she needed his assistance dealing with that shipping creep, he was sorely mistaken. They were laughing as if they were old friends. As usual, she had the man in the palm of her hand. That was the thing about Alexa: she never let you know what she was actually thinking, too busy making sure you were having too good of a time to actually wonder why her smile sometimes never quite reached her eyes.

"No," Henry agreed. "But investors like stability and now that you're engaged, the stock price is going up. So you can imagine what would happen if you were to get unengaged right when you're opening a new office and rolling out a new product?"

Carter sighed. Alexa wasn't going to like this news. Hell, he wasn't sure he liked this news, but she was the one who'd gotten them into this mess. "So you think I should stay engaged indefinitely."

"Of course, married would be better, but engaged is good, too."

Alexa turned then, looking for him in the crowd and sending him a commiserating smile when she found him. He returned the gesture with a nod, his damn bow tie clenching even tighter around his neck. He never forgot how damned beautiful she was, but sometimes that crooked smile was like a punch to the gut compounded with a pulsing electrical shock to his cock.

"I'll take those suggestions under advisement," Carter told Henry before ending the call.

A black-tie waiter walked by and Carter grabbed

a flute of champagne from his silver tray, downing it in single pass. It wasn't the scotch he usually preferred, but then, they weren't pouring five-hundred-dollar bottles of that for the general public.

Pulling out his cuffs, he returned to Alexa and her uncle, who had moved on to a group that included the owner of the Tropicana and the CEO of Elysium.

"Ah," Larry Green said, "there's the other half. I was just apologizing to Alexa for that unfortunate video leak."

Under different circumstances, Carter would have punched the Elysium owner in the face since it was on his instruction that the video had leaked in the first place, but tonight apparently wasn't about who he wanted to punch. As it was, he already planned to pull his contract team from the man's casino as well as continued support for the software every single computer in his building used. The inconvenience would be paramount and Carter couldn't wait. Larry Green could suck a dick as far as he was concerned. He was going to bury the fucker.

"It's so difficult to find trustworthy employees these days," Larry continued, with absolutely no sign of guilt or shame for the fact that he was lying through his teeth.

Carter could tell that John wasn't happy either, but they all knew a charity gala was not the time or the place for a scene. No, his revenge would be much longer and more satisfying.

"No need to apologize," Carter said smoothly, putting an arm around Alexa's waist to bring her closer. "It was the push we needed to announce our engagement."

Alexa smiled up at him, every bit of the wide-eyed dewy expression an act that made him twitchy. Alexa had always been the only person in his life that he could be absolutely himself with, and the fact that their whole relationship was now tainted with this bullshit ruse was irritating. He was already wishing that she would look at him like that for real, which was idiotic and dangerous.

"There never seemed to be a right time to tell the world," Alexa sighed, lovingly straightening his lapel. "We wanted to enjoy it by ourselves a little while longer."

She leaned up to give him a peck on the cheek then and he whispered in her ear, "End this."

Giving his hand a squeeze, she returned her attention to the men with a wide grin and waggling eyebrows. "Excuse us for a moment, gentlemen, I'm afraid I need a moment alone with my fiancé," she gushed flirtatiously, letting her reputation allude to why they were leaving the conversation. She was relentless.

She led him to a quiet corner, and after making sure no one was paying attention, she ducked behind some heavy drapes. The darkness coupled with the muted background noise was a definite improvement, and he felt a good bit of tension subside.

"What are we doing back here?" he asked, vaguely amused.

"You looked like you needed a minute," she explained, pulling her phone out of her small black purse. "Would you rather go outside? Because there are a lot of people out there, too."

He shook his head. It was just like Alexa to know exactly what he needed without making a big deal about it. "Does behind this curtain still count as public?"

"What?" she asked, distracted by something on her phone as she gave him a confused glance. "I mean, yeah, I guess."

"Good," he grunted, pulling her roughly against him and setting his lips to hers.

She responded, but whatever she said was lost in the kiss. The feel of her lips on his again was intense and lush and like a secret in the dark. Embers of lust smoldered into fire as her hands worked their way under his coat and up his back, her manicured nails scoring his skin. That she wanted him just as badly as he wanted her fueled some beast inside him, the one who used to be an insecure kid in love with his friend and finally knew what it was like to get what he wanted. That beast wanted to open the drapes and declare that she was his.

He hiked up her skirt and found her completely bare, already wet and waiting for him. He let two fingers slowly and deliberately caress through her slick folds, letting her know that he saw her. Knew that they could deny themselves all they wanted, but this desire was always going to be between them.

"Carter," she panted, squirming against his hand, greedy with need.

"I know sex is against the rules," he murmured wickedly in her ear, "but that isn't even the best thing on the menu."

The desire to torture was high and before she had any idea what was about to happen, he slid a small vibrator into her.

She squeaked and met his eyes, hers wide with surprise. "What are you—"

He pulled out his phone and opened the app that controlled the toy. Pressing the vibrate button on the screen, he drew them out of the drapes and back into the ballroom.

"You made the rules," he reminded her, giving her a light kiss on the forehead to soothe the ire so clearly telegraphed in her slammed brow and severe frown. "But you forgot I'm really good at games."

He turned and spotted an old colleague, Connie

Lipman, making her way over to them. Flipping the switch to increase the speed of the vibrator, he heard Alexa whimper right before Connie greeted them.

Carter navigated the conversation with ease, having turned off the vibrator as soon as Connie began congratulating them about the engagement. She asked Alexa a question, but before she could respond he put the vibrator on full blast so she ended up just being able to smile and nod while he picked up the slack.

He wasn't an animal, he just thought it would be fun to play with her, take the control out of her hands for once. It wasn't very often he was a step ahead of her and he intended to enjoy this moment for all it was worth. He was most intrigued by the fact that she could leave, could excuse herself from the conversation, go to the restroom and take it out, but she remained by his side. He wouldn't have stopped her. But she was still here, which meant one thing—she liked it. Liked the anticipation, being just a little out of control, and the public aspect of it. Just like he'd known she would.

Discreetly, he tapped at the cell phone in his pocket, letting it go for just a second before turning it off again.

He felt her stiffen beside him and smiled. The conversation with Connie finally ended and Alexa whispered to him, "I can't believe you did that."

He shrugged. "Maybe you don't know me as well as you thought." If nothing else, after this month was over, they weren't going to be the same kind of friends they'd been before. For once, Carter wasn't going to hold back the man, even though Alexa only ever wanted the boy who'd trailed after her like a service dog, always there to support her when she needed it.

Her glare continued through their next conversation, which was satisfying on a lot of levels. He made a show of putting his hand in his pocket without actually turning on the vibe, making her twitch in anticipation. Ten minutes later, just when she'd loosened up and started engaging more in the conversation, he turned it on again.

She stepped on his foot.

He put his arm around her and drew her close, turning off the vibrator.

"Had enough? Ready to call me the winner?"

There'd been no bet, nothing to lose, but Alexa would never admit he'd gotten the best of her.

So he tortured her for the rest of the night. And in the end, perhaps he'd been wrong—he could get used to galas.

CHAPTER TEN

FOR THE WEEK after the gala, Alexa flat out avoided Carter. He'd finally let her go to the restroom to remove that damned vibrator, but only after a good hour had passed. He had tortured her with it as they spoke to every person they remotely knew. People whom, otherwise, he'd have paid money never to interact with. He hadn't kept the device running the entire time, and in truth hardly at all, but the anticipation had driven her to the point of madness. And that had been exactly his plan.

Unfortunately, the workweek was over and they were attending a wedding they'd agreed to go to as friends months ago, only now they were engaged friends, which meant they had to put on another show.

He was waiting for her in the foyer again, looking dapper and relaxed in a charcoal suit complete with a vest, a burgundy tie and a matching burgundy-and-aqua plaid pocket square.

"Long time, no see," he drawled, crossing his arms over his chest as he looked her over.

She'd gone a little more conservative this time, choosing an A-line, tea-length baby-blue Monique Lhuillier with a dreamy tulle skirt adorned with glitter. It was delicate and ethereal, the exact opposite of what she'd worn to the gala…and tonight would also be the opposite. She would not be touching Carter. At all.

Because touching got her secret vibrators and she wasn't going to be caught off guard again. She'd had all week to examine the implications of what he'd done, namely she acknowledged that he was purposely ignoring the rules. One time, they could dismiss, but it would be a problem if it happened again.

She'd been attracted to him before, but he'd opened a door and now everything he did turned her on. Even walking in on him last weekend while he brushed his teeth had revved her girlie parts.

Luckily, he was engrossed in something on his phone for the majority of the ride and she found herself drifting to the other disaster in her life, worrying about what she would do if the casinos actually sold. Her uncle wanted to retire in France, and if Carter was leaving Vegas, maybe she would open a casino there. She loved wine, cheese and crepes so it could be perfect. Except she couldn't imagine living in a place Carter wasn't, but then maybe she just needed to accept that that would be her new normal.

By not having sex, she was keeping their friendship the way it always was, which meant he was leaving in a few short weeks. She needed to get used to it and figure out her own life instead of making sure she wasn't screwing up Carter's.

They sat companionably through the wedding ceremony and navigated the first two hours of the reception without touching or discussion of what had happened last weekend. Alexa couldn't have been happier. More or less.

Except she couldn't help but feel the loss of companionship. The careless touches they used to give each other were too fraught now that they knew they were attracted to each other. Their old friendship seemed to already be over, and the realization ached.

She was just about to suggest they leave when the groom came to greet them.

"Carter Hayes and Alexa Lawson," Matt boomed, his voice loud enough to draw attention from the wedding guests in the vicinity. He was clearly already shit-faced. "Congratulations. I heard you crazy kids went and got engaged!"

He pointed at one of his groomsmen at his side. "Didn't we have a bet on that, Sam?"

Sam shook his head. "Probably!"

Matt grabbed Carter up into an exaggerated

bear hug before moving on to Alexa. His dark brown hair was mussed from his previous run on the dance floor—tux jacket, vest and tie had disappeared hours ago. With his light blue eyes twinkling with good humor, he was still the same guy from college. Always up for a laugh and looking to get into trouble.

"Congratulations, Matt," she told him, giving him a peck on the cheek. "Sophie's a lucky lady. And you're an even luckier man."

"That I am," Matt said, his big grin stretching even wider. "She's my best friend and love of my life."

At the words *best friend* she struggled not to meet Carter's eyes, and wondered absently if anyone would ever speak about her with such naked love and devotion. Mostly the best guys did was offer her eggs for breakfast on her way out the door.

"So when are you two lovebirds doing the deed?" Matt laughed.

"We just got engaged last week," Carter said, his voice dry. "Give us a minute. You and Sophie were engaged for three years."

Matt gave Alexa a wink and pulled two champagne glasses from the passing tray, handing them to her and Carter. "Yeah, well, she needed a lot of time to plan this shindig. Y'all have a good time, now, okay?"

Then he left them with another wink and a pointed look at the drinks he'd just put in their hands.

Carter gave him a mock salute.

Alexa nodded and threw back her third glass. There were lots of drapes here, and God help her, she couldn't stop thinking of Carter sliding that vibrator inside her again. Not that she had the thing. She'd immediately hidden it when they'd gotten home that night, but she had to admit it was probably the hottest thing that had ever happened to her, and it wasn't as if she didn't partake in a little kink every now and then. All her senses were on high alert waiting for what he might do. Kiss her on the dance floor? Go down on her under the table? Make her come in the photo booth? The possibilities were endlessly fascinating and terrifying in equal measure.

And yet he showed no inclination to do any of it. Content to shoot the shit with old college dudes who she'd only ever known through him. He was largely ignoring her, which from their infamous Elysium stairwell incident, he knew she hated. Once upon a time, he'd drop everything to hang out with her.

She stepped away from the group, but he caught her hand, leaning down to give her a quick kiss on the forehead.

"Could you grab me another whiskey from the bar?"

She wanted to scream at the no-contact contact. "Of course," she said with a tight smile.

Waiting in line at the bar, she gave herself a pep talk. She would not lust after her best friend, she would not imagine taking all his clothes off and climbing on top of him in the middle of a wedding. *She would not.*

"Alexa Lawson?" a female voice asked, soft and tentative.

Alexa turned to see a fellow Entrepreneurs Club member from college, Kaylee Shepherd.

"Kaylee!" she greeted, enveloping the girl in a hug. They hadn't been close, but it had been so many years and it was nice to see a familiar face unconnected to Carter. "It's wonderful to see you!"

Kaylee's smile widened as well. "You, too," she said as she stepped back from the hug. "And congratulations on your engagement. I always thought you and Carter should get together."

Alexa nodded mechanically, something about the statement catching her off guard. So many people had been saying that to her that she wondered if they'd ever really been normal friends. Had they always been a little too close to be considered normal?

"Yeah, we finally did it." She smiled.

"And you'll get to do the marriage thing, too," Kaylee said, gesturing to the wedding at large.

"Yeah, I guess so," she allowed, but then realized someone in her position should be excited about getting married. Which made her vaguely uneasy because she and Carter would never be together, and yet talking about their wedding made it seem extremely real. "I mean, yes, I'm excited to start planning."

"Well, this one was beautiful. Vegas beautiful, but still beautiful."

Alexa laughed. "It was a great wedding. Though I could have hooked them up at one of my casinos."

Kaylee nodded, a crease in her brow. "That's right, you own casinos. I knew that."

"I guess they met here," Alexa explained. She looked around at the plaster walls and arches. The Aurora was pretty enough in that it tried to look like a Venice church, but it wasn't her kind of place.

"Ah," Kaylee said.

Alexa saw an impressive ring on Kaylee's finger. "Are you engaged, too?"

A pretty pink blush bloomed on Kaylee's alabaster face. "Yeah."

"Congratulations," Alexa said, grinning.

The bartender handed over their drinks, two whiskeys for Alexa and a ginger ale for Kaylee.

They left the bar together. "Is your fiancé here tonight?" Alexa asked.

Kaylee pointed at a man who was making his way over to where they'd stopped near a fountain boasting what appeared to be an upside-down pineapple on top.

Alexa briefly glanced over to Carter, who was talking to a girl she recognized as his college girlfriend. They'd dated for two or so years, which in college time was virtually a lifetime. She hadn't been Alexa's biggest fan, though Alexa had liked her well enough. She'd been good to Carter and that was all the info Alexa had needed back then.

But now that Alexa thought more about it, she was really the only serious girlfriend Carter had ever had. Since he'd graduated from college, gotten super ripped and become a millionaire he'd been playing the field. Maybe his perfect-for-him ex-girlfriend would be the one to nail him down again. The thought made her a little murderous. Faceless girls could be ignored, but if he slept with someone he actually had a connection with, that was something else entirely that she didn't particularly care for.

Her mind drifted back over that time he'd told her he had more-than-friend feelings for her, but it seemed so long ago. Like a vague fragment of a dream forgotten and remembered. Seeing all their college friends was dredging up old memories, but she couldn't remember what she told him after he'd admitted his feelings. She knew they'd never spoken of it again, though, because the very thought of it was making her sweat. All she remembered was the fear of losing him even then. That she'd end up with nothing more than a memory of Carter instead of him. And the thought of a lifetime without him even then had been unthinkable.

She'd never allowed herself to consider whether or not she felt the same about him. She'd just known that they were too young and their friendship too important to waste on a relationship neither of them was ready for.

Alexa knocked the entire whiskey back in one swift pull. The burn felt good. She might already be a little drunk, but that slow whiskey warmth hit the spot.

"Have you two set a date?" Alexa asked after Kaylee had made the introductions. Her fiancé, Bruce, had been in the military but now owned his own security company.

Bruce shrugged at her question, glancing at Kaylee with an indulgent grin. His close-cropped dark hair worked well with his strong facial features. "Kaylee wants the big wedding, so it might be a long time."

"You know, I own three casinos, so let me know if you need a venue. I can give you a great deal," Alexa offered. "All three of my casinos are gorgeous, if I do say so myself, but Halcyon was practically made for weddings."

A furrow appeared in Kaylee's brow. "Oh, we'd

love to get married here, but I live in Seattle now so the wedding will probably be there."

"Unless," Bruce started, taking Kaylee's hands in one of his while placing the other one over her stomach, "you want to do it right now."

Kaylee blinked rapidly. "What?"

"Who knows when we'll ever be in Vegas again?" Bruce urged, getting into the idea now and squeezing her hands. "We can have a big reception later, anywhere you like. A ceremony, too, even." He pulled her into a hug. "I just want to start our forever right now, K."

Alexa blinked back an unexpected tear. Frankly, she fell a little in love with Bruce at the moment.

Kaylee drew back, her hand going down to cover the one he was still resting on her stomach. Alexa's eyes widened. Holy crap, Kaylee was pregnant.

"Okay," Kaylee said softly. "Let's do it."

"Well, I'll let you go get married," Alexa laughed, moving away. "Double congratulations on the engagement and the wedding!"

Kaylee laughed, as if she couldn't believe she was going to do it either, but then waved Alexa back. "No, you have to come! We'll need witnesses."

Alexa opened her mouth to protest, but Kaylee grabbed her arm. "Please, I don't want to chicken out."

Nodding, she squeezed Kaylee's hand. They

hadn't been close, but Alexa was one drink away from either needing a nap or taking her shirt off on top of a bar, so why not go to two weddings in one night? Her emotions were already streaming out in all directions, like her heart was a wet kitchen sponge being squeezed. Why now of all days was she remembering Carter telling her that stuff, now when he was refusing to make out with her and talking to his ex-girlfriend? To hell with him, then, she thought, going ahead and drinking his whiskey, too.

She caught his eye and waved him over, not bothering to interrupt his conversation in person. She didn't need to prove to some ex-girlfriend that she'd always be Carter's number one. When he finally joined their little group, she explained the situation about Kaylee.

However, he still didn't seem to have a complete handle on what was happening, even after they left the reception and got a ride to the Blue Angel Chapel.

"Are you drunk?" she asked, confused.

He looked at her blankly. "Just a little."

She shook her head. "We're here to see Kaylee and Bruce get married."

"I don't know who Kaylee and Bruce are," he stage-whispered.

"Well, you would if you hadn't been ignoring me the whole evening," she told him with a raised eyebrow. "How was your conversation with Amber, anyway?"

"Good," he said, not responding to the first part of her statement. "She's still single, living in Phoenix. She actually heads up a small tech company there, so we were sharing stories. It was good to see her."

"That's nice. Maybe you two can strike things up again after the month is over." She nearly rolled her eyes at her own completely transparent bullshit. Keep pretending that they were friends and that they'd both just return to normal after this was over. It was the only thing Alexa was holding on to, that things would go back to normal.

Alexa felt Carter's eyes on her, but she kept her gaze out the car window. Why in all these years had Carter never been in a real relationship and why hadn't she been waiting for it? He dated lots of women and she'd never been jealous before, and yet now the thought of him dating someone he'd had an actual connection with felt like someone was poking at her insides. Like when he'd asked about dating Monroe, someone she respected and he had a lot in common with.

"Maybe," Carter finally said.

The car stopped at the front of the Blue Angel Chapel and they followed the group inside. Kaylee pulled Alexa up with her and Bruce to the registration office to fill out the necessary forms. Carter

followed and she squeezed his hand as a thank-you
for being a good sport.

A tall young man worked the reception desk and
his eyes got huge when he saw Carter approach.

"Oh my God," he whispered. "You're Carter
Hayes."

Carter nodded, somewhat used to nerdy guys
recognizing him.

"I can't believe this!" He grinned. "My first
day on the job and Carter Hayes is here! That's,
like, so meta because I'm writing this app that
turns people into superhero cartoons. So like you
can send emojis of yourself as a superhero or put
yourself into a comic."

Alexa held back a snort.

"That's cool," Carter told him, even though she
knew Carter hated comic books. "Keep it up. And
if you want to intern for us, you can apply on my
site. We're always looking for new people."

"That's so awesome! Thanks!" he chirped.
"Hey, are you getting married tonight? I read that
you just got engaged to your high school bae."

Alexa cleared her throat beside Carter and the
kid looked over at her, his eyes widening even
more as he took her in. He reminded her of Carter
a little when they'd been in high school, the too-
long hair, ill-fitting glasses and button-down uniform, except Carter would never chatter away like

this guy was doing. He was way too self-contained for that. Even as a kid, he'd been serious.

"Hi, I'm Carter's fiancée."

The kid, James, opened his mouth to say something, but couldn't get the words out. Carter pulled her into his side. "It's okay. Alexa makes me speechless, too."

She nearly rolled her eyes because it was over-the-top, but a traitorous part of her also kind of wished he meant it.

She saw Kaylee and Bruce heading to one of the private rooms and remembered they were on a mission.

"We need to sign the paperwork so our friends can get their marriage license mailed to them. We're the witnesses."

"I think they already filled them out," James informed.

He pulled out a form on a clipboard from under the large reception desk and placed it on the counter. Alexa got distracted by Kaylee's squeal of pleasure as the attendant showed her one of the available ceremony rooms.

"Are you guys getting married tonight, too?" James asked, writing something down on the paper. "That would be, like, so cool. Carter is like Google or something and I could tell all my friends I was, like, at your wedding."

Alexa held back her rolling eyes at the guy's

hero worship, but she didn't begrudge Carter for it. He'd worked hard and deserved recognition wherever he found it.

Carter said something to James, but Alexa wasn't paying attention.

"Just sign here," James instructed.

Absently, ready to get this show on the road, Alexa signed where James pointed and headed out to find Kaylee and leave Carter to his fan club.

Kaylee had changed into a puffy white dress she'd found in the shop of the Aurora. She looked beautiful and in love as she and Bruce took their places at the front of the small chapel room.

After a few minutes, Carter appeared by her side.

"Remind me again how I agreed to two weddings in one day?"

"You did it because you're the nicest person I know."

He raised an eyebrow. "You're the only person who thinks I'm nice."

"Well, me and James," she said, smirking. "Besides, I know the real Carter, remember? The guy who once sat with me all night long when I got dumped by Kyle Roberts after his fraternity dance."

"Kyle was an idiot."

Alexa grinned up at him. "Exactly."

"Whatever you say, Alexa."

Winking, she left him on the groom's side along with a couple of other guests who had migrated over from Matt's wedding. Taking her spot beside the bride, Alexa felt a strange sense of alarm come over her. How many times had she been a bridesmaid just like this, standing up before two people who vowed to spend the rest of their lives together? Far too many. She witnessed weddings on nearly a daily basis in her own casino and yet she'd never taken the time to truly consider her own. It had been one of those things she just assumed she wouldn't have. A vision of herself in white in the gardens at Halcyon appeared, Carter standing at her side.

She shook her head at the image. Watching Bruce take Kaylee's quivering hand and professing his love and vowing to stand by her forever was cracking open some vault of emotion in her chest that she normally kept locked up. It was probably just the alcohol talking, but maybe she was ready to settle down. Maybe she would move to France to open a new casino and finally find a man who would feed her cheese without judgment. Maybe selling the casinos was a good thing. Maybe the life she'd cultivated was just one big—oh God, did she just hiccup out loud?

Eyes darting, she witnessed the inescapable truth. All fifteen guests and the bride and groom were staring at her, arrested expressions on their faces, not quite believing a grown person could hiccup during a wedding ceremony. Even a quickie Vegas one.

"I'm so sorry," she whispered furiously.

She waved at the officiant to go ahead with the ceremony, but she could feel the laughing eyes on her. Her mortification was real, but mostly because she knew no matter what grand plans she made for her future, the only thing she really wanted was for everything to stay the same. For Carter to not leave Vegas.

Thankfully, the rest of the vows were brief and Alexa was able to quickly escape to the bar for another glass of champagne to ease the embarrassment.

Carter followed. "Hey," he laughed, his face looking wavy. "That was the funniest thing I've ever seen you do! I don't think I've ever heard you hiccup at all, let alone in public."

"I'm here all night, ladies and gentlemen," she mocked, attempting a wobbly bow.

"Everyone's dancing," he told her, taking her arm. "We should, too."

She nodded, walking into his familiar arms. The last thing she remembered was her eyes closing as she nuzzled against his chest.

CHAPTER ELEVEN

CARTER WOKE UP with a profound pounding in his head and in a bed that didn't belong to him. As far as his mornings and waking up went, it was puzzling. Also, he was naked beside an equally naked Alexa. So there was that.

Disoriented, he reached out to the nightstand for his phone, but got the regular hotel landline. He tried again, but only found the cool lacquer of the wood.

He croaked out a voice command, his throat dry and crackling. After his second try, a dinging sounded from somewhere across the room. His phone's digital voice was loud in the quiet of the room, but it gave him the time he asked for.

A groan came from the Alexa-shaped lump beside him. "Shuuuut uup."

The sheets shuffled as she readjusted. Carter struggled to move his head through the pounding but glanced over to see that she'd drawn the sheets up over her head.

"It's already two in the afternoon," Carter told her.

"I know," she croaked groggily. "I heard."

Carter rose to his elbows, shielding his eyes from the sun streaming in through the floor-to-ceiling windows, and took in the room. They weren't at Alexa's house and judging by the generic furnishings, they were in a hotel room.

Christ, what the hell had happened last night?

Getting out of bed, not giving a shit that he was naked, he went in search of his clothes.

Finding his boxer shorts near the bathroom door, he slid them on and faced her, throwing her his button-down shirt since her dress was nowhere in sight and she wasn't wearing it.

"Last night was like college all over again," she said, her voice muffled as she put on his shirt under the covers. "I drank too much and am sure I regret most of my decisions."

"Same," he said, sliding on his undershirt.

"Let's just get out of here."

Carter called for his phone again, following its response and eventually finding it inside his shoe, which was inexplicably inside a dresser drawer. He quickly opened the messages crowding his screen. There were at least thirty congratulating them on their marriage. The first one was a link from his sister to an article with their picture and the announcement that they were married at the Blue Angel Chapel, the place they were last night. His sisters and his mom had messaged him multiple times, their texts increasingly angry and confused as to why they hadn't been invited.

"Shit."

"Fuck," Alexa echoed, looking at her phone, too.

Their eyes met, the same confusion and fear written in hers that he felt.

"I don't understand," Alexa breathed. "I was drunk, but not blackout drunk. We did not get married. What the hell is going on?"

"I don't know," Carter said, lowering himself back onto the bed, possible solutions racing through his mind.

"Oh God," Alexa gasped, her hands dropping to the mattress as she leaned forward urgently. "Could it have been James? Did he have us sign the wrong thing or on the wrong place on that form?"

Carter was on the line with the chapel immediately, obtaining picture proof to confirm that, yes, he and Alexa had signed the marriage license as the spouses, not the witnesses.

"Fucking James," Alexa growled, flinging off the covers. "I'm going to end him. He will rue the day he met Alexa Marielle Lawson."

Carter met her eyes. "It could have been an honest mistake. We were all distracted and he did say it was his first day."

Alexa snorted. "And how did it get out then? He just accidentally took a picture of it and sent it to the newspaper? He's the only one who would have known the signatures were wrong."

Alexa looked like she was one second away from riding a flaming motorcycle into the Blue Angel Chapel and setting it ablaze.

"I'll call my lawyer and we'll have it annulled," Carter assured her. "This will all be taken care of as if it never happened. There's no reason to worry or enact the revenge you're plotting."

"Uh-huh," she said doubtfully, rubbing at her head.

"Let's just get the fuck home now, okay?"

He slowly rose, on a course to find his pants and wallet, dreading the fallout of this fuckup. Without a doubt, this was going to push Alexa away. He just didn't have a plan on how to stop it.

Alexa was typing away at her phone. "My uncle is thrilled," she informed. "He has an offer for one of the casinos."

"Um, that's a good thing, right?" Carter asked, knowing it wasn't. She'd pretend that she was okay with it, but it was hurting her and that meant it was hurting him, too.

Alexa took a moment before answering. "Yeah, it's what we wanted. I just want to get a good deal. Set Uncle John up, you know."

He nodded, trying to be supportive even though his mind was elsewhere. Now that they'd figured out they were married, Carter couldn't overlook the fact that they'd woken up completely naked.

Alexa put down her phone finally and met his eyes, his own thoughts echoed there. "Do you think we—"

He shook his head. "I have no idea. But there are no condom wrappers anywhere so we might need to make a drugstore stop on the way home, just in case."

Eyes wide, Alexa rolled out of the bed and made her way to the bathroom.

"I'm on birth control, Carter. Jesus," she muttered. "Are you clean?"

"Of course. I never don't use protection," he told her. "I'm not an animal."

She turned, rolling her eyes. "That doesn't mean anything. Have you gotten tested?"

"Last month."

She took a deep breath and let it out. "Super."

The door to the bathroom shut and Carter groaned. He would remember sex, he thought, and definitely remember sex with Alexa. Christ, he'd been imagining what that would be like for the better part of his life; it wasn't a thing he'd just forget, hammered or not.

He pulled on his pants and jacket from last night and folded her dress before laying it on the bed. He was fucking married to Alexa. A state he'd always subconsciously thought might be his future.

He definitely couldn't imagine himself married to anyone else.

A knock sounded at the door and Alexa emerged from the bathroom, looking hot as hell in his shirt with no bra. Yeah, he would definitely remember sex.

"What are you doing?" he asked as she went to the door.

She opened the door to a woman holding a bag of clothing.

"We're in the Landmark. There's a store downstairs. I texted the concierge to bring me some clothes," she explained, taking the bag back to the bathroom.

The shirt barely covered her ass and if he didn't feel like the textbook definition of shit at the moment, he might take advantage of the situation. As it stood, however, he was one gag away from vomiting.

He pulled up the car service app on his phone and ordered a ride, wishing he had a pain reliever. He pulled a bottle of water from the mini fridge and drank it down.

The bathroom door opened again and Alexa had pulled her hair into a messy-looking bun and changed into a pair of black yoga pants and an Landmark sweatshirt.

"You ready?" she asked, taking a bottle of ginger ale from the fridge. Her stomach must be the same as his.

The car was waiting for them outside, and when they got home they took the stairs slowly to their rooms.

Once they reached the upstairs hallway, he turned to her. "I'll call my lawyer now so we can get this sorted."

She gave a slow nod and they went to their respective rooms, where he showered and gave in to sleep.

When he woke up, the sun had gone down and he felt like a new person. His stomach grumbling, he made his way downstairs and found Alexa in the kitchen, cooking something on the stove top. The image stopped him in his tracks, because they were married and he wondered if this was the life he was giving up by leaving. The cozy, quiet evenings together where they could just be. But he had to remind himself that his leaving was the only thing that might get him closer to that future. Alexa had to know life without him to realize that it was what she didn't want. Having a heart-to-heart emotional conversation with her wasn't going to work. She'd shut down the instant he tried. He knew that beyond a shadow of a doubt.

After her parents died, he'd read lots of books on how to support people in grief. He knew she had attachment issues from childhood and that's why she avoided emotional entanglements. He also knew what his role was and had been forever, to just be there for her when she needed it and not ask for more than she could give.

But fuck it, he wanted everything and he literally had it all right now and every single piece of it was bullshit. It was like a living fucking joke.

"Hey," she said, turning to face him.

"It smells good in here," he returned, rolling his shoulders to fight off the tension gathering there.

"Chicken noodle soup."

"Are we sick?"

"Are we not?"

He mustered up a half smile. "So, are you ready to unpack this nightmare?"

"No." She grimaced. "I will never be ready for that. Uncle John came over a little bit ago so I could sign the papers. We officially sold Wild Nights."

He took a seat on one of his island stools. Now he understood the chicken noodle soup—she needed some comfort food.

"You feel okay about that?"

She gave him a lopsided smile and a shrug. "I'm very rich."

He laughed. "You were already pretty rich."

"Yeah, but now I'm like in a totally different category of rich. Like buy-a-town kind of rich."

"I would suggest we go out and celebrate, but maybe another time."

"God, yes. I never want to smell alcohol even

from a long distance ever again. Let's just eat and watch television tonight."

"Agreed, but congratulations anyway," he told her, pulling her into a quick hug. The kind they used to share all the time before everything changed in that stairwell. "At least this ruse is bearing fruit."

"Well," she said, ladling the soup into bowls, "it's technically no longer a ruse. We are, in fact, married."

"Yep, that does happen to be a fact."

She gave him a confounded headshake before heading into his media room. Pulling up the documentary series they'd started months ago, they ate in silence; the only sounds were their soup spoons knocking gently against the sides of the ceramic bowls and the monotone voice of the male narrator educating them on the Vietnam War.

When the episode ended and they'd finished eating, Alexa turned to him.

"I got a little bit more information about what happened last night," he told her, taking her cue. "My assistant spoke to the management at the chapel and James has been let go. They did suspect him of sending the picture of the license to the paper and posting it on social media."

"No shit," Alexa said. "I'm the one who demanded he be fired."

Carter scratched the back of his head, a headache forming there at the thought that he'd been party to getting the kid fired. "That's pretty harsh, Alexa. He's just a dumb kid. It's not like he was trying to extort us for money—he was just excited."

"First of all, he should absolutely be fired for violating the policies of his workplace, which obviously include posting private company documents on social media. My own lawyer was able to take a screenshot of James's post of our marriage license photo so there's no doubt it was him."

Carter shook his head. "Yeah, okay. But that doesn't mean I hate him. He was probably just trying to get more recognition for his app. We should have paid more attention to what we were signing."

"Well, since you're clearly ready to go to bat for this kid, I think you'll be happy to know that his new employer will be a better fit."

"I'm not hiring that kid," Carter told her. "I don't want him to be fired, but I'm pissed as hell."

"I hired him as my new junior assistant. He'll be working directly under Margaret."

All the hair on Carter's neck rose at the mention of Alexa's drill sergeant head assistant who oversaw all the assistants for Alexa's casinos. She was literally a former air force lieutenant and she did not fuck around. In all the years Carter had known her, he'd never once seen her smile. She was just the person to set James on the straight and narrow.

"Jesus. That's diabolical."

Alexa gave him a crafty smile. "Yeah. It's the best revenge, but also maybe he'll learn how to be a decent human being instead of a crazy person who posts stuff on social media for attention. I also talked to Kaylee. She sent me a video that might be illuminating."

His head swung to hers. "A video?"

"Yup," she said, handing him her phone.

He pressed Play and watched as he and Alexa kissed the shit out of each other as they danced, off in a far corner of the room sometime after Kaylee and Bruce said their vows. The kiss went on forever, as if they'd been the ones to have gotten married. It was hot as hell to actually see Alexa kissing him, her hair wild and curled, arms flung around his neck as if she couldn't get close enough to him.

Loud hooting and hollering from the guests filled the quiet room as he picked Alexa up in his arms and carried her through the pews and out the door to the lobby beyond the ceremony room, which is where the video ended.

So the whole *how they got to the hotel* and *did they have sex* were all still up in the air.

"I don't think we were coherent enough to even have sex," he reasoned, but that video scared him.

Because it showed him acting how he always wanted to act, but couldn't. He'd spent so long holding back his own feelings, making sure he didn't spook Alexa, that seeing that one moment of inhibition on his part was heart-wrenching.

"Remember when you asked me to date you?" she asked, as if she were somehow reading his thoughts.

"Um, it was pretty difficult to forget," he said slowly, his pulse kicking up. What the hell was she doing bringing up the subject they'd purposely not talked about for ten years?

"Were you attracted to me then, too?"

He stilled, every muscle on alert, because this was dangerous yet familiar territory where he had to act as if every atom of his body didn't want to throw her to the ground and fuck her.

But then a kind of calm came over him. Maybe it was just a really bad hangover, but he didn't care what happened if he said the wrong thing anymore. He was so damned tired of protecting this friendship that he answered her question honestly. "What the fuck do you think?"

"What kind of answer is that?"

"I told you I was in love with you back then, Alexa. Did you think that meant I wasn't attracted to you, too?"

Rising from the chair, she pulled her sweatshirt

off, revealing that she wasn't wearing anything underneath.

"What are you doing?" he asked, setting his bowl aside, blood rushing to his head.

"It was a rough night, we're accidentally married so I couldn't cheat even if I wanted to, I just sold a casino I spent the whole of my twenties running, and I'm horny as fuck. Are you up for this or not?"

"This is against your rules," he pointed out, taking care not to look at her chest in case she changed her mind. Her bare breasts weren't something he could unsee.

She pulled off her pants next and stood stark naked in front of him. "Fuck the rules."

Carter allowed himself a moment to stare because her body was unbelievable. The chance to be with Alexa almost didn't seem real to him. He'd imagined being with her so much over the years that now that it was possibly finally happening it wasn't computing in his brain. Only his dick, which was way ahead of him and ready to go. But that kid who once asked her out and was rejected was still in there somewhere, wondering if all he'd ever get from Alexa Lawson was the same inconsequential hookups she was famous for. Either fucking way he was taking the opportunity, but part of him told him to be cautious because she'd run at the first sign of them getting serious.

"I'm not fucking you for the first time in my media room," he told her.

"I don't give a shit where we do this, just as long as we do it."

Well, he'd given her fair warning.

He hoisted her into his arms and carried her up to his bedroom.

FRIENDS WITH BENEFITS

CHAPTER TWELVE

ALEXA SAT DOWN on Carter's bed, for the first time completely unsure of how to behave in a man's bedroom. Except that it wasn't just some guy's bedroom. It was Carter's. Which meant something. It meant a hell of a lot and she was vaguely terrified, but at this moment she was tired of fighting her attraction to him. The gamble was the gamble, and if they slept together and it ruined everything he was leaving anyway. Either way the outcome was essentially the same, with her alone in Vegas, so they might as well have as much fun while they were sober as they'd had in that drunk wedding video.

She watched as he strode away from her instead of kissing her like she wanted him to. "Are you planning to deliver amazing sex or what?" she joked, trying to lighten what had become a serious mood.

Carter ignored her and opened his closet, pulling at a door inside.

"What are you doing?" she called.

He came back out with something in his hand that she couldn't see.

"Scarves?" she asked when he turned around. He didn't answer.

"Carter, what are you doing?"

"Lie down."

"Are you doing some BDSM shit right now?"

He raised an eyebrow.

She raised her own eyebrow and waited. After that move with the vibrator in public, who knew what he was capable of, and she was curious to find out. Was it this seductive anticipation that kept women in Vegas chasing after him?

"Am I getting the Carter Hayes treatment?"

"You're not going to get anything if you keep up the snark."

"I'm not just another girl in your bed, you know," she said, for the first time experiencing some insecurity where Carter was concerned. "I'm your wife."

"Trust me. I know exactly what you are." He stood at the foot of the bed, watching her expectantly.

Slowly, she scooted to the top of the bed and lay down.

His eyes raked slowly over her body, starting at her toes. Her stomach clenched, nerves she hadn't expected hijacking her sexual buzz. She'd initiated this with Carter, but the reality of it was just hitting her. She was so vulnerable lying there with everything visible to him. He was her best friend who knew everything about her, including the story of how she lost her virginity, which made this feel far more intimate than her usual sexual encounters. She'd wanted this to be fun, but the way he was looking at her right now, his eyes dark and hooded as they crept over every inch of her bare skin, was anything but. This brilliant plan to distract herself from selling the casinos was becoming the thing she needed to be distracted from.

He drew out a blindfold and she sucked in a breath.

"Is that all you got?" she asked, trying to even the playing field again.

He walked to the side of the bed, staring down at her, his blue eyes serious. Holding up the blindfold, he gestured for her to lift her head. When she did he tied the black silk scarf tightly around her head and heard something click into place. It smelled like the cedar of his closet and Carter, that freshly clean man scent. She wondered where he'd obtained such an item and then the pieces started falling into place, and the scarf he'd given to Maggie made more sense.

Holy shit, he really did blindfold all the women he slept with. "Is this scarf mine now?" she asked.

"Of course."

It was harder to breathe and her heart started pounding. What the hell was she doing? Could she ever look Carter in the face again after knowing he was the mayor of depravity? A little voice in the back of her head reminded her about the whispers, the veiled comments he sometimes made that she ignored. The part of her brain that saw Carter as a man had been locked up with chains and an electric fence but now it was wide-open.

Her world was dark and she struggled to stay still and not fidget. He clearly knew what he was doing. This was a Carter she'd never known before, and she thought she'd known everything about him. Not being able to see him was somehow opening her eyes to what and who Carter really was. And she knew he was smart enough to have known that when he'd brought out the blindfold.

Deliberate footsteps got quieter as he moved away from the bed. She dragged her fingers over his soft duvet cover; she'd been there when he'd bought it, which grounded her in their actual, prosaic reality instead of the wild scenarios she was building in her head.

Muted clicking came from somewhere in front of her and she suspected he was in his closet again, but for what she had no idea.

The footsteps got closer again and she got a whiff of him as he leaned over her, lightly caressing her stomach, rough hands smoothing over her waist. Surprised, she sucked in a breath.

"Do you trust me, Alexa?"

Normally, she trusted Carter with her life, but right now there was so much uncertainty that for the first time around him she didn't know how to answer that question.

Finally, she nodded her head.

"Good," he said, rubbing a reassuring thumb over her hip bone.

His fingers moved then, traveling down to her lasered mound. Only a small strip of hair remained, so she felt every small touch. Slowing, he rubbed a thumb over her crease, taunting and exploring, before sliding into her slick heat.

She was already so wet, could feel it heavy in her core. Then just as she was relaxing into the experience, something bulbous was being pushed into her.

"What the hell?" she coughed.

"They're just balls, Alexa."

He turned the two connected balls around inside her, the silicone brushing up against that rough patch there, making her suck in a breath of intense pleasure.

Then the warmth of him was gone, leaving her cold and vulnerable, having no idea where he was or what he was doing. She heard footsteps leave the room and she sat up, trying to take the blindfold off, but found that it was stuck.

"Don't take the blindfold off," Carter called from somewhere in the distance.

"What are you doing?" she demanded, hands going to the balls deep inside her, wanting to take them out.

Then the vibrating started. The balls started to pulse and spin, hitting the walls of her vagina in a rhythmic dance, each going a different way, reaching a different piece of her sensitized flesh. Clenching, she tried to contain the pleasure. Why wasn't Carter here?

A moan escaped her as the balls' gyration got faster and more intense. She couldn't tell where one ball ended and the other began; her vagina just felt used, the depths never plumbed so thoroughly before. Her hips bucked of their own volition, seeking out some kind of contact, some relief from the unrelenting pressure and sensation driving up from her core and branching out to all her nerve endings.

"How does that feel?" Carter's voice asked, but he wasn't in the room. Instead it sounded like it was coming through a speaker system.

"What the hell, Carter? Where are you? And why can't I get this blindfold off?"

"The blindfold has powerful magnets in the back."

She started snorting at that, but then one of the balls shifted and pinged against her G-spot and the sound morphed into a mewl of pleasure and surprise. The fact that she couldn't see was intense, making her much more aware of what was going on inside her, and the fact that she had no idea where Carter was or what he could see.

"Where are you?" she pressed, a little breathless.

"There are cameras in there and I'm watching in a different room," he finally allowed.

She opened her mouth to say how creepy that statement was, but the speed increased again, thrumming against her softness. "Carter!" she yelped, feeling her orgasm climbing up from her toes and lighting bonfires along her skin.

"I'm here," he said, but he wasn't there, and she was caught between this weird state of needing to come, but needing his touch, needing to feel someone else. Just one brush of her clit would send her into oblivion, but she'd never gotten there before like this.

God, which Carter knew. He totally knew she'd never had a orgasm from penetration alone.

"Please," she moaned as the balls rotated again, her thighs gripping tighter, desperate for relief.

And then it was happening, the slow, hot coiling in her middle, moving into a rich lava of pleasure as she came apart in slow motion, the sensations jerking at her entire body, milking the pleasure from her until she was replete and exhausted.

Breathing heavy, the balls felt too big inside her now, like an invasion. She started to pull them out, but then Carter was moving her hand away.

"Let me," he instructed, gently tugging them from her, his thumb casually brushing her engorged clit. She jerked, grabbing at where she thought he might be.

"Are you going to take this off now?" she asked.

"No."

"But I want to see you."

"Just trust me, Lex."

She blew out an irritated breath and she heard his muted chuckle. He knew she hated being told what to do.

His footsteps faded again and she was left by herself in the afterglow of an epic orgasm, struggling to figure out how she'd never realized that Carter was into this kind of sex. It was almost as if he knew she liked being on display as she'd been, knowing he was somewhere watching her writhe and moan and come, and while he held the power of the vibrating balls, she held the power over him.

It was a power dynamic they skirted frequently. They were both stubborn and liked to be in charge and while Carter often let her bossier tendencies go unchecked, it was clear that he was in charge now.

Alexa had done her fair share of fucking, but she'd never been tended to like this before. Like he'd thought every moment out, orchestrated a plan of action and was enacting it on her. That piece of her always looking for something to fix was finally quiet. All she needed to do was feel and Carter would take care of the rest.

She gave in to it then, ceded whatever control she was trying desperately to hang on to, and lay back onto the bed just as his footsteps returned to the room.

"You knew I'd like to be watched, didn't you?" she asked, her voice languid with pleasure.

"Yeah."

"How do you know that?"

The mattress moved as he sat down. "Are you serious? You love being looked at."

"Do you love looking at me?" she asked, maybe not quite as ready to not be in control as she thought.

"Of course."

"Did you like what you just saw?"

He drew a finger down the middle of her breasts to her belly button. "You're sweaty."

"You didn't answer my question."

"It was a stupid question."

She pursed her lips.

"Did I like seeing you come apart in my bed? It was like every fucking wet dream I've had since I was fifteen."

She took a breath then, wishing desperately that she could see his face.

"You're still flushed." A fingertip lightly ran

over her cheek, making her shiver. "The last time I saw you like this we'd just hiked at Red Rock and you poured water over yourself like we were in an '80s car commercial. You knew then you were turning me on and didn't give a fuck."

She remembered that day well because they'd both been hot and sweaty and she'd wanted him, too.

"You've been provoking me for years, Alexa, and this is your payback."

He flipped her over then, his weight vaulting over her back so he was on his knees straddling her ass.

He drew something cold and hard down the length of her trembling spine. "Do you feel helpless now?"

"Yes," she breathed, squirming below him. His legs were pressed against her sides, the soft fabric of his pants rubbing on her skin, which meant he still wasn't naked.

"Good."

Taking her hands, he pulled them up above her head, and wetness pooled at her center. She was so ready for him. He clipped her hands to something so she couldn't move them.

"Are you going to spank me?"

"No. I don't do pain play. You?"

She shook her head. She didn't do any sex play, really. Her encounters were straightforward. She liked to get off without emotional attachment and that was pretty much what she did. In and out and she was done. Figuratively and literally.

"Didn't think so," he said, tightening the fabric around her wrists.

Lips brushed the back of her neck, rustling the delicate hairs there and sending delicious goose bumps up all over her skin. She was so aware of her entire body, the curling of her toes at his every surprise yet gentle touch, the clean smell of his duvet pressed into her nose, the fact that his hands felt far larger and more powerful than they looked.

But she was also impatient and hot and needy and could barely stand the wait anymore.

"The point is, Alexa, we see each other every day to the point that we've stopped actually seeing each other."

He slid a finger inside her, twirling it until it hit that sweet rough patch, already abraded from the toy. She bucked up, needing more, needing him.

"And I want you to know who I am," he murmured in her ear, almost sounding like a threat.

He picked up her hips so she was on her knees with her arms stretched out in front of her. The vulnerability of it, the fact that he could do anything to her and she trusted him completely, had her quivering.

She felt him position himself at her greedy entrance for just the tiniest moment before sliding deep into her with one sure stroke. Crying out, she took his length, her muscles stretching and adjusting to accommodate his cock.

"Carter," she sighed, moving against him, willing him to give her what she needed, but he didn't move.

"Carter, please," she moaned, arching her ass against him.

"I like hearing you beg," he growled, pushing into her one more time before deserting her completely. The darkness was ever-present as she tried to tame her raging want and desperation for more.

Then her legs were being held and he was opening up her folds from his position behind her, letting the cool air flow over her heat. His tongue was on her, separating, exploring, excavating her from the inside out. He sucked at her clit, the first time any real attention had been paid to it, and she cried out, the bud engorged and inflamed.

Sensation radiated outward like a warning signal, waves of electric need streaming out over her body. He tongued her, treating each side of her clit to the same torture, but the angle was so different from what she was used to, the new intimacy, knowing what he could see made her even wetter. He bit gently, his fingers digging into her hips, and she flew over the cliff at warp speed, shaking with the weight of her own pleasure.

He was moving behind her again and entered

her with one clean thrust. Carter was big, and in the back of her mind, where it still worked on some level and wasn't completely buzzed out in a blissful haze, she was kicking herself for not doing this sooner. But that was her last thought, because he was jackhammering into her, the walls of her insides clinging and begging for the rough pressure of him, addicted to the width and texture and weight of his cock.

After two orgasms, her slickness was on her thighs, on the thatch of hair as he pounded into her. They were one sexual being now, instead of Carter and Alexa living separately. He was part of her, part of this hungry beast that couldn't get enough.

A hand went to her hair, tugging gently. It sent her so close to the edge she was basically hanging there by a manicured fingernail.

He hit that spot again and she hurtled toward paradise, crying out as she contracted around him.

He wasn't far behind, body spasming in four hard jerks.

Their shared breathing was the only sound in the dark room as they came down from the high. With a soft caress down her spine, he slid gently out of her. Familiar hands unclipped her wrists and removed the blindfold.

Turning onto her back, she gazed up at him, barely believing that the man who had indeed delivered the best sex of her life was Carter Hayes, her best friend and roller of clothing. She knew it was because he wasn't just a guy she was dating. It had been good because he was hers and she was his in all the ways that mattered. And that was more than she'd been willing to admit before.

"Hi," he said, meeting her eyes.

She grinned up at him. "Yeah, I'd say that was one hell of an introduction."

CHAPTER THIRTEEN

IT WAS LATE when Alexa finally got home from work, already completely dark outside. The smell of Carter's house welcomed her instantly; bright and woody spices wafted from the kitchen and made her mouth water.

She'd seen Carter only briefly this morning on his way out the door so they hadn't had time to touch on all the sex, but it had been pretty damn epic. The fact that it had been with Carter was problematic because she wasn't going to continue with her regularly scheduled life knowing what things were like with him. But it wasn't as if she and Carter could casually date each other now that they'd had sex either. They were best friends who were technically married and now they had a physical relationship. That was some real-as-fuck emotional entanglement that she wasn't equipped for.

She just didn't know what life looked like if she fucked up her friendship with Carter. Except lonely. And she'd been so lonely for so long after her parents died. What had been a house full of laughter and *noise* when she was growing up had so quickly gone quiet after her parents' death. Her uncle had been a single man who was away a lot and Alexa was just alone all the time. Beyond the devastation of her parents being gone, what she feared now were all the hours of silence and solitude without Carter. He'd always known how to cheer her up, bring her out of that place.

Not that it mattered either way since he was leaving. A fact that she kept trying to push away, but was creeping up as each day passed. Her insides were already shredded up like an old napkin by it.

Entering the kitchen, she stopped when she saw Carter at the stove, stirring a medium-sized pot with a wooden spoon. He was barefoot in a pair of gray jogging pants and a T-shirt, his glasses slightly foggy from the steam rising from the pot. He looked sexy as hell, and she wondered if she'd have to make the first move again or if they could just go at it. She didn't know that anyone had cooked her a meal before and the fact that he was doing it sent a heat wave through her.

But it also made her feel at home, like this was where she belonged even though she knew it wasn't real. Within the course of a second she'd gone from wanting to jump him to nearly bawling right there in his kitchen at the thought of losing this in her life.

He spotted her in the doorway staring at him like a lunatic who'd never experienced human emotions before.

"Hey," he said, his voice gravelly. "Long day?"

"Not any longer than usual. You?"

He held up a razor-thin chrome laptop on the island. "Technically still at work."

All things considered, he didn't look as happy as he should be considering what they'd done last night. And again early this morning. Had it meant something different to him? She wasn't one for having the "where is this going" talk, but maybe she needed to check in with him just to make sure they were on the same page.

"You okay?" she asked. "Did I take advantage of you last night?"

He snorted and raised an eyebrow.

"Seriously," she pressed. "You look mad."

"I'm pissed off," he allowed, but he didn't elaborate.

"At me?"

He shook his head and she felt a measure of relief that they were cool. "Some douchebag in my company leaked code for a new product to our biggest competitor and now the new office might be in jeopardy."

"So you think this other company can go to market faster than you with your code?"

"Maybe."

"Well, shouldn't you hack their system or something and steal your property back?" That's what would happen in the movies, anyway.

"It won't matter if we get it finished before they do if ours is better," he finished, apparently deciding against breaking the law. He poured her a glass of Chianti. "Besides, they won't finish as fast as we can. It's just an irritation."

She took a sip of the wine he'd placed on the island in front of her. "Are we having Italian?"

He nodded. "Bolognese."

"Sounds delicious," she purred, hoping a little flirtation might take his mind off his problem and lighten the mood. They *had* had sex last night and while she wasn't in a big hurry to hash it out with him in any meaningful way, she would have liked it if he'd at least acknowledge it. He'd said he'd wanted it since he was fifteen and now they were talking about spaghetti and work? It just wasn't what she'd expected.

He filled two plates with pasta and pulled some bread out of the oven, completely ignoring her invitation.

She met his eyes, her suspicion suddenly growing. "You hate cooking. Is something going on?"

"First of all, spaghetti is hardly cooking. But yes, there is something we have to talk about that you won't like."

"Well, after producing five orgasms last night,

there's really not going to be a better time for you to bring it up."

She expected a reaction to that, but got nothing from him except a muscle twitch in his jaw. So, he didn't want to talk about last night in any capacity. That was fine by her. Or at least she thought it was, but she felt like he could at least say something along the lines of, it was the best sex of his life, thank you for your patronage, your body was the stuff of dreams. Anything was better than this.

"I spoke to my board this morning and of course, they were preoccupied with the fact that I'd gotten married. Considering the leak, they think it's best if we stay married for now."

Her attention snapped back at "stay married for now." "Oh. So we can't get an annulment."

"We can," he allowed. "Just not right now."

"So longer than the month we'd originally planned to be engaged?"

"A monthlong marriage doesn't look good, no."

She fell silent, not sure what to make of this news. "This is what your board wants?"

"Yes."

"Is this what you want?" She both wanted the answer to that question and didn't. Of course, she didn't want to be married to Carter through their own absentminded blundering on paperwork, but whatever angst she was supposed to feel at being accidentally married to him was strangely absent.

She didn't know exactly what that meant, but if someone had told her a month ago that she'd actually be married to Carter she would have flipped out. But she wasn't. Not that she wanted to stay married, but being tied to Carter wasn't sending her screaming in the other direction, either.

"I don't want to be married to anyone against their will, but I also want to open the San Francisco office."

She sprinkled some Parmesan cheese onto her plate, staring out his French doors onto his terrace and the moonlight reflecting off his pool.

"Do you realize that we're legally married now?" she asked. "Like, actually married."

"It had crossed my mind," Carter said wryly, taking a seat at the end of the island.

She gave him a small grin. "I guess somebody had to be my first husband." That some deep part of her had assumed Carter would be her last husband remained unsaid.

He laughed, shaking his head.

They ate in silence until his phone rang and he left the room for several minutes as she poked at the pasta, waiting for him to return.

When he came back, he looked even more bothered and started typing furiously at his computer.

"What's going on?" she asked.

"Our internal network was almost hacked. We're locking it down."

"Can I do anything?"

"You could clean up dinner while I deal with this? You know I hate old food smells."

She did indeed know that about him and she would get on it as quickly as possibly because she'd never seen such a stressed-out look on Carter's face. Something bad was happening.

Sitting a beer beside him on the island, she got to work. She scooped up the leftover pasta into a glass container and put it in the fridge, then loaded the dishes into the dishwasher. By the time she'd gotten out the disinfectant to wash down the counters, he'd gone back up to his office.

For over an hour after changing into yoga pants and a sweatshirt, Alexa sat outside Carter's office. She listened as he barked instructions that sounded as if they were in a different language to his employees while she read news and thumbed through social media on her phone. Mostly, though, she thought again about the fact that she was married, *really married*. It wasn't a state she thought she was even ready for, let alone to Carter. That it wasn't real didn't make it any less problematic because what she and Carter were to each other was extremely real. The realest, most tangible thing in her life.

She listened as he fixed the problem for the company he loved. A company that made her life easier—a fact that had never been lost on her.

Carter was a man who, when she'd told him about employees stealing from her, had come up with a program to catch them and then built an empire. It had all started with him wanting to help her out. Remembering that made everything very clear to her because she wanted Carter to have everything he wanted, and if that included moving to San Francisco without her, that's what he should do.

And that's why she needed to end the marriage. To set Carter free once and for all. A tiny voice inside her head called her a liar. She accepted that it wasn't completely selfless of her and that it saved her from taking that final crucial step into a real relationship with him, but it was better for both of them in the long run.

Also, the child in her that dreamed of a perfect, magical wedding was screaming to get out of this as soon as possible. She'd imagined wearing a white dress and walking down the aisle with her dad. Not that she'd really ever have that dream wedding, since her dad obviously wasn't there. Their sham wedding was just one of many milestones her parents had missed in her life, but that memory she never allowed herself to have anymore was resurfacing now and she just had to get out of this.

Carter finally appeared in his office doorway looking exhausted and strung out.

"Fixed?" she asked.

"Yeah, but it's going to be an ongoing fight apparently."

She smiled. "Isn't it always?"

It would be a dick move for her bring up the annulment now when he looked like death warmed over. She decided it could wait until tomorrow.

"Have you been sitting here the entire time?"

She nodded. Quiet and stillness seemed to blanket them in the dark house. Only the light from his office illuminated them in the hallway.

He was looking at her strangely.

"We can't stay married," she blurted. "I'm really sorry, but I've just been thinking about it and I just can't do it. I've been sitting here feeling sorry for myself that I had a wedding and my parents weren't there and even I don't remember it."

His held tilted and he held out his hand to help her up. "Come on, let's go get a drink and talk this out."

"Do we have to?" she asked. This was why she never talked about her parents with anyone. Because it opened up "a conversation." Her entire past was brought into the present again as if she could never escape the weight of it.

"Yes, Alexa," Carter told her, his voice dry. "It's what adults do when they have a problem."

They took the steps together and when they made it to the kitchen he passed her a bottle of her favorite beer that she noticed had been stocked in the fridge. Yet another example of his thought-fulness was not what she needed right now.

"That wasn't your real wedding, you know that, right? It was Kaylee and Bruce's wedding. I'm not sure I understand the problem."

"If we stay married that was our real wedding," she told him.

Carter swallowed his beer. "But you don't want to stay married, so we won't."

Alexa ran her hands through her hair, agitated. How could she fucking explain that the thought of being married was like a vise around her neck. She felt immobile and trapped, but there was no way to say that to him without it sounding like she hated him. "I just don't want to be married, Carter. I shouldn't have to explain it."

His whole body tensed as he stared her down. "You're really doing this now?"

She tried not to cringe. She wasn't going to feel guilty about this. "I didn't think I was going to, but I couldn't not do it now."

He ran a hand through his hair in frustration. "So you're reneging on our earlier deal to stay married."

"I guess so. Yeah."

Lockjawed, he pulled out his phone, scrolled to something, then held up the phone's face to her. As he drank his beer down, she watched a video of her begging him to get married at the altar of the Blue Angel Chapel. Saw him back off and try to talk her out of it, but she badgered him until he kissed her, and that was the part of the video she'd already seen.

"So what?" she said, crossing her arms over her chest. "I was *drunk*!"

"You just saw me working upstairs for over three hours on an additional problem unrelated to the one I shared with you earlier and you're going to fuck me over like this?"

"What does it matter if we're married or not? Your company still has the problems."

"It's the optics, Alexa," he gritted out. "I cannot get married and divorced within the same damn week! It makes me, and therefore my company, look unstable! Britney Spears is only a pop star and her quickie Vegas wedding and divorce is still the advent of her crazy."

"Oh, it's just the press," she dismissed. "Blame it on me, say whatever you want. Just give them a story that sounds good and I'll corroborate it. You're making too big a deal out of this."

He stood, his face red. "You're such a goddamn coward, Alexa. I've fucking turned my whole life upside down for you to clean up your reputation and you can't do me this fucking favor that you got us into in the first place? You're an awful friend."

The last mark pierced her heart like a rusty knife, the wound messy and jagged.

"Being married indefinitely was part of no plan that we had, Carter, and you know it. You're pressing an unfair advantage here and I'm not some newb who will just take the first deal offered."

But he was finished fighting.

"Cut the shit, Alexa," he said. "Quit pretending that this has something to do with our agreement. This has to do with the fact that you're scared as fuck that when you found out that we were married it wasn't scary at all. It was the rightest thing you've ever fucking felt. Add in the best sex of our lives and you're running at the first chance available."

"Oh, are you Dr. Phil now, just handing out pop psychology advice whenever you feel like it? Maybe you're just pissed that I don't want to stay married to you in the first place."

Carter could barely remember a time that he'd been so angry, but it was probably at Alexa, too. Especially because he knew he was right. If he was afraid of being married and what their physical relationship meant, she had to be absolutely terrified. Between the two of them, there was only one emotionally well-adjusted person in the room and it wasn't the one who'd just claimed that her reason for wanting an annulment was about a dream wedding.

But he wasn't a fool, and knew there was no arguing with her when she'd only dig her very high heels in. Which was just fine with him, because he was so fucking tired of talking.

He pulled her roughly to him, meeting her eyes in challenge. She kissed him in response, her tongue lashing at his in a fury, desperate to prove that he was wrong, that they were just friends and that everything was the same between them. Part of him wanted to believe it, too, wanted to wake up and not feel the yearning for her so deep in his bones like it would never leave. And he knew it wouldn't. So he gave in to it, accepted that together or not together, he was hers.

He took over the kiss, soothing her assault with the same considered patience he applied to their friendship, letting her know that everything was okay. *They* were okay. She could stab him in the heart and they would be okay. He would make sure of it.

Lifting her onto the island, he pulled off her sweatshirt, bra and leggings and threw them to the ground. He tugged a hard pink nipple in his mouth and feasted like he hadn't gotten to last night. Tonight he wanted her to see just who the fuck she was dealing with, wanted her to know just who was going to fuck her.

She squirmed underneath him as he sucked just to the point of pain, how he knew she liked. They both played on the edge and he didn't suppose sex would be any different. His free hand pinched her other nipple and she bucked against him, but he ignored it, kept up his sucking until she cried out, convulsing beneath him.

He rose, letting her nipple pop out of his mouth. Their eyes met again and he raised a knowing eyebrow at the shocked look on her face. She'd come just from nipple stimulation alone, so that was two firsts he'd delivered.

Still keeping her gaze locked with his, he drew his tongue all the way down from the valley of her breasts over her abdomen, around her belly button and to her clit, gently easing her down from the edge while amping her up again. She got antsy against his mouth, whimpering with need, and he'd never heard anything so damned good as Alexa falling apart, letting everything between them disappear into nothing but the two of them needing each other.

He dived in, licking and sucking at her core, moving his tongue in her like it was his job.

"Carter," she moaned, her hands clenching in his hair, something he'd imagined countless times when he jerked off.

He was hard as steel and didn't want to wait anymore. Reaching for his wallet, he unearthed a condom, catching her gaze again as he took himself in his hand, stroking just the slightest bit. He slowly slid the condom on, drawing it out, reveling in the look on her face. She wanted him like her next breath and he couldn't get enough. All the years he'd been waiting for this moment crystallized in her gaze; time didn't exist anymore, not the years between them, not the minutes before when they'd been fighting.

Opening up her legs, he slipped them over his shoulders and slid into her heat inch by slow inch. Her moan was like a cattle prod and he lost control, driving into her over and over again. A bowl of her oranges fell to the ground as she grasped wildly looking for purchase, but he'd placed her specifically so she had nothing to hold on to. He wanted her exposed and helpless and unable to wrest the reins away from him. He'd been living in the wake of her willful oblivion to his feelings for so long that he wanted her off-balance.

Alexa's muscles gripped at him, the fluttering warning him that she was close to coming apart again. And so was he, the pressure building like a freight train behind his balls. The feel of her around him, tight and wet and hot, was filthy pleasure personified. He pulled his length out to the tip, waiting until she looked up at him again, her chest rising and falling as she breathed hard for air. He slid back into her to the root, banging against her, her harsh gasp echoing in the empty kitchen.

He pumped furiously then, watching again as she came undone.

"Eyes here," he commanded.

Her familiar hazel eyes popped open, looking wrecked, and that was when he lost it, impaling her wildly until he exploded in a wave of pleasure so intense that his whole body shook from it.

He stayed there, buried in her, until he was able to breath semi-normally again.

Leaning over, he gave her a soft kiss, soaking up her breathlessness.

Gently lowering her legs, he stepped back and out of her, caressing her leg as he did. Quickly, he threw the condom away.

She watched him from tired eyes as he readjusted his clothes.

"I'm sorry about earlier, Carter," she said quietly. "I don't want to argue. It's not only about the wedding, but I just imagined mine different is all. Like one that actually happened and that my parents were at. That's the last time I really thought about having one."

She pulled on her sweatshirt, but accidentally got her head caught in the oversize sleeve. He pulled it out, readjusting it for her, and her head finally appeared. He drew a finger over her cheek and kissed her on the forehead.

"Hey, people fight. We were overdue. And I get it about your parents."

He flicked off the bright kitchen lights so only the one over the stove remained, its soft glow catching the gold in Alexa's hair. For a second, time got away from him. She looked so young standing there in her beat-up college sweatshirt.

"Carter," she said, her voice soft and considered as she looked up at him. "This, us, whatever we are now, means a lot to me, too. Just because I'm not ready to be married doesn't mean it doesn't."

"I know," he said, bringing her into the crook of his arm.

For now, it would have to do.

CHAPTER FOURTEEN

ALEXA USUALLY LOOKED forward to the monthly dinner with Carter's family, but this was the first one since their fake engagement (and marriage) and there would be questions. So many questions to which she didn't have answers. Considering the state of her and Carter at the moment, the probability of losing them along with Carter was mounting and had all her anxiety systems in high gear. She should have already been over here to explain what was happening and had been dodging calls from Carter's mom and sister for weeks.

His younger sister, Kara, turned to Alexa at the dinner table, her blue eyes so similar to Carter's. They were filled to the brim with curiosity, which didn't bode well. Dinner had ended an hour ago and the three of them had been sitting around just catching up.

"So let me get this straight," Kara pressed. "You guys got fake-engaged to clean up Alexa's reputation, then you *accidentally* signed as the bride and groom at the chapel instead of witnesses and you *accidentally* got legally married."

"That about sums it up," Carter told her, looking at the face of his phone as if what Kara had just said wasn't absolutely ridiculous.

She and Kara watched as he took the call into another room, his ass looking bitable in a pair of fitted jeans that hugged all the right places. In her former life those kinds of thoughts hadn't seen the light of day, and it almost felt sacrilegious to be having them at his parents' house.

Kara popped a kettle chip into her mouth, crunching loudly as she considered Alexa.

"Just say what you want to say, Kara," Alexa issued bluntly.

"And you're going to get an annulment."

"Yes," Alexa said for the tenth time tonight. His parents had asked the same question. Because the date might be pushed back, but the annulment was happening. If that was still a possible thing to do now that they'd consummated the marriage. A lot.

During dinner, the Hayes parents hadn't seemed upset or surprised by the unexpected news of the abrupt wedding. Being informed that their missing invitation wasn't on purpose seemed to put to rest any questions they might have had. Kara, however, was relentless, trying to ferret out the secrets of Alexa's soul one noisy potato chip at a time.

Carter strode back through the door and returned to his vacated seat at the same buttery oak dining room table they'd sat around in high school.

"The annulment won't be soon, though, because the board doesn't want the Hayes Tech CEO to look reckless," Carter clarified, referring to their previous conversation.

At the mention of it, Alexa's blood heated in irritation. She hated losing ground. Even if it was to Carter. She also didn't appreciate that they hadn't discussed it further. Underneath that anger, though, she knew Carter had been right about what he'd said in the kitchen that night. She was scared. Being around his family now, seeing the thing that she'd lost so up front, drove that point home for her in a way his words couldn't. Once upon a time, she'd dreamed of having this kind of life again, but somewhere along the way she'd told herself it wasn't possible because she wasn't strong enough to lose it all again.

"Huh," Kara said, crunching on another chip while regarding them speculatively.

"Jesus," Carter barked, "can you at least close your mouth while you do that?"

"Nope," his sister chirped, fully opening her mouth as she chewed, a move expressly designed to annoy him. Everyone knew Carter hated chewing noises.

Alexa snorted a laugh, shrugging when he raised

an eyebrow in disbelief. She couldn't help it—he deserved his sister's torture and more.

Kara glanced at her brother and then at Alexa, before pinning them both with a look. "You guys are totally doing it," she proclaimed.

"That's gross, Kara. And untrue," Alexa protested, and did a pretty good job of it, too.

Kara crunched on another chip. "Yeah, you are."

"If you don't quit doing that," Carter warned, "I'll break into your Bumble account and do a lot of indiscriminate swiping as payback."

Kara got in a few more crunches before her eyes widened and she stood up abruptly. "Oh my God, you've done that before, haven't you?"

Carter shrugged, a twinkle of guilt and satisfaction in his eyes.

"I keep getting messages from a full-blown practicing mime. I never would have contacted a mime! You know I hate silence and white face paint!"

Alexa snickered, but then thought about her own accounts, trying to remember if anything out of the ordinary had ever happened.

"Not yet," Carter told her, reading her thoughts, "but it's been tempting."

"Don't you dare," she warned.

"Also, you two," Carter addressed both of them, "it's not hacking if I can just guess your password, okay? Be safe out there."

"My password is super complicated," Kara protested.

"Your cat's name and your birthday?" Carter asked doubtfully. "One-sixth of all people use a pet's name as their password and nearly half use their birthday."

As Alexa watched the back-and-forth between Carter and Kara she got that squeezing feeling in her chest that there would be another woman sitting in her place someday enjoying their sibling camaraderie. That Carter was leaving town and she wouldn't be at his side for these dinners anymore. She'd just be the old neighbor who stopped by for dinners sometimes while Kara and Carter moved on with their partners and families. This vision stretched out in front of her, depressing and empty.

Kara rolled her eyes at Carter's directive. "Stay out of my stuff or I'll post naked baby pictures of you on Instagram."

"I was a cute naked baby," he said, shrugging. "Do your worst."

Kara looked to Alexa for support.

Alexa sprang into action like any good female friend. She was also just glad that the conversation had shifted from their sex life to Carter's bad behavior.

"I have it on good authority that one of his former girlfriends has a video of Carter doing, well, you know…" She shrugged and let the words hang there for them to draw their own conclusion. It wasn't so far-fetched considering there was a camera in his bedroom.

It was a total bluff, but if Carter was breaking into accounts he needed to know there were consequences. It wouldn't hurt to give him a taste of his own medicine, either.

Carter's head swiveled toward her, eyeing her speculatively. "Who?"

Alexa just shrugged. "Not telling."

"You're lying," he said dismissively, but still looked wary.

"I never lie about bootleg pornography."

Kara slapped a hand on the table and laughed. "Wow, family dinners *just got interesting!*"

Carter grabbed Alexa's hand under the table and gave it an encouraging squeeze. Just that simple physical contact was enough to put her back in dangerously lusty territory. Could they make it home in five minutes? Should she analyze why the brush of the calluses on his fingers from typing turned her on? Was she now just turned on by everything he did? She'd been enjoying a rather vivid fantasy of having him in his boardroom, on top of the sleek long table where he ran meetings with the most powerful people in the country. Was her underwear tighter now? She needed to get out of this house.

"I think Mom would take offense to that statement," Carter drawled, letting go of Alexa's hand.

Kara just laughed. "You guys are totally doing it."

On the way home that night from dinner, Alexa turned to Carter. "Do you think it was weird that your parents weren't more shocked about the marriage?"

"I think they'd be more shocked if we weren't going to have it annulled."

"I guess so."

"They're probably hoping we stay married. God knows Kara isn't going to give them grandchildren if her brother keeps breaking into her dating apps."

Alexa laughed. "I'm serious about mine," she growled, pointing a finger at him.

"Technically, you really shouldn't even be on dating apps right now. It would have been a bad look when we were engaged and it's an even worse one now that we're married."

"I've been off those sites for years."

His brow furrowed. "Really?"

"Yeah. So it turns out you have no leverage over me and that incriminating video of you," she said with a cheeky grin.

He neatly steered the car into his garage and she helped him carry the leftovers into the house. When the small plastic containers were stashed away, they stood staring at each other for a moment in the kitchen. Besides the show they'd put on for his family tonight, things between them hadn't been quite the same since their fight.

And the dinner tonight hadn't been any easier. The familiar camaraderie she enjoyed with his family felt forced and fleeting. Maybe it was just her being paranoid, but would his family be just as welcoming if they thought she hurt their son? It made the connection she'd always had with them seem extremely fragile.

"Come up to my office. There's something I want you to see."

She grabbed her purse and followed him upstairs, stopping in her room first to change into some yoga pants. To actually do yoga, she decided. That would be the perfect balm to her overactive libido. Heavy breathing and awkward bending.

When she made it to Carter's office, he was sitting behind his streamlined glass desk. Two walls were completely made of windows, while the other two were covered with crowded bookshelves holding literature titles as well as some older tech manuals that he kept around for sentimental value. Pictures of his family were perched on the shelves, as well as vacation pictures and a couple of the two of them. Her favorite was one of them at the Grand Canyon. They'd driven there the day after high school graduation because it'd been her parents' favorite place and had been where the three of them were supposed to go on vacation the year they died. That Carter had been the one to go with her meant a lot. It still did.

"What do you want me to see?" she asked, returning her attention to him. He'd also changed into a pair of black jogging pants and a white Google hoodie.

"Just that I was able to get the entire video of Kaylee's wedding night and I wanted you to see something."

He pulled up the extra chair beside him and gestured for her to sit.

He hit Play and the video started, footage she hadn't seen of the end of Kaylee's wedding and what happened after.

It was mostly boring, the minutes ticking by as the few guests milled about in the aisles. Eventually, the camera got a close-up of Carter getting down on one knee, looking as if he was proposing to her. It should have been odd to the other wedding guests since they'd technically already been engaged, which may be why whoever it was had chosen to record the moment on their phone.

Carter looked so serious and handsome, down on one knee, and the look on her face was like any woman being proposed to, excited and shocked. She glanced down at the ring on her finger, a flutter of nerves in her stomach, because she looked like a woman in love in that video. Drunk in love, maybe, but in love nonetheless.

"Wait. You proposed for real," she said slowly, understanding finally dawning.

Then her phone rang. Seeing that it was her uncle, Alexa answered with a cheery hello. His big voice shattered her eardrums and Carter laughed at her grimace.

"Alexa, I sold Hard Eight, honey," he boomed. "We did it. I'm willing to bet that you're about to be the wealthiest woman in Vegas right now."

She clutched the phone in her hand. "Congratulations, Uncle John!" she chirped as genuinely as she could. Her ever-present mantra, *Halcyon is still mine*, played out a backbeat in her head, calming her enough to keep her composure because inside it felt like she was falling apart. Every part of the life she'd built and loved was unraveling thread by thread.

Carter came up behind her, wrapping his arms around her waist and giving her a kiss on the top of her head. She took another deep breath as her uncle went through the particulars of the sale and set up the meeting with the lawyers for tomorrow at Hard Eight to set everything in motion.

"It was a movie studio," she told Carter, explaining who bought the casino.

"I'm sorry, Alexa," he said, giving her a squeeze before disengaging. Taking his seat again, he gave her a cheeky smile. "Any chance you're looking to diversify your investment portfolio? I know a successful security software company that is seeking to expand."

Alexa shook her head and laughed. "You know I'm already an investor in your company, right? I did that a long time ago. Both Uncle John and I did. We believe in you, Carter."

She flopped down on the black leather couch in the corner, dramatically covering her face with her arm. "At least I still have Halcyon."

"Why didn't you tell me you invested in my company?" he asked.

"I honestly thought I did."

"I think I would have remembered."

"Well, we did. You're the safest bet in Vegas, Carter," she said, raising her head to give him a warm smile. "Always have been."

He met her eyes, his brow furrowed in thought as he watched the video again, another sound chiming in to draw his attention away.

"What's the matter?" she asked, sitting up on the couch to look at him. He didn't look happy.

He shook his head. "It's nothing."

She sat fully up then, her feet dropping to the floor so she could meet his eyes. "You're lying."

"Trust me, you don't want to know."

She rolled her eyes. "Give me a break, Carter. If there's anyone I trust with my most mortifying secrets, it's you."

His blue eyes rested on hers then, a weird intensity she'd never seen before in them. "I remember you said yes."

"What?"

"When I proposed," he clarified. "You said yes."

"That's it?" Alexa shrugged. "I was drunk."

He leaned back in his chair, considering her. "So not even a small part of you wonders if maybe we should stay married? That maybe we're actually meant to be together?"

Alexa's pulse rate entered into a danger zone and her throat constricted, making it difficult to breathe. A relationship wasn't part of the deal. They'd promised each other they would always be friends. "What?"

Carter's eyes pinned her to her seat. "You heard what I said and know what I meant. We know we get along, now we know that there's unparalleled sexual chemistry between us, and we're already married. Explain to me why we're not trying to make this an actual relationship again? Because from where I'm sitting that sounds like a no-brainer."

Alexa's fingernails dug into her palms. "We've discussed this already. Because our friendship means too much to both of us to fuck up with a casual relationship."

"We're married, Alexa. News flash, it's not casual anymore."

She rolled her eyes. "Yeah, but we're not really married."

"And yet, when you were drunk you were fine with getting engaged for real."

"I also went to bed with you completely naked in a hotel room on the same night and yet I have no recollection of it. Shit happens when you're wasted. It doesn't mean anything."

"Do you think my family will hate you or something if we break up? Because they won't. With or without me, you have them."

Alexa threw her hands up in the air, so mad she couldn't even scream. "I'm worried about losing you, not your family, you idiot! Neither of us has had a real adult romantic relationship. I have no idea how it works and I'm not going to let the most important person in my life be my relationship guinea pig. It's not worth it."

He rose from behind the desk, his big body swallowing up all the space in the room.

"Scared Alexa isn't what I expected to find after all this time. Do you think I couldn't have had a real relationship? I didn't have one because I knew I wanted you."

"That's ridiculous."

Crossing his arms over his chest, so only the top of the logo was visible, he seemed almost menacing. He was not hiding his rage at all, which was something she was still getting used to.

"I have wanted you for as long as I can remember, Alexa. So much that I agreed to this whole engagement charade. You don't want to believe me? Fine. But we're in a real relationship here, and both our feelings are and have been involved since the beginning. I'm sick of pretending otherwise just to make you feel safe."

"Oh, don't do me any favors," she bit off.

"I just said I won't," he threw back.

His angry gaze raked up from her bare toes, over her snug Lycra pants, to the tank with the built-in bra she was wearing, finally resting on her face. Heat pulsed from his eyes to her core, goose bumps dancing over the skin of her arms. It would be wrong to sleep with him now because she knew this had to end, but she didn't think she had that kind of willpower. She needed him right now.

"And for the record, if I were such a safe bet you would have taken it a long time ago," he gritted out, stalking toward her.

She gasped as he picked her straight up off the couch and into his arms. He ran his hand through the back of her thick hair and pulled her lips to his. He took his time with the kiss, his exploration deliberate, and she felt every swipe of his tongue, the taste of mint on his breath, the familiar mountain spring scent of his long-preferred laundry detergent. He sat her down on the couch.

Leaning back, she pulled the tank top and bra

over her head, revealing breasts that were peaked and aching for his touch.

He drew a thumb over a dark pink tip and she watched him smile at her shiver.

"I can't tell you how many times I've imagined these," he murmured, closing his lips over her nipple. He sucked harder as she squirmed against him, her head falling back with a moan. He let her go, running a thumb over her wetness. "But nothing lives up to the real thing."

He pulled off his shirt, the soft glow of the desk lamp casting shadows over his pale abdomen. Her fingers glided up his chest to his shoulders, reveling in the fact that touching him this way still felt so new.

"You don't feel like I imagined, either," she admitted, her voice hushed in the quiet room. "You're more."

Then she pushed at his shoulder and reversed their positions, needing to take control. Sliding his pants down slowly, her eyes met Carter's and they were different than just her old friend's eyes. Now they were serious and wicked and unbending. A shiver of anticipation raced up her spine.

He helped her pull his pants down and off and she hesitated, enjoying just being able to look at him for once without rushing to touch him. The moment stretched and she felt him watching her watch him, his cock bobbing against his smooth stomach, waiting for whatever she chose to do next.

But he took advantage before she'd had her fill, kissing her hard, letting their desire rage out of control. Her thighs grew heavy and languid against his as she leaned into the kiss, fingers tangling in his thick hair.

Finally breaking away, she licked down his chest to his cock, teasing him with playful nips and sucks before taking him into her mouth. She loved the feel of hard softness in her mouth, like a living piece of Carter that was hers alone. He grunted when she took in the length of him, tasting, sucking, caressing until his leg muscles tightened in thick bunches under her hands. Her core squeezed in pleasure as the first drops of come greeted her tongue.

His hands pulled at her hair in warning, but she didn't care. Letting him come apart in her mouth was something she wanted because she wanted all of him, wanted to take care of him like he did her. There wasn't a day that Carter didn't make her feel loved and wanted, and she'd been denying him that in return. The realization fucking wrecked her.

Lifting her head, she met his eyes, the blue dark and tumultuous.

He levered off the couch, picking her up and sitting her down again.

"Condom," he explained, then strode over to

his desk to pull one out of a drawer. She didn't want to speculate why he kept condoms there and concentrated instead on what a spectacular sight it was. Thick thigh and bicep muscles contracted and bulged as he walked, his semi-erect cock glistening from being in her mouth. More than their other times together, the energy between them tonight felt far more intimate and theirs. If this was a real relationship, she guessed it wasn't that bad.

Then he was pulling the drawstring out of his hoodie and her brain froze.

He returned to stand in front of her in all his buck-naked glory, the thin white string dangling from his hand.

"Are you going to use that?"

He raised an eyebrow.

She swallowed. "I don't think you're ready to go again yet."

He took hold of himself, keeping their gazes locked as he slowly stroked, his big hands lazily moving over the ruddy shaft. Heat jackknifed to her core, her insides pulsing as wetness pooled. Giving his cock a final squeeze, he was back at full staff.

Grabbing the condom from his hand, she pulled him back onto the couch and straddled him. She slid the condom over him, wishing she could feel him bare inside her. Lifting up and over him, she sank down, inch by slow inch until she realized the

only person she was torturing was herself. When
he was buried in her to the hilt, stretching her inside, he kissed her with such a sweet, gentle kiss
her heart ached with it.

Then he was pulling her hands from around his
shoulders and behind her back, where he tied them
together with the drawstring. It drew her shoulders
back so her breasts thrust out for his mouth and
also took the control she'd thought she'd so handily had away from her.

Now the only thing she could do was feel as his
rough hands gripped her hips, moving her where
and when he wanted. Starting slow at first, he increased the rhythm, faster and faster, her upper half
completely within his control as she could barely
balance on her own. It was a weird sensation, to
be so helpless and on display for him. Her breasts
bobbed in his face, but he kept his eyes on hers.

His thumb brushed against her clit and she
flamed higher, so ready to come. Her muscles
gripped at him and she could feel the hair of his
thighs rough against the soft skin of hers as she
rode him, the intimacy of it decadent and lush. The
unraveling hit her whole body at once, wave upon
wave of drugging sensation dragging her under
so the only thing she knew was Carter inside her
and the feel of the heat they were making together.

When he convulsed underneath her, he still
didn't let her fall, the fingers gripping her hips so

hard that they'd probably leave marks. Part of her wanted a tangible reminder of Carter on her body.

Coming down from his own release, he gently lowered her to his chest, where she nuzzled into his neck.

He untied the string on her wrists and rubbed the skin there. "You okay?"

"Yeah," she murmured.

"You like being tied?"

She nodded because he knew she did; she liked power for herself and liked giving it to him, too. Most of all, she liked that she was able to trust Carter implicitly, without doubts and hesitation. He would never hurt her. He caressed her hair, dropping a kiss on top of her head.

They sat that way forever, until her body had cooled and the reality and weight of what had gotten them to this point started to penetrate her sex brain.

Eventually, he went to the bathroom to get rid of the evidence. Spotting his water bottle on the desk she threw her clothes back on and collapsed, exhausted, into his desk chair and downed nearly the entire bottle. The movement accidentally bumped his mouse and his computer screen woke up.

She glanced over at the screen, not intending to read anything that was on his personal computer, but she saw her name and did a double take. His email account was open, displaying an email from a board member suggesting that the expansion would look better to investors if he was married. Not new news. However, there were several emails in the chain and the original was dated before they'd even gotten engaged.

Sitting back, Alexa's brain raced over the events of the last couple of weeks trying to figure out what the fuck this meant.

Considering the date of the email and the subsequent events, it sure as hell looked like Carter had actually secretly been angling for a fake engagement. She couldn't help but think he'd pulled her into that stairwell knowing they'd be seen, effectively backing her into a corner so she had to use him as her fake fiancé. It didn't make any sense because he'd turned down being her fake fiancé at first, but then why did he drag her into that stairwell? Why that day of all days had he chosen to cross that line?

Her gaze returned to the emails, double-checking the date, the sender and the content. The facts were there right in front of her. The week before Carter appeared in her casino with news about her general manager stealing, his board suggested he get married.

And when she clicked on the email before that, it was as if her worst nightmare was coming true. The board also suggested he distance himself from her completely because of her reputation.

Holy shit. Holy shit. *Holy fucking shit.*

CHAPTER FIFTEEN

ALEXA SET HER keys on her foyer table, thankful to be home for the first time in nearly a month. She hadn't been able to fit all her stuff in her car, but she definitely wasn't going back to Carter's house, not after his betrayal. The closest person in her life had basically just gut-punched her emotions.

How long had she been an embarrassment to him? She couldn't help but wonder if that had been the reason they hadn't been hanging out as much. She'd been busy with work, but maybe he'd been deliberately taking a step back from their friendship, and San Francisco was a part of that.

Alexa wasn't ashamed of her reputation. She treated men how men treated women and if people had a problem with it, well, that was kind of their problem. But the thought of Carter agreeing with his board or being ashamed of her had settled so deep. Regardless of whether or not he agreed about her reputation, he hadn't stuck up for her and had been about to create the distance his board wanted by moving to San Francisco. He'd chosen something else, even if it was his company, over her and she hated it. She mostly operated under the assumption that she was the most important thing in Carter's life, and the fact that she wasn't was breaking her heart even as she knew how fucking messed up it was.

That little annoying voice piped up in her head again saying that she put her business before him all the time, but why wouldn't he have at least told her about the stuff with the board?

Either way, she couldn't live there. She couldn't think about it anymore, either. She'd been up all night wrestling with how to deal with all of it, then in the morning met with her uncle to sell Hard Eight, and on top of that worked a full day at Halcyon. Her exhaustion was complete.

Carter had texted her encouragement throughout the day about the sale, but she hadn't responded. Who knew, he'd probably orchestrated the sale of her casino, too. He operated completely in secret, apparently. While she opened every part of her life to him from pictures of her breakfast sandwich to what she'd wear to events to top-secret casino operations, he was just over there in Carter-land being ashamed and plotting to get away from her.

She blew out a breath. She was being irrational

and needed to get with it. Or get to bed. That was the better option. The smart option.

Instead of doing the smart thing, though, she changed into an old pair of pajamas and pulled her laptop onto her lap to read the email chain from Carter's computer that she'd sent herself last night. She'd copied the email text and sent it as a document instead of forwarding the actual chain to her own address. So there was at least a chance he wouldn't know what she'd done.

She was halfway through the emails when she heard the front creak door open.

"Fuck," she breathed, knowing exactly who it was.

Locking her bedroom door, she went over to her window to consider how far the drop to the ground would be. As soon as she pushed the window out, ready to make the jump, Carter banged on her bedroom door.

"Alexa! Open up!"

"Go away!" she yelled, the hurt and anger and panic she'd been fueling bubbling to the surface before she even had a chance to contain it.

"The document you made of my emails was in my trash. You have to delete that separately, you know. Do you want me to teach you how to use a computer?"

Alexa's fingers dug into her palm. He was such a dick to try to make a joke right now.

"If you're so embarrassed to be my friend, then

explain why you took us into the stairwell when you knew there were cameras in there."

"I have never for one moment been embarrassed to be your friend. Can you open this door so we can talk like normal people?"

She blew out a breath and skipped to the really important question, the one that had kept her up all night. "Are you leaving Vegas to get away from me?"

She stared at the door between them, waiting for his answer.

"I don't want to mess up your business," she added, giving him permission to tell her the truth.

"Are you kidding me? We're still married because you're good for my business. That email about your reputation was a direct result of the news article about how you'd gone nude watersliding with an entire country's soccer team."

"Well, that just sounds dangerous," she huffed. "And not true." She'd partied with those guys and maybe she'd been topless for a portion of the evening, but certainly not on a waterslide.

Carter continued. "Can we talk about what this is really about? That I told you I have feelings for you and now you moved out of my house and believed that I am somehow embarrassed of the person I'm most proud of in the world and want to get away from her?"

Alexa wasn't so emotionally stalled as to not

recognize the truth of what Carter was saying. And maybe it was cowardly of her to run away, but really, exactly how honest did she need to be with herself about her feelings anyway? She and Carter had gone from friends to spouses in under three weeks; was she so wrong in looking for ways to create some distance? Of course, she loved Carter as she always had and adding the sex had been fucking amazing, but jumping from sex to a real committed relationship was huge. There'd be no casually dating Carter; they were already at date one thousand.

"I don't want to talk to you right now," she entreated, needing some time to process.

There was a pause and she could hear him slide down the door and sit on the floor.

"Listen, I know yesterday was a lot, but I'm scared, too, Alexa. I mean, fuck, I'm the one who laid it all out there. And yeah, I thought going to San Francisco would give me a chance to get over you, but it wasn't because I was embarrassed."

"Okay." Her heart clenched at how defeated he sounded. He wanted her to say she'd wanted him all this time, too, but she wasn't ready. She didn't know if she'd ever be ready. That was the problem.

Her phone rang, her Uncle John again. The urge to let it go to voice mail was strong because she was exhausted and didn't want to talk business.

But she had a responsibility so she pressed the green button.

"Alexa, you'll never believe what has happened!" Uncle John boomed in her ear.

She held the phone away and turned it on speaker to save her hearing. "I got a huge deal on Halcyon!"

Alexa's pulse was frantic. "But the deal was that I was going to buy you out."

"Of course, you can say no," he stressed, "but it's customary to bring all offers to the table. Now that the news is out that we're looking for buyers, we got a lot more than we needed!"

The excitement in his voice was electric as he rattled off an insane purchase price from a British corporation.

It was almost too good to refuse. But Halcyon was her raison d'être, and without it, what would she do? Live off her money and tan by the pool every day? That wasn't who she was. She *loved* her job.

She took a deep breath to try to settle herself and focus, but the pain in her chest was relentless, like she was seriously about to lose part of herself. She'd never even allowed herself to consider losing Halcyon for real, so the possibility of it was insane. It was her last link to a life that had been slipping through her fingers for the past month. She couldn't get a grasp of anything solid. Not even Carter.

"When do they want an answer?" she asked.

"It's up to you, Alexa. Give it all the time you need."

She nodded even though her uncle couldn't see. Disconnecting the call, she opened the door for Carter.

"That's a shit-ton of money."

She managed a laugh, but the sound that came out was wan and anemic.

"You don't have to take it."

"I know," she said, "but not taking it would be stupid."

Carter took her by the shoulders and locked eyes with her. "You're allowed to make decisions based on what you want for yourself, Alexa. You never know how those people will treat the employees you care about. Just because it makes the most financial sense doesn't necessarily mean it makes the most sense completely."

Her head fell forward onto his chest. "Why are you being so reasonable?"

"Because that's who I am."

"I know," she sighed. "I just hate it."

Carter laughed and drew her into his arms.

"I'm sorry I ignored you," she said against his chest, which was smooshing her face, so the words came out in a garbled mess.

"It's okay. I know why you did it. It's been fast. I hate to pile on, but with all that stuff going on with the code leak, opening the new branch is going to happen sooner than I thought. I've got to leave for San Francisco this weekend and I wanted to make sure we were okay."

Alexa's stomach dropped. "You're leaving now?"

He nodded.

"For good?"

"Yeah, for the year."

Tears sprang to Alexa's eyes and she buried her head harder into his chest, not wanting him to see. "Do you have to?"

He ran a gentle hand over her hair. "Yeah, I have to."

"But your wife doesn't want you to," she complained. "And neither does your best friend."

"You could always sell Halcyon and come with me."

"Or you could stay and we could try to make this marriage work," she tried with a hopeful expression, knowing it was a cheap move because she wasn't at all ready. He needed to go and she should let him. She should be as good a friend to him as he was to her.

Carter touched his forehead to hers. "If I thought you meant that, I would stay without a second thought, Lex. But I'm not the consolation prize for having to sell your casinos."

"You're the most important person in my life,

Carter," she told him, touching her lips softly to his. "You'd never be a consolation."

He pulled back to meet her eyes, his thumb drawing lightly over her cheek. "You'll be fine, Alexa. You're the strongest, bravest and smartest woman I know. Within a week, you won't even know I'm gone. Plus, in a month or so the office should be up and running and we can get the annulment. We can both get back to our regularly scheduled lives."

"But this weekend is so soon." Tears threatened. Ruthlessly pushing them back, she met his eyes. If he felt like he needed to go, she wasn't going to stop him regardless of how it was ripping her apart. Her whole Carter-less life was stretching out in front of her like a laughterless black void.

He took her hand in his, the calluses so familiar that it made her heart ache to know it might be the last time. "Why don't you come back to my house at least? Until I go?"

She shook her head. "The casinos are selling," she said. "My reputation is good. You've done me a favor and then some, but now that you're leaving I can't keep pretending that we're married." *It hurts too much* was what she needed to say, but couldn't. Couldn't say the words that might make him stay because friends didn't manipulate each other like that. He wanted her physically, but he hadn't said he was in love with her and she knew better than anyone that physical attraction and love were two completely separate entities.

"So that's it then?"

She shrugged, pulling away from him because his touch was clouding her judgment. "You said you were leaving, what else do you want me to say?"

"Come on, Alexa. Don't do it this way."

She met his eyes. He stood in the middle of her bedroom, the dim light of her lamp burnishing his hair in melted gold. He looked so lovely and dear and he was exiting her life for what may as well be forever.

He brushed a piece of hair behind her ear and she shivered with awareness. The moment was fraught with all the things she wanted to say, but couldn't get past her cowardly lips.

"You know this is our last night for the foreseeable future," he said, his voice low and tinged with the same sadness that was swallowing her up.

"I guess we'll have to make it count," she whispered, then touched her lips to his.

Alexa didn't hold anything back. She put all her cards on the table, taking over the kiss, holding his head just where she wanted it. She poured all of her pent-up anxiety and need and want into the kiss, as if it were their last one.

He lifted her off the ground and to the bed, her heart beating fast in her chest. She didn't know how she'd live without being in his arms again.

He climbed on top of her and she pulled him down for another kiss. It was gentler this time, sweeter, an homage to all they meant to each other and would always mean to each other.

He pulled back and his eyes never left hers as he drew a thumb across the corner of her eyebrow. There was no fight for dominance here, no need to show the other one up; this wasn't even fucking anymore. It was them, for once, just the two of them together. Pinpricks of desire alighted on her skin as he traced a line up her side. Reverently, he kissed the top of each breast, his hands caressing them as if she would break under the weight of him.

He left her then to pull off his brown-and-coral paisley tie and his white button-down, then went for his pants. Leaning over her, he drew a finger across the bared skin of her belly, making her shiver.

"I've seen you shiver a thousand times," he whispered, right before he gave her a soft kiss on the side of her belly button. "But I've never gotten to be the one to cause it."

"You're wrong about that," she murmured, her hand running over the coarse patch of hair on his chest. "You've made me shiver a lot over the years. Especially once you found a good tailor."

"Too bad you didn't tell me," he said, nuzzling her ear. "We could have been doing this a long time ago."

He took her mouth again and her hands buried in his thick hair as his arms, the muscles chiseled out, bracketed her head to support himself. The kiss went on forever, the mingling tastes of scotch and mint on Carter's breath, the alcoholic zing on his tongue, the mellow and salty scent of his bare skin, all of it was hers tonight. Maybe he'd get some tech girlfriend after he left and this would just be the thing they pushed under the carpet in the future, but for now he was hers alone.

"It's never been like this for me," she admitted quietly, not being able to hold in the words and also wanting him to know. Despite the fact that their physical relationship was ending, it had meant something to her. It had meant a lot.

His head lifted, their eyes joined like they had so many times before, but she felt it in her bones. Over the past month, their relationship had shifted forever, but it wasn't anything they hadn't antici-pated. Where she thought they'd fight or they'd lose their friendship, something else entirely was happening. Their old friendship paled in compar-ison to what it had become. They'd worked as a team to build their businesses, been true room-mates and lovers.

"Me neither," he said, kissing her lightly on the forehead, then going lower, dropping sweet kisses on her neck, across her collarbone, down the middle of her chest to her belly button. "I'm going to miss you like crazy, Alexa."

"Me, too," she managed, a lump in her throat forming around the words.

She reached over to her nightstand and pulled out a condom, handing it to him. It was a cop-out, ending the moment where she could have truly asked him to stay or he could have asked her to come to San Francisco, or just admitted that, yes, this was a real relationship and real future he was leaving behind. But she didn't say any of that.

He took the foil from her and ripped it open, deftly rolling the latex over his straining erection. His hand moved down to her center, swiping deliciously slowly over her slit, finding the wetness there.

"Alexa," he said, placing himself at her entrance, "you mean everything to me."

Then he slid home. Gasping at the luscious stretching, she dug her hands into his back, wanting more already. The moment was too intense. Her body was saying too much without words, just trying to hold back the desperation she felt that he was leaving. And part of her knew that it might be forever, that he might find someone else to start a life with. A life that she'd never be part of.

He drove into her again, fighting against her inner muscles for space and completion. Arching against him, she came in a rush of hot and cold, their eyes locked on each other. She was still coming when he let go, spasming inside her as she milked him for everything.

Hours later, she lay there in the dark, with Carter wrapped around her, able to admit to herself that after all these years, she'd fallen in love with her best friend.

CHAPTER SIXTEEN

ALEXA DIDN'T HATE MONACO, but she thought she should like it more than she did. She was in Monte Carlo, one of the most romantic places on the globe, and all she could think about was eating at the shitty diner she and Carter used to go to on Fremont Street. Instead of flirting with the hot casino dealers or suave hoteliers or handsome bankers, she ate crepes in her hotel room. Instead of enjoying a day at the Grand Prix or going out on a truffle hunt, she sat outside at a bistro, texting back and forth with Carter about television shows.

Another night at the Casino Monte Carlo and she was one step closer to opening a casino right on the blue Mediterranean Sea in the playground of the world's rich and famous. It was what she'd thought she'd wanted when she'd sold Halcyon— a fresh start, a chance to make something all on her own. But she wasn't so sure what she wanted anymore. She understood why her uncle hadn't been as sad about selling the casinos as she had. They were just buildings. What she really needed was a purpose.

Her phone lit up, another text from Carter.

It was a picture of the fog rolling in over the San Francisco Bay, his hand in the corner of the frame obviously in mid-wave.

She sighed. She'd royally fucked up. Not as much as he had, of course, since he'd been the one to actually leave and go to San Francisco first, but they were both idiots. So Alexa had packed up and gone to Monaco. Except now that she was there, it wasn't exactly working out the way she'd thought. She missed Las Vegas too much. And she missed Carter too much.

Dialing her uncle's number, she held her breath until he answered.

When he did, the words rushed out of her mouth. "I don't want to build a casino here."

Her uncle chuckled. "There's no reason why you can't do it here in Vegas, darling. I'll stay in town for a while yet and I miss you."

"I miss you, too."

For the first time in the past two weeks, Alexa felt like she could breathe again. She was going to go home. Even if Carter wasn't there, Vegas was still home to her. But she really wanted him there, too, and maybe she should explain to him just how much she needed him around.

"Why don't you take a vacation?" Uncle John advised. "Take your mind completely off business for a while. And off Carter. Then when you come back, you'll be full of ideas and ready to build what you want."

Alexa didn't even bother to deny the fact that her current ennui was a result of missing Carter.

"I didn't think he really meant it," she admitted quietly. "I didn't think he'd really go." Even as they stood saying goodbye outside her house the day he left, she hadn't believed it. He was always, always there for her.

"He didn't leave you, Alexa," Uncle John told her. "He just left Las Vegas for a little while."

A tear threatened and she blinked it back. She knew, rationally, that Carter hadn't left her, but it still felt like there was a hole in her chest. Part of her believed she'd never see him again. She knew it was a crazy part of her, but her parents had disappeared in a matter of seconds as if they'd never existed at all. On some level, she'd been waiting for Carter to do the same. And now he had and she was wrecked.

The decision made not to open a casino, the hours stretched even more slowly in front of her on what was now a vacation. She went out with a fellow casino friend a couple of times, but dancing on tabletops wasn't really interesting to her anymore.

Today was the anniversary of her parents'

death, and she knew exactly the time they'd died, dreaded every minute up to the one where they'd finally left the world. She'd had an early dinner with a friend and drunk far too much, but went back to her hotel early so she could observe the day on her own. Last year, she and Carter had gone to Chicago together and it felt weird to not have him by her side now.

Another friend called, probably to go to a bar for the night, but she ignored it as the elevator slowly climbed up to her floor. All she wanted to do was to crawl into bed, eat Thai food, feel sorry for herself and then go to sleep not caring that there would be cupcake crumbs inside the bra she was too lazy to remove. Was that too much to ask?

When she got back to her room, a bouquet that dwarfed the round table in her living area had been delivered. It was the same arrangement of flowers she always had in her office at Halcyon, delicate cream roses, peach peonies and blue hydrangeas. She didn't need to read the card to know they were from Carter, but his message was equally comforting. *Here for you.* Tears she'd been holding back seeped out and they weren't even about her parents anymore; they were about the fact that she'd pushed Carter away and she hadn't really understood what that meant when she'd done it. She hadn't expected it to hurt this much once he was really gone.

It'd been sixteen years since her parents' death, which meant she'd officially been alive just as long without them as she'd been with them, which on top of losing Carter was crippling. But it also reminded her that life was short, and she'd wasted so much time pushing away the best, most thoughtful person in her life. The one person she should be holding on to forever and never letting go because she was stupidly in love with him.

She'd been in love with Carter for so long, she wasn't sure she remembered a time when she hadn't been. It had just been her default state since high school that she'd talked herself out of acknowledging because she was an idiot and a coward. She'd been afraid to allow herself to be happy because she knew all too well how it felt to have that happiness ripped away without reason or warning.

But accepting the risk felt like claiming a destiny she'd ignored instead of jumping off the cliff like she'd feared. She planned to text Carter as much and also thank him for the flowers, but she looked crazy from crying and needed a nap before tackling that mountain. Unfortunately, she'd had a lot of alcohol fell asleep as soon as her head hit the pillow.

The next day, she woke up with a pounding headache and a video message from him. He'd donned the Jon Snow costume he'd worn for Halloween the previous year and was pretending to ride a dragon. For the first time since she'd been in Monaco, she laughed.

She might be hungover, but she knew what last night's revelations meant. The time had come for her to go home and get her life back together. She'd allowed herself to wallow long enough; she was ready to build the future she'd been stupidly denying herself.

Carter was in Vegas for his mom's birthday, but also to meet with Alexa's uncle to finalize the sale of Halcyon. He obviously respected her decision to sell, but he hated the look on her face when she talked about giving it up and knew she was only doing it for her uncle. She loved Halcyon more than anything and Uncle John agreed that she should have it. Carter buying it was the perfect solution to her getting to keep it and her uncle getting the return on his investment.

Unfortunately, he hadn't gotten a chance to talk to her about it because she'd gone completely off the grid and hadn't answered any of his calls or texts since yesterday. And sending a text saying he bought her casino just wasn't the thing to do.

After two weeks of moping around San Francisco during what should be an exciting time in his life, he knew what needed to be done. If he had to move back to Las Vegas to have Alexa, he would do it. He was not prepared to fuck around anymore. He wanted Alexa and he was going to go for it. For real. Not some half-assed, doing-it-for-show bullshit like they'd been doing. He wasn't giving her any more space. Shit was about to get real.

So when she appeared in his media room right in the middle of the football game he'd been half paying attention to, it at least saved him a trip to Monaco to see her.

"Carter?"

"Alexa?" he asked, his heart seemingly beating somewhere outside of his chest.

She looked so completely un-Alexa-like in a pair of jeans with stains on the front and an old UNLV sweatshirt with the collar torn out. Dark circles rimmed her eyes and her mascara was smudged on her cheek, and most startling, she had two different shoes on. Both were sneakers, but one a red Converse high-top and the other a regular maroon canvas shoe. All signs indicated that she was not okay.

"You flew here from Monaco?"

Where do you think she flew from, genius? He just hadn't expected to see her yet and wasn't prepared for the onslaught of emotion, joy, fear and acceptance all mingling in his chest like an out-of-control feelings bonanza.

She nodded and took the seat next to him.

"You don't look great," he joked, brushing a

tangled piece of hair from where it had snagged on her lip.

She laughed, the sound tight in her throat. "I've been drinking too much and I didn't get a lot of sleep on the plane because I got a middle seat."

"You didn't take your Uncle John's plane home?"

She shook her head. "I couldn't wait for it to fly back to France from Vegas so I just took my chances. FYI, airline attendants do not like to be bribed."

He grinned at the image of her trying to bribe her way into a better seat. "Why was it so important to get back so fast?"

"I remembered it was your mom's birthday and I wanted to see you."

"You wanted to see me?"

She shrugged. "Yeah, I missed my friend."

He met her eyes. "Your best friend."

"Damn right," she agreed, a corner of her mouth lifting in a wry smile.

"Alexa," he said, his tone serious. "I think we need to talk."

She toed off her shoes, frowning when she realized they were different from each other.

Now was the time to come clean about Halcyon, but she needed to know something first.

"I missed you and I love you," she said, the words so soft he could barely hear them.

"I love you, too, Alexa."

She turned to meet his eyes then, her hazel ones determined and serious. "No, that's not what I meant. I love you. As more than a friend. And though I'd really prefer an actual wedding that I'm at least sober for, I want to stay married."

Carter stared at her, not quite believing what she was saying. Also, a little dumbfounded that she'd completely stolen his thunder.

"Wow," he said, grinning, "I should have moved away a long time ago."

She pushed at his shoulder. "I can't believe you actually left."

Laughing, he shook his head. "You know, you couldn't even let me have this, could you? You're the most selfish best friend."

Her eyes grew comically large. "What? Do you know how nerve-racking this is? I flew all the way around the damn globe with a hangover to get home to you. The man next to me farted every time he moved and a small devil child threw up on my pants. But I didn't even care. I just wanted to get back here to tell you that I am hopelessly in love with you and the thought of not having you in my life is not acceptable."

"Again, your hyperbole is misleading. Monaco to Las Vegas is not nearly all the way around the globe."

She crossed her arms over her chest, waiting.

He stood and pulled her up and into his arms. "You know you're the love of my life, Alexa."

"I did not, in fact, know that."

He scanned her face, looking for any sign of a joke and didn't find one, but could it have been possible that she really didn't know how he felt about her? It seemed ludicrous.

"Of course you did," he prodded.

Her eyes widened. "I did not," she said, poking him in the chest with a chipped white nail to accentuate the truth of her statement.

"Maybe you need glasses because I feel like every time I look at you I've got those cartoon heart eyes."

She shrugged then, meeting his eyes. "We saw what we wanted to see, not what was there."

Wasn't that the fucking truth.

"Well, Lawson, you waited long enough to tell me since my sister is here and upstairs making a cake for my mom we can't do anything."

A corner of her mouth lifted. "You could always just get me an Hermès scarf and we could call it even."

"Right," he drew out, thinking about how all his savings were tied up with his purchase of Halcyon and how it would be a good time to tell her about it. And yet, he didn't tell her. It was definitely a symptom of brain damage, but goddammit, she'd just told him she loved him and couldn't he have that for a damned day before it all went to shit?

"Will you accept the best kiss of your life instead?"

"I would if I thought that was forthcoming," she snarked.

He took her mouth in a gentle kiss, caressing her back in slow strokes, adoring the way she felt against him and the way she smelled, the same green apple smell he'd come to associate with simply home. Which brought up another issue they needed to sort out.

Slowly ending the kiss, he set his forehead against hers, taking a deep breath. "If you want me to move to Monaco I will."

She shook her head. "I'll go to San Francisco. There's nothing for me in Monaco."

He gave her quick kiss. "So it's settled. We'll live in Vegas."

Pulling back, her left eyebrow winged up in question. "What?"

"You were right, San Francisco sucks. You know I hate yeast. Plus, Greg is more than ready to open the office there on his own especially after I made him a full partner in the business."

"You did it for me so you could come back here," she stated, asking, but not really asking it as a question.

"I did."

"Because you're in love with me."

He nodded, raising an eyebrow.

"And you'd do absolutely anything for me no matter what."

"I mean, within reason."

She made a tsking sound. "Love isn't reasonable."

"What do you want, Alexa?"

"I'm just testing how unconditional your love is."

"You're cracked," he laughed. "And you look like that one time in college after you vomited all night from too much grain alcohol."

The couch shifted as Alexa flopped down into her seat again. "I know, it's bad. But I don't have anywhere to be because I am officially unemployed."

"Speaking of unconditional love, um, there's something I need to tell you." He took her hand and squeezed and hoped for the best. "I bought Halcyon."

Alexa's jaw tightened with rage. She literally could not believe what she was hearing right now. Just a second ago, she'd thought her life was finally on the right track and now just as fast it was a shitshow.

"I knew you didn't really want to sell it, but would never admit it to Uncle John so I bought it for a higher price than the original buyer," Carter tried to explain.

But this was typical Carter behavior. Always thinking that he knew what was best for her. Since the moment she'd told him about her parents, he'd been protecting her in one way or another. Maybe she'd needed his protection all those years ago, but she just didn't anymore. Especially not in her professional life.

"If I hadn't wanted to sell Halcyon, I wouldn't have."

He raised a doubtful eyebrow. "You'd do anything for your uncle."

"Yeah, that was then. This is now. I didn't open the Monaco casino for him, did I?"

He ran a frustrated hand through his hair. "You're never going to let yourself be happy, are you?"

Her rage grew exponentially, but a tiny piece of her recognized his words as the truth. Of course, she did not appreciate his phrasing or word choice because it wasn't as if she wanted to feel guilty about her parents' death. It was part of her. But she didn't want to fight with him. She picked up her bag, intending to leave.

"Oh, there you go," Carter scoffed. "Running away again."

"I am not running away," she gritted out, turning back around. "But I guess you're right, maybe

I don't want to be happy. Tell me, how much I owe you for Halcyon so we can get on with it?"

"Jesus Christ, Alexa, it's not a fucking dinner check. You can't just owe me that kind of money."

"So you want to run the casino with me? I'm not sure what you're saying."

He stood then and blew out a frustrated breath. "Do you think I waited half of my life to tell you I'm in love with you to have it end like this? Why are you doing this?"

A part of her heart ripped then, because it felt like all the joy she'd been able to touch for that short moment earlier was evaporating before her eyes and she had no idea how to contain it.

"I'm doing this because I'm the richest fucking bitch in Las Vegas and instead of coming to me with a problem that affected both of us, you thought you had all the answers. And that's just not the way I fucking operate as you well know. So maybe you're just mad at me to distract from the fact that you don't want to be on my team. You want to be the coach."

"You're really reaching, Alexa."

She put her hands on her hips, facing him down. "Am I? Greg has been more than capable of running your company for over a decade and you just now gave him a partnership."

"Are you calling out the way I run my business?"

"Well, apparently you want to be business partners now, so maybe I am."

"You have no idea what you're talking about."

Alexa took a few steps toward him. "You talk a big game about being in love with me for all this time, but I was the one who said it first."

"Only because I left Las Vegas," he drew tightly.

"You have sat back and worked behind the scenes of my life, so far as to create software for the casinos I ran, to the point that you have never paused to consider what being with me really means."

He rolled his eyes. "I think I have a fairly good idea."

"If you had, you wouldn't have bought the casino out from under my nose when one simple phone call would have solved the problem."

His jaw clenched, the muscle ticking there like the steady wand of a metronome.

"I love you, Carter, with no expectations."

"What are you trying to say?"

"I'm saying that you don't have to buy me a casino for me to love you. You don't need to do anything besides be yourself."

"That's not—"

"I love you."

"I love you, too, but that's not—"

"Even when you thought you were unlovable, I loved you."

"Alexa, whatever it is you're trying to do, it's not nec—"

She strode toward him, pulling him to her and finding his lips with hers. It was a kiss born out of frustration and confusion and bone-deep longing. His arms came around her, the heavy muscles of his biceps curling her into his warmth.

Breaking the kiss, she met his eyes. "I'm not some fantasy girl that you've built up in your head and you don't have to treat me as if my love is contingent upon you doing something outrageous."

"For fuck's sake, Alexa, I didn't think it was some grand romantic gesture. I'd like to think I could come up with something with a little bit more imagination anyway. I knew you'd be mad as hell, but time was of the essence."

"I was better equipped to handle the situation than you were, seeing as how it's my damn casino and the person who offered for it was someone I'd been working with for years."

"I'm sorry for interfering," he said, his eyes earnest. "I wanted you to be able to start fresh if that's what you wanted."

"Why can't you just admit that you're scared?" she asked, almost laughing in frustration.

His eyes grew incredulous. "Of course I'm scared as hell! Every time we get remotely close to something real you sneak away without another fucking word! You think I have some kind of hang-up because I was chubby once? I don't give a shit about that and you're just using it as another excuse to not be with me."

"Don't be a dick, Carter."

"In case you haven't been paying attention, I am a dick, Alexa. People aren't exactly knocking down my door to be friends with a moody, sarcastic, semi-malcontent. And yet you're the one who seems to think I have this hang-up about my old self."

Carter pulled her roughly into his arms then. She could feel the heat radiating off his body as one overwhelming and continuous wave of anger.

"You want to be in charge, the ball is all yours, Alexa."

Then he kissed her and the fire ignited instantly. The love and hate and resentment and insecurity, all of it flowed through them like a flooding river of emotion, no longer contained or placid or waiting for them to examine the meaning. Alexa's hands fisted in the back of Carter's tailored white dress shirt, the thread busting with each flex of her fingers.

She couldn't breathe, but didn't care. He was taking her whole, his tongue delving deeper, hard cock grinding against her clit showing no mercy. God, she'd missed this. For weeks, she'd been out in the cold without his smile or voice or this mad, sweet, dirty rush of pleasure only he was able to deliver.

Her arms went around his neck to take it further and hopefully to the bedroom, but he caught her hands in his and put them back down at her sides as he broke the kiss.

"If you honestly want this to work for real, prove it," he challenged, eyes sparking. "I'm tired of wasting my fucking time."

Then he was gone, the front door slamming shut behind him.

The fact that he'd stormed out of his own house to get away from her was not lost on her. She did the only thing left to do and went to the kitchen to help Kara with the cake. At least there was his mom's birthday to celebrate, even if Alexa would rather shove Carter's face into a bowl of frosting.

CHAPTER SEVENTEEN

CARTER DIDN'T EXPECT to see Alexa anytime soon, which was fine with him. She acted like she had her shit together, but Alexa Lawson still had the best poker face in town and inside she was just as fucked up about relationships as the day her parents died. He'd been by her side like an unwavering sentinel since the day it happened, but his watch was officially over.

He threw an old keyboard from his garage into the trash. Turned out when you gave some of your work to your partner, one had a lot of time on one's hands. The new office was still in the hiring phase and he'd sat in on all the interviews via Skype while running the main headquarters in Vegas. His stock was up again after he'd made several public appearances since opening the new branch. It would have been better if Alexa had been there for those appearances, but she'd been too steeped in her own angry delusion about Halcyon to give a shit about something he wanted.

It pissed him off all over again that he was the one having to do the heavy emotional lifting in their relationship. Except that, if he were honest, maybe she did have a point. Her uncle had advised against buying the casino, obviously knowing Alexa's temperament when it came to business, but Carter had ignored him. He'd been in San Francisco, miserable and alone while she sent him photo after photo of her sunning on the French Riviera and updated her social media feeds with various calendar-caliber dudes. For the first time, his connection to her had felt tenuous and paper-thin. When he'd left her house the last time, he'd literally had no idea when he'd see her next. He'd been so damn desperate to have her in his life again—to have her in his life forever—that he hadn't thought about the consequences, just that maybe she'd come back to Vegas if she had a reason.

Well, she was in Vegas now, but she was pretending as if he may as well not exist. One stupid mistake in their entire friendship and she was ready to call it quits? Fuck that.

But it still didn't change the fact that he wanted her and would take her back with open arms if she came through his garage door right now.

He threw a chunky '90s era mouse into the recycling bin with enough force to make an echoing clank on the metal can. How did he even have this much shit? It wasn't lost on him that he was cleaning up his actual baggage instead of his emotional baggage, but he wasn't in the frame of mind to be sensible. He just wanted to break shit.

He chucked another old notebook into the trash, the contents opening up inside the can. Peering into the bin, he noticed the old spiral-bound book had opened to a conversation he and Alexa had written in high school. He'd recognize her swirly handwriting anywhere. Plucking the notebook out of the trash, he tried to determine a year and found that it had been the same year her parents died.

He read the conversation, a smile tugging at him despite his shitty mood. Nothing important was said, just what are you doing after school, want to go swimming, did you talk to so-and-so at lunch. Kid stuff, but something tugged at the back of his memory. He flipped the page over and saw the yes or no boxes where he'd asked her to junior year homecoming. She'd filled in every space of that yes box, leaving no white visible. They'd never made it to the dance, though, because her parents had died the week before.

Taking a deep breath, he set the notebook aside, wondering if Alexa remembered it. Probably not, since he'd forgotten, too. But at the time it had been a big deal for him. Months of preparation had gone into those two boxes precisely measured on the back of a piece of notebook paper. That year, world history had been their only class together and he'd planned to ask then because she sat in front of him, so he wouldn't be able to see her face and she couldn't see his if she said no. But she'd said yes. Between that day and college they'd become best friends, though, and everything had changed.

Was it possible that they'd been on a trajectory to being together romantically with that homecoming, and after her parents died he'd become something way more precious than just another transient high school boyfriend?

He threw more cords into the recycling bin, determined to stop thinking about Alexa. The garage wasn't air-conditioned, and a bead of sweat fell into his eyes. He wiped it away and by the time he was finished throwing stuff away and reorganizing the remaining boxes, his head was marginally clear.

Grabbing a beer from the fridge, he sank down onto the sofa, contemplating his future, when John Lawson called.

"You really screwed the pooch on this one, C-dog," John blustered when Carter answered.

Carter bit the side of his cheek. "You don't say."

"That girl is still on a warpath about you buying the casino."

"I'm aware."

"Well, you'll excuse me for saying I told you so. I saw your point, that she was only selling it to appease me, but son, we all know that I have more than enough money to retire. All she needed to do was say the word and I would have given it to her. She wanted the money, son."

Carter ran a hand through his hair. John hadn't wanted to sell, but Carter hadn't really given him much of a choice.

"So she's still in Vegas?" he asked. At least she hadn't run too far away from him.

"Yep. She'll be at Halcyon tonight in case you were looking for her."

"I'm not," he said, emphasizing the words to prevent any of John's future meddling.

"Now, boy, that's a damned shame. A woman like Alexa Lawson doesn't come around your house declaring her love for you every day. I know you're some big-time stud in the city, but you two were just kids when you fell in love. Don't take that for granted."

Carter closed his eyes against the wave of guilt that threatened to undo his resolve. "I'll keep that in mind."

John coughed, but didn't end the call. Then he cleared his throat.

"Just maybe go on over there to Halcyon tonight. She might be in a mind to talk."

John ended the call, but Carter had no intention of going to Halcyon anytime soon, especially if Alexa was there.

Except if she was in trouble of some kind. But if she were, John would have just said so. Fucking hell. The last decade of uncomplicated, no-strings-attached sex flashed before his eyes as some kind of utopian existence he'd previously failed to appreciate.

He took a deep pull from the beer bottle and put his feet up on the coffee table. Flipping on the television, he decided he'd finish that documentary he and Alexa never got around to. Halfway through, his sister appeared in his kitchen.

He really needed to reprogram his locks.

"I'm fine," he told her. "I don't need a pep talk."

"I don't care about you," she grumbled. "I just quit my job and I know you have beer. Now that I'm unemployed I can't afford to buy it."

She pulled open his fridge and took out two bottles, joining him on the couch in a defeated slump.

"Care to share?" he ventured.

"Not really."

"Well, you can always work for me, you know. If you don't want to do tech stuff, there's always human resources or sales."

She turned to him, her blue eyes full of indignity. "I wouldn't work for you if you paid me a million dollars."

"If that's a salary negotiation, I'd advise you to start lower, since as a community theater director you lack a certain skill set."

She rolled her eyes. "Bite me. You're impossible to be around and that'll only get worse now that Alexa had the good sense to toss your pestilent ass to the curb."

"You know, you can just take the beer with you when you go."

He flipped the documentary back on.

"I'm sorry," Kara muttered. "But this crap between you and Alexa is stupid. And, you know, I also might be homeless soon, so forgive me for the bad mood."

"You're not going to be homeless. Are you sure you just can't go back?"

"I probably could, but I don't want to. I want to direct new stuff by local writers, not tired and dated stuff that everyone already knows. But the theater owner isn't interested. I'm done with it."

"Just hold acting classes and charge for them," he told her. "Then you can do what you love most, working with people and putting on whatever plays you want."

Kara stilled beside him, beer bottle poised in midair. "Oh my God, you're a genius."

"Yeah," he agreed. "Glad you've finally figured out what the rest of the free world already knows."

She glared at him.

"And why don't you ask Alexa if you can use one of her theaters at the casino? She'd love to have you. Don't know why you haven't thought of that before either."

Carter could feel Kara's eyes on him.

"I do have an IQ of 142, you know. I've been a member of Mensa since I was sixteen."

Kara groaned. "I wonder how many more birthday candles I need to blow out for you to finally become mute."

"Barring a freak accident, the chances of me suddenly becoming mute at this stage of life are very slim."

Her lips pressed in a thin line, Kara glared at him again.

He shrugged. "Any more of life's quandaries you'd like me to effortlessly solve for you?"

"Yeah, are you going to man up and go get Alexa or are you going to continue sulking here like a little baby?"

Okay, he'd quite literally asked for that.

"I think you should be directing that barrage of nonsense to Alexa."

Kara rolled her eyes again. "She did the scary thing and told you she loved you first—"

"Yeah, and at the first sign of trouble, she tried to cut me loose."

"It doesn't matter. She went first and that takes guts. Then you lied to her about the casino and instead of figuring out a way to make it up to her you just yelled at her and walked away."

That was an extremely skewed version of events, but he didn't feel the need to justify it to his baby sister.

"You guys have been friends ever since I could remember, especially after Alexa's parents died. She really relied on you, on all of us, but she was never *one* of us."

"Is there a point to this verbose Hallmark card?"

"Yes, you asshat. The point is that we've never lost anyone and have no idea what it's like to feel so alone in the world that losing a friend feels terrifying. So why don't you go be nice to your best friend. You know, the one who sold casinos she loves more than anything in the world to make her uncle happy and stayed married to you to help your company so you could expand to San Francisco even though she asked you multiple times not to move there. And she did all that without asking her own best friend for any support and then watched as that same best friend walked out on her a second time instead of talking through a problem. Maybe you should go see how that person is doing instead of sitting here like the world's biggest douchebag."

He stared at her, blinking.

"Who's the genius now, jerk?" she said, cackling, downing the rest of her beer and cracking open the other one.

"Talk to her about a job for me when you get there, won't you?" she called, but he had already left the room.

CHAPTER EIGHTEEN

ALEXA HAD NEARLY everything ready. It had taken her a couple of days to think of a plan, but once she'd set her mind to it everything had fallen into place. After a couple of sleepless nights imagining herself alone on the floor of her house surrounded by teetering notebooks of her own bad poetry and empty plastic buckets of ice cream, she finally went to work. She still wouldn't mind some ice cream, but she was going to make sure she got her happily-ever-after if it meant dragging Carter to the altar herself. She wasn't above it.

Eventually, she'd calmed down about him buying the casino, gained some perspective over copious bottles of wine with friends, including Kara, and realized that Carter was right. She wasn't alone because her parents were gone and it wasn't her fault they were gone, either. Those were easy enough words to say and feel, but more difficult to accept. That way of thinking was just a bad habit and she'd just been using it as an excuse to not commit fully to Carter. But she was determined now. Fear and guilt were not things she was going to let destroy the best part of her life.

When he came racing into Halcyon three days later wearing a black suit with a white shirt and black polka-dot tie, she knew she'd made the right choice. The man had definitely learned how to dress. His tortoiseshell glasses were on, too, and her heart fluttered a bit.

Her home was here and she'd been waiting for so long to feel safe again, she couldn't believe she'd denied herself for so long.

Eyebrows drawn together, he looked serious, carrying an enormous Hermès bag as he strode across the casino floor.

"Please hear me out. I just want to apologize," he said, stopping in front of her.

Upon closer inspection, he looked tired, bags under his eyes, skin a little paler than usual. It was nice to know he'd been miserable, too.

"Alexa, I'm an idiot, but you already know that about me and you're still around. The truth is that I was the one afraid of losing you. I feel like every time you dated someone I lost you a little. Every year we weren't together felt like more distance between us because I wanted you so badly. You left all those guys so easily, without a backward glance. I needed to know I was different, and even though you've shown me that over and over, part of me still didn't believe it."

She shrugged and tried to look bored even though a lightness had taken hold of her chest, like all the pieces of her life were finally falling into place.

"I don't ever know the right things to say to people, specifically you in this instance if that isn't clear, but also to most people. I'm not good at being jovial or charming or easygoing like you, but you wouldn't like it if I were those things. It's fair to say I'm not a people person, but you're the one person who has always made me happy."

His eyes searched hers then, quiet desperation in them, but she waited for him to continue. "So you can tell me to go to hell or whatever else I definitely deserve, but just know that I am never not going to be a part of your life. Even if you want to marry a goat or whatever, I'm here for the long haul, for every day, and for forever."

He lifted the Hermès bag and a corner of her mouth lifted.

"This is all the scarves they had in the store, so I figured it was a start. I won't be needing to buy them for anyone else now."

She was trying to really pay attention and remember the moment but when she still didn't speak, he continued, "Which now that I had to buy a casino at an exorbitant rate was a bigger hit to my wallet than it might have been in the past."

That pulled her back to her plan. "You're selling Halcyon," she finally managed, pointing to a lawyer sitting at one of the empty roulette tables. She'd cleared the whole top floor of the casino for this. "So your net worth will be restored shortly."

He dropped the bag to the floor.

"Do you mean selling it to you because that's the only way I'm parting with it. You love Halcyon, Alexa. You should have what's yours."

"I do love Halcyon," she admitted, "but I'm ready for a new challenge. I loved Halcyon so much because I designed it, but my uncle helped, too. I've got a concept for a new one that's all my own, the design, concept and money."

Carter still looked uncertain and off-kilter, which was such an anomaly in itself that she nearly laughed.

"Who is buying Halcyon?"

"Let's just say I charmed a certain shipping magnate."

Understanding dawned on his face as he remembered one of the investment creeps he'd been forced to meet, a crease forming in his cheek.

"Nicely done, Alexa."

She nodded. "Sorry if you were really looking forward to being a casino owner," she told him.

"I was not," he confirmed with a slight grimace.

She laughed at his quintessentially Carter understatement.

"I'm sorry, too," she said, acknowledging his apology. "You were right, I was scared. Not the best defense, but I'd rather cut my own arm off in a cave than not have you in my life."

"You need to stop watching that movie."

"I can't help it. Sometimes I get an overwhelming urge to go hiking at Red Rock and need a sufficient excuse not to go."

He gave her a soft kiss on her forehead. "Makes total sense."

"I'm glad you see it that way."

"You know I had a good plan that you screwed up," he complained, drawing back and looking in her eyes. "I had that bag of scarves and I was going to have us play roulette to see who took Halcyon. Of course, I paid that dealer over there to fix the wheel."

"Subterfuge," she nodded knowingly. "I expected nothing less."

"You knew," he deadpanned. "I literally just thought of it two hours ago."

"It's what I would have done." Alexa shrugged, giving his tie a playful tug. "Were I the total douche who bought my best friend's casino without telling her."

He scowled, which was adorable.

"Also, my employees tell me everything," she

admitted. "Especially that one, since along with most of my staff, he'll be opening my new casino with me."

He shook his head at her plans. "Can we get out of here? We have a lot of lost time to make up."

She nodded. "But I have question first."

Alexa's heart beat double time as she pulled the piece of paper out of her pocket. She was about to do the unthinkable and that included possibly vomiting and peeing her pants at the same time. It was the total wrong sequence of events for what she was about to do.

She met Carter's impatient eyes and held out the piece of paper for him to see.

When he saw it, his eyes widened in surprise and then sheer delight.

"You're just always going to steal my thunder, aren't you?"

"You already got me the perfect ring," she explained. "I just created the perfect proposal."

He crushed her into his chest, their mouths meeting in desperate happiness, a mixture of relief and joy in her heart.

"I couldn't wait any longer to be your wife for real," she murmured against his mouth when the kiss ended.

"Well, can I get a pen?" he laughed.

She pointed to the closest table on which were a pen and an empty picture frame.

Taking the pen, he filled out the yes box after her written question: *Will you marry me?*

She swiped it out of his hand before he could change his mind and placed it in the frame and gave it to him.

"Just so you always remember that I went first."

Carter picked her up and kissed her as her uncle and some of her employees filtered in from the hallway to watch the show.

When he put her down, he whispered in her ear, "We both know that's not true considering the very nature of the proposal. I'm the one who asked all those years ago."

She rolled her eyes. "Shut up and go sign the papers. I have a new casino to open."

"Yes, ma'am."

* * * * *

COMING SOON!

We really hope you enjoyed reading this book. If you're looking for more romance, be sure to head to the shops when new books are available on

Thursday 31st October

To see which titles are coming soon, please visit

millsandboon.co.uk/nextmonth

MILLS & BOON

LET'S TALK

Romance

For exclusive extracts, competitions
and special offers, find us online:

f facebook.com/millsandboon

🐦 @MillsandBoon

📷 @MillsandBoonUK

Get in touch on 01413 063232

For all the latest titles coming soon, visit
millsandboon.co.uk/nextmonth

MILLS & BOON

THE HEART OF ROMANCE

A ROMANCE FOR EVERY KIND OF READER

MODERN

Prepare to be swept off your feet by sophisticated, sexy and seductive heroes, in some of the world's most glamourous and romantic locations, where power and passion collide.
8 stories per month.

HISTORICAL

Escape with historical heroes from time gone by. Whether your passion is for wicked Regency Rakes, muscled Vikings or rugged Highlanders, awaken the romance of the past.
6 stories per month.

MEDICAL

Set your pulse racing with dedicated, delectable doctors in the high-pressure world of medicine, where emotions run high and passion, comfort and love are the best medicine.
6 stories per month.

True Love

Celebrate true love with tender stories of heartfelt romance, from the rush of falling in love to the joy a new baby can bring, and a focus on the emotional heart of a relationship.
8 stories per month.

Desire

Indulge in secrets and scandal, intense drama and plenty of sizzling hot action with powerful and passionate heroes who have it all: wealth, status, good looks…everything but the right woman.
6 stories per month.

HEROES

Experience all the excitement of a gripping thriller, with an intense romance at its heart. Resourceful, true-to-life women and strong, fearless men face danger and desire - a killer combination!
8 stories per month.

DARE

Sensual love stories featuring smart, sassy heroines you'd want as a best friend, and compelling intense heroes who are worthy of them.
4 stories per month.

To see which titles are coming soon, please visit

millsandboon.co.uk/nextmonth

WANT EVEN MORE

ROMANCE?

SUBSCRIBE AND SAVE TODAY!

'Mills & Boon books, the perfect way to escape for an hour or so.'

MISS W. DYER

'Excellent service, promptly delivered and very good subscription choices.'

MISS A. PEARSON

'You get fantastic special offers and the chance to get books before they hit the shops.'

MRS V. HALL

Visit millsandboon.co.uk/Subscribe and save on brand new books.

JOIN US ON SOCIAL MEDIA!

Stay up to date with our latest releases, author
news and gossip, special offers and discounts, and
all the behind-the-scenes action
from Mills & Boon...

 millsandboon

 millsandboonuk

 millsandboon

It might just be true love...